DYNASTY OF SPIES

ALSO BY DAN SHERMAN
The Mole
Riddle
Swann
King Jaguar

DYNASTY

OF SPIES

BY DAN SHERMAN

ARBOR HOUSE
New York

Library of Congress Catalog Card Number: 79–54012

ISBN: 0–87795–255–8

Manufactured in the United States of America

10 9 8 7 6 5 4 3 2 1

The author wishes to acknowledge the following for their help in the research and preparation of this work:
S. Ganns for his advice and support. My publisher and editor Donald I. Fine. Richard Curtis for his overall guidance. David K____, Susan H____, and others who trusted me with what they knew about the secret world. Further credit goes to the Citizens Commission on Human Rights for their untiring efforts to expose the abuses of the American Intelligence Community. Finally to Manon Alarie who was with me from the beginning to the end.

D. S.

PART 1

PART 1

CHAPTER ONE

PERHAPS THIS story rightfully belongs to the historians, to those who kept the records of the secret world. Certainly it was their conception of events that remained, a conception summarized in a single paragraph found in one of the last reports. The passage compared the Dancer family to a spinning bobbin wound round and round with lies. Only when the last thread unraveled was it clear that the truth had been hidden for eighty years.

Yet however one chose to conceive of the story, this much was undeniable. The past was vital. Everything depended on that which preceded it, for there were three generations of the Dancer family, and the last was a consequence of the first.

To begin with there was John who left London in 1917 to cross the Finland Station into Russia. Even today no one fully understood exactly what had happened. They only knew that he had been recruited by the British Secret Service, and that his mission had been connected with the Allied effort to keep the Russians in the war. Also, the job had gone awry and a man had been shot against a Petrograd wall. But this was so very long ago. What really mattered was that John Dancer had been the first spy.

Next there was Allen, the consummate spy. He was suave and elegant, and had that famous Cheshire smile. One always had the impression that he was perpetually leaving for distant cities. One would see him striding down the halls of CIA headquarters, calling good-by over his shoulder. His clothing was always perfect.

His career began in Spain on the eve of the Second World War. There he claimed he had befriended Hemingway and Jean-Paul Sartre, which might have been true, because even as a young man Allen understood that friendship was only a means to an end, not an end in itself. Or a judgment. Following this dictum, he also befriended several Nazi intelligence officers. Later he used these Nazis in an effort to make a separate peace with Germany. Allen has always played both sides against the middle, his colleagues would say. They also said that he had no morals, and no politics. He lied to everyone. Yet for all this Allen was forgiven, because he was the first and only one ever to tap the Kremlin. They said his Kremlin link was magic, and so they called it Magic. Source Magic. Then everything that Allen did he did with impunity, since all that mattered in the secret world were results.

Finally there was Allen's son Jessie. He was not the sort of boy that one would have thought was a Dancer. They said that Jessie was a grim and scary shadow man. They said that when he spoke to you, you had the feeling that he was light-years away. They joked that he slept with his eyes open, and that if he hated you he would genuinely and wholeheartedly wish you were dead.

Some said that Vietnam had destroyed Jessie Dancer. They recalled that once he had been a serious, polite young man with

4

a fragile smile and disarming way. But the war had been like electroconvulsive therapy. It had apparently rearranged his personality until he became locked into a still-point. They said that Jessie looked as if he had been suckled by wolves.

Others believed that Jessie had gone bad because he had not been able to live up to the legend of his father and grandfather. The stigma of the Dancer name had crippled him. Too much had been expected. First there was John and he had been a leader within the American intelligence community for nearly fifty years. Next came Allen, the mercurial, quicksilver king of the Soviet desk with his crown Source Magic. And so what was left for Jessie? All the mountains had been climbed, all the rivers crossed.

Then there were those who believed that Jessie had always been evil. They said that he had been born with teeth—again the wolf image. Before Vietnam the evil had been concealed, so that when it finally emerged later everyone attributed it to the war. But Vietnam, said those who believed this theory, had not destroyed Jessie—it had nourished him.

And finally there were those who simply said that the last generation of the Dancer family was merely a consequence of the first. Take it from there.

So much of Jessie's story was to occur during the winter that it was fitting that everything began in the fall. November was gray then, and the rain kept hissing through the West Virginia forests. Finally there was even an early snow, killing the late-blooming roses and blanketing the lawns of the Langley complex.

Jessie had been away some years. The war was well over, and most of those who had fought it were gone. Some had been fired in the great purge. Others had quit in disgust. At the Company helm stood Stansfield Turner. Sturdy Stan, they called him. Sturdy Stan the Navy man who hadn't the foggiest idea of what he was doing. About eight hundred, the cream of the clandestine services, were fired by Turner. Thereafter things were slow. The

5

old order had been gutted, and the new one lacked fire.

After the failure to predict the fall of the Shah, many lost all confidence in Langley's ability to produce. Yes, Turner had cleaned up the Agency's image. No longer did one fear that the CIA would eat a man alive, but instead of muzzling the beast, Stan Turner had pulled its teeth.

There were, however, still pockets of real brilliance. Turner had not sent a pink slip to the famous Lyle Severson, nor was little Humphrey Knolls fired. And of course no one could touch a force like Allen Dancer, not even indirectly through his father or his son.

So when it all began there was premature snow among the brambles and dark wood, and the snow lingered between freezing and melting. It was a gray time of the year, and three generations of the Dancer family were still employed by the Central Intelligence Agency.

There was a storm on the night that Jessie's story began, a storm that became a factor in the opening moves, because the first pawn in play was a nasty jungle fighter named Dusty Yeats, and once he had reached the Langley forest there was no stopping him in the wind and slanting rain.

Until that night of the storm little was known about Yeats. He was a quiet simple boy with red hair and a child's face. He had been transfered in from an outstation near the Cambodian border in Thailand. Few knew what he had been doing there, and still fewer even cared. Mostly Dusty kept to himself, eating alone, living alone. On Saturdays he lifted weights. He was fairly short, but he was built like a boxer. No one at this stage had even dreamed that he had a conspiratorial link with Jessie Dancer.

They put him to work in the Watch Tower, logging incoming telex reports from the field. It was a dreary job, and worse, he had the graveyard shift—midnight to eight. His traffic intake was light, but that was not unusual. Most agents in the field did not

6

feel secure with the telex lines, nor the sleepy juniors who manned them.

Next they posted him in Operational Services, where he handled second-class intelligence from Soviet bloc nations. His job was to classify and file for analysis. Again the work was dull. Incoming reports were tagged according to country and source and then given a rudimentary rating. In reality Dusty was just a clerk.

Personnel had him living in a drab one room apartment off a bad street in Washington. There was a burger stand on the corner where he usually ate, or else he heated frozen dinners and opened cans of meat. Those who knew Dusty said he was polite enough, and his seniors found his work passable. He was slow, but he often stayed late to catch up.

Supposedly Dusty had stayed late on the night of the storm to finish sorting a sheaf of reports just in from East Germany. This was a lie. The arresting watchman, a lanky Marine named Jasper, found Yeats going through the Central Reference files. Jasper had been strolling the half-lit halls when he saw Yeats through the double glass doors. The boy was stuffing a plastic folder into his jacket. Jasper asked to see the folder, and Yeats made his move. The first blow was a stinger for shock, a whipping back-knuckle to the face. Then Dusty swung again with a roundhouse to the ear. Jasper crumpled, and Yeats ran.

Outside the whole night was rocking miles of surrounding forest. The rain fell in flapping sheets. Trees shook and gnashed together. Limbs tore off, and branches sailed across the lawns. Once he had faked his way past the door guards, Dusty sprinted two hundred yards for the blackest hole between the thrashing pines. Then he went knee deep into the mud and clawed back up a low ravine.

The search lasted seven hours. Some thirty guards were involved, tearing through the underbrush in the cross beams of jeep mounted floodlamps. Overhead lightning kept tattering the sky, filling the forest floor with bluish shadows. A truck was lost when the road washed out. A man's face was slashed by branches. The guards finally packed it in at dawn. Yeats became the quarry of the professional hunters.

For Dusty that night was reduced to the crudest, most fragmented images. First stumbling through the dripping forest, then out on the black highway, flapping his arms at passing cars. But, there were no takers for his nightmare. He must have looked too ghastly in the headlights and rain.

Three miles down the road a pickup finally squealed to the gravel shoulder. Behind the wheel was a scary kid with straggly hair and the worst shabby grin.

He said, "I'm Dog. Where you headed?"

The cab was dark. The dash lights were out. The whole night was a wet smear through the rain splattered windshield.

"Can you take me as far as the city?" Dusty asked.

"City huh? You don't look like a city boy. You look like a country boy."

"Is that right?" Yeats laughed, but he was straining it. There was something foul in the swaying cab.

"Lots of mean people in the city," the kid continued. "Guys that will rip you off as quick as look at you. You should go back to the country."

Where I should go, Yeats suddenly thought, is back to the jungle. Thailand, Vietnam, Cambodia—even the worst jungles weren't as bad as this.

"On the other hand," the kid snickered, "sometimes you need the city. Like now, I need the city to get myself a little dream dust."

"Huh?"

"You know." The kid made a fist so the veins stood out along his arm. Then he jabbed the mainline with his finger. "Skag."

"Oh yeah," Dusty slurred. "Well, that's cool. That's real cool. Nothing cooler than skag."

8

"Nothing this side of heaven, and that's the whole truth."

"So you're out to score now, right?"

"Sure."

"And you got the bread on you?"

Then Dog grinned again. "Watch it, brother. I'm a mean prick."

"Oh I can see that," Dusty smiled. "I see that for sure."

But as they slowed into the next curve Yeats braced himself against the dash. The kid was rapping his fingers to the clack of the wipers. Shadows from overhead trees swept the cab, and Dusty's coiled arm finally snapped, his open palm jabbing to the kid's pinched face.

The rear window shattered, and the truck went skidding. Sheets of water flew over the hood, but Yeats kept driving his elbow into the ribs. When the truck finally stalled out, the kid lay curled and moaning.

Dusty had started prattling, mumbling, all while he rifled through his victim's clothes. Then he was kicking the door open, dragging the kid to the side of the road. When he jammed in the clutch and went off he had one nasty vision of the kid on all fours, a wounded animal. Old times.

Dusty left the truck in a garbage alley somewhere in the city. His clothes were still damp and caked with mud. There had been eighty dollars in the kid's wallet. It was more than enough to see him through the night, but when he had counted it out he felt deeply ashamed.

He took a junkie's room in a trashed out hotel where the desk clerk asked no questions. A night cost twelve dollars, but there was only a lumpy bed, a desk, a chair and a lamp. He would have given blood for a television set, but then he remembered that junkies didn't need the tube. On smack one could sit in a closet all day and, so to speak, dig it.

Out on the street again at midnight, Dusty felt badly wasted. The muscles in his legs kept tightening. Down the block was a bar, but it was filled with jive blacks and he didn't like the glares he

9

got. Finally he found a dirty, little market, bought a box of chocolate cookies and the cheapest gin they had, then scurried back to
his room. Waking in the morning with echoes of old plumbing
through the walls, blinking into the pasty light, he could hardly
believe what had happened. Then in a wave of panic he suddenly
remembered that he was still holding the plastic folder he had
taken from Central Reference. It was unforgivable folly to carry
it now.

He grabbed his jacket, and pulled out the folder. Inside it were
about twenty sheets of paper, neatly typed and stamped with red
numerals along the margins. He knew he should have read them,
but he was too afraid. He only wanted to get rid of them. For a
long time he stood, half-naked, glaring at the ceiling and floor.
Then he decided that the room was no good, so he dressed and
moved down the foul staircase.

Behind the hotel lay a vacant lot, half paved and filled with
trash. The end of the lot faced a sooty brick wall. He made sure
that no one was watching and began to feel for loose bricks. Then
he saw the length of exposed pipe which ran along the bottom of
the wall. The pipe was rusty, but bone dry. It must have served
no purpose. He rolled up the folder and stuffed it as far into the
pipe as he could. Then for an instant he was vaguely elated. He
even grinned. It was a perfect dead-drop. God doesn't help, Jessie
used to say. You've got to be your own engine, make your own
breaks. So Yeats took his first real chance and called a hustling
flake named Danny Grimes.

Yeats and Grimes had known each other from the war. Grimes
had been a Saigon dealer, now he ran errands for Special Operations. He terrorized people, but rarely hurt them.

Dusty had to plead, balled up naked on the bed with the telephone pressed in tight to his ear. Finally Grimes agreed to meet
him in a bar nine blocks away. Then came more frantic minutes,
trying to wash the mud from his clothes. When the dacron tore
at the shoulder, Yeats gave it up.

10

The bar was a sultry hole with a pool table and plastic booths. Not even noon and there were seven drunks slouched on the stools. Grimes was waiting at a table in the rear. He was a wiry little man with a long face and immature teeth. He had lost some hair since Yeats had seen him last.

"I appreciate this, Danny. I really do," said Yeats. He scrunched into the booth to face Grimes. He couldn't help digging his nails into the pool of dribbled candle wax.

"I shouldn't even be talking to you, Dusty boy. You're on the hit parade. They're after your ass. We're supposed to shoot you on sight."

"Yeah well I'm in a little trouble, you know? Got to get away till this blows over. So I figured maybe you could help, you know?"

Grimes frowned. "Oh man, what is this? Charity? You need a passport, some bread and ticket to ride, but you don't even have the dime to call me up again."

"Look, Danny, what can I say? I need it bad. I need it real bad. Soon as I get it together I'll send you some bread, but right now I need it."

"How much you got in the bank?"

"I don't know. A couple of grand. But I can't go to no bank. They'll be expecting that."

Behind the bar a sullen black was swabbing the floor. Dusty suddenly realized that he must have been on the take from Grimes. This is one of Danny's places, he thought. That's why he's got me here. The black man kept glancing over.

"I'll tell you what," said Grimes. "You be straight with me and I'll be straight with you."

"I am being straight."

"Yeah? How come you called me in the first place? You don't even like me."

Yeats shook his head. "Look, just tell me yes or no. I need a passport, some money, some clothes and a ticket out of here. I'll

11

get it all back to you and then some. Whatever terms you want. So just tell me yes or no, Danny. I can't screw around any longer."

"That bad, huh?" Grimes smiled. "Okay, it'll go like this. The passport will be one of the standard escape books. I know a guy who can do one up for you. Without the proper clearance you'll only be safe with it for about two days, but at least it'll get you out. I can give you about a grand in cash, and a ticket to Mexico City. The clothes you can buy yourself. I'm no errand boy. The whole package will run you ten. Call me tonight, say about eight."

"I appreciate this, Danny. I really do."

"Sure, everyone owes me."

"And I'll get the bread to you. I swear I will. I got friends elsewhere."

"Yeah, I know about your friends. There's Jessie Dancer for starters."

"Ah, Jessie is okay."

"Yeah? Is he in on this?"

"Come on, Danny, don't ask me things like that."

"Because if Jessie Dancer is in on this one then you're in a lot more trouble than you think. Jessie is the devil's only son. Know what I mean? He'll put you right between a rock and a hard place. You got Jessie on one side and his old man on the other, and now you're talking big establishment. Allen Dancer has long arms, Dusty. You know what I'm saying here? Rock and the hard place. Jessie Dancer is around the bend."

During the next hours Dusty Yates might have been living in a cracked glass jar. Impressions were disjointed. There was the roar of traffic, and jagged light off the chrome. Women hung from tenement windows. Fierce kids drank wine on the stoops. White boys could live their whole lives on the streets and never have a clue what the secrets signs of the blacks and Hispanics meant.

Yeats spent the afternoon riveted on the bed. When he tried to sleep he just kept seeing that boy by the side of the road, down

12

on all fours. Finally he was pacing, checking the window, listening for footsteps in the hall outside. His mouth felt gummed with chocolate and gin. He wished he had a toothbrush.

Nightfall, and Yeats just let the room fill up with shadows. At eight o'clock he telephoned Grimes, then walked out the door, down the hall and back into those streets. Now the ghetto had a bombed out feel. There were vacant shops and gutted storefronts. Buildings were spray-painted with the anagrams of local gangs. Three blocks down he saw Grimes glaring from behind the windshield of a Cadillac.

Grimes drove erratically, punching off from dead stops, then riding the breaks. They were moving through a neighborhood of factories. The streets were badly lit. End of the line was a loading dock, squeezed between two brick walls. They were hemmed in by chain link and cement.

"The dude who does the passports works up there," Grimes said.

"I don't know, Danny. Couldn't you just go and get it yourself?"

"He's got to take your photograph. What do you think? Passport needs a photograph."

They passed through an alcove and up a flight of wooden steps. Dusty's heart had started pounding. All down the filthy corridor he kept wiping his hands on the seat of his pants.

They stopped at a battered door with a pane of frosted glass. Grimes rapped twice, then smiled. "Be happy you're almost home now."

But Dusty's stomach was inexplicably knotting. Then came the merest slip of a falling shoe from down the corridor. Yeats started to turn, but now there was a squating shape at each end of the hall. Both were balled-up and stiff armed. It was real when Dusty saw the sweeping pistols. He would have shaken the whole world to fuck them over one last time, but all he had was Grimes. He

13

wrenched up the man by his shirt, pushed his face through the glass. And everything exploded.

In the end time became liquid. There were only soft slow shapes. He saw the smooth head of a Langley hunter, another in a red checked sportscoat stood behind. Grimes was kneeling, swabbing blood with his sleeve. He himself had crumpled, heard himself panting from a kick to the groin that he had not even seen coming.

And now he too was on all fours, like the kid.

They took Dusty Yeats to the holding tank in a compound of low, solid buildings. All was concrete and flat gray. But beyond the chain-link fence lay an open land of tall grass and hollyhock. Further still there were the trees, evergreens and laurels. The days were cold, but mostly clear. Wispy clouds sailed, unraveling with the tradewinds. Then too these clearing days must have been omens for Yeats, because he soon passed into the hands of the gentle Humphrey Knolls.

They said that Humphrey once loved an extraordinarily pretty girl who loved him back but only as a brother. She used to call him Humpty Dumpty, and in the end she ran off with a silent killer named Robin Turner. Now Knolls was prematurely caught in middle age. He was a round, faintly grubby little man with a chubby face and thinning carrot hair. He lived in a flat with a kitchenette and clumsy furniture. He wore cheap stay-press shirts and had a dozen quirky habits. Only truly compassionate women were kind to him.

Langley historians have always seen Humphrey's role in the Dancer story solely as the prod, the one who questioned Yeats and later drafted the first reports. But years before Humphrey had been an historian himself, and he had loved those chronicles as only a quizzical scholar could. He had even loved the great, dusty hall where the files were then kept in a warren of tall shelves, and even though Knolls had been with Lyle Severson's counterintelli-

14

gence group for fifteen years he had never really lost that historian's sense of the past. It would serve him well from here on out.

Officially Humphrey's entrance into the Dancer story came the morning after Yeats was caught, because that was when counterintelligence was first called in. But Humphrey's own sense of a beginning came before all that. The night of Yates's capture a sparrow had flown into his bedroom window, shattering the glass, killing itself. The terrible thump and tinkling shards had frightened Knolls so badly that he had not been able to get back to sleep. When they had telephoned at dawn he was still sitting on his rollaway bed, staring through the jagged pane of glass. The bird lay in the sooty rainspout. Beyond hung a sculpture of black oak. Through those branches lay neat lawns and garden walls. The windshields of parked cars were frosted over. Nothing moved in the neighborhood. Especially that dead sparrow.

You had to drive past the Langley complex to get to the prisoner's compound. A ribbon of black tarmac wound through the wooded dingles. Knolls took this route now in his battered Rambler. Low mist lay among the rolling hills.

Not far from the gate house he parked, and in the distance was a watery vision of Lyle Severson, bent, chatting with a uniformed guard. His breath was fogging the air. Then he must have heard Humphrey's leather soles grinding on the path, because he turned to watch, and Humphrey was moving toward the gaunt man on the path between wet grass and ferns.

Lyle was an old man, nearly as old as John Dancer. He lived alone in a drafty house with creaking stairways, groves of burnished furniture and rooms that he hardly ever entered. He often had difficulty sleeping, and the night of the storm had been especially bad.

"Thought my roof would fly away," he told Humphrey. "It was the wind." Now in the cold and weak light he looked especially skeletal. He wore a black coat and a muffler that somebody had given him years ago.

15

The two men had walked a little ways past the guardhouse further into the compound. Just ahead lay the concrete building. Beyond was a dreamy view of red leaves and green grass through the low mist.

"Haven't been sleeping much myself," Humphrey replied. He thought of the bird in the rainspout.

"You might have a few more sleepless nights," Lyle said.

"It's as bad as all that?"

Lyle nodded. "Ever heard of a boy named Dusty Yeats? Stocky. Special Forces in Vietnam, then knocked around Cambodia until they brought him in as junior."

"No," Humphrey sighed. "I don't know him."

"Didn't think you did. I'd never heard of him either. He was just another kid in from the East. But he's a mean little fellow. He beats people up all the time."

From somewhere along the edge of the black circle of pavement a dog began to howl, and the wind moved through the tufted grass beyond the fence.

"It started in Central Reference," Lyle said. "Nightwatch caught him rummaging around. He was trying to conceal some papers under his jacket. When the guard tried to take him in he got nasty. There was also a bit of drama during the escape. Apparently he flagged down a pickup truck, and beat the driver very badly. They finally got him as he was trying to buy a passport. He contacted one of the local stringers, but the stringer set him up. The boy received a face full of stitches for the trouble."

"What did he take from Central Reference?"

Lyle shook his head. Strands of his snowy hair were blowing in his eyes. "We don't really know yet. We haven't retrieved them, and the inventory check isn't finished. However, it appears that he took a product list. Out of date, of course, but it may be one of the Magic lists."

"Why would he want a product list?"

"First he claimed that he was acting on orders of Herold Pimm.

16

When that one fell through he shut up entirely. My theory, however, is that he simply went dirty. He wanted to make some money on the open market, and took the first item that looked interesting."

Knolls sighed again. "Poor, stupid fool. He could have done better than Central Reference if he was after something marketable. He should have gone for Science and Technology. There's always a buyer for that stuff."

Severson shrugged. "Apparently he's not all that bright."

Far across the windswept grass moved the rippling figure of a guard and his dog, which reminded Humphrey of his floppy basset hound, long since killed by a gang of boys. Dogs, sparrows . . .

"I'm not sure what sort of leverage we have," Severson was saying. "His parents are dead, so there's no hope of using that approach. He does, however, have a sister, and I gather that they're fairly close. On the other hand, she's only sixteen, I wouldn't like to drag her in unless we absolutely have to. You might want to mention it, though."

"His sister?" Knolls said vaguely. "Yeats has a sister?"

"A waitress in a coffee shop, lives in California."

"I'm afraid I don't see the relevance."

"Well, you might want to mention her to shake him up, so to speak."

"Oh." Sometimes Humphrey Knolls passionately disliked his work.

Interrogation began that morning. Humphrey asked the questions while Lyle played over the tapes in the next room. The cell was small and square. The walls were dark green, and the steel door was buff. There was a bunk bed, two chairs and a rudimentary desk, The single light was fitted to the ceiling. Of course, no windows.

The cell was cold so Humphrey left his raincoat on. It was an old brown rumpled thing with missing buttons and frayed cuffs. The tramp across the dewy grass had soaked his socks, and now he could hardly keep from shivering. Worse, however, were the boy's eyes.

Yeats was bunched up in the corner of his cot. His knees were drawn up to his chest. He might have been waiting to kill someone, and certainly he didn't seem afraid of Knolls, not in the least. When Knolls stepped into the cell he had had the thought that he had come too early. I should have let time soften him up, he had told himself.

The first hour was prickly. Yeats was tough. Knolls asked what happened to the papers that Yeats had taken, and Yeats, without a pause, said that he had lost them running through the forest.

"Where in the forest?" Knolls asked.

"How the fuck would I know? I said they were lost. Lost means you don't know where."

"Well, do you suppose they fell out of your jacket?"

"No, they jumped out. They couldn't stand the smell. Shit! Of course they fell out."

"When did you notice they were gone?"

"I don't know. The next day I guess."

"What made you take those particular papers?"

"I don't know. They looked important, like they might be worth something."

"Do you know what they were?"

"No. I didn't get a chance to read them."

"Well, they were product lists, Dusty. Do you know what a product list is?"

"Yeah, it's a list of stuff that's been taken in from the field."

"That's right. Each item is numbered and synopsized as to content. Lists are compiled according to project headings or operation headings, and they're usually chronological. Now, Dusty, why do you suppose you thought the particular list you took would be worth something?"

"Because it had red numbers on it."

18

"Red numbers?"

"Yeah. There was little red numbers stamped on each page."

"And do you know what those numbers stood for?"

"Yeah. They meant the stuff was secret."

"That's right. They were secret, and do you know why?"

"Everything's secret around this dump."

"They were secret, Dusty, because the product list was one of the Source Magic lists."

"Oh I get it. I'm in hot water, huh? I was fucking around with Source Magic, and now the big guns are coming down on me. Is that why they sent you, Knolls? You a big gun?" The second stage was smoother. Knolls found the thread of a story and drew it out slowly. The boy said that he had broken into Central Reference for product. It had been a solo job. No one had put him up to it. The plan had been to take anything of value, and sell it to the first buyer.

"Did you have a buyer in mind?" Humphrey asked. His voice was still soft, but his glasses kept fogging. Whenever he took them off to clean them his eyes felt naked, moist.

"There's a guy in Paris," Dusty said. "A fence. Lots of guys sell him stuff. I thought, you know, I would try him first."

"I wouldn't imagine you'd get the best price," Humphrey said, and for a moment it seemed that he genuinely cared.

"Yeah well you take what you can get, don't you?"

"What about the product? Was there a shopping list, anything you specifically had in mind?"

Yeats smirked. "I'm no damn syndicate, for Christ sake. I don't make plans, I just do things. I was just going to take whatever looked good, you know?"

"Then why Central Reference? It seems to me that Central Reference is way out of the current field. I mean it's a storage bin, some of that material goes back . . . oh I don't know . . . fifty years or more. Surely you would have found more valuable items in Technical?"

"Well, surely you're an asshole, Mr. Knolls, I may be a dumb

19

fuck, but I'm not a creep. I wasn't out to get anyone hurt, I didn't want to blow some poor jerk out of the water. I just wanted to sell some stuff that no one could care less about anyway. Okay? I needed a little bread. I'm not a heavy guy. I love this job," and he smirked again.

"Why did you need the money, Dusty?"

"Cause I'm sick of living like a nigger."

"Was it for your sister, Tracy? Was the money for her?"

Yeats rolled his eyes and breathed hard. "Yeah, I needed it so I could pay for the operation, get her out of the fucking wheelchair. Didn't they tell you? Trace and I are orphans, and she's the poor little cripple."

Knolls came back as calmly as before. "Does your sister know what you do, Dusty?"

"Yeah, sure. I tell her everything. She thinks I'm James Bond."

Before Knolls left he asked once more where the missing papers were, but once again Yeats said that he lost them in the forest. Then Knolls rose, walked to the cell door, and knocked twice for the guard to let him out. When the door was shut again, Knolls told the guard to give the prisoner anything he wanted. Cigarettes, chocolate, magazines. The guard was to provide anything the boy wanted. True, this was a classic interrogator's procedure, but it was also more than that. Kindness had always been a border to Humphrey's incongruous life.

The days were toppling into one another. Humphrey moved into one of the compound rooms, hardly less austere than Dusty's cell—the same sort of cot, the same crude, metal furniture, the same drab linoleum floor. But Knolls did have a window, one square of glass that looked out across the blacktop through the fence and out to the rolling hills. Two miles beyond the forest you could see the Langley towers above the trees.

The days were gray again. Sometimes there was rain, sometimes light snow. After the first spell of cold, Knolls had an electric

20

heater installed in Dusty's cell. The boy did not thank him for this, and the softening that Humphrey had hoped for never came. Yeats remained the rock. He still claimed that he had acted alone, that all he had wanted from Central Reference was something to flog on the market.

So Knolls went to the records. He worked nights mostly, often into the small hours. By the end of the week the strain was beginning to show. His skin was pale. His eyes were ringed with red. Severson told him that he looked bizarre, but Humphrey did not care, for he had already begun to sense the magnitude of what lay ahead. Later he would write that the path of the Dancer story had begun to widen at this point. Soon he would glimpse a landscape as limitless and forbidding as the bottom of the sea.

Humphrey's first clue came from the Watch Tower book. There in Dusty's schoolboy hand every incoming telex had been logged. Yet even among these routine entries Knolls detected the beginning of a pattern. More intense nights followed. Humphrey had taken to reading on his cot in the yellow spray of a tensor lamp. Some nights rain came pounding off the corrugated roofs. Other nights there was wind humming in the chain link fence. Snow fell once, and when Humphrey padded to the window he saw the whole glowing landscape just before the dawn.

But mostly the files kept him wedged in the corner of his cot. He was well past the Watch Tower now, into Operational Services. Dusty had mainly handled second-class stuff, but again the log gave up a pattern. There were certain reports that had slowed way down whenever his interest had been aroused. Further, the boy had been given certain research rights so that ambiguous points could be checked against the master files, and Humphrey was able to follow the trail through the record of call slips.

First there was Dusty's request for Allen Dancer's study of European courier links. Then he was asking at the research desk for a Kremlin brief written years ago by old John. Finally he had taken a look at the personal files of top Dancer aides, and so it went night after night until Humphrey's tiny cement room was filled with possibilities and the looming reflection of all the Dancers.

In the end the days cleared again, for a while at least. Tradewinds swept the sky of clouds, and the meadows and the forests seemed crystallized, or gently tossed by the breeze. Knolls had reached the first plateau. The records would one day bear this fact when the historians eventually got hold of his memo to Lyle Severson, the one which contained the first reference to Source Magic.

On the morning of this, the first clear day, Knolls met Lyle at the compound. They followed the fence as far as the first trees. Before they quite realized it they had trudged off the road and into the sea of wet grass.

Trees stood bare and steaming with dew. The sun was a pale oval. At the rise of a mound they stopped, Humphrey panting. "It's a question of emphasis."

"Sounds pretty flimsy to me." Lyle frowned.

All around them was open greenery of high grass and shaggy ferns.

"Look at it this way," Knolls said. "Yeats was a rat. He kept gnawing away at things. He was especially obsessed with certain lines, certain Soviet bloc lines."

Lyle was facing the wind with stiff lips and watery eyes. "I suppose you know that you look like hell," he said.

"What do you expect? I've been up all night."

The sound of the wind in the grass was oddly haunting now. They might have been standing at the edge of the world.

Finally Knolls said, "Why don't I run down the sequence?"

"Sure, the sequence." Lyle coughed.

"Okay, it's six months ago," Knolls began. "Yeats is living in Thailand. He's loosely attached to a backwater listening post but he was also involved in some sort of paramilitary. I'm not sure what. Then one day he sends a petition into Placement. He says

22

that he's tired of living on the fringes. He wants to make something of himself, wants to be part of the Company proper. Well, Placement is sympathetic, but they turn him down. They tell him that there are no available positions at the moment. You know the sort of letters they write. Actually he's denied on psychological grounds. His profile is too unstable. But of course Yeats eventually petitioned again and he was given a post out here. What's important is that now we come to the first curious knot. The Dancers. Allen, John, and finally Jessie. Jessie particularly. He's the one I couldn't fit into the picture at first. Then I checked Dusty's service record. Jessie and Yeats knew each other in Thailand. They had even known each other in Vietnam. When Placement first turns Yeats down, Dancer writes his father Allen and asks him to give Yeats a job. So now we have the makings of a neat little knot."

Lyle had grown stiff. His hands were jammed hard in the pockets of his coat. He was looking out across the landscape of bending grass.

"I'm talking facts, Lyle. We've got to come to terms with the facts, and facts are that Yeats stole papers listing material which Source Magic took in over a nine-month period. Yeats claims that he had not known that the material related to Magic, and I'm sure he's lying, because everything points to one thing. Yeats never wanted to make it as a Company boy. He wanted information. He was trying to find out how Allen Dancer ran the Soviet desk, and more particularly he was trying to find out something about Source Magic."

Suddenly Lyle's head turned sideways. "You're on a very dangerous road. All sorts of snakes along the way. Do you understand that, Humphrey? Do you fully understand?"

"Oh, I think so, I think I know the implications—"

"All right." Lyle sighed. "Then just how far do you want to go?"

Humphrey might have been a stodgy schoolboy now. His cheeks were flushed by the wind. "I'd like to ask the big question,"

23

he said. "I'd like to hammer away at Source Magic and see how Yeats reacts. I also want to ask him about Jessie. I think it's important that we find out just how Jessie fits."

Lyle began nodding before he spoke. "I'll want a guard posted outside the door when you do it. And don't feed him. You can toss out the line, but if he doesn't bite, don't feed him. Also, don't expect me to tape it. I bloody well don't need Allan Dancer jumping down my throat."

Dusty seemed calmer. Humphrey Knolls found him squatting on the end of the cot, tossing pennies against the wall. He did not glance up when Humphrey entered. He just sang out, "What's happening, Knolls?"

"How are you, Dusty?"

"Me, I'm smooth, Knolls. You pricks have got me moving smooth now."

It must have been true because Humphrey felt particularly clumsy and fat.

"I'd like to go back a bit this morning," he said. "If that's all right with you, Dusty?" The pretense of friendship was by now a firm part of the ritual.

"Back, forward; makes no difference to me. I'm an open book. I've seen the light." He was jangling the pennies.

"All right, let's go back to Thailand."

"Sure." Dusty shrugged. "I'm a hero over there. I'm helping the nationalists kick ass against the Pathet Lao and Vietnamese."

"Actually I'm more interested in your friends. Your American friends?"

"Ahh. Give the fat man a medal. Big break, huh, Knolls? You found out about Jessie Dancer. So now you know that I was hanging out with the famous Allen Dancer's kid, huh? Well, big deal."

"You were rather close to Jessie, weren't you?"

"Sure. I was his best friend."

24

"And he got you placed here, didn't he? He used his influence with his father to get you into Langley. Is that right?"

"You got it, Knolls."

"And did you ever talk to Jessie about his father?"

"Yeah, you know . . . now and then Jess would bring up the famous Al Dancer."

"And did he ever tell you what Allen does?"

"Sure. He fights communism. Don't we all?"

"I mean specifically, Dusty. What does Allen Dancer do specifically?"

Dusty had tossed all his pennies away. Now he was picking at the olive-green army blanket. His nails raked through his hair.

"Look, Knolls, what do you want? Huh? How could I know anything? I was in the fucking jungle sticking gooks for a grand a month. How could I know anything?"

"But, Dusty, you knew about Source Magic. That much is very clear."

The room was suddenly very still. Then Yates said, "I trusted you, I really trusted you, Knolls. And then you pull that kind of shit. Why didn't you just tell me straight that I was busted? You didn't have to play that crummy little game . . ."

Humphrey bit his lip until his skin turned white, but then his voice was soft and even. "All right, Dusty, I'll tell you how I think it happened. I think it began in Thailand, and Jessie put you up to it. He got you a job in his father's group so you could check it out from the inside."

Yeats seemed to sag. He was squinting at the scuffed linoleum. "Jessie said that he never used to think about Magic too much. He said he wasn't interested in it. All he really knew was that the operation was his father's big gun. It's what put Al Dancer at the top of the heap and kept him there for what? Thirty years? He also knew that Magic's roots went back to the old man, John Dancer. So Jessie tells me, 'Go to Langley and work yourself in. Then we'll bust them wide open.' "

25

"How do you mean, Dusty?"

Yeats began to tap his knuckles on his thigh. "Jessie knows a lot about Magic. He knows how the retrieval system works, who brings the product in and from where. He also said he knows who Source Magic is. I mean who the guy in Moscow is. He didn't tell me how he found all this out, but he did say that he couldn't bust it unless he had a product list, or something that came from Moscow. So that was the game he wanted me to play here. Anything else I could get on Magic was gravy."

"So that's what you were doing in Central Reference? You went in there with the purpose of getting the product list and you got it."

"Yeah, I got it."

"And before, all the work you did before was only so that you could locate where they kept the product lists?"

"Hey, pin a medal on yourself, Knolls. You're a real smart fucker."

But Humphrey would not be shaken, although that spindly chair wobbled whenever he shifted his weight. "I only wonder," he said, "that is, what made you do it? You must have known the risks involved. So why?"

"Because Jessie Dancer is a friend of mine," Yeats scowled.

"How do you feel about him now?"

Yates looked at him. No smirk now. "Why don't you save that question for the day that Jessie comes back."

Humphrey waited twenty-four hours before he went back to Yeats. In that time he doodled, mooned around the compound grounds and out along the road through the open grassy hills. In the evening he went walking with Lyle, and they both agreed that the basic facts had now been established. Jessie Dancer's role became defined. He had sent Dusty into the heart of his father's world, and his intentions had been decidedly unfriendly.

In one day Dusty seemed to have strangely aged. He had not shaved. The cell had a new odor, perspiration. Knolls found the

26

prisoner supine on the cot. When the boy sat up his nose began to run. He was blowing and coughing into a wad of tissue.

"We need to know about Jessie," Humphrey finally said.

The boy sniffed again and wiped his sleeve across his nose. "Jessie Dancer, huh? Well, you never met anyone like Jessie. I can assure you of that."

No, Humphrey thought, he supposed he hadn't.

"Besides, Jess wouldn't like you, Knolls. He hates fat people."

Humphrey only swallowed. He had been living with such comments all his life. As a child he had always been tormented . . . "What about his father?" he asked. "Does Jessie also hate his father?"

Dusty smiled. "Ah, so that's your missing piece. You can't figure out why. Jessie sends me to turn his old man's operation inside out, and you can't figure out why."

"They tell me that Jessie had a break with his father."

"A break, huh? Is that what they call it? A break? Jesus, Knolls, you don't have a clue, do you?"

Humphrey felt the way he looked, a dumpy man on a wobbly chair. "I've never met either of them," he said. "The grandfather, John, I've met him briefly, but I've never met either Allen or Jessie."

Dusty's eyes looked directly into Humphrey's. "Let me tell you something, Knolls. They say Jessie Dancer is out of his mind, off his cork. Well, if he is, he sure makes sense about one thing—when he tells how much he hates his father."

With confession came new freedom, and Dusty was allowed to prowl the compound so long as the guards were posted. On restless mornings he and Humphrey would lope the circle of the chain link fence. On other mornings the guilt got to him, and they would sag on the bench beneath the corrugated awning. But he was generally talking freely now, and Humphrey taped their conversations with a microphone hidden in his coat.

By the third week they were well into the Asian days, and the

27

unifying thread was Jessie Dancer. Dusty had met him first in Vietnam. Jessie had been heading a delta station in a land where the Communists ran freely every night. The station was white-washed and old colonial. There were black iron grills on the windows and coils of barbed wire on the outer garden walls. The portico had been hung with screens to deflect grenades and a poplar grew in the courtyard.

Dusty said that he and Jessie used to waste the days, just stretched out on rotting mattresses, tracking the rotations of an overhead fan. After a joint or two of the local grass the mouldings on the ceiling seemed to blister in a steamy, yellow haze. Dusty used to love to stare at the corners of the room until the plaster started undulating. Jessie, however, did not take dope. He said that drugs destroyed his night vision, and there on the delta every-thing happened at night.

There were clean, stark images of the perverse drama that Yeats and Dancer played out when the sun went down behind the jungle hills. Snaking through the forest, pulling down the enemy—the evil—with knives and bits of piano wire—it was like some perverse religious mission.

Yates remembered how they would sit on the bamboo porch, solemnly smearing their faces with night-fighter cosmetic. When they felt right, they would lope out into the fading green. By the time the forest floor was black they were already hanging from the trees, as motionless as snakes. Then the V.C. came, and Dusty said that you would flip right into a trance with the leaves shivering and all those shapes scattering below. "Took a second to zip through a clip with an M-16 on full automatic. Then three more to reload, but in that first second you really shot your wad."

After a month of night patrol the war became exclusively their own. They lived nocturnally like vampires. Regular station busi-ness fell by the side. Jessie hardly bothered with his weekly intelli-gence briefs. Nor did he stay in touch with his Province Advisor. As far as the Advisor was concerned Dancer's unit was a lost

28

cause. "But as far as we were concerned," Dusty said, "our job was getting done. We knew what the game was no matter what kind of shit they tried to give us. They sent us over to kill dinks and that was just what we were doing."

It got pretty hard to stop killing. Dusty remembered how Jessie hadn't wanted to leave even when the North Vietnam regulars started pouring in. "He wanted to stay. He wanted to pull back into the jungle and keep cutting them down . . ."

But the war did end, and Jessie had to leave. Then followed the lost years. Jessie returned to London and worked in the American embassy. They gave him a job which did not demand the slightest thought. Dusty went back to California. His mother had died, and he had to take care of his sister. He worked evenings as a security guard in a bank. "Sometimes it was all I could do to keep from blowing away jerks with that Mickey Mouse .38 Special they gave me."

Then Jessie came back. He came in the fall, at the end of a freak weather stretch—a heat wave. Yeats had just stepped out of his trailer house, a beaten, gray, tin sausage of a thing he shared with his sister. He was heading down the dirt path for his Chevy. It was dark, and the crickets were throbbing all over. Then a finger brushed his ear. He whirled, but there was only Jessie, smiling from the hollow of leaves. "I got another war for you, Dusty boy."

The job, Yeats explained, was helping Cambodian guerillas harass the Vietnamese. Ever since the Vietnamese had invaded Cambodia anticommunist refugees had been striking from the Thai border. The forces were small, but Dancer had said that with CIA support the conflict would grow. He believed that there was no better inspiration than modern weapons.

For obvious reasons the project was top secret. No one wanted the word to spread that American Special Forces were involved in another Asian war. Weapons and supplies would be filtered through Bangkok, and Jessie had imagined that the money would also be laundered there as well. Pay was two thousand a month,

29

but the Company would not cover their insurance.

Action was sporadic and quick, mostly light firefights with communist patrols. Morale among the guerillas was high. Most were young, sixteen to twenty. In defiance of a Cambodian edict they wore their hair long. Some tied it back, others wore head bands, Che Guevara style. Dusty could not get over the irony. In Vietnam he had been the invader, fighting the ragtag so-called idealists. In Cambodia the situation was reversed. He even began to believe in the ideals himself. Jessie, however, had no beliefs one way or another. Once he told Yeats that he liked combat because it was the only time he felt involved in something that could free him from his own mind. It was a relief, he said.

Dark days followed. Clouds kept churning in from the east, and the air grew tepid and damp. Broad leaves went limp, and often there were thunder showers. By now Yeats was speaking freely. Humphrey hardly had to prompt him anymore. But with each confession, through each passing day, Dusty seemed to die a little. Eventually Knolls could find him listlessly slumped at the far end of the compound.

On the twentieth day Yeats didn't even bother to turn around when Knolls approached. He just waited for the footsteps on the blacktop, then said, "You guys are going to throw me away pretty soon, aren't you?"

Humphrey stepped to the prisoner's side. Now they both stood facing the grass and trees beyond. "What gives you that idea?"

Yeats shrugged. "I get up this morning and start banging on the door. Jake lets me out. I take one step and some fucking bird shits on my hand. Right here." He held his fist to Humphrey's face, then let it slap back down to his thigh. "Bad sign, Knolls. Ever calculate those kind of odds? One bird and one jerk in all this open space. Maybe that bird's entire life was running on a sort of parallel track to mine. Then a day comes when I walk outside and he gets me. It's a bad sign. You know?"

He's feeling the guilt again, Humphrey thought. A lot of them felt guilty after they talked.

"I may be a stupid little fucker," Dusty went on, "but at least I can see the signs."

"What about Jessie?" Humphrey asked. "Could he see the signs?" It was a weak opener, but he felt he had to change the subject quickly.

"Jessie doesn't have to see the signs. He makes his own."

They had started traipsing the perimeter of the compound. Dusty had wrenched off a strand of creeper vine and was letting it drag and coil behind him. Eventually he was rambling on about Jessie again. He said that his friend had no superstitions, or at least not the usual ones. All Jessie feared were things.

"What sort of things?" They were facing the tree line again. Humphrey's hands were jammed in his pockets.

"Just things. You know, objects. Maybe it would be a doorknob, or an empty bottle. He could walk into a room, and maybe there would be nothing in that room but a table and a couple of chairs. And maybe on that table there would be an empty bottle and a dish. And he'd sit down at the table, and just look at the bottle and the dish, but he couldn't touch them. Once he told me that everything you touched was covered with this invisible slime. Only he didn't say it like that. He said that there was just this sort of evil in things. And they disgusted him. He used that word a lot. Disgust. He said that he hated objects because they were more real than he was. Bottles, tables, chairs—they were too solid, too real. They just stood there existing, and he hated them for that. It was weird, but like I told you, Jessie is pretty special, far out . . ."

"Did he feel the same way about people?"

"Sometimes, but it was different with people. Jessie hated people for other reasons. I remember once we caught a dink line in a mango grove. They were just marching into this little grove, and we caught them right in the open—prime selection. But about

31

three of them got away. Well Jess tracked those three down for a mile until he finally took them. So I asked him why. Why all that sweat for just three dinks? And he told me that he had to get them because they were bad. That's all he said. They were bad men. I thought it was a joke at first, but then I realized that he really believed it. He believed there were really bad people in the world."

"Did Jessie believe that his father was bad?"

"Sure. What do you think?"

"What about Source Magic? Did Jessie believe that the operation was bad?"

"Rotten to the core."

"Did he tell you why?"

"Jesus, Knolls, you don't quit, do you?"

A wind had risen, bringing the scent of the damp forest and the coming rain. Already there were mounds of black, wooly clouds above the distant hills. Soon the landscape would grow taut in the muggy stillness, then thunder.

Finally Knolls said, "We could take a break if you like."

"No, I want to get it over with."

"Okay, then how about Source Magic again? Can we talk about that for a little while?"

"Yeah," Dusty sighed. "Magic. Magic was the big time. Jess told me that everything his family had was because of Magic. Even when Jess was a kid, Magic paid the rent. No one could touch Al Dancer as long as he controlled Source Magic."

"And what did he tell you Magic was. Precisely I mean."

"Precisely, huh? Okay, Knolls, this one's for you. He said that Source Magic was a highly placed Moscow Center intelligence officer who fed product to Allen Dancer. The product was delivered through a courier system that ran through one or more safe-houses. The main one was called Sorcerer, and it's supposed to be in Zurich. The couriers and safe-houses are all funded and operated under a program called Enchanted Forest. Jessie said that anything I could get on the Enchanted Forest would be good,

32

but what he mainly wanted was a product list."

"Did he tell you why?"

"No."

"The list you took was about three years old, did you know that?"

"Yeah, but Jess said it didn't matter. He just wanted a list of stuff that Allen Dancer got from his guy in Moscow. He said I could either get a whole list, or even just a sample of the Magic product would do, but I swear to God I don't know what he wanted it for."

Knolls had grown still. He was taking small quiet breaths. "What about the origins of Magic?" he finally asked.

"What do you mean?"

"Well, did Jessie ever talk about how it all started?"

"He didn't know how it started. He said that Magic had just been around as long as he could remember. Even when he was a kid there had always been Source Magic, like this big family secret, the treasure chest. Source Magic, get your hands on that baby, he used to tell me, and you could run the whole show."

"And is that what Jessie wants? He wants to control Source Magic?"

Yeats lumped up his cheek and smirked. "I didn't say that, Knolls. I was just telling you about the Magic myth—that's how Jessie used to describe it. He said that Magic was like this old myth. Like the Golden Fleece or something. Did you ever see that movie? Well everyone is trying to find this treasure that will make them rich and famous, and that's what Source Magic is like. But Jess never wanted it for himself. He just wanted to wreck it."

Then again, in his softest voice, "But why, Dusty? Why did Jessie want to destroy Source Magic?"

There was a long pause. Then Yeats whispered something that Knolls could not hear entirely. It was something about a girl.

"A girl?" Knolls replied.

"Yeah, there was a girl."

33

"What girl, Dusty? Who was she?"

"Sara."

"Sara? Sara who?"

"Moore. Her name was Sara Moore."

"And who was she?"

"Just a girl. Jessie met her in London."

"And this girl is the reason why Jessie wants to hit Magic?"

"Yeah, that's the reason."

"But why?"

"Because Magic fucked her over. That's what Jessie said. He said that Magic fucked her over, just like it's fucked over lots of people. He said that Magic was all wound up in lies and people got hurt for no reason. He said that Source Magic was how the real pricks of this world control everyone else. Crazy, huh?"

Humphrey did not return to the compound that night. In the early evening he tramped for miles down the winding road until he stood surrounded by quivering pines. The glade was alive with falling dew. Endings were always moody, and this one seemed especially sad, because Knolls had come to like the boy, though he was not sure why.

Later he drove to the city and ate in a dismal, little Italian place he had never been to before. There were red table cloths and Chianti bottles dribbling with wax from the candle stubs. The pasta was gummy. The waiter was a sullen boy. The only other patrons were wizened old men.

Afterward he walked the streets through a neighborhood of factories and industrial plants. Everywhere the trash spilled over the curb. Once he saw a youth slouching under a streetlamp. It was a cloudy night and cold, but he was sweating when he finally returned to his apartment.

He began typing the Yeats interrogation summary shortly after midnight. It went smoothly at first as he pecked it out two fingered on his battered Royal. Then he started slowing. One whole hour

34

was lost somewhere just hunched at his plywood desk, cramped by the litter of books and paper, clothing tossed over the chairs, wads of candy wrappers. Then too he may have also been cramped by an overwhelming image of that elusive Jessie Dancer.

Then it was Sunday, and Knolls returned to Severson's cavernous home. Lyle served him runny eggs, toast and weak coffee. They ate on the terrace in the midst of a haphazard garden filled with weeds and trailing ivy.

"I started writing the summary last night," Humphrey said, but could only half explain how it had been wrestling with the spirit of Jessie.

"Don't tell me things like that." Lyle frowned. "I hate those reports where they talk about coming to terms with concepts and all that. I hate vagaries." He looked a little vague himself today, bony and fragile.

Only the light was clear. The shadows of the vines were distinct against the grass. Insects were darting through tunnels of vegetation.

"I'm not trying to be difficult," Knolls replied. "I'm only trying to give you some idea of the problem."

"Oh I think I know the problem," Lyle said impatiently. "There's twenty pages of a Magic product list floating around, and if that list winds up in Moscow Center it's not going to take them very long to find out who has been passing material to Al Dancer."

"Yeats still claims he lost it in the forest."

"Well we haven't found it, have we? I've had the whole damn forest searched, and still haven't found it."

"That doesn't mean Yeats isn't telling the truth. After all there was a storm, wasn't there?"

"There's going to be a hell of a lot bigger storm if that list makes its way to Center."

"Yes I understand that, sir, but at the moment I think we should forget about the list and focus on the larger questions."

"Which are?"

35

"Well, Jessie Dancer for one."

"Oh, Humphrey, can't we leave him out of this."

"No, sir, I'm afraid we can't. He's the one who sent Yeats here in the first place. He's the one who told him to get the product list. We know almost nothing about him, and quite frankly it would be a tragic mistake to ignore him at this juncture.

Severson sighed. "All right, Humphrey, what is it?"

"It seems there was this girl. Sara Moore. English. Worked out of Whitehall."

"You mean in the trade?"

"Yes, files or something. She and Jessie met while he was working at the London Embassy. Apparently they became quite close."

"Sexually?"

"They shared a flat together for over a year. Then it seems she went East on a job. Germany, I think. She's there a few days and the Abteilung picks her up. They make a show out of the trial and she gets thirteen years. Naturally Jessie is fairly upset about it all. That was eighteen months ago."

"And Jessie blames Allen?"

"Apparently Jessie went to Allen and asked him to use his influence to get her out. Well it was a tall order even for Al Dancer, and he couldn't pull it off. Jessie, however, got the idea that Allen didn't try hard enough and has never forgiven him."

"It doesn't seem like a particularly rational reason to hate one's father, does it?"

"Yes, well Jessie doesn't seem to be a particularly rational person. In fact I'd say he's not quite right at all."

Lyle suddenly began pulling his walrus mustache, brushing crumbs off the table. "It's extraordinary, really. Did you know that I once knew Jessie fairly well, and I can't recall a consequential thing about him. I saw him last. . . . Oh it must have been ten years ago. Always thought he was nice enough, but quiet. He was a quiet boy, and he had his mother's looks. She was a very pretty woman."

"Well she apparently didn't have a pretty son." Humphrey

grunted. "I'd say he comes off as a near-pathological killer."

"Oh come on, Humphrey."

"Well how else do you describe a person who wakes up in the morning, takes massive amounts of vitamins and then spends the day shooting handguns and throwing knives?"

"Did Yeats tell you that?"

"And a lot more."

Lyle was staring at a bumble bee hovering by the trellis of snapdragons. "I don't want you to put that sort of thing in the report," he said.

"Why not?"

"Because I can't give that sort of thing to John. We happen to be dealing with his grandson here. Can't you at least tone it down?"

Passing clouds were dousing the harsher reflections in Lyle's garden. Now the light was blanched among the crooked rows of fuchsia and geraniums.

"This girl," Knolls said absently. "Sara Moore. I see her only as the catalyst. Jessie is living with her. She goes to East Germany, gets arrested and gets thirteen years. Yes, Jessie is going to feel frustrated, upset and the rest of it. But I think the problem goes much deeper. I think that the girl was only the spark that ignited the flame, and the flame has been burning for a long time. Do you see what I'm getting at? Jessie hasn't liked Allen for years. It's psychological. The boy hates his family."

"Is that what Yeats says?"

"Yes, more or less. Yeats says that Jessie sees his family—particularly Allen—as a kind of symbol for all that's wrong in the world. There must be a word for that."

"A word for what?"

"For a person who sees things, people, in terms of symbols. I mean it's some sort of emotional condition, isn't it? I'm sure there's a name for it."

Lyle became stiff and fussy all over again. He started smearing his toast with marmalade. His fingers were trembling slightly and

37

the crumbs were spraying everywhere. Finally he asked, "Does the Yeats boy have an equally ambiguous motive?"

Humphrey shook his head. "Jessie told him that once Allen fell Dusty could have whatever he wanted. And what Dusty wants is a sixth-floor office. He wants to wear a suit to work and have a key to the executive washroom. At least that's what he says. Personally I think he's doing it because Jessie asked him. Period. It seems that Yeats worships Jessie."

The garden seemed so still just now they might have been sitting in a bell jar. Every leaf and twig was motionless. There was only that droning bee to give the entropy a razor's edge.

Then Lyle was speaking through. He was staring at the melting slab of butter. "I've given the whole matter a great deal of thought, and I've decided to keep this report off the normal lines for a while. I'm simply going to hand it over directly to John. I think John will understand. Besides I don't want him finding out through the grapevine. If it's going to spread I want him to be the first to know."

"Sure," Humphrey nodded. "John's a friend of yours."

"There's more to it than that. John is . . . well, connected with everything. I mean he is as responsible for Source Magic as Allen. It's all tangled up. John, Allen, Jessie—you can't hope to understand one of them, unless you understand them all."

"What are you trying to tell me?"

Severson's eyes were milky. He was still gazing into his wild garden. "Go easy, Humphrey," he finally said. "You have no idea how many twists and turns the road you're on has. So go easy. I think you should explain Jessie's condition in terms of Vietnam. Yes, I think John would be able to understand how a young man could lose his perspective on things through a particularly horrible war. So that's the approach. That's the way you handle it."

"But the war was years ago, Lyle. Vietnam has been over for years."

"No, you don't understand. Time has nothing to do with it.

38

Memory can keep rising up years and years after the events. So you just write it like I told you. Even if you don't understand, John will. He knows what it's like to have things pop out of the past."

Lyle received the Knolls report on Yeats the following Sunday, a full week after that breakfast in the garden. The report ran ninety pages. It was poorly typed and bound in a cheap buff folder. It's completion would later be seen by Langley historians as the end of the first stage.

All in all the Knolls report was a comprehensive study of what had happened on the night of the storm and the subsequent Yeats interrogation. There were, however, two areas which would eventually prove critical, but were sadly neglected in the work. The first was the girl, Sara Moore. Her name was only mentioned twice in the report. Once in reference to Jessie's motives for sending Yeats to Langley, and then again in the conclusion as a recommended area for additional research. The recommendation, however, was never followed and for the time being the girl was largely forgotten.

Secondly there was the actual material that Yeats had stolen. The Magic product list, now determined to have been twenty-six pages, listed thirteen Soviet documents which Magic had taken in during the spring and summer of 1977. There was no indication in the Yeats report that Knolls actually believed Dusty's story that the product list had been lost during the flight. However, Knolls did tend to underscore the document's importance. He would later be severely criticized for this.

Knolls delivered his report shortly before noon. He handed it to Severson at the doorstep, and would not come in for coffee. He just shoved it at Lyle's chest, and then padded back down the garden path. Lyle thought he looked a little ill, a little swollen and very pale. His sweater was inside out, and he had probably slept in the pants he wore, Lyle thought.

Lyle began reading the report that afternoon. Again there was

39

clear light in the garden, so he sat in one of his ratty straw chairs with his coffee on a wrought iron table, and the pages in his lap. He would read while sucking on a tooth or twisting his mustache ends, but mostly he tried to keep very still. It was the only way to keep the years from cascading down . . .

Lyle remembered how, decades ago he had come together with all three Dancers. It had been John's birthday and the family had gathered at their Norfolk home. The light was much like it was today. Stone and marble had looked very white. Soft ferns grew along the paths. There were willows on the broad lawns.

That day Lyle saw branches of the Dancer family he had never met, some old goat named William who dressed like a tropical planter. There were also scores of beautiful women in chiffon, and those Dancer children hovering at the buffet table, snitching melon balls and iced crab legs.

John had looked especially dapper with his blue blazer, red handkerchief and creamy, silk shirt. He told Lyle that he hadn't felt so well in years. They strolled off together past the formal garden and down to the bamboo groves. He said that he was happy because his son Allen had come to his birthday. The old Allen would never have come, but all that had changed. Now there was a new Allen. "We've become very close," said John.

They had come to the mossy bank of the pond. For a while they only talked of simple, inconsequential things. Red lips of fish kept breaking the green water's surface. Finally John could not help boasting. "I suppose you've heard about Allen's new Center line."

"Source Magic," Severson said, lowering his voice. "Isn't that what they're calling it?"

The name had not yet acquired its near-legendary ring.

"That's right. Source Magic brought to us by way of the Enchanted Forest. Allen came up with those names himself. I rather like them. He could have called it Ramrod or something. But Source Magic from the Enchanted Forest. It gives it a sort of mysterious, misty feel, a sort of . . . oh I don't know, a timelessness."

40

"Yes," Lyle said. "Timelessness. Out of time."

Later in the softer light of afternoon Lyle even saw Allen. He was far more elegant than he had ever been. Severson watched him striding up the path, leading young Jessie by the hand. The boy was a lovely child with very blond hair and fey eyes. When Allen sent him off to play with the others, he only lingered by the hedgerows.

Toward evening the guests gathered in the dining room. John sat at the head of a long oak table to receive his gifts. Every present made him respond with joy, and he held each one aloft so that all could see. Allen gave a polished glass ball, a crystal ball really. One of the children began to cry because he wanted it for himself. An inscription cut into the glass read: *May the Magic Never Dim* . . .

When Lyle had finished reading the brief he continued to sit in that unraveling wicker chair. Once he even mouthed John's name. Then he got up and limped back inside. The screen door banged behind him. There were long shadows in the garden.

His house too was filled with shadows, and even worse there were patches of clotted darkness. He had to hold tight to the banister as he climbed the stairs. Once he had fallen and had been lucky not to have broken his hip. People were always breaking hips. Hips were what you broke in old age. In fact, John Dancer had once broken his hip, falling down stairs no less.

John. The hardest part would be telling John.

CHAPTER TWO

LIKE LYLE Severson, John Dancer lived alone in a large house filled with cool, still furniture. It was a gabled house with a co-lumned portico and broad steps. Allen had grown up in this house, and his mother had died here. Upstairs there were rooms that had not been touched for years.

There was still Mary's piano in the drawing room, although no one ever played it anymore. Nor had John ever had the heart to sell her pillbox collection, even though he had always hated the gaudy little things, jewel encrusted and redolent of illness. So the seat of the Dancer family remained fairly much as it had always been. Maids and gardeners saw to that. They kept the Chippen-dale furniture polished and the parquetry waxed, the hedges trimmed and the lawn mowed. Every few years the siding was whitewashed, and for some reason, not long after Allen had established Magic, John had ordered the shutters painted bright green.

John often used Source Magic as a kind of reference point for the passing years. It was easy to remember things as occurring before Magic or after Magic. Lyle used the Second World War the same way. But if Lyle believed that all good times ended with the war, John thought that the best years had not really started until Source Magic. Before Magic John rarely saw his boy, and when he did they fought. Magic changed all that. The secrets fused them together.

John supposed that this house also fused them together. After all, time counted for something. Allen had become a man in these panelled rooms. The spirit of his childhood still more or less stalked the halls. And sniggered some from the balcony. Allen, truth to tell, had been a rather nasty boy sometimes.

Still, John loved to linger in his son's old bedroom. It was a circular room with a dormer window high in a basket of laurel leaves. Sometimes John just liked to sit on the window box and watch the branches sway, or root around and lay his hands on books and clothes that had once been Allen's. There was that old coat from his college days, a dozen silk ties, even a pair of curling penny loafers. Yes, John liked being in the room where Allen had lived as a boy.

So he took the Knolls report up to that room now. Severson had dropped it by, then scurried off, and now John took it to Allen's old room. He propped himself up on the window box with a couple of corduroy pillows. First he read by the milky light that fell through the laurel, then he switched on Allen's lamp, the ceramic one with the buckskin shade. It was a real boy's lamp.

When he finished reading he slipped off his glasses and sagged back. All through the house ticked the cooling timber. Finally he was dozing into the creaking wood and the rustling of the branches outside. Then he shivered with a fairly rattling thought;

for all the memories gummed up in this house, for all those odd mementos there was not even a trace of the essential Jessie left, only that haunting photograph on the mantelpiece.

Once, six or seven years ago John recalled how he and Allen had virtually written Jessie off. Allen had just come in from Switzerland. John met him at the airport, and they drove through the countryside for an hour. Then they stopped by a meadow to stretch. A ruined church lay in the distance. The day was cold and gray.

Allen did not speak until they tramped well into the grass and came to the stone wall that ran across the hill. Then he explained that he had recently seen Jessie in Saigon. The boy had not looked well. Allen wondered if he had been taking drugs. In the valley below there was fog curling in from the sea.

"Why don't you get him a job out here?" John had suggested. "There must be something he could do."

"No, dad, there's nothing he could do."

"Allen, I can't believe that. There's always something."

"If you saw him for yourself, then you'd understand. I think he may be the most brutal person I've ever met. I don't know him."

Later father and son soothed themselves with claret in the neo-Tudor drawing room. Allen sat in the wingchair, all bundled up in a tartan comforter. John used to find him lounging like that as a boy, a little leggy boy with protruding ears. Allen was forever jotting down memorable snatches from his history books. He used to be afraid that these scraps of notes would blow about and then he would have to explain them. Just as he was afraid later that the day would come when he would have to explain Jessie.

"Jessie," Allen said, "isn't one of us . . . he never will be. I'm glad he's . . . well, unhinged." . . .

That was six years ago, and John had tended to agree with Allen. He too became convinced that Jessie had walked a divergent path, and would never fit into the scheme of the family. Yes, you kept his photograph on the mantelpiece, for nothing was so outré as disowning a grandson. Then too his name would occasionally come up, usually dropped by someone who had no idea what sort of life he had led in Vietnam. But mostly Jess was forgotten.

Now, however, Jessie could not be ignored. His presence filled the house whether you liked it or not. For a while John tried to stalk that spirit. He padded cautiously over floorboards that sent his steps reverberating. He peered into rooms where the furniture and paintings loomed in the darkness. He even drew back curtains to see the sculpture of white oaks in the moonlight. Finally he stopped and heard his footsteps trail off. Jessie's photograph stood before him, eye level, and accusing.

Over the years John had felt himself occasionally haunted by a ghost of his own youth, a questioning doppelgänger with still-brook eyes. Yet only now did he realize how like Jessie he had once been. There were the same raw eyes, the same delicate features. And what else have I overlooked? he thought.

Only this: if it had been said that Jessie did not fit in with the scheme of this family, it was only because no one had ever considered the whole story. They had not looked back far enough. They did not understand that events had not just happened. They were the result of deeper, secret passions.

So this was Jessie's beginning, and it was really just a continuation of a larger story, and not even all that different from John's own beginning. . . .

John Dancer had also been to war, but by 1916 he had left it. He was living in London then, living for nothing really. In the afternoons they sent him to the clinic. In the evenings he drank at the pub on the corner. Sometimes he would just sit by the open window of his dirty little plaster room and watch the crowds flow down King William Street.

His room lay up three flights of narrow stairs. The building dated from Victoria. The skirting board was slipping from the dry rot. The plaster had browned. Below John's window ran a narrow strip of gnarled hedge. Then came the bricks that vines had cracked, and beyond the wall were cobbled streets of sooty tenements.

John's neighbors rarely spoke to him. He supposed it was because they were afraid. They must not have liked the way he slinked over the ratty, flowered carpet in the hallway, or the way he lingered on the creaking banister. They also must have known he slept badly, hearing him pace the floorboards and stumble to the watercloset in the bleakest hours before dawn.

Then too they may have been afraid of the way he looked at them. He had a cracked oval mirror on his dresser. It had been in his room from the beginning. The frame was a gilt arabesque, but the paint was flaking. He used to gaze into that mirror and practice greeting people. He experimented with all kinds of faces, but none of them ever seemed natural. It was the eyes. Morphine dilated the pupils so that his eyes looked like plugs of dull glass. It seemed that there were medical reasons for everything in 1916.

These were his February days. Actually he had been living here longer, but he always thought of this time of the year as February. There was rain and coils of dirty fog that wound through the streets. All in all time was slow. Nothing of consequence ever seemed to happen, but then John never read the *Times,* so he only remembered things he saw. There was the night the zeppelins came, huge ghostly phantoms. When they shot one down John saw it flame above the city. Then there was the polio scare, and the day the boy from the Royal Welsh Fusiliers died.

The boy had been John's only friend in London. He was Marlow. John never knew his Christian name. They had met at the clinic, although Marlow swore that he had seen John before in Flanders. This may have been true, because Marlow had known that John was a correspondent. John's uncle had gotten him the post, against his father's better wishes. John's father had wanted him to finish up at Princeton. He had told John that there was no need to rush off. There would always be a war to see. And wasn't that the bloody truth? Because in John's head there was always the war.

Marlow had lost his legs in Flanders. There was also some internal damage, but the doctors never told him what it was.

For a while John visited Marlow every day. He would stop by in the afternoons, usually with the *Daily Mirror* and a pack of Players cigarettes. Clinic nurses thought John was a genuine love to spend so much time with the legless case. But John did not come only out of kindness. He also came because talking to Marlow was better than talking to himself. For a few weeks it had gotten pretty bad. There were always these prattling voices in his head. It had something to do with the dwindling doses of morphine they gave him.

Marlow's room was entirely white; white walls, white tiles, even the bedframe was white. In an alcove stood a light blue vase from Harrods. The nurses usually kept it filled with daisies. By the door hung two travel posters. One advertised George Lunn's Magic Mountain tours of the Alpine glow at Grindelwald. The other read, "Come South where sunny hours await you!" In the background was a dreamy landscape of printless sand and a striped cabana, all in the aura of the setting sun.

Marlow was obsessed with the Alpine tour and the holiday at Cooden Beach. "When they let me out, John," he would say, "you and I will go straight down to Wigmore Street and fix it. And if George Lunn won't give us a good time, there's many another that will."

Marlow's second obsession was John's home in New York. Dancer had grown up in his father's Fifth Avenue pile. There was also a summer house in Newport, but Marlow loved the ivy walled brownstone. Once he had seen the photograph of John on the broad steps, he could not get enough of it. The portrait showed a vague, unsmiling John, the light in his fair hair. Beside stood two stone dogs, and above hung the Gothic trim through the beeches.

Something in that picture touched Marlow very deeply. John would find him munching on biscuit, staring at the photograph propped up on his knees. "If your dad has a packet then how come you live like you do?"

John hardly knew the answer to that one himself. Unless it was the morphine. How could you explain morph to old dad? Then too there were those thousand little compulsions, and every night there was a war in his room, complete with rolling mustard gas, boys coughing like hags, and a trench full of rats. The captain was a Scottish kid with zinc teeth. He had lost his boots and his bloody feet left tracks across the bedspread.

Marlow's death was as simple and matter-of-fact as any story John had ever written for his uncle's paper. John walked into the room, found the bed had been stripped, the travel posters taken down, the vase of daisies gone. He asked a nurse, and was told that the patient had died. John's stories had read like that. There were brief accounts of offensives and the number of dead and wounded. The real story he kept inside himself. It came out at night.

The night Marlow died John wandered. He rode the double-decker into Piccadilly, then got drunk at the Hambone Club. Further down the line he picked up a girl named Stella, and she took him back to her flat in Chelsea. He sat by the fire escape and watched her undress. She was a sallow girl with a bruise on her thigh and dark, stringy hair. On the wall hung fake Oriental prints from Oxford Street. Stockings and camisoles were draped across a chair. When she spread herself on the low divan, John could still not get up from his seat by the window. The torpor of the evening made him sluggish. Outside the last light was an ugly gold, soaking through the haze. Finally his cigarette ash dropped on the mat. She said, "Well, what did you pay for if you don't want a good time?"

The days ran on. Weeks smeared together. Some nights John spent slumming through the red brick boroughs. He could crouch on the stoops for hours and watch the chimney smoke curling into a violet sky. When it was too much to grope downstairs he ate out of tins. He would lay on his bed, then get up, smooth down his hair and put another record on the gramophone. Every scratchy note put him deeper into his trance.

Then came the night at the Tiger Club. He was fairly well along on gin when a voice beside him at the bar said, "What's your dilemma?"

"Huh?" It was Thursday night, and he was just another simple loiterer in this tawdry basement cavern. Why should a stranger ask him questions?

"I said what's your dilemma?" the stranger persisted.

John turned his head slowly. It was a kid about his own age, thin, in tapered flannels and a spotty silk shirt. His cuffs were undone, and the boy was a little red around the eye. It made him look faintly like a nasty rabbit.

"You must have a dilemma, because I've seen you at the clinic with all the other morphos," the boy continued.

All John said, was, "My name is Dancer. How do you do?"

They took a table at the rear, one of the high-backed pews. When more drinks came, the boy introduced himself as Andre Belov. He said he was Russian, which explained the accent.

"Russian," he smiled. "And that is my dilemma. That and the sailors."

"What about the sailors?" John was only getting out words mechanically. The gin had numbed his lips.

"The sailors because I'm amphibious. What do you think?"

"I don't know," John said. "I don't know what amphibious means in this context . . ."

"It means I live on both land and water. It means that I like boys too. So go ahead, give me a fat lip for it."

"I don't think I care about that," said John seriously.

"Wonderful, then we'll be friends. Now tell me, what's your dilemma?"

"Haven't got one."

"Of course you have. You're a morpho aren't you?"

John shrugged. "Sometimes I can't stop the pictures in my head. And there're the voices, I can't stop the voices either."

"Ah, now we're getting somewhere. What do those voices say?"

John thought for a moment, then started smiling. "They say, come south where the sunny hours await you!"

Belov lived in a snug little flat over an eating house in lower Richmond Road. His bedroom led through oval doors to a lilac patio with sky-blue tiles. A legitimate garden of roses and geraniums grew below. Sometimes John drank tea in that garden, or else they would hang over the balcony and watch the light turn to shadows across the city.

Talk was mostly political, because politics were Belov's passion, that and the Russian Revolution. He claimed royal blood by way of an archduke. "But we lost everything. You can imagine the Russian Revulsion, that's what that little episode was. Now you're going to have the workers rebelling all over Europe. Imagine, all those bleak hordes stampeding through the streets."

But John could never imagine. Even London was unreal. It was just slate roofs and a changing sky . . . By the end of the month they were friends, more or less. Belov always called him "lover," but the boundaries of their relationship became defined one night on a harder note. Slumping back from the Tiger Club, and John had come up for brandy. They were lounging on Belov's Kula rugs. There was a fire in the grate. The clock began to chime, then London's greater bells. Andre stretched like a snake, yawned and laid his hand on Dancer's thigh.

John could have chopped it off. "Don't ever do that again." He had the white thing twisted back at the wrist.

Belov tried to squirm free. "It was a test, just a test. Let me go —"

John let the wrist pop back, and Belov rolled away. They were both very still.

50

"Don't even think it again," John said. "It's revolting. I hate it."

"Alright, lover. Just wanted to know where you stood on the issue." Although he was clearly hurt.

So John deflated. His head slumped. He began toying with the tassles on the cushion.

"It's not that I have the usual prejudice," John said. "I just don't like to be touched. I don't even like women to touch me. I suppose it's part of the condition."

"What condition, lover?"

John shook his head. "I don't know. I'm just strange now. I've become a strange person."

"Oh we're all strange. It's the fall of the natural order. Haven't you read Nietzsche?"

"No, it's the war."

"In that case you need to find love, John. You need selfless love like from a child. I'm being serious. You need to meet a beautiful young princess. And if that isn't possible then you need a cause. There's nothing so purifying as a social and political cause."

"How about morphine?" He smirked. "Why can't I make morphine my cause?"

"Because in between the dosages there are always bad dreams. I know, I've been there. So it must be either true love or a reliable cause."

Belov began smoothing his hand on the arm of his velveteen chair. His eyes were glassy. He was smiling like a fish, or that clever rabbit.

"I think it's about time that we made the rounds," said Belov. "There are people I'm just dying to have you meet, lovely, lovely people. And who knows? You may even find that young princess, or that cause."

The following week they attended a party held at the West End home of some duchess or countess. A centerpiece of soapstone nymphs danced on the dining room table. All the women had bare

51

white arms. One girl in a simple frock played Chopin preludes, but every note was like dripping water. When he couldn't take another minute, John went out to the terrace and gulped the night air, then watched the lamplight grow clearer through a curtain of vines.

Next were the dinners at the Savoy, and John wedged himself into brocaded chairs to pick at the bones of roast duck. It seemed that everyone had Belov's nightmare of a human flood of workers pouring through the streets. There was one shy boy from Petrograd who had lost his hand in the Revolution. He had been a Czar's cadet, and a mob had pinned him to the streets. Then a girl had sliced off his hand with his own saber. He had kept himself from bleeding to death by packing the stump in snow.

Finally there was lunch at the Thimble Club, and Belov was unusually sober for this one. John was told only that they had been invited to dine with two English gentlemen. One would be elderly and kind, the other would be young and cold. If John was offered a drink he should ask only for dry sherry.

The club was a vast, shadowy hall filled with red leather chairs and oak. Belov's friends were waiting at a corner table. The older one was round with a plump face, he wore country tweeds and his name was Sutherland. The other was sleek and dark, he might have still been in his twenties, only a few years older than Belov and John. He was introduced as Harper.

Chops were served with dollops of mint sauce and steamed asparagus. Everyone sliced away the fat; Sutherland was particularly precise about it. He had warm, clear eyes. His mustache ends had been twirled into saber points. He kept pressing more wine on John.

They discussed the war. Sutherland asked about John's eighteen months at the front, although he might have been asking about the weather. Next it was politics, but only in the abstract. The conversation wound through words like intervention and commitment. Proper names were never mentioned, except once. Sutherland asked John Dancer if he had read Marx. John said that he had only glanced through it. Then Sutherland wanted to know what John had thought about it. John told him that he did not believe in fairy tales.

Afterward John and Belov took a cab to Hyde Park. Dusk was falling now and the lawns were vacant. They strolled along mossy paths into a tunnel of leaves.

Finally Belov said, "I think you made a very good impression on them."

"Who were they? The fat one, who was he?"

"They're my sponsors. Terribly important that you made a good impression."

"What do you mean by sponsors?"

"They're going to help me restore the natural order. Moderation is the word."

A thrush was rattling high above them in the branches of a yew tree. Another was calling from across the maze of hedgerows. "But what are they? Beggermen, thieves, politicians?"

"They're manipulators, lover. They're puppeteers. They pull strings for people, people like me and you."

The leaves about them were strung with pendants of swinging dew. More birds darted through the underbrush. The chill seemed to rise up from the sodden grass . . . "I'll tell you," Belov said suddenly. "Yes, it's time that you joined the club. Tonight, I'll tell you."

John Dancer would always remember this first briefing. Even decades later he would recall how they walked with the flowing crowds through warrens of filthy streets. They moved with tramping factory girls and swayback horses pulling dray wagons of flour and beer, watched urchins sitting on stoops, eating out of paper bags.

For the first mile Belov hardly said a word. He kept his head down and his fists jammed into his pockets. Once they passed a scaffolding and a group of laborers milling around a tub full of coals. Their clothing was covered with lime. Their heads were

53

cropped. Their sleeves were rucked up over their elbows.

Belov watched them for a moment, then said, "That's the revolution for you. Dirty feet and dirty hands. That's about as romantic as it gets."

He continued this theme in a dark, brick pub. Beyond the leaded glass traffic was still thundering over a bridge. you could hear the girders trembling.

Belov spoke slowly, evenly now. The jokes were gone. He said, "My father was a monarchist, but he was also a liberal, I think. At least he understood a need for change. We lived in Moscow first, then Petrograd. We always spent the winters in the south. I had a pony, and even my sister was not permitted to ride him. But one could see a need for change. One could travel anywhere and see this terrible need, because the peasants were very badly treated. So I would say that my father was a monarchist, but also a liberal. Yes, I sincerely believe that he was a liberal in his heart."

Belov went on to recall his childhood in tiny, crystaline impressions. There was his Petrograd apartment with white tiles and tooled pine. In the rolling hills southwest of Moscow his father had owned a summer lodge that lay on a windy bluff above a lake. They would sail in the mornings along the wooded banks, and in the evenings the moon would be bone white.

As for the fall, one hardly understood events even as they were happening. Belov had only the sketchiest sense of cause and effect. There had been breadlines for as long as he could remember. You would look down from a window, and there were the black shadows spread across an open square of snow. In time the lines became less symetrical. Instead of a single rank, there were clusters of dark figures. Shops closed. One could not get even the simplest things: sugar, nails, soap. Then came the street fights.

Belov still wept whenever he talked about his sister's death, and he was crying the night he told John about it. He was staring across the smoky pub, and his eyes were filled with tears. He said that she was murdered for no reason other than the fact that she

54

was clearly not a peasant. Her clothing was too expensive for the taste of the revolutionaries, so they dragged her into an alley and someone killed her with a shovel that had been used for clearing the snow. He said that her murderers must have seen her as a symbol of all they hated. "Well, now I have my own symbols too," he said bitterly.

Belov left Petrograd nine days after the fall of the Czar. He hitched rides on trucks, took trains when he could. Deserters heading east gave him potatoes and tea. Occasionally there was horse meat. At the end of six weeks he had reached Switzerland, and friends. There he lived in a timbered villa for another month, but all the while he knew he was only waiting for the chance to return and avenge his sister's death. Then he met Sutherland at a British affair, and Sutherland took him to England and told him that his chance had come.

Long after the Revolution John Dancer's recollections of this, his first formal briefing on the embryonic Soviet State, were recorded and the fragments of these notes, some written in John's own spidery hand, eventually formed the basis of Langley's Russian files. Even today there were historians who still sifted through these notes in the hope of finding some fundamental key to the Western mind's attitude towards communism. Belov, to be sure, was a fanatic. Many of his notions of the communist movement were plainly garbled. His vision of the early party leaders such as Lenin and Trotsky were also stilted. Yet for all his faults, Belov did possess a certain feel for history. He felt he understood what he considered the destiny ahead. He seemed to know, as John Dancer himself later wrote, just how the cards were really stacked.

Belov's portrait of Russia in 1917 was, though, perhaps simplistic. Factions were too clearly cut, issues too black and white. According to Dancer's notes, Belov began his talk with the first Provisional Government under Prince Lvov. This was the state of affairs immediately after the Czar's fall. Belov explained how civil unrest and popular disenchantment with the war soon began to undermine the Prince's rule until the first government finally fell.

Belov described the situation with Alexander Kerensky's Second Provisional Government, and although his explanation was still too simplistic, he nevertheless seemed to understand the fundamental issues. He said that Kerensky had pledged himself to keep the Russian troops fighting the Axis in return for Allied support. The Allies, of course, had been horrified from the beginning that the Revolution would mean an end to Russia's war effort and thereby free some million German and Austrian troops from the Eastern front.

Wavering on this question of whether to continue fighting were the Soviets. Soviet, meaning council, had at that time none of the stigma that the years would later attach to the word. There was merely the Soviet of workers, soldiers, and peasants. Every city, town and village had its Soviet, which was not so much a political body as a popular organization. What Belov feared then were not the Soviets, but the Bolsheviks.

The Bolsheviks, as Belov saw them, were a small group of radical communist agitators. They stood for immediate land reform, an eight-hour workday, and the end of Russian participation in the war. For this last reason they were the sworn enemy of Kerensky and the Allies.

Of the party's eventual leader, Nikolai Lenin, Belov sketched a mad little man who loved to argue all night and then sleep until noon. Belov claimed that he had actually met Lenin in Zurich. The exiled Bolshevik had then been living in a shoemaker's home, a gloomy place that stood across the courtyard from a sausage factory. Belov remembered how Lenin had complained about the stench, no matter how he scrubbed he had not been able to get the smell of sausages out of his clothing and hair.

When the Czar fell, Lenin was still living in that dismal shoemaker's house, and Belov drew him as the frantic revolutionary poring over the foreign newspapers, crying out to his wife that the tide of history was passing him by.

56

Yet as a testament to Lenin's sway with the Russian people, Belov pointed to those midsummer riots later called The July Days. Here, Belov said, was a classic example of the bolshevik threat.

Not long after the Czar's fall, when Kerensky was still trying to consolidate his new government, the Germans decided that if Lenin and his followers were placed back in Russia they would ignite a second revolution, one that would topple Kerensky, bring the Bolsheviks to power and so end the war on the Eastern front. Contacts were made, meetings arranged, and the result was Lenin's return to Petrograd in the now famous "Sealed Train."

Just as the Germans had planned there was indeed a revolt, two days of vicious street fighting. In the end, though, Lenin and his group were defeated. Trotsky was jailed and Lenin was forced to escape again.

Here then was Belov's real brilliance, and even years later he would be remembered for this insight. For although the July Days had ended badly for the Bolsheviks, Belov felt certain that they would soon be back. He said that Lenin was merely waiting in Finland for the right moment to strike. Government charges that Trotsky and others had conspired with the Germans were not totally believed by the public. Indeed, Belov said, there would come a day when the masses would once again look on Lenin as their savior. So where many saw the July Days as the end of the bolshevik movement, Belov saw them as only the beginning.

Of all that John would remember about that late summer night in London nothing would come back quite so clearly as Belov's final pitch along the Thames. They had left the pub when the cigarette smoke and jumble of voices had started smothering them. Out in the streets the sky was glowing from backed up smoke in the night. John and Belov followed a crumbling river wall until they came to a footbridge where the water lapped against the pilings.

"I'm not sure how I should approach you," Belov began. They

57

had slumped to the low, stone wall. "For example, are you a pacifist? I would imagine that one could become pacifistic after a particularly gruesome experience in war. Or possibly you no longer feel committed one way or another? I often sense that in you, John. I sense a certain . . . oh, let's call it apathy. So if I were to appeal to you on strategic grounds, I'm not sure that you'd be responsive. Still, the fact remains that should the Russians pull out of the war there would be all those hordes of Germans free to fight on the Western front. But as I said, I'm not sure you will find this a personal factor—"

"Why don't you just ask me," Dancer said sourly. "Just say it, okay?"

"All right . . . here is the game. I'm going away soon. I'm going a long way to do something that I believe is very important for the British and the Americans. Mr. Sutherland is helping me, and I'd very much like your help too."

The turning tide was bringing in patches of scum, and an oil slick filled with empty bottles, driftwood and sandwich papers.

"I don't think you want me, Andre. I feel empty. They may have gotten me off of the morph, but I still need it—"

"I think that I already know your shortcomings, John. What's important is that I trust you. Besides, Mr. Sutherland likes you. He thinks you have a level head. That's how he put it. I told him that I wanted you, and he thought I had made a wise choice."

"Oh, I see." John frowned. "Sutherland is a bloody spy. He's His Majesty's Secret Service. I know about their sort from the war. They buy people—"

"No, John. Sutherland is an English gentleman. He doesn't buy people. He convinces them. In my case it was easy. I hate the Bolsheviks."

"Lots of ways to buy people, friend. Lots of ways."

"So then how does one buy you, John?"

"Ah, the great mystery. Hell, I don't even know the answer to that one myself. Wish I did though, then I might be able to join up in the ranks of normal society. Whatever that is . . ."

Belov smiled. "What's today? Tuesday? All right, John, you come round to my flat next Friday morning and tell me what you want to do."

"How can I decide if I don't even know what it's all about?"

"Oh come on, lover, don't give me that line. I know you. You're not the type for deductive reasoning. You wouldn't weigh the odds even if you had them. They're sending me to Russia to stop the Bolshies. You come round next Friday and let me know if you want to go along." . . .

On Friday the sky was dead clear. Every leaf and petal in Belov's garden seemed unnaturally distinct. John stopped on the flagstones, tore off a rosebud and shredded the thing. He rang the doorbell. When Belov answered all John said was, "I'm going." And that was it.

They settled into the burlap. Andre's furniture always sort of absorbed one. The teapot, sugar bowl and tiny pitcher of cream were arranged on a japanned tray.

"I'm going to have to tell Mr. Sutherland your reasons, John. He's very keen on the reasons why people do things."

"Reasons?" John echoed, and then went blank.

"Yes, your reasons for coming."

"I don't have to have reasons for everything I do."

"Fine with me, but I'm afraid that's not enough for Sutherland, John."

Dancer was rattling his spoon inside his cup. Some of his tea went sloshing over the side. This was just like that morning when he had told his dad that he was going off to war. All through their sensible talk he had wanted to twist the flimsy silverware until it snapped . . . "Then tell him I'm tired of rotting in London like some Cheapside doper. Tell him I want to be a hero. Tell him any damn thing."

Belov ladled more sugar into his tea, and just as casually asked, "Is it your family, John? Do you want to prove to them that you're

59

not the prodigal after all? Is that why you're going?"

John hated being figured out. "Tell Sutherland *anything* you like."

On the wall hung a gloomy landscape of Sheffield. There were also prints of Dublin streets and some haunting photographs of children. Belov was speaking slowly, tonelessly. "This commits you then. If you try to back out now they'll make it very tough on you. They'll take you away somewhere, and keep you there until they're satisfied that you'll never compromise the mission."

John just looked at him. "I'm going. There's nothing else to say."

"All right then. We'll be leaving in about three weeks. I suppose we'll take a northern route into Petrograd. You'll be my American comrade. They'll accept that. The cause has attracted several Americans. Just be innocent and beautiful, and everyone will trust you. The whole idea is that you must help me establish the cover, because on the other side of the coin I'll be meeting with some people—they're cossacks actually. I don't know if you're familiar with the cossacks, but basically they're royalists. Czars have used them as their personal corps for, oh, since the Middle Ages. They've always been pampered. Of course some of them have joined the Revolution, but these, the ones I'll be seeing . . . well, let's just say that they'll go a long way to stop the Bolsheviks."

"What's a long way?"

Belov's eyes had dropped. He was wedging sugar into small mounds.

"What's a long way?"

"Past political solution," Belov mumbled. "Past any compromise or reconciliation." But he was still ploughing the sugar with his fingers.

"Look, why don't you just say it?"

Belov shrugged. "Very well, John," and he couldn't have been primmer. "We're going to murder Lenin. That is, if Lenin leaves Finland and enters Petrograd, then we're going to kill him."

60

They trained at Oxford. There was a black shingled Victorian house with nearly an acre of wild garden. Huge chandeliers hung from the coffered ceilings. The downstairs rooms were filled with portraits of an unknown family. There were sketches in sepia, miniatures and vast oils. A bell clock in the village struck every hour. At the end of the day Belov liked to relax on the terrace. He once told John that this training house upset him . . . somehow there was a quality of old age and inconsolable grief.

Training lasted two weeks. Generally the sleek and quiet Harper served as instructor. He taught codes and ciphers, how to run networks, debrief informers and service the messenger routes. There were detailed maps of Petrograd, and the street names had to be memorized. On clear, starry nights Harper ran a combat course in the garden, placing emphasis on silent killing with both knives and hands. Belov and John Dancer spent hours tracking one another through the hedgerows and weeds. John always scored the highest, but then he had always been athletic.

Sutherland played headmaster, overseeing. He also conducted the games, games in which he played the cossack's leader and Belov had to recruit him. Or there were cover games, and the pupils had to convince their instructors that they were really quite dedicated to the movement. Everything was acted out in mock tearooms like the ones they would see in Russia.

Sutherland seemed to grow especially fond of John Dancer. Toward the end of those Oxford weeks the two often strolled together down the evening lanes. Once they walked quite far, north past the Tudor cottages where figures moved across the lighted windows. Streetlamps glowed in swatches of mist. Old women were out with their dogs.

For the first few shadowy blocks they only mentioned inconsequential things. Sutherland asked about John's childhood, his mother and father, then abruptly said that John had a special feel for the world of secret intelligence.

"I'd say you have the wits for it," Sutherland said. "Most lads are either too enthusiastic, or else they don't have the stomach. But you, John, you seem to have just the right touch."

"Thank you, sir." Although he couldn't have cared less. He had been feeling pretty shabby, just living from day to day.

"Oh it's not a compliment. It's a fact. I'm not the sort that butters one up, not anymore. I'm too old for that. I'm only wondering if you've given any thought to a career."

"A career, sir?" It sounded pretty formidable, and John couldn't help wincing at an image of Harper's stupid night-combat course.

"Yes, a career as an intelligence officer."

John Dancer saw it in brass letters, stuck on an office door.

"True, it's a rather long, special road," Sutherland went on. "But I think you'll come to love it. I know that I do. Oh, my lord, I love it. I love every long, dark inch of it."

As it happened, the road to Petrograd was indeed a long, special one. Belov and John Dancer left on an early morning train. Sutherland and Harper stood in the coiling steam to see them off, but they did not wave. The game had begun and cover was everything.

At first came the gray seas, and Belov was as sick as a dog. He hung all night on the railing while their liner went lurching east. Then trains took them through open steppes. Stockholm was temperate and neutral. They lived three days anonymously in a white pine room above the harbor. Beyond the old stone bridges Baltic freighters were unloading. These arctic summer days seemed eternal. They might have entered some kind of vacuum.

Through most of the journey Belov was tense. He drank pots of railroad tea and chain-smoked. John was the opposite, sullen and quiet. Whole hours would pass when he hardly spoke or moved as they rode through an enormous, still country of desolate waste.

Finally came Petrograd. Their train arrived in the evening, and they took a carriage into the city. The air was cool and moist. From the rise of a bridge they saw a slim, spired skyline. Few lights burned, but the tram was running. There were peasants sweeping the mud from the cobblestones.

They took a double room at an old hotel—Russian baroque, long gone to seed. There were gnomes carved into the moulding and flaking gold cornices on the lobby walls. Stuffing bulged from the satin chairs, and the ball-and-claws were gone from the bathtub; now the porcelain rested on slate.

Rain fell that night, and the lamps blew out. Belov found candles in the Oriental dresser, and they drank, talked and finally dozed . . . Then the milk carts were clattering below, and the charwomen sang from the streets. John, who had slept on the sofa, now rolled off and stumbled to the window. When he yanked back the heavy drapes and stretched himself across the panes, he saw this city of peaked roofs, cut stone and the onion domes of churches. It was still and surreal for miles.

People in Petrograd seemed caught up in forces beyond their control. Apathy mingled with hysteria, all in an undercurrent of fear. Crime was rampant. Apartment houses had to be guarded all night. Food was scarce. One week there was no butter, the next no milk. In some quarters they just laughed . . . there were gambling clubs open from dusk until dawn, and the stakes ran as high as twenty-thousand rubles; prostitutes were hoarding small fortunes in furs and jewels; speculators played on the flux of bread . . . Each night brought suicides and murders. And there were the mystery agents—drab little men in woollens who prowled the food lines, whispering that the Jews had cornered the grain.

Every night Dancer and Belov made the rounds at cafes where the Bolsheviks met. Belov played the slightly flippant bourgeois convert, while Dancer was his sober protégé, an American journalist—a little sympathetic and a little skeptical. They drank tea, attended basement lectures. The prevalent mood was hope, and party leaders claimed that the popular fear of the Bolsheviks that had raged since July was now over. Time, said the believers, was on their side.

As counterpoint to these cafe nights there were furtive meetings with the cossacks. These occurred at odd hours, in crowds and along back streets. Once Belov met them among the brooding passengers at the station. John came along to cover the rear. The cossacks turned out to be two burly men in leather coats. John had expected lithe horsemen, but these men just looked like killers, the sort you'd find in any city.

One of them kept asking about a rifle with a sniper's scope. The other kept telling the first to shut up. All around were the pinched faces of waiting factory workers. Afterward Belov's face was ashen, and his shirt clung to his back. Next contact with them was down by the canals. Belov left in the early evening. When he returned his hand was bandaged. He said that the cossacks had slashed his palm with a dagger to seal the pact with blood. While he talked John poured gin over the wound until there was an ugly, reddish puddle on the bathroom tiles.

There were days when life in Petrograd seemed as directionless and vapid as life had been in London. Belov tried to keep John's spirits up by telling him that they were making progress, moving closer to the center of the Bolsheviks. Eventually they would have a window on the inner circle, and Lenin could not pass unseen. But through these weeks of parties, the coming and going, the cups of sour tea, all John saw was the void.

They usually woke at noon when the cannon sounded from St. Peter and Paul. The cafes were always filled with the same faces, laughing, or crying, at the same jokes. In public one discussed the Revolution in terms of weather. Rain and snow meant violence from the left. Occasionally there were more formal meetings, mostly held in an unfinished brick apartment. Hundreds packed around the scaffolding, heaped on piles of mortar and lumber, or perched high up in the rafters.

One night the speaker was a fierce gunner just back from the

64

Austrian front. He had been wounded in the throat, and his voice came rasping out. Afterward John followed a party leader down to the Sobornost cafe and found himself jammed at a table with half drunken men and women. A bottle of vodka was passing from hand to hand. The women always laughed and shivered whenever they had to belt it down straight.

By nine that evening the mood was sleepier. The windows had grown silvery like the streets outside. John was pulling on his lips, half listening to a skinny boy in wire glasses talking about someone he had slept with the previous night.

Suddenly John raised his eyes. "Who's that girl?"

"Huh?"

John nodded to a slender figure weaving through the crowd. Her hair was a filmy halo in the cigarette smoke. "That one. That girl over there."

"Ah," the skinny boy smiled. "That's Anna Servana, the actress. She used to sleep with everyone but now she only sleeps with First Party members. Which is a pity really, because everyone is still in love with her."

"Do you know her?"

"Sure, everyone knows her. You want an introduction maybe?"

John didn't know what he wanted.

"If you want an introduction, I can fix it. There's a party tonight. You come by, and I'll introduce you to her."

By midnight he found himself in someone's cramped apartment in the exclusive district near the Winter Palace. Candles burned on the mantel and in the plaster alcoves. There seemed to be no furniture, only a crude, block table piled with bottles and a basket of crackers. The skinny boy was tugging on his sleeve, pulling him through the teetering crowd. They plowed right into a circle of drunken soldiers. A glass shattered, and a soldier started howling. But finally there was that girl again, leaning on the ice box, wrapped in a long fur coat.

"I'd like you to meet this beautiful American," he said. "This

65

is Dancer, Anna. He saw you in the Sobornost."

She smiled and took his hand. Hers was cool and dry. "Dancer? Is that what you are? You love to dance?"

"No, it's just my name. John Dancer."

"Okay, John, you can dance with me anyway. Of course you can dance with me."

She was drunk, and they had to waltz slowly in the tiny kitchen to the strains of an old Victrola. He held her body close to his, and she laid her head on his shoulder. There was something wonderful about her perfume, and the way her body swayed into his. Now and then she muttered in his ear, but only in Russian and he could not understand. Still, it knotted up in his stomach.

Finally a sailor cut in, and it was over. Except later as the guests went reeling out he had the chance to ask, "Will I be able to see you again?"

At first she only scowled. "Don't be rude. I like only to dance, but it doesn't mean you can sleep with me."

He shook his head. "No, I only want to see you again. Maybe we could have lunch or something?"

"Oh, you want to play cat and mouse. Okay, Mr. Pussycat, you can come to my house." Then she brushed her lips on his cheeks and whirled out the door.

It nearly paralyzed him. "But I don't know where you live," he called after her.

And she, laughing back, "Ask anyone. I live on the moon!"

Later that night the real moon was faintly blue above the Petrograd skyline. John walked with Belov through the empty streets. There were only a few hooded figures in the doorways, and a group of soldiers huddled around bonfires in the broad squares. John said that he had met the girl, and Belov called it a stroke of luck.

"She's just a girl."

"Hardly just a girl. You must cultivate this relationship. This will prove very useful. She knows people, lover. She even knows

66

Lenin. You have no idea what's pumped away between her legs."

The image grated.

"She can get us into the thick of it, lover. She knows the leaders."

"I only talked with her a moment."

"Then you'll have to see her again. I'll arrange it if need be. Because you *must* cultivate her. She's the best we have so far, the only one who can really get us into the inner sanctum."

They had come to the chapel of the Iberian Virgin. There were no lights but several plump women were lingering on the steps. One of them was cupping a candle in her hands.

"You like this Anna Servana, don't you?" Belov said, but it wasn't the sort of question that Dancer ever answered. "Oh I know she's very pretty. She's the princess of the universal worker's movement. Maybe she'll be the first Communist saint. Saint Anna of the bed—"

"Shut up, Belov."

"Ah, you do like her."

At the end of the narrow lane they saw half a dozen figures bent over the blackened carcass of a horse. The animal's legs were stiff in the air. One of the peasants had rolled up his shirt sleeves to hack away at the rump.

"There's a bolshevik symbol for you," Belov said. He was watching the peasants toss back hunks of meat. . . .

Anna loved the Revolution as if it were a man. She loved it physically, not intellectually. There was much she did not understand. Whenever she spoke of the movement she spoke only in terms of platitudes, phrases she had heard tossed out at cafes and parties. But she had a breathless, windy voice, and John Dancer could listen to her for hours.

They met for a second time in a cake shop near the University Square. There were tables on the patio filled with students. John and Anna spent the afternoon chatting and sipping sweet tea. She

67

told him that her parents had died, and that the theater had been her life since she had been quite young. Shakespeare was her favorite, next came Shaw, and one day there would be a great Russian film director who would change history.

In the white evening light they walked along the Ekaterina Canal. A breeze came rippling in from the west. When they said good-by, she pulled him into the shadow of a stone arch.

"You should know the truth about me," she told him. "No one ever read me all of Karl Marx, and I couldn't read it myself because the print was too small." Then she kissed him full on the mouth and ran off.

The next time he saw her she wore a pleated skirt and gray sweater. She looked like a schoolgirl. Also the coyness was gone. They went to the Mars Field where the April dead had been buried. Workers, soldiers, all who had died in the Revolution all went into that common grave. John stood by her, and she leaned against the iron railing, surrounded by the open grass. She talked in broad gestures. She might have been telling him a fairy tale . . . "Coffins were painted bright red," she said. "Everywhere there were big red banners floating above us. Everyone could see that we marched in perfect steps, and without the need of police. There was great silence, except when the cannons boomed. It was a great day for peace and victory, but mostly I remember how much we all loved each other. Have you ever loved like that, John?"

There was a blue-gray tinge to this afternoon. Overhead hung a solid cap of clouds. Far across the field there were dumpy forms of women.

"I haven't loved anyone for a long time," Dancer finally said. "I'm not sure why."

"What about your friend, Andre? They say you love him."

His teeth clenched together. "They say that, huh?"

"So I thought you were like him. You know?" She was pulling at a thread on her sweater. "I thought you only liked other boys."

"Uh, no."

68

"So maybe we could go into the bed together?"

"What?"

"Well if you're not like Andre, then maybe you would like to go into the bed with me?"

His stomach was seizing up.

"You see, John, this is something I have thought much about, and I have decided it would be good for you. Good for you in here." She put two fingers beneath her breast.

"Why?" At least he managed to get out that.

"Because people should go into the bed with people they like. And I like you, John."

They were both still staring across the open field to the marble stones of the grave.

"Do you like me too?"

The grass went blurry, then the trees beyond. He kept trying to swallow the knot in his throat, to hide all those months of backed-up tears.

She took him to her apartment, high in a concrete block with a window overlooking the river. Her rooms were cleanly furnished with simple geometric chairs and couches. He watched her comb out her hair in the bedroom, and it crackled and sailed after the brush. Her body was framed against the tooled octagons in the headboard.

He was shivering, and his joints were stiff. He could not even manage the buttons on his shirt, and finally she had to undress him. They lay together, unmoving under the eiderdown quilt. The sheets were rough and cold.

She began to kiss him, softly following his collarbone. Once she whispered, "Do you know any Russian at all?" He told her his only phrase, which meant, "I'm tired."

They made love carefully, formally. Her body was long and firm, although he touched her as if he were afraid he would break it. But Anna knew her own strength, and she kept squeezing his lips to her breast, clamping him between her thighs. He couldn't

69

help gasping at the curve of her spine. Then their bodies hardly mattered anymore, and they started coming together. Sometime during that night he felt himself unraveling into her. Then came only stillness, and relief. It seemed as if his soul was hovering above him, stretched across the ceiling. . . .

September and October turned bad. It was dark from the early afternoon until late the next morning. Hard rain fell incessantly, mud filled the streets. Each dawn you heard the workers tramping by, their boots tracking the mud all over the city. Damp winds blew in from the Gulf of Finland, and when there was no wind evil clouds of fog rolled between the buildings.

Zeppelin raids increased. Damage and casualties were light, but the people were terrified. Blackouts were common, sometimes to discourage bombers, sometimes merely because the power died. One night John saw the sausage shapes looming out of a cloud bank in the west. Searchlights swept the sky, but only a few guns fired. In the morning there was the blown-off leg of a man in the gutter.

Week by week food grew scarcer. Bread rations fell from a pound and a half to a pound, then to only a quarter of a pound. A chocolate bar cost nearly the equivalent of a dollar. Only half the babies had milk, there was no sugar. Finally the first real snow fell, and then the food lines stretched for blocks down iron-white streets.

Politically there was also chaos. Things were moving apart, whirling in an ever-widening circle. John only vaguely understood the shifting themes, and would not gain real perspective until decades later.

During the late twenties scholars drafted several careful studies of this period. The idea had been that the pattern of all leftist revolution had been laid in these pivotal weeks of 1917. Some of the material used had been circulating around the academic community for years. Most, however, came from State Department

70

records and John's own chronicles, which eventually found their way into the archives of the CIA.

Yet given their resources, the scholars' work was sadly disappointing. Their conclusions were prosaic. They found no revelatory thrust, no previously unseen forces. Much of what was secret then became common knowledge later.

Causes for the revolution, wrote the scholars, seemed to be several. First they cited General Lavr Kornilov's aborted attempt to seize the power from Kerensky. Kornilov, who had then been commander-in-chief of all Russian armies, was the flower of the Mongolians. He had been a great hero on the Austrian front, and a capable leader of men. Yet he deeply overestimated his own popularity when he led his army to Petrograd. Not only was the general defeated without a struggle by infiltrating Soviet propagandists, but his aborted coup gave a powerful boost to the Bolsheviks. After Kornilov's army had dispersed it seemed to the masses that their real enemies had not been Lenin, Trotsky and the like, but the liberals and conservatives. Further, when Kornilov was finally arrested he left a military power vacuum that was easily filled by the Red Guard.

The scholars also noted the indecisiveness of Kerensky. True the end of the Czar had meant an end of the physical autocracy, but the essential issues remained. The nation was still torn between a possessing class and the hordes of peasants and workers, while Kerensky wavered in the middle. During the Kornilov crises, when the general's troops were nearest to the city, Kerensky became so panicked that he issued weapons to the Bolsheviks, weapons that would later be used against him.

One interesting by-product of the 1927 study was a validation of Andre Belov's uncanny ability to interpret the winds of change. Scholars found that Belov's predictions, as later reported by John Dancer, were nearly always on the mark. He understood that the Kornilov affair would end in new Bolshevik strength, and further guessed the October election results almost down to the last vote.

The elections were held for seats on the presidium of the new Petrograd Soviet. Voting was by the usual method of having all deputies leave the hall who were in favor of overturning the old Presidium and replacing it with Bolsheviks. As more and more deputies left the hall the minutes grew taut. When it was finally clear that the Bolsheviks had seized the day the hall at the Solomnly Institute erupted with cheering. For Belov the day was a nightmare.

He had ridden twelve muddy blocks by streetcar. The seats had been taken and the aisles were jammed. He had to hang on the running board. When he reached Solomnly he was told that the hall was filled so he had to huddle by a bucket of coals on the steps. Five kopecks bought him tea in a tin cup, and there were hunks of meat in a foul broth, but not enough to go around. About noon clouds passed over, then the light turned smoky and the wind picked up. Before the day ended, he was fairly certain that he saw Leon Trotsky and his bodyguards striding up the steps.

That evening the election results swept through the city. Trotsky and the other Bolshevik leaders who had just been released from prison now had control of Petrograd's council. There were rumors concerning Lenin. Some said he was on his way from Finland, others that he had already arrived. Kerensky was sounding the alarm, but there was little he could actually do. There were victory parties in all the Red quarters.

Belov spent the night drinking in a raucous cafe on Liteiny Street. By the small hours he was numb and sick, so he threw it all to the wind and took a cobbler's son back to his hotel. The boy was a sultry, dirty scamp, with a clipper ship tattooed on his ribs.

He picked up more boys, kept them for a night, then kicked them out. Once a sailor got nasty, and Belov woke up in his own blood. That afternoon he started in on morphine again. The local chemist had a fairly clean supply, but it was expensive what with the war and all, you understand . . .

Through these days John Dancer only saw the Russian inter-

72

mittently. They would sometimes meet when Anna was away, but mostly John tried to avoid his friend. Finally Belov cornered him and they took a long walk by the banks of the Neva. The river streets were still this darkening afternoon. There was ploughed snow along the cobbles, and a view of the empty white boulevards. When they reached the black iron fence above the river, Belov said that the day had come.

He meant that Lenin had arrived.

"He came in disguise," Belov added. "He wore a wig and shaved his beard, but I know it's him."

"I see," was all that Dancer said. He was wearing a tawny leather coat. It had belonged to one of Anna's old lovers.

"So now we have to move," Belov continued. "Now. The time has definitely come."

There were low clouds of snow and fog moving across the landscape. The wind was sounding above the rooftops.

Finally Dancer said, "I've been thinking. I've been thinking that maybe we should just let it be."

"What are you talking about?"

"Lenin, the movement, everything. Maybe we should just let it *be.*"

"Oh I understand. She's gotten to you. That Servana girl has gotten to you, and now you want out."

"I don't really know what I want." He might have just turned to ice.

"Oh I understand you, lover. You don't know whether you're a coward or just a lovesick doper. Well I know. You're both. But if you're still confused, perhaps you should just take a nice holiday and think it over. Yes take your princess away and discuss it with her. Meanwhile I'll stay here, and change history. How does that sound, lover?"

Dancer thought it sounded a little bitchy, and pretentious. "We don't have a chance, Andre. You were right a long time ago. There's a big wave coming—"

73

"Don't talk to me about waves, lover. Let me tell you one thing. Let me tell you how one bullet can change history. One bullet in the brain, lover, and then let them discuss their dialectical materialism."

"What do you want me to do?"

"What difference does it make. You won't help me anyway."

"No, I said I'd back you and I will."

"Yes, lover, you'll back me all the way to hell."

Then Belov cocked his head to the sky. Huge blackened clouds were swirling and tumbling above. "What's that sound, John? Like soft screaming, what's that sound?"

"It's the wind," Dancer told him and he was watching Belov's eyes, his hollow cheeks. "You're into it again, aren't you?"

"Yes, I have the need again, lover. You have a need, and I have a need. Women and morphine, it's all the same need."

"Then get out," Dancer said. "Get out while you're still ahead. Go south."

"Too late for that, lover. I'm selflessly committed to the cause. Logic is down the drain. The cossacks are gone too. It's just me now. Lenin and me. He calls it the class struggle. I call it the blood feud."

Flurries of snow were still sweeping across the open land. Some had oddly human shapes, or ghost shapes.

When the wind died Dancer asked once more, "What do you want me to do?"

Belov answered quietly. "Find out where Lenin is staying. I need to know when he comes and goes. You know the sort of thing. Ask the girl, I think she'll be able to tell you."

Before they parted Dancer was left with one last vision of Belov. The boy was leaning on the black fence, his arms were coiled through the grill. He was grinning at the clouds of snow on the plain.

Later more snow fell, but the night was windless and there was only soft brushing against the glass. John built a fire, and Anna

74

roasted sausages that she had brought home in newspaper parcels. When she had first returned she had smelled as clean as the snow. The sun had also browned her face and bleached her lashes so that her eyes seemed a darker green. After eating they made love. John had never felt so desperate.

Now they lay in one another's arms, wrapped in the quilt. Outside the vacant streets were glowing. Their clothes were heaped beside them on the floor. There was Anna's peasant dress and her bulky sweater, also John's old, leather coat. For a long time neither spoke. Then John asked her if she loved him as much as she loved the revolution, except he posed the question obliquely . . . he asked if she cared more about history than people.

"People cannot deal with too much history," she replied. "That's why the propaganda is written in simple words."

"No, I mean do you care more about individuals than ideas? I'm asking about us, Anna."

"Oh I see. You maybe are starting to get serious."

"Yes."

"You crazy, baby." It was one of the phrases she had picked up from the theater people. "I have enough love for both you and the movement."

"But if you ever had to choose, then what?"

"Why would I have to choose?"

"But if you had to, Anna?"

That cornered her, and she chilled. "No person can ever be as big as the Revolution, darling. This is impossible. The Revolution is as big as the whole world."

"Then to hell with the whole world."

"No, John. You mustn't say that." She even put her finger to his lips, just like in a play.

Sometime well after midnight as they lay in the goose-down bed, he finally asked her about Lenin. He asked where the man was, what his schedule was and the rest of it. He tried to make it sound natural, but the words sounded ugly and lumpy to him.

He had to spit them out as if he were some kind of machine mouthing sounds. What she told him hardly mattered, at least to him. The asking was decisive. It was the first time he had ever used her. . . .

Soon everyone seemed conscious that the breaking point was very near. There were always loitering men about. The twilight crowds were the worst. The morning streets were always littered with signs of violence from the night before: an overturned car, blood on the snow. Squads of government shock troops often skirmished with Red Guards. There were meaningless crimes— shops were looted. Jews were beaten. Roving gangs of boys killed for a few kopecks.

For John it seemed as if he were living inside a bottle. Events merely happened around him, and he could not control them even if he had wanted to. And he did not want to. He did not want to change anything, because to move an inch in any direction was to shatter that bottle, and the bottle was where he lived with Anna.

Toward the end Belov looked very bad. His skin was pasty, and there were dark circles around his eyes. When he spoke his lips drew back from his teeth. Years later, this was how John would remember him, standing in the dirty snow on the steps of Saint Isaac's Cathedral, his face terribly white against the turned up collar of his fur coat.

"Lenin is at the Solomnly," John said. "I think he has a room in the north wing. He works nights mostly, and he's always surrounded by people."

"You have done a good thing. I already had heard all that, but you have done a good thing anyway in coming to me and telling me this. You confirm it."

"You can go to hell, Andre."

But Belov may not have even heard. He was watching a rank of choirboys file across the snow-packed square. "You have no idea"—he smiled—"what it's like to feel so totally committed to

76

a cause. This is something that you must experience one day, lover. It is bliss. I guarantee you."

One straggling choirboy bundled in a seaman's jacket was mooning about the square. When he kicked at the snow, the powder seemed to turn to gold in the light.

"Jesus, Belov, don't you understand that it's hopeless now. There's just too many of them. When it started the picture was different. The party was small. Everything was dependent on the leaders. But now it's too big. It's moving with its own momentum. If Lenin were gone there'd be Trotsky. If Trotsky were gone . . . can't you understand, Andre? There are millions of them now."

"One at a time, lover. You take them down one at a time."

Now the child across the court was heaving snowballs against the rectory wall. He may have been pretending they were bombs.

"Well I'm out," Dancer suddenly said. "I've done all I'm going to do, and now I'm stepping out."

"Of course, lover. Agreed. Besides, I don't need you anymore. So you go back to that slut of yours and be happy. Yes, I truly want you to be happy. And by the way, there's no need to worry about that girl. She won't even care if she finds out how you took advantage of her. If it's real love, you can get away with anything." . . .

Eventually these days would be called the Final Hours. Historians would argue that the Bolsheviks had already consolidated, and that the movement had "a linear thrust." They would cite the mass rallies of early November, and Kerensky's frantic backlash as clear signs of the impending upheaval.

But all John saw was the pandemonium. There were soldiers everywhere, and mobs with kitchen knives and lead pipes. They loitered in groups, smoking and chewing sunflower seeds. Brick walls were smeared with red paint. The trams ran erratically.

Through it all John lived within a deteriorating routine. He would wake in the mornings with Anna. They usually ate black-market pumpernickel, tea and marmalade. Some days he walked the streets, went nowhere in particular; he just walked. Everyone's eyes seemed turned down to the asphalt. The wind swept through the broad boulevards. The first thing that numbed were your feet.

At midnight before the final day, John and Anna knelt on the window box to see the city in the bluish glow of still another snowfall. She had been away from him since early that morning, and he had spent hours waiting. It had seemed as if his nerves were metal wires, strung almost to the breaking point.

She drew his face to her's and kissed him. Then she pressed his hand to her breast, but he could not make love tonight. All he wanted was to hold her. He just wanted to hold on tight. They ended up on the rug by the fire, and he coiled himself around her.

When she fell asleep he lay with his eyes shut and listened to the pinging clock until he could not stand it anymore. So this had been the problem all along, he suddenly realized. You couldn't stop time. Even when he jammed the swinging pendulum and smashed the crystal dial; even when the mainspring snapped— there was still that ticking inside his head.

Of that last day, John would only remember a smear of wild impressions. He would remember waking in the morning and finding Anna gone. Then there were the long hours of rooting around her apartment, gnawing on bread and an oxtail. At noon there were gunshots from across the roofs, and someone slashed the tires of a neighbor's car. The neighbor was an old man, a French painter who had lived in the city for thirteen years. John heard him crying in the hallway after the vandals had struck.

By nightfall John was pacing at the window, running his fingers through his hair, even digging his nails in his scalp. Then came the tolling bells, and John said Anna's name out loud. Something was happening to her. Something bad. The thought was like a bolt suddenly driven through his chest. Blood drained from his face. His stomach heaved, and finally he was stumbling out the door.

All around were the barricades; crude, haphazard walls of pack-

78

ing crates, scrap lumber, stone and mattresses. Red streamers flew from the balconies. Something was burning. There were long trails of smoke above the tenements.

Beneath a sputtering streetlamp he saw the face of some acquaintance, a poet he had met at one of Belov's late suppers. The boy was passing vodka with a dozen ragged others. They were all slouched around an armored car.

"You're seeing raw history tonight," the poet shouted as soon as he recognized John.

Dancer ignored him. He just kept moving forward until he had the boy by the arm. "I'm looking for Anna. Anna."

"Here. You'll find her in this," and the boy tried to jam the bottle into Dancer's mouth.

John pushed it away. "Just tell me if you've seen her."

The boy shrugged. "Try the palace. They're all moving on the palace tonight. They're making raw history."

Six blocks further on he was swept into a flood of tramping figures, and their heads all blurred together. Shots broke from the top of a bridge, and a woman crumpled with her elbow blown away.

An aura of light glittered above the palace, and for a moment the crowd was wavering. A three inch gun exploded and rocked on its side. Then a truck rumbled through and rammed the gates. The engine blew, white steam billowed out, and they were pouring over the walls.

John caught only the merest glimpse of a blonde girl through the bobbing heads, but he was screaming her name anyway. Then the flood became a riptide, pulling him over the rubble and into the light.

He would never forget how he swayed with vertigo high up on the landing of the palace staircase. Below they were swarming across the gleaming parquetry, battering down doors, pulling curtains off the rods. For a long time he must have been frozen there, watching. Then he started limping, limping because his thigh had

79

a cramp. So he was moving very slowly, first toward the fuzzy light of the chandeliers, then back into the night . . .

Somehow the next hours passed, although he would never remember them. He walked for miles through the half-deserted city. Who knew where all the people went? There were only chips of fallen plaster, twisted iron and overturned cars. Once he thought he saw Anna among the gray shapes huddled beneath an arch, but when he shuffled forward shouting, no one responded.

It was dawn when he returned to the apartment. He crept up on doors, pushed them back and called for her, but every room was an empty shell. The pretending was over. She was gone.

In the kitchen he tipped a few bowls, searching for scraps: a stray sausage, milk, a little cheese. There was nothing. So he finally just sat down on the window box, wishing he hadn't smashed the wall clock because now there was no sound at all to drown out the ringing in his ears.

For the rest of that day he barely moved. Once or twice he padded through the empty rooms as if there were something important he had overlooked, but he always returned to the window. He slept a little, badly, and when he awoke he was clammy and warm. He supposed he had a fever. Toward the end he was only half awake, even though his eyes were open. The edges of the room were blurred. The walls were undulating.

Anna returned as the light began to fade. John did not hear her climbing the steps or opening the door. Suddenly she was just standing there in her coat and riding boots. Her eyes were vacant. Her skin was pale. She might have just turned to wax.

He heard her say, "Have you eaten, John?"

He shook his head. "There's nothing to eat."

She ran her hand through her hair. "I'll make some tea then. Yes, we can have some tea."

He would have thrown himself around her hips, but her eyes put him off.

When she had settled into the sofa, she told him that the government had fallen during the night. "Everyone is very happy. The trams are running again. The shops are open. I even saw an exhibit of paintings by my good friend Leo Stolpin. You know him, I think?"

"Where were you, Anna?"

"What do you think, baby? I was working for the new government. It has a wonderful name. It would be in English, uh, The Soviet of People's Commissars. Don't you think it has a wonderful sound. It makes me very happy just to say it."

She knows, he thought. She knows everything. Then her cup and saucer started rattling. Tea went splashing. Finally the china crashed to the tiles.

Anna was hunched over, sobbing. "Why? Why, John?"

"Was it Belov?" he asked. "Did Belov tell you?"

She spoke to her lap, or the fragments of her teacup on the floor. "Our new president is Lenin. Early this morning he left his bedroom. He has been working day and night. Perhaps he slept for a few hours on the little bed that they made for him. But early this morning he left his room, and there were many people around him. All these people walked down the hall. That was when Andre Belov ran up beside and fired his pistol at Lenin. Only, his aim was poor, or some say his arm was pushed. Then they took Belov away, and explained everything, even you."

"I see," Dancer whispered. It was all that came out.

"No, you don't see." "You don't see anything."

"Yes I do," he said, looking into her eyes. And then he was rising, gliding toward her. He might have been wading through water. The whole room had grown watery and she was so very light in his arms. For a long while they were simply swaying together, just as on the first night they met.

An hour might have passed, although it couldn't have been more than a few minutes. Finally she was saying, "You must go, they're looking for you. You have to go. Now."

The room was washed with shadows. A white pool of moonlight

lay on the tiles, projecting rectangles on the wall. Anna moved softly. She gave him money, clothing and a tiny pearl-handled revolver. When she sank to her knees he fell with her, so they were facing the glowing window together.

"Here," she said, and ran a finger along her hairline. "You must strike me here and make it bleed, because they will be here soon and I must have a story to tell them. So do it now, John. Strike me here. *Do* it."

He would always have this single memory of their last moment together: he kneeling beside her, then kissing her, she wincing to take the blow.

The image would remain for sixty years. . . .

John fled west, back through the Finland Station and out across the tundra. There were three nights of blizzard spent in a reed hut with a Mongolian trapper. He rode for miles in a boxcar jammed with peasants, and saw the narrowing rails slide together behind him. Often the going was harrowingly slow. The Germans had torn up the tracks. At night they burned human dung to keep warm. When he finally reached Archangel he had lost fifteen pounds, and his face was raw from the wind. Later he would write that he felt as if he had aged a hundred years.

CHAPTER THREE

LANGLEY HISTORIANS generally saw John Dancer's first Russian sojourn as a convenient beginning for America's modern intelligence apparatus. Yet as John himself grew older, it seemed that the past ceased to be mere sequence . . . there was another, secret pattern. People were linked in devious ways, small events had great importance.

When John read about Dusty Yeats and Jessie and the rest, he felt more convinced than ever that his own life was merely a small fragment of a cycle. He had had this perception before, but it had always been fleeting, more intuition than logic. Now it seemed clear and undeniable. Jessie, he told himself, will bring this house down with him.

John slept fitfully the night he read the Yeats report. At some point he went to bed, from habit, then lay for an hour, and got up again. There was whiskey in the cedar chest downstairs, but tonight he was particularly frightened of those creaking steps. So he prowled the upper rooms, inspected a vase, browsed through Allen's old history books. There was one rather good one on great naval battles. The moonlight was shifting over the carpets and paneling.

By morning a breeze was sweeping through the neighborhood. Allen used to climb that rustling oak in the garden. John brewed a pot of coffee, then telephoned Lyle Severson. When Severson arrived the two old men lumbered out to talk beneath the windy trees among the vines and hedges.

"I'd like to see this Yeats," John began. "I'd like to ask him a question or two."

Severson grunted. "He's not a very nice person."

"Who is these days?" He lowered his head to Lyle's ear. "It's not that I think your Humphrey Knolls hasn't done a good job of it. It's just that there are a few things I'd like to ask the boy myself. In order to get a better feel of the situation. In order to . . . oh I don't know. I suppose that I can't quite come to terms with it. I'm afraid I'm terribly ashamed."

They had come to the coolest, darkest end of the garden. Here the path was mossy and the grass still wet with dew.

Dancer said suddenly, "I remember when Allen first came to me with Magic. I remember how proud I was. We had been trying to find an effective Kremlin link for years, and all of a sudden here comes my own son. What especially pleased me was that he had developed Magic out of my own contacts. I remember thinking how symmetrical it was. Father to son and all that."

"Magic was a big event for all of us," Lyle said. He had to say something.

"And now you tell me that my grandson, Jessie is out to destroy everything my son has built. Well it's the same sort of symmetry.

Oh, the paths are different yes. Jessie goes off to Vietnam, then battles it out in Cambodia, but in the end he's come back to his family. So there you have it. You have this . . . oh, what should I say we all are? Jessie, Allen, myself. What, Lyle? A dynasty, but of what? A dynasty of spies?"

Severson was frowning at his brogues. They were studded with droplets. "You know it may not be as bad as we think," he said. "All we have now is the word of Dusty Yeats."

"But Knolls wrote that Yeats was found in Central Reference. Do I have that right, Lyle?"

"Yes, it all started in Central Reference."

"Well, there you have the answer."

"I don't follow, John."

"Central Reference. That's my slot, isn't it? That's where they keep all my old papers. All the early groundwork that eventually led to Magic is still in Central Reference."

"We've looked at all that, John, but it doesn't necessarily prove that much."

"It proves that Yeats knew what he was doing. He was trying to trace it back. He wanted to go back all the way until he found out just what Source Magic is."

The garden had begun shivering with a new gust. Leaves were sawing away at one another. Behind them lay the tunnel of foliage back to the white frame house.

"Anyway," John said at last, "I'd like to talk to this Dusty Yeats. Do you think you could arrange that for me?"

They drove to the compound in Dancer's old gray Mercedes. He parked just inside the gates and waited in the car while Lyle spoke to the guard under the steel awning.

"How is Dusty today?" Severson asked.

"Fine, sir. He's just fine."

The guard was a trim boy, and Lyle had taken his elbow for that paternal touch. They were facing the cement building, a depress-

85

ing view of asphalt and corrugated roofing.

"Hasn't given you any trouble then?"

"No, sir. Dusty's been a good boy."

Lyle glanced back at the battered sedan, at old John, sitting stiffly behind the wheel. "In a few minutes," Lyle said, "that gentleman over there is going to have a few words with Yeats. Now I want you to make sure that Dusty behaves himself. You understand me, son?"

Severson took John down the scuffed linoleum hall and up to the prisoner's cell. Then the two friends parted, the guard slid back the bolt, and John stepped in alone.

Yeats was crouching on his bunk, leafing through a magazine. Yeats was grinning. "Hello, don't think I've had the pleasure."

Dancer lowered himself to the chair. He had seen the naked thigh of a girl as the pages of the magazine flipped by in Dusty's fingers. Now he was rubbing his hands together.

He said only, "I'm Jessie's grandfather."

"Ah, yes. I've heard of you. Yeah, John Dancer. Well okay. I've finally hit the big time. Guess I'll have to write them back home about this one."

They were supposed to have broken him, John thought. His heart was pounding.

"Yeah," Yeats prattled on, "Jess liked you. He said you were the nice one."

"I'd like to talk about him," Dancer said.

"Sure, I'm an open book now. I've been reformed."

"Can you tell me about that young lady Jessie had an affair with in London?"

Yeats shrugged. "What do you want to know?"

"You told Mr. Knolls that Jessie was very fond of her."

"Yeah. They were pretty close."

"Did you ever meet her?"

"How could I have met her? She was in London. I never went there."

86

"Well, did you ever see a photograph of her?"

"Yeah. Jess had a picture."

"Can you recall what she looked like?"

"Yeah, she looked good. Blonde hair. Kind of a kid's face. Real pretty."

"Did Jessie talk about her very much?"

"No. He didn't like to talk about her. He just sort of kept it to himself."

"I see. Thank you." John rose from the chair and started for the door.

"That's it? That's all you wanted to know?"

"Yes," John smiled. "That's all I wanted to know."

Well beyond the compound John and Lyle rested in the grass at the top of the hill. They had walked out along the black road. When they had begun to run short of breath they stopped.

"He seems like a rather tough character," John said.

"Yeats? Yes he is."

"And I imagine Jessie must be similar. Tough I mean."

"Yes, I'm sure he is."

The wind was sounding in their ears, quivering in the grass. This open space was always the center of a tiny storm, thought Lyle, and there was something pathetic about two old men standing on a desolate hill.

Suddenly John said, "I feel very awkward about this. I mean they never told you the entire Magic story, did they, Lyle?"

"It wasn't my area."

"Still, they should have told you. I mean, I would have told you if it had been up to me. But as it happened I had very little control once it got rolling. Allen picked up what I dropped and ran with it. Next thing I knew he had built my bit into Source Magic. Then, of course, they clamped the lid on tight. That's why I could never tell you about the details. I'm sorry."

"Well, it hardly matters now. I think we've both been left in the

87

dust by it. Magic is a young man's institution now. The last great intelligence network . . . I've heard it called that somewhere."

"It's in the Yeats reports. Knolls wrote that."

"Yes," Lyle said. "I remember now. Humphrey has always had a way with words. And a flair for history. Did you know that? He used to work with archives himself."

They had started climbing down the hill again, slowly feeling their way through the tall grass. The whole landscape seemed to be swimming around them in the breeze. When they finally reached the compound gates, Lyle stopped and touched his friend's arm.

"There is one thing that I'm curious about, John. Why did you ask Yeats about the girl?"

John lumped up his cheek and shook his head. "I don't know, really. It just seemed important somehow. Young men will go a long way for a girl. I know I did. I once went a very long way for a girl. And she did for me."

When he returned home that afternoon he tried to keep his mind on simple tasks. He spent a few hours tidying the house, sorting laundry and stacking dishes. At dusk he put a slightly bruised chicken in the oven. The raw skin was revolting, but even when the bird was cooked he couldn't eat it. He just sat at the head of the dining room table and let the past drag him back in time.

It was wholly true that the source of the Dancer power lay in his past. So yes, John told himself, Jessie was a cunning boy. Let them speak of him how they would, will, but no one could deny that he was a cunning boy. When he sent Dusty Yeats to Central Reference he was starting at the beginning and marching forward on the only path there was.

But Central Reference only contained the sketchiest record. There was nothing in the files that spoke of the deeper human feelings, nothing of how he had really been when he had first returned from Russia. There was nothing even of Anna Servana.

So in a way the real beginning of the story was lost, because in those early days everything depended upon passion, and there was no sense of passion in the files.

The records placed him back from Russia in the spring of 1918. There was mention of the job he took at his uncle's magazine, and his testimony on Russian affairs before a board of military intelligence directors. Historians also noted that he had been interviewed by the FBI and representatives of the State Department. All these talks were conducted informally, and their only significance later was that they constituted John Dancer's first real link with America's fledgling intelligence community.

As for John's motives, he had told them about Russia because they had asked. There was hardly any deeper sense of duty than that. How they had known about the affair in the first place was anyone's guess. Probably there had been a leak from London to the American Embassy.

There was particular interest in British training methods. The military was especially keen on that point. Otherwise the questions put to John were pretty general. He was asked to describe his impressions of the new Soviet regime and estimate its potential strength. Of Andre Belov, John said very little until he learned that he had been shot. Then John described his friend as an idealist and a humanist. Anna was kept out of the narratives completely. She was buried inside of John's chest, and they would have had to cut it open to get at her.

For a while John lived with his parents in that ivy brownstone on Fifth Avenue. He had his old room back, with the brass bed and the pennants on the wall. There was also that globe that his father had given him years before. It was set in a lovely steel frame, and John could sit at the rolltop for hours, spinning the earth until his finger landed on Petrograd. He often read until late at night. In the morning the cook left a tray by his door—coffee and a poached egg. His parents were concerned about his state of mind. His father complained that he did nothing. John felt as if he were

89

living in another dimension of space and time.

When his parents became unbearable he took the job from his uncle and got himself a two room flat near the park. Then came the drudgery. He got up in the morning, took a bus to the office, maybe had a donut and coffee at noon. His uncle had him editing, which he had no feel for, but no one ever said anything. Then it was back to his room, or maybe down to a corner bar. He was waiting for something to change; waiting, not hoping.

Fridays he had dinner with his parents. They always asked if he had met anyone special. For a few weeks he told them he had a girl named Anna, but they kept pestering him to bring her by, so he finally had to tell them that he and Anna had fallen out. It was around that time that his mother insisted that he take out Mary.

Mary Brown was the daughter of John's father's partner. John had known the girl for years. Once they had even kissed underneath the honeysuckle in the garden. She was a pert, bouncy girl with golden red hair. John always pictured her in pale pink taffeta and fur muffs. He had also always disliked her name. *Hail-Mary-Mother-of-God.* It sort of stuck in your throat.

On their first night together he took her to the Continental and they dined on squab in orange sauce. Later they rode a carriage through the park. The sky was clear and filled with stars.

"Tell me about Russia, John." She had a young girl's windy voice. When she snuggled into his shoulder her crinoline gouged his ribs.

"It's a big place," he said. He was numb from the wine and a little nauseous in the rocking cab. Also, the smell of horses reminded him of war.

"You must have been cold there." She laughed. "I heard that Russia's very cold."

"Yes, it was cold."

"But colorful too. Imagine being in the middle of a revolution. Weren't you frightened?"

90

"No. I was never frightened."

She figured it was a joke and giggled. "Well, what on earth did you do there, John?"

"Do there?"

"In Russia, silly. What did you do in Russia?"

For an instant he went blank. Then his lips spread in a too wide smile. "Didn't they tell you? I was a spy."

It was the first time that John had ever given himself the identity that was to mark him for the rest of his life.

He continued to see Mary Brown, because there was nothing else to do. True, there were a couple of possibles at the office, but he avoided them. Mary at least was harmless. He also liked the way she wore her hair swept back with tiny china barrettes. Anna had sometimes worn her hair that way . . .

In time he found himself toying with an image of a naked Mary, perhaps before the mirror in the ochre light of the late afternoon. Her hair would be following the brush in filmy strands, just as Anna's had done. Or else he saw her on the bed, looking a little scared. Oh, sin of sins. Her body would be plumper than Anna's, but who cared?

On their seventh evening he took her to a ball. Some friend of hers had turned eighteen and was going up for bid among *society*. Mary made him whirl across the floor in celebration. Then he had to bring her punch and ladyfingers from the buffet. But afterward they rode another carriage through the park, and this time the shadows were more inviting. The trees formed black tunnels. When he kissed her, she pressed his hand against her breast. "I'd like to see where you live now, John."

His mother had filled his apartment with bulky furniture. There were lamps with tassels on the shades and Oriental rugs. Still, the place had a shabby feel what with the grime on the windowsills and the lingering odor of stale tobacco.

Mary spread herself on the sofa. Her shawl was slipping over

91

her shoulder. John brought two glasses of sherry. The decanter stood before them on an ebony table. He crossed his legs on the wing chair and ran his thumb along the crease in his flannels. She was winding her fingers in the end of her shawl.

"You're a strange man," she said, and stretched so that her bracelets went clinking down her wrist. "I never know what you're thinking."

He was thinking that they would sleep together, and afterward he would be caught. He was also looking at the curve of her arm in the lamplight, and the thin straps of her frock.

"You're not at all like other boys, John. Why I hardly know if you even like me."

"I like you," he said.

"But I wonder if you truly mean it. A girl needs reassurance you know."

He took a mouthful of sherry, then slipped off the chair. Now he was on his knees before her. "I'm actually just a normal person," he said in a voice so low she barely heard him. "I'm just like everyone else."

"Well," she breathed, "I suppose I'll just have to find that out for myself." Then she pecked at his lips with hers.

Now they were melting into one another. She had sunken into the cushions. He had dropped on top of her. His hand was sweeping back her dress to the thigh. Hers was pressing into his chest. Finally her breast slipped free, and she arched, sucking in long breaths.

It was not the last time John slept with her. They even spent a weekend at her father's hunting lodge, a rough pine cabin that lay in a dingle by a lake. At twilight deer grazed by the grassy shore.

On the last evening of that weekend Mary told him that she was pregnant. They were standing by the water's edge. John was skipping stones off the glassy surface. When she spoke he just kept arching stones over the water. His only thought was, so this is how you fall back into life.

"We don't have to marry," she said. "I know a girl who's a nurse. She can fix it for us. She has some pills or something."

The wind was blowing through the trees. The lake was turning a deeper blue. It was said that the lake had no bottom.

"Because I don't want to get married on that sort of basis. I won't live the rest of my life wondering if you really wanted me as your wife."

"No," John told her. "We'll get married." It seemed inevitable anyway.

"Are you sure that's what you want?"

What he wanted hardly mattered. This was just how you fell into life.

"I mean, do you feel that this is right in terms of your . . . existence?"

His *existence?* Good lord.

"We're discussing our future, John. This is important. Please."

Suddenly she looked so fragile and silly, facing him on the edge of that bottomless lake, that he had to take the easy way out. "Yes"—he smiled—"I want to marry you. I'm sure I do."

It was the first time he had ever lied to her. Ever needed to.

He was, after all, a gentleman.

They were married in a cool high vaulted cathedral in windy autumn when the streets were filled with red leaves. Nearly a hundred guests attended, including the friends of both families. Best man was a fellow from the office, some chap who occasionally had a five o'clock beer with John. He was asked to serve because there was no one else. It was slightly embarrassing.

The ceremony was oddly somber. Mary stepped to the altar as softly as a breath. They stood beneath a blue velvet canopy while the priest read a standard service. Everyone craned over the balustrade to see John slip the gold band on his bride. But when he finally lifted the veil and closed his eyes for the sealing kiss, all he saw was Anna's face, and he felt like he was killing her.

In the beginning the young couple lived in a plain but clean apartment near the river. Every morning they drank coffee on the balcony and watched the barges pass. Life became regular, and after eight months Allen was born. Allen, named for John's grandfather, although he had his mother's features. When the child became ill, John walked the floors every night for seven weeks. He dreamt of Anna a lot.

Within the chronicles of the secret world the next phase of John Dancer's life became known as the dark years. Historians have always had difficulty following the thread of the clandestine services between the wars, because with isolationism as American policy the foreign intelligence professional had nothing to do.

Yet even through these dark years the torch still flickered. Those who believed that the nation needed some sort of intelligence capacity often met informally. Most were civilians now, although there were a few with government posts. Now and then a member of this secret community would look John up. Then he would spend an evening at the club, chatting, drinking. The talk was always ambitious, but it never came to much.

Whether John stepped in knowingly to this intelligence subculture, or was drawn in by happenstance was never fully determined. He himself probably did not know. Merely the fact remained that by the second decade John was once again in the secret world.

For several years the extent of his relationship with the intelligence community remained hazy. Records show that he was the occasional advisor to the army's chief spy, Ralph Van Deman, and was loosely connected with Herbert Yardly's New York code and cipher office. There were also tacit links with the State Depart-

94

ment, and even a line to the White House. But currently all that seemed important of this period was simply that the groundwork was laid.

Through those years of evenings at his club, the dinners of burnt chops, the coffee and biscuits, Dancer slowly came to know them all, all who would later fill the ranks of spies. There were the Dulles brothers, and Wild Bill Donovan, who would eventually head the OSS. William Stevenson, who was later dubbed Intrepid, first met Dancer at this stage of the story. Some would die, some fade away, and some would go on with John's son Allen to form the CIA.

They were fairly quiet years for John. He continued to work at the magazine, and events were hardly anything more to him than a few inches of copy, although he still read the foreign press to keep himself in touch with Russia. When the economy crashed his life changed little. His father's trust remained intact. None of his wife's friends' fortunes were seriously hurt. The Depression meant only that there were whores along Broadway and Times Square was full of derelicts: pushcart vendors, ragmen, children munching apples and all the other dispossessed. It was a little like Petrograd just before the Revolution, a little unreal.

Summers the family still spent in the country. John had purchased a farm in the Berkshire mountains. It was called Twin Willows and lay on a broad lawn under maples and elms. When Allen was old enough, John would fish with him for trout in the nearby brook, or maybe swim in the pool downstream. Mostly they loved the first weeks of spring. Then the willows turned yellow and the pale shadblow filled the surrounding meadows. There were big clumps of dogwood and more formal white flowers. But Mary's second child was stillborn at the farm, and then she never wanted to go back there again.

The years were marked by regularity. There were dinner parties among friends, and Mary had her charities. As John grew older the lines deepened in his face. He managed to stay fairly thin and people always thought he looked nice enough. But also with age the world seemed stranger to him. History, politics, economics—all that he understood as well as anyone. It was his own life that remained a mystery. I have wasted twenty years, he told himself, twenty years largely wasted, and the oddest part was that when he had been younger he had thought himself dead. All through those months with Anna, he had thought himself dead when in fact he had never been more alive.

But to all this came the turning point. It came in the fall, during an Indian summer. John was boating on the Chesapeake with a friend from his club, an eccentric old lawyer named Greyson Dow. Years before, Dow had chatted with John about Russia. At that time he had had some sort of connection with the navy. Lately his contacts seemed more political. They said he had a White House link.

Greyson was a snowy, round man with red cheeks and bushy eyebrows. He and John had a sort of father and son relationship. They dined together and John was never permitted to pay. Christmas, and Greyson sent a case of whiskey. There was also candied fruit for Mary and Allen. Finally John was asked out for that day on Greyson's sloop. It was called the *Mata Hari.*

There was low fog on the morning they set out. The wind was light, and skirting the shore they smelled pine and heard the thrushes singing. There was also the gentle slap of the sea on the bow.

As always they fell to talking politics. These days there were the Fascists on the right and the Communists on the left, and Greyson was proud of his moderation. He often said that he liked a man who could hate both Stalin and Hitler. Hitler especially, for Greyson had become one of those who early saw the writing on the wall.

That morning as they sailed the coves and stretches of windblown beach, Hitler had been on Greyson's mind. The night be-

96

fore he had attended a party in someone's country home and the place had been filled with fascists.

"There was one brat from the *American Review,*" Greyson said. "He kept talking about liquidating people. Liquidating. Where the hell did he pick up that word?"

"From the latin, *liquidus,*" Dancer said.

"It's a disease, John. You've never heard me say that about anything. There's the Reds, yes, but one can at least talk to them. They're artists mostly, or artist types, anyway. You have a lot of artist friends, don't you, John? Hang about the magazine, don't they. Who's that chap I met at your place?"

"Auden. W.H. Auden."

"Yes, well he's a Red, isn't he? But at least you can talk to him."

"I don't know where Auden stands. I really don't know him very well."

"Well there's others, and the point is that one can talk to them, reason with them, if you understand me. The fascists are different, John. The fascists sit squarely on a sense of profound, and ugly, delusion."

They were almost just drifting now, following the wooded shore. Among the blacker rocks the water was luminous. There were fingers of seaweed waving below.

Greyson was crouching at the tiller. His face was very red against the purple of his sweater. "Do you have any Jewish friends?" he asked.

"I'm sorry?"

"Friends that are Jewish. Do you have any?"

Dancer shrugged. "I suppose so. Yes."

"I've always admired the Jews. Energetic people. Use their minds. They place a lot of emphasis on the intellect. Albert Einstein, he's a typical Jew in a way. Which is why it's somehow symbolic that the Nazis hate them so. The Nazis can't exist in the face of questioning intellect. Their basic theory is nonsense. The race theory, I mean. A bunch of trash, that's what it is. At least

97

the Reds have a certain intellectual footing. Economics and all that. You can read Marx and make *some* sense of it. Not true with the Nazis."

Seagulls were skimming the water ahead, and further out a buoy clanged. There were more gulls watching them from the grassy dunes ashore.

"The other day I had lunch with one of the President's people," Greyson was saying. "Can't tell you who it was, John, but suffice it to say that the fellow is well connected. He asked me who I favored in Europe, the Nazis or the Reds? Well I told him I didn't favor either, not on principle anyway. So he told me, principles aside how would I stand. 'All right,' I said, 'I'll take the Reds.' You see, John, one must sometimes make a choice. A lesser of two evils kind of choice. Well, the Nazis are a disease. You can't deal with them. I think the President agrees. I think if push comes to shove he'll side with the Russians."

"The Russians?"

"Yes, the Russians. That's what I want to talk to you about, John. Russians. You see something has just come up with them. They've been putting out some feelers. Embassy route and all that. Of course they're very timid at the moment, but it's clear that they want to talk. That much is very clear. The Russians want to talk to us about the Germans. Oh I know what you're thinking. You're thinking about the treaty Stalin just signed with Hitler. Time, John. Stalin was just buying time for himself. He knows there's going to be a war, and he needs time to prepare. No, the Russians are as frightened of Hitler as anyone. That's why they want to chummy up with us. They're looking for friends, and let me add that they come bearing gifts. Oh yes, the Russians are bearing gifts, all right."

They were coming about, pulling hard on the line to draw out the luff, then ducking under the swinging boom. Then came the sudden calm again. There was only the lapping sea and crying birds.

98

"Wilhelm Canaris," Greyson was murmuring. "Know who he is, John?"

"Hitler's intelligence head. Abwehr, I think they call it. Military stuff for the most part. They're clumsy, I hear, but there's a lot of them."

"Mmm." Greyson nodded. "Canaris is a highborn Junker. A real stereotypical son of a bitch. Wears those riding boots when he hunts. Drinks dry sherry. Takes chances too. For instance, Hitler told him to stay clear of us. Keep his agents out of New York. Don't poison the wells, don't dirty the sheets. Hitler has too many pals in New York to risk spoiling the pot with illegals. But Canaris is a fanatic, and with fanatics anything is possible."

The gulls had begun wheeling above. Some fell and broke the water, then rose again with fish in their beaks. Otherwise the sloop was easing into a still and silent mist. They might have been sailing a phantom sea.

"If we can believe it," Greyson continued, "here is the story. The Russians have a girl inside of Abwehr. Pretty girl and uses it. Maybe she's the type that sleeps with anyone. Maybe she's got a steady man. At any rate she knows how to make them talk, because the Russians claim that they've gotten their hands on the one thing we want—Canaris's New York network. The Russians have names, courier routes, the whole business. See what that means, John? Do you?"

"The Russians are willing to trade with us?"

"Not trade, John. It's a gift. I said the Russians are bearing gifts. All they want is to be our pals. Don't want us sleeping with Hitler. Get the point?"

"Yes, I guess I do."

"I knew you would. That's why I recommended you. You have a feel for it."

"Recommended me for what?"

"To go, of course. Moscow, John. We want you to take the ferry across the sea and meet with some people in Moscow. Well, we

99

have to accept the gift, don't we? I mean somebody has to do it, and we need a man who has the credentials, but not the official connections, if you get my drift. Need a man who isn't officially tied with Washington, but someone that Washington can trust. And I trust you, John. And if I trust you, Washington will trust you."

"But Moscow" John Dancer laughed—"Moscow? You're really serious, aren't you?"

"Of course. You know the choreography there. No one else I know does."

"But that was twenty years ago. I was just a kid then."

"You're still a kid to me." Greyson smiled. "Besides, twenty years isn't so long. You'll still find a few friends there."

"Enemies more likely."

"No. That's all forgotten now. Forgotten and forgiven. You got into a little trouble there on that British show during the Revolution, but that's all over now. No one even remembers anymore."

"I remember," Dancer said to himself, and silently mouthed her name again. Anna. It could have been written in the sky.

"What was that?"

"I said I'll have to fix it with Mary."

"Yes, tell her that the magazine is sending you off. Tell her you have to do a story on the Eskimos."

By the day's end they had returned to the dock. Now on the very edge, dangling their feet above the sliding tide, Greyson passed a hipflask of whiskey. The fog never did lift. It was still curling all around them.

"Tonight, tomorrow, maybe the next day," Greyson was mumbling, "there may come a point when you'll start to waver. You'll get cold feet. You'll want to telephone and call it off. When that moment comes I want you to think of something, John. I want you to think of spending the rest of your life knowing that you had the chance to go back but didn't take it."

100

"There's no need to sell me, Grey. I want to go. It's time. Besides there's someone in Russia I'd like to see."

Greyson shook his head. "You won't have much time there, John, and it's best not to get involved with old shows."

"It won't take long, an afternoon maybe. This is just something I have to do. It's an old debt that has to be paid."

"Sure, old debts . . . I understand. Nothing can wreck a life like old debts." He was speaking to the flat expanse of sea.

In the next three weeks John met several times with Greyson Dow. Occasionally Dow brought others along, nameless men, some in military uniform. Briefing could not have been simpler. John was merely to sail for Russia. There he would be met by a General Josef Serov. The rest would follow. As an aside John was told that Serov was old Russian, a gentlemen. Greyson said that the general had the intellect of a poet, and Dancer got on well with poets.

On the last day before departure, John lunched with Greyson once more. They ate in a gloomy loft where the walls were bare brick and the visceral pipes stretched across the ceiling. Wine bottles were stuck with candle stubs, and the tablecloths were splotched with grease.

For a while they spoke of the war in Spain. Then Greyson asked about Allen. There was little John could say. His son had been away at school for what seemed like several years. Also, Dancer had no idea that Allen had already become entranced by the spell of the secret world.

The last night John spent with Mary. They hardly spoke, but for years now they had never had much to say. Time just kept passing. Habit kept them living together, that and all the things that John had never dared to tell her. Later, after lying awake for several hours, John got up and went into the dining room. He meant to pour himself a glass of wine, but passing by the oval

101

mirror he caught the quick vision of his younger self. He could have been nineteen again for an instant there. Then he understood at last. The wheel had indeed come full circle.

The voyage took weeks. John walked the decks a lot, read a canvas bound edition of *The Brothers Karamazov*. He had found the ratty copy in the captain's personal library, and something about the Grand Inquisitor kept him going night after night.

Sometimes fellow passengers were a touch too friendly. They must have seen him as a lonely professional, maybe a novelist or a veterinarian. His suits had that slightly rumpled look, because the salt air made his creases sag. No one seemed afraid of him as they had before. This time he was always being asked to sit at people's tables.

Toward the end the last of the season's ice ground them to a halt. The liner lay bogged some twenty miles off the coast. At night the running lights could be seen for miles. Finally the ice-breakers led them in, but two days had been lost.

There were too many backed-up memories. Even just stepping onto the Petrograd docks, John had a terrible urge to turn his head as if someone were calling him from far away. Petrograd all over again, although now they called it Leningrad (well, he'd survived there). Still, the place hadn't changed much, and the scent of the air and the blocks of rectangular buildings kept John bouncing back and forth between two decades.

Impressions were crashing in on one another. First came General Serov and his entourage to welcome John. The general was a stocky, gnarled little man with a long moustache and grizzled hair. He spoke English well, and said that he loved the Americans. John was to call him Josef, and there was a silly greeting where they all shook hands for the camera.

Next came a banquet in some converted ballroom. The tables were packed with officers and bureaucrats in dumpy suits. The

102

waiters were cadets and they served black caviar, sturgeon, and finally lumps of skewered mutton. Later there was vodka, and the general became maudlin. He kept toasting the future dead, then beauty and sadness.

And finally John was alone. Now was the uncertain hour. His hotel room, done in a sort of random baroque, only aggravated old memories. There was a ghastly reproduction of a landscape that he could have sworn he'd seen before. Who could forget those stylized trees and that gloomy shading? Also the flowered chintz was the same sort of stuff that had covered the sofa in Andre's room. But worst of all was the simple black telephone. What if it went off before you were ready?

For a while he could not move from the window, because there was that haunting skyline again, there the palace, there the glowing onion domes. He could have howled at the moon.

Then it was midnight, and John was driven down to the streets once more. The boulevards were dead. The place was like a ruin. There were windows boarded up and vacant shops and empty shelves. Six blocks from his hotel he was lost, wandering aimlessly. Then he found the Nevsky and walked as far as the Anichkov bridge. Skirting the quay led to the old section. Home, Anna used to say, was only where you started from.

By the time he reached her courtyard his mouth was dry. He felt as if his knees would buckle, or his vision go. The building had never looked this bad before. No lights burned, and the central fountain was dry. High above and all around were only the blackened windows.

Then it was up the rotting, wooden staircase, through a fire door. The hinges moaned. There were no longer even the threadbare carpets in the corridor, just the floorboards.

Now he was trembling at the door. He had to stop, catch his breath and hold his ribs. There didn't seem to be enough air, only the smell of cabbage and cleaning fluid. He knocked, banged twice. A muffled voice came back. Padding footsteps, the locks slid back, and a woman's face glared out from the crack. But she was old. Her eyes were black circles.

"Anna Servana?" Dancer whispered. "Does Anna Servana still live here?"

The old woman ran her hand across her mouth, then shook her head.

"Anna Servana," he repeated, then again in Russian "Does she live here? Anna Servana?"

"Go away."

Dancer stuck out a fist of crumpled bills. "Anna Servana, please."

But the woman only sucked in her lips and shook her head. "Go away. Go away."

A second door slid open behind him. John turned, and there was a beefy man in underwear framed in the light. He had a purple scar, and his head was entirely shaved.

"English?" Dancer pleaded. "English?"

"Yes, English." The man frowned. "What do you want?"

"I'm looking for a woman. Her name is Anna Servana."

"She does not live here."

"But do you know her? She used to live here."

"No one like that lives here. Now go away."

"But how could I find her?"

"Go away."

Now both tenants were chanting it. Their mouths seemed to have become rubberized. "Go away. Go away." Until he was stumbling back down the hall.

The rest was no less a nightmare. He had to bribe the doorman to get back into his room, only to lay sweating and shivering under a mound of covers. In the morning Serov fetched a greasy meal of eggs, then it was into the trains.

They rode all day, past villages and small towns. There were no signs and no lights. Serov had a private compartment, but you couldn't shut the door on the aroma of disinfectant. . . .

Moscow rose up out of the night. All John saw were the darkened sections; the empty frames of half built apartments, the skeletons of office buildings. An old Lincoln met them at the station. Everywhere flowed crowds of men and women in cheap coats and boots. All moved without speaking, most with their eyes fixed to the pavement.

They put John up in The Savoy, in a once elegant room that had been poorly repaired. Now the window frames did not quite fit, and the bedsprings sagged. The furniture was crudely jointed, but there was a view through a cavern of walls to a broad cobbled square with trees.

Talks began the second day. There was a conference room deep inside the central cluster of the Kremlin, and every time John passed through the gates and brick battlements he felt as if he were being swallowed up. The corridors were long and windowless. An elevator cage seemed to rise for miles. The room was bare with only a long table and red leather chairs. Clerks kept the glasses filled with water, and there was tea and canapes for lunch.

In all, seven attended. There were four officers from the military intelligence group, two civilians and Serov, who seemed to run the show. The first day was casual. Hors d'oeuvres were served, black caviar and wine. The mood was jovial. Even the translators kept laughing. The favorite word was brotherhood, and half the jokes were sexual.

The next session was moodier. Serov led a formal discussion on Nazi radio links and the seamen networks along the New York docks. Much of the talk centered on funding. The Russians said that courier routes could always be traced through the money flow. The word of the hour was *Kreigsorganization.* K.O., Serov called it, and defined it as any German intelligence ring. The New York end was supposed to have been similar to those uncovered in Moscow and Leningrad. Agent masters were buried in the embassy, and agents were drawn from all over. A lonely girl in a high security typing pool, a minister with debts and a mistress— the Nazis were masters at recruiting those types. There was also a sobering lecture on Abwher muscle. Serov knew of three people who had been murdered in New York by Nazi hunters. Two were sympathizers who got cold feet. One had been a girl who was knifed in the spine and left in an alley where that sort of thing happened nearly every Saturday night.

Afterward, in the banter, the coughing and the scraping chairs, Dancer felt Serov's arm linking through his. The squat general had never looked this sly before. He said confidentially, "Come . . . a sight you must see."

They hurried down the tiled hallway, then through an arch of blocked stone and finally out high above the bastions on a little windy parapet.

"There," Serov said. "See?" He was pointing to a dreamy vision of the crenelated walls, the domed cathedral of Assumption and the warren of stone.

But it was cold, and John held his collar tight around his throat.

"Very few people ever see the Kremlin from just this angle," said Serov. "Only the highest officials and guests like you. The others must stand over there."

"And it's not as nice over there?"

Serov cocked his head for a halfhearted shrug. "Who's to say what is the best view?"

Far below, a line of guards was moving across the open square, first out of the tower's shadow, then into an open patch of weak light.

"Everything depends upon the angle," Serov continued. "That's why I never draw conclusions until I have seen both sides of an issue."

Dancer was leaning on his elbows between the battlements. The wind kept sweeping his hair in his eyes.

"It is the same with people," Serov said after a moment. "One cannot judge too quickly. That's why I have reserved my judgment of you, John."

"Of me?"

"Yes, of you. Because I see things that make me wonder just what sort of fellow you are."

"I'm afraid I don't follow."

Serov bent over. He was very close to Dancer now, whispering, "Where did you go one night in Leningrad, my friend?"

"Oh I see." Dancer smiled. "The doorman at the hotel. I must not have tipped him enough."

"This is no joke. I very much want to have you tell me where you went that night."

"If I told you the truth, I'm not sure you'd believe me," Dancer said.

Serov pulled away. Now he was just scowling at the tedious lines of massive wall.

"I went to see a girl," Dancer said suddenly. "Someone I used to know. I went to her apartment but she no longer lives there."

"A girl? A girl you once knew?"

"A woman, now she's a woman. Her name is Anna Servana. She used to be a famous stage actress. Now her apartment is a ruin, and no one has heard of her."

"I've heard of her," said Serov softly. "Once a long, long time ago."

"And if I wanted to find her . . .?"

"You don't want to find her, John. You would discover that the angle has changed. It would not be the same. Better to have a good memory. Better for lots of reasons."

"No," Dancer said. "I want to find her. If you'll help me I'll be very thankful. If you won't, then that's all right too. But I have to find her."

"Then what? You have a drink? You talk about the old times and remember?"

"I don't know. I just have to find her."

Serov looked like some brooding statue fixed to the stone. The wind was shivering through the fur of his collar. His eyebrows were pinched together. He's just like me, Dancer thought. He's afraid every minute of his life.

"If I help you, John, you must promise to be discreet."

"Yes, I understand."

"No, you don't understand. We are here in a dangerous place, in dangerous times. You have no understanding of how people can suddenly vanish off the face of the earth, vanish without a trace. I've seen this happen before, so you must always be very discreet."

"Yes, but—"

"Don't talk anymore, John. From now on you will be quiet and wait."

Three more days passed in that Kremlin room, and Dancer lived through them with the simple amenities that were expected of him. The Russians sometimes treated him like a child. There were charts to illustrate the Nazi command chains, and long lectures on the accessibility of information in a free society. Published shipping movements, loose talk among government workers, talk among the longshoremen—all this was the meat of a clever foreign agent. The Russians were particularly appalled that American defense contracts were so easily available.

Evenings he spent with Serov. There were parties and nights at the theater. The mood was always reserved. The more the general drank, the more depressed he got. It seemed to be the same with all the Russians. The singular theme was cold determination in the face of disaster. When he walked the streets, people did not look at him. Only once, in a half deserted twilight, he saw the fleeting image of a man walking behind.

Twice more that week John saw figures that seemed to be lingering after him. The pattern was always the same. When he was with Serov or another of his hosts he was safe, but when he walked the streets alone there was always someone following a block or two behind.

Put it down to Russian dramatics, John told himself. Or you

108

could play the indignant guest and complain. Except that he was never sure if these phantom-men were wholly real. He had never learned the finer points of shadow-war in the streets. It would be Allen's generation that would bring that art to America.

Then one night, quite late after dinner at the home of some ranking party member, John returned to the Savoy and found that his room had been searched. Or so it seemed, because small things looked out of place. His shirts were not quite folded right. The spine of a book had been broken.

He sat very still in the darkness. Once he even crept to the window, drew back the curtains, but there was no one in the gloom below. Finally he dropped into bed and a patchy sleep. Greyson had never said anything about this.

When the door slid back, knocking gently against the wall, Dancer woke and thought it was some maid coming to clean. But there was no light, not even enough to see the faces of soldiers who stood at the foot of his bed. Three ghouls watching, this had to be how people vanished. For an awful minute no one spoke. Then one was shaking Dancer's leg, and another dragging clothing from the closet.

No one spoke while he dressed. The soldiers only stood and glared at him. Then came the casual march out to the waiting van. The back windows were covered with wire mesh, the door was bolted from within. When he finally broke and swore, no one seemed to notice. Or to care.

The van stopped in a courtyard. All around were blank, brick walls. There were seven more soldiers waiting. He was led through a steel gate, then down a concrete passage. Still no one spoke.

The cell was clean, not really even a cell, but the door was locked. There was a cot in the corner, a tap with no basin and a table and chair. The window above had been painted over so that the only light came from a bulb in the ceiling.

They took his coat, his watch and his cigarettes. Then he was alone—and at first afraid, horribly afraid, but soon the fear gave way to some kind of shame. He desperately wanted to smoke and kept glancing at his wrist, forgetting that his watch was gone. When they come, he thought, just tell them what they want to know.

He was scrunched on the cot when the locks slid back and the officer stepped into the cell. For a moment they just faced one another. Not much was revealed. John's only thought was that he was young. He couldn't be much more than twenty.

The boy was slim and neat. His uniform was freshly pressed. He had a smooth face and the slightly wistful look of a painter John had once known.

His voice was also soft. He said his name was Diderot, and held out a pack of Turkish cigarettes. The first drag made Dancer ill, and he had to slump back down to the cot. Then his limbs were tingling, and suddenly there were no pretenses, no unspoken thoughts. There was merely this unshaven, middle-aged man, and a serious, blond boy.

"They'll miss me if I'm not back soon," Dancer said. He meant it as a fact, not a threat.

"No they won't," said the boy. "I've sent word that you have been invited to speak with Jan Brezin's chief advisor, and would be in conference for several hours. No one will question Brezin's office."

The boy was sitting very still. His hands were folded in his lap. The uniform no longer seemed to count for much.

Suddenly he said, "You have no idea why you're here, do you?"

"No, I have no idea."

"Well, possibly some betrayal has occurred. Do you think that? Or possibly you think that some mistake has been made. This is not the case at all. I merely wanted to speak to you so that no one in the world would hear us."

"I'm afraid I don't understand any of this," Dancer said coldly.

"It's my English. One rarely gets a chance to practice these days."

110

"Oh no, your English is perfect, better than anyone I've heard since I've been here."

"Better even than Josef Serov?"

"Yes, your accent is better."

The boy smiled and rocked back. "You see how funny life can be. I wanted to speak to you about something that happened a long time ago, and instead we discuss my English skills."

"A long time ago? What happened a long time ago?"

"You were here before, not Moscow, but Leningrad. You were in Leningrad twenty years ago."

"I see," Dancer sighed. "So that's it."

"Not that, only a woman you once knew. It's about a woman you once knew."

"Anna . . . ?"

"Yes, Anna Servana. You tried to find her. No one will tell you where she is, but still you want to find her. Will you tell me why?"

"I just want to see her again."

"But why?"

Suddenly Dancer jerked his head back. His eyes were shut. "Look, what's going on?"

"I have a vital interest in the matter," Diderot said softly. "Naturally I would not have taken such a risk unless I had a vital interest."

"I was very much in love with her. I don't know what else to say."

"So you were compelled to find her? Is that how one would say it? You were *compelled?*"

"Please," said Dancer. "I'd like a glass of water."

The boy nodded, looked around, but then said, "May I first know a personal fact?"

Dancer winced, waited.

"Tell me," Diderot continued. "Did you love Anna Servana the way any man loves a woman?"

111

It made John clench his teeth. "Do you mean, did I sleep with her? Yes, I slept with her."

"And before you left Russia, just before you left, did you sleep with her then?"

John could have smashed something. "Look, what do you want?"

"What do I want? Nothing really, except that you should know that Diderot is not my real name. Diderot is merely a name that I sometimes use. You might say that it is a professional name, but it is not my real name. Because my real name is my mother's name. You see I took my mother's name, because I never knew my father."

"What are you trying to tell me?" said Dancer softly.

"The truth. You see, my real name is Servana. I am Valentin Servana, and Anna Servana is my mother."

"I . . . I don't know what you're talking about."

"Yes you do. Anna Servana is my mother, and I use her name, because my father was an American who was forced to leave her before I was born."

"Me?" Dancer whispered.

Then the boy shut his eyes and nodded. "Yes, you."

And for the second time in Dancer's life it seemed as if his soul had left his body and had spread like a membrane across the ceiling. Some kind of passion rose for an instant. Then it was still again.

Outside in the courtyard the light was faintly amber. Dawn was breaking. The cobblestones were slick with drizzle. An empty truck, a discarded oil drum, even the distant city seemed suspended in time.

John and the boy had passed the sentries. Now they were treading aimlessly. The boy spoke formally, slowly, as if he had all the time in the world. He said that for years he had believed that Anna had had an affair with a man named Diderot. The man was

112

supposed to have been an adjutant to Leon Trotsky, and then a major in the civil war. The story also said that this Major Diderot had been a great hero but finally died of influenza at the base of the Ural Mountains. It was not until Valentin had turned sixteen that his mother had told him the truth, the truth about John Dancer.

As for his own life, Valentin said that he was the aide of Jan Brezin, head of the army's Fourth Department. John knew only that his group was called Razavedurpr, or the GRU, and that they handled foreign intelligence. He also had some vague notions that the GRU was at war with the State Police, but one never ever talked about that. Only later would Valentin offer details, and these would one day form the basis of Dancer's classic paper on the thirties war within the Soviet's secret world.

For close to an hour the boy spoke of himself and his mother. He said that they had lived together in a two room apartment off Serdobolskaya Street. For many years she had taught English. They made ends meet. Sometimes she had lovers, often from the Soviet Central, so at Christmas there were apples and chocolate, occasionally even nylon stockings. None of her men ever lasted very long. Life was neither good nor bad.

Primary school was a red brick hall. Valentin was one of the serious boys, the sort that instructors liked. Now and then they would have him to their offices for bread and coffee. Once Valentin was a model for a dental hygiene poster.

At sixteen he was in the army, typing orders. Then one morning Jan Brezin needed a temporary boy to run an errand, but Brezin must have taken to Valentin's open blue eyes and the way his hair fell over his forehead, not to mention the boy's flair for organization. Within the week it was permanent. Valentin was in the Fourth Department.

Brezin required discretion. One had to know when a letter was to be misplaced, an order ignored. You had to understand that power was always shifting, that friends could be enemies, and that

113

he who was first might soon be last. Sometimes the head of Razavedurpr only wanted an ear to listen. Whole nights could pass and the general and his aide did nothing more than sip neat vodka.

Through these two years Anna was not much more than a young mother. Valentin still lived with her, although for weeks he was often away. She had her pass to the officers' stores and no longer had to wait in line for food. Sometimes in the evenings, maybe kneading dough or cracking sunflower seeds by the fire, she would even talk about John. John, she would say, he could have been only yesterday. . . .

As for his own thoughts, Valentin said that he often used to lie awake at night and try to imagine what his father had been like. There was a photograph, and the stories his mother had told him, but mother only talked about the strength, never the weakness. Valentin admitted that there had been moments when he hated the man for having left him, and as he had walked down the corridor and approached the cell door, he wondered if that resentment would surface again. It did not.

There were bells sounding when Valentin had finished. He and John now sat on an iron bench in a little strip of the People's Park near the Pushkin Bronze. The day had fully dawned. It would soon grow cold.

Dancer stretched his neck. He let his head fall back, so he was really just speaking to the trees.

"I'd like to see her," he said softly. "Your mother. I'd like to see her."

All the boy said was, "Yes."

"Is it far?"

"No, not far."

John's entire life, he suddenly realized, had been syncopated by just such matter-of-fact voices. This one was, technically, his son's. Anna's son.

114

They walked through the morning crowds on Gorki Street, past opening shops and factory girls waiting for trams. Once again John's knees felt weak. He asked, "Will I recognize her?" But Valentin must not have heard. They were moving through the market street, over hacked-off vegetable stalks. A gang of boys were splattering a paling fence with discarded fruit. The sky was almost purple.

Then came a long block of oblong apartments, some had pre-Revolution fronts with grills and balconys. Others were just plain gray with rows of tiny windows and strings of wash lines. The gardens had been turned into potato patches. The stairs were concrete. The hallways were lined with green carpet, the trash neatly stacked in bins.

Now they were climbing to the second level, down another blank corridor. Flat light fell through a square of glass. Dancer was walking close behind. There were hand posters in crude block letters, something about noise. The walls were thick plaster and whitewashed. Odors of boiled meat and liquid soup came lingering by. Finally they stopped at a half-glazed door, just one in a row of several.

Valentin had the faintest smile as he slipped in the key. John felt the hand on his arm. Then he was stepping across the door-mat, reeling a little, because the climb up three flights had winded him. He was totally breathless when he finally saw her bent over a blue porcelain basin.

Once ten years ago he had stupidly, half consciously scrawled Anna's name on his steamed-up bathroom mirror. He had to rub it out quickly so that Mary would never know, but now those letters were looming at him—*Anna*—and he called her now.

"Anna?" She turned slowly. They were facing one another, and her hand went quickly to a stray lock of hair. Then he heard his own name and it nearly sent him toppling forward, splintering a tiny wooden stool. Every object seemed so fragile now. The room

115

was shrinking, and when they finally fell together a secret muscle inside his chest began to unknot.

It had been twenty years.

There were forces in that room that none of them could grapple with. When John had rocked her in his arms, he felt as if the decades would snap back and fuse them together. Their son had left on some halting excuse, but his intentions were pretty clear. So John was alone with her now, but his throat was dry and his voice strained. He kept trying to swallow the lump while he nosed about her room, eyed her old sketches.

"I remember this one," he said. "Hadn't you had this one before?" It sounded pretty artificial, stilted.

"Oh that." Her laugh wasn't much better. "That was a gift from Palo Slansky, and we all thought he was going to be a great painter, but he never came to much."

The room was full of reminders. There was the sofa and wing chair, both a little tattered. Her curio cabinet was still filled with those china figurines, although one was armless, and a crystal pane was gone. There was even that evil wall clock, the one he had disemboweled. But most of all there was Anna. She kept falling back into the corner of his eyes no matter how he tried to glance away.

"You look well," he finally told her, and it was true. Even in her flannel housecoat he could see that her body was still lithe and firm.

"You look well too, John."

"I haven't had it too bad." Although right now he could have screamed.

They were moving too close to things that mattered, to the past, to wives and husbands, so John went back to nodding at a meaningless still life of fruit on a rucked up tablecloth.

"This one never came to much, did he?"

"No, not that one either."

116

"But there's your friend Eisenstein," John suddenly remembered.

"Yes Eisenstein is a very great filmmaker, only I don't see him any more."

Now she was perched on the sofa exactly as he remembered her best, with her arms linked around her knees and that vaguely lost look in her eyes.

"I know a few poets," he said. "From the magazine I work on, I mean. There's Auden. Have you ever heard of him? And Robert Frost, I've met him too. You'd like him, I think."

But it was hopeless. He couldn't keep muttering forever. So he just sank down with her on that worn sofa. Then her head was dropping to his shoulder.

"Anna?"

She was crying, but softly. He felt the dampness through his shirt.

"Anna, I won't leave you again. It's set. I'm not going away without you."

She still smelled of lilacs, and her shoulders were still firm.

"What ever else we've ever done . . . all the useless things . . . I don't want to regret the next twenty years . . . Anna. Anna . . . ?"

They slept together that night, and the next and the next after, but she would not go away with him. She said that they had no place to go. Worse, so much worse that he actually cried because he knew that it was true, she told him that they had had their chance and missed it. So the clock kept ticking and there was no way possible to turn it back. He should have guessed that one from the start.

Still, they had two weeks together. They took long walks down Gorki Street. The days were growing shorter, the twilights lasted for hours. They strolled through the dusk, lugging straw bags filled with groceries. They did not speak much. Sometimes they were the only people on the broad streets. So John would always

117

remember walking with Anna under the street lamps in the valley of gray stone apartments.

On his final day in Russia he and Anna rose early. Valentin brought a car around, then waited in the hallway while his mother and father said good-by. For a while John just pressed her body close to his. Then they stood together with their fingers intertwined. The last of his vanity dropped away again, and he cried. He couldn't help it.

But just before hefting up his bags, it was as though she had some vision. "Listen to me, John . . . we could be fulfilled through our child. Then it will be like us living together forever."

So the seeds were sown, first with Anna, then in the barrel-vaulted station with Valentin. He and John had an hour before the train departed. They spent it sipping tea on a marble bench between the massive pylons. They felt safe among the crowds and all that dim, airy space. Outside it was raining.

Just before boarding they stood together on the steamy ramp, and the die was really cast.

"There's going to be a war," John said. "I believe that we'll be allies, but whatever happens I want you to know that you can count on me. There are people I know, things I can do. We won't even speak of it again. It will just be something between us, that's all."

And the boy said he understood.

So this was both the end and the beginning of all that would follow. Nothing of it was to remain in the records. Only that John returned to New York on a cold fall afternoon. There was wind off the bay. Allen met him at the docks. Europe was on the verge of the Second World War.

PART 2

CHAPTER FOUR

NINE DAYS had passed since Humphrey Knolls had finished his summary of the Yeats interrogation, nine vapory days of suspended drizzle. Then one evening churning thunderheads backed up in the north and more rain fell.

For Humphrey these were dreary, lingering days. He spent the afternoons just nosing around his office, poking through old files, drifting between reverie and regret. Nights he would grope about his cluttered flat or shamble downtown as if to search among the crowds for someone he once knew. He thought a lot about Yeats, and in the visionary hours before deep sleep there was also Jessie Dancer.

It was during these brooding days that Humphrey first conceived of the spinning bobbin metaphor. It was found in a scribbled memo to Lyle Severson. Also it was about this time that Knolls began his own diffident walk into the Dancer records. It was not an orderly, formal search. He just more or less felt compelled.

So Humphrey gradually slipped into a parallel world of secret signs and compressed time. The files had always had a way of pulling him under like a whirlpool. But he loved those records. He loved seeing people's lives as if through the wrong end of a telescope. Once he had envisioned charting years of events in crayon on large sheets of Plexiglas. One sheet for every story, then you would set them in rows and the whole scheme would appear as multileveled as the truth.

The night of the rainstorm was a restless night for Knolls. He had driven to the city with the thought of maybe catching a movie, or just mingling with the crowds. But everyone's face looked so strange, eyes seemed so vacant. Under a neon sign faces were slightly green and he thought: this is how it must be for Jessie. The whole world must seem ugly to him.

Around nine o'clock he left the city and drove into the suburbs. Soon the streets became blackened tunnels through overhanging leaves. The night was liquid, what with the wind pouring through the gardens. It was only a half-conscious route he was taking. He might have just been blown through the streets, but he was hardly surprised when his Rambler squealed to a stop out in front of old John Dancer's home.

How long Knolls remained in his car across the street from the Dancer home, he did not know. He had parked in the darkness under a maple tree. He sat until the radiator stopped ticking, until the miscolored moon had moved a few degrees in the sky. He sat behind the wheel and watched the lighted windows.

The house stood in mottled shadows. Branches were moving on the shingles. Twice Humphrey saw a silhouette glide across the drawn curtains. Finally he saw the valance draw aside, and the

122

outline of a tall slender man. Weeks later, as this story progressed, Humphrey would find himself dwelling upon the image of the man he had seen in the lighted window. It was his first glimpse of Allen Dancer.

Allen Dancer had flown in from Switzerland about four hours before Knolls saw him. He had flown in with his personal aide, a smooth young man named Tony Nugent. Together they came on Langley like a storm, and now everything was sealed tight.

The first thing that Allen did when he arrived was to have Yeats moved from the compound to the Neuropsychiatric Testing Center. This was a large, red brick building on the far end of the Langley square. Here Yeats would be interrogated on an intensive basis. He would be given hallucinogens, barbiturates, amphetamines, ultrasonic and electroconvulsive shock treatment. These were techniques which had been developed by Company psychiatrists over three decades, and they were said to be infallible. In fact they were not infallible. They could destroy a man's memory and his ability to think logically, but they could not always make him tell the truth. In reality the truth was closer to something Jessie had told Yeats years ago. He had said that the Langley psychiatrists were really nothing more than black magicians who had no conception of the spirit. He also said that they deserved to be hurt.

After Yeats had been transferred to the Testing Center, Allen met with the head of Langley security. They discussed the Yeats case while Tony Nugent took notes.

Nugent was a tall man with sandy hair and broad shoulders. It was said that before he came to work for Allen he had been an undercover agent for the Internal Revenue Service. The rumor further said that as an IRS agent he had killed a man out of spite. Allen had then saved him from a jail sentence and ever since Nugent had been fiercely loyal. Nugent was also efficient and tireless. He prided himself on being a completely modern young man.

123

It was three o'clock when the meeting ended. Nugent and Allen walked out into the afternoon and strolled along the paths between the vast rectangular lawns. The sun behind them was turning the leaves silver and leaving reflections everywhere. Allen said that he was tired and would return to his father's house. Nugent said that he was going to find a girl, any girl.

Allen liked to wander in his father's house. He liked to come downstairs early and see the morning break through the honeysuckle. As a boy he had had a tree house in the garden. Dad had helped nail the planks. He used to spend hours up there with a box of graham crackers and an old canteen full of lemonade. He liked to watch the people passing on the flagstones below. He liked to spy on them.

Yet there was a darker side to coming home. Allen often found that he lost his bearings in this house. Then he would have to remind himself that he was *the* Al Dancer, driving force of the Soviet Desk, instead of just a boy prowling through old dad's house.

When Allen returned home from Langley time seemed especially warped. He and John did not seem to know what to say to one another. They sat in the library and watched the garden darken. Long wads of inky clouds were passing in the sky. John said that he had had a dream about Jessie the night before. Allen grunted. His father was always having dreams and trying to pass them off as meaningful.

Later, well after John had gone to bed, Allen found that he could not sleep, so he wandered through the gloom, sniffed at the canisters of old tobacco, touched the furniture, gazed at photographs on the mantelpiece. And yes, just as dad had said, Jessie's face was somehow haunting.

It seemed to Allen that there had always been something near-spectral about Jessie. Even as a little boy he could be frightening. One never knew what he was thinking, whether he was happy or

124

sad. He often had a vaguely elfin look, as if he had been a change-ling. He hardly ever cried.

When Allen had finished reading the Yeats report, a kind of rage had risen inside him. He had even had the urge to shred the pages. He could have also wrung Jessie's neck, except that fifteen years ago he had tried to slap the boy, slap him hard across the mouth, but Jessie had caught him by the wrist and nearly broken it. It was the last time that Allen had ever tried to deal with Jessie on a physical basis.

The last time they had argued was in Saigon. Allen would never forget that yellowed plaster room where Jessie had been living. The air conditioner did not work, and it was sputtering water and filling the room with a bad odor. There was trash everywhere: cigarette butts, empty bottles, plates of congealing food. A dis-mantled automatic rifle lay on the rumpled bed. Some of the shells had rolled onto the tiles. The bayonet, however, was gleaming. Jessie wore some kind of black, native outfit, and sandals.

This was how Allen recalled his son tonight: Jessie leering at him from a half-open door against a background of suggestive violence. On that muggy Saigon evening it seemed that the boy had achieved his final stage of development: he had hit rock bottom.

Initially the boy had been polite, at least outwardly. He served green tea and almond cookies. They discussed the inconsequential aspects of the war. Allen asked if Jessie had made any friends. Jessie said that he had, although this was a lie. Jessie rarely·spoke to anyone. Finally the conversation turned political, and Jessie launched into a long, garbled tirade against the American foreign policy, Richard Nixon and a host of other government institu-tions. He skipped from one subject to another. Allen had the impression that if Jessie had suddenly died his jaws would have kept on working for another hour.

Allen came away from the Saigon encounter with the feeling that he never wanted to see his son again. He believed that they

125

had nothing in common and that they would only move further and further apart. Now, however, he realized that he had been wrong. They would not continue to move further apart. They were like two points traveling in opposite directions on a circular track. Eventually they would meet head-on.

This realization came to Allen shortly after midnight. He had wandered to the window, pulled the drapes aside and seen the waving branches of trees that he used to climb as a boy. On the landing behind him the moonlight was shifting over the sandal-wood. In this house where it all began, Allen too finally came to understand that the story was a vast circle.

Years ago this house had a different feel. Mother used to tie back the window sashes to let the nickle-colored light flood in. Allen always used to think of this house as his mother's house. Dad was never around much. Except in the evenings they would occasionally play a game of chess. Once Allen dreamed that the chessmen came to life and he had to play to the death.

Allen had always been closer to his mother than to his father. They had all sorts of secret, unspoken rituals. When he was very young she used to let him wind the clocks. Then they would seem to tick religiously all through the cool, timbered house. She also used to let him sleep in her bed when dad was away. Then one day she caught him kissing the bathroom mirror, just to try it out. After that he was too old to sleep in his mother's bed.

Even later dad was never a figure of great importance in Allen's life. Dad was too mysterious. He was a reader, and often used to bury himself in books for hours, rocking in his bentwood chair by the fireplace. Sometimes he even used to trace the printed lines with his finger. He always wore an old, green smoking jacket, and his thoughts seemed screwed up tighter than a jar.

John had also never counted for very much around the school yard. He did not hunt, he did not even own a gun, and even though he had been in the Great War he never talked about it. Finally Allen had to make up stories about his father. The best one had

126

dad blowing up Huns in France, but nobody believed it.

One day when dad had gone away for a few weeks mother told Allen something that he would never forget. They were in the kitchen. Allen was perched on the draining board, knocking his sneakers against the cupboard. Mother was making a cake. Her wedding band lay on the counter.

"So if he's not going away for the magazine," Allen said, "then what's he going away for?"

Mother wiped her brow with the back of her wrist. "Your father has another job," she replied.

"What sort of job?"

"Well, it's a secret job."

Allen had been twelve when he understood that his father had a place within the secret world, although for many years his conception of that world was foggy. He imagined dark figures lurking in the alleys of distant cities: Bagdad, Budapest, Macao. He envisioned complex codes on the backs of postage stamps. He supposed that poisoning people was common practice.

Later he came to understand that the title was not "spy" but "intelligence operative," and one did not sneak about in alleys. One read papers and chatted with people. The whole game was learning how to cultivate the right people, and to this end Allen began to court Greyson Dow.

Allen knew that Dow was John's most substantial link to the secret world. He could tell because whenever they were together they would talk behind closed doors. Also Allen had heard snatches of their conversations, and there were always words like "military capability" being exchanged. So Allen made a special effort to impress Greyson Dow. He would always shake the man's hand firmly, and gaze directly into his eyes. Eventually Allen's efforts paid off. Greyson sent him candied fruit on Christmas, and sometimes they would linger together in the hall before John came downstairs. If they only exchanged polite conversation, Allen was still certain that some deeper understanding passed between them.

He came to believe that Dow was only waiting until the right time.

Gradually as the years passed Allen came to perceive his intended path. He learned to speak in euphemisms. He learned that history often repeated itself, and that politicians were usually only puppets of hidden forces. He would later tell his friends that he had learned things early in life that his father had learned late.

By the time Allen was eighteen he knew Greyson Dow very well. They would often lunch together during the spring and winter holidays. They had a special table in Greyson's club. It was mutually understood that Allen would eventually join the ranks of America's intelligence community.

Allen's actual entrance in the secret world came two years earlier than he had originally planned. It was then 1937, and civil war was raging in Spain. To some, the war was seen as a struggle between fascism and democracy, while others believed that it was really a struggle between communism and fascism. Generals Franco, Mola and Sanjurjo together with the Spanish power base of monarchists and the Fascist Falange clearly meant to overthrow the freely elected Republican government. In response to the fascist threat the Republicans organized the militia, and volunteers who were out to stop the march of fascism had come to Spain from all over the world.

In cafes, among schoolmates, along the shady walks of Harvard Yard, it seemed to Allen that the war in Spain had become a symbol for his generation. They said that Spain would test the mettle of the idealists. They said that freedom was at stake. Allen, however, tended to view the war as a showcase of modern weaponry. He was particularly interested in watching the performance of the German air force.

It was January when Allen and Greyson met formally to discuss the possibility of Allen going to Spain. Snow was falling. A log was burning in Greyson's fireplace. Through the window lay a somber view of the Potomac River and the skyline in twilight. Allen was

128

a leggy boy who had grown up too fast, although he had learned to slouch like a man three times his age.

"You came to me a year ago about Spain," Greyson began. "Do you remember?"

"Of course I remember. You told me that I was too young."

"Did I really? You must have resented that terribly."

"I was devastated, I ran home and tried to grow a mustache."

Then they were both laughing, and staring at the glowing ends of their cigars.

"Well, the fact is you honestly may have been too young then. But you're not now. So I pose the question: would you still like to go to Spain?"

"Are you serious?"

"Never been more."

"In what capacity? Or shouldn't I ask yet?"

"Oh, let's just say that there are some people I know who would very much like to have a special correspondent there."

"When would I leave?"

"As soon as possible. We wouldn't want the war to end before you saw it, would we?"

"Ah, so you're one of the nonbelievers."

"I'm a realist, Allen, and as a realist I simply can't imagine a few thousand artist types and peasants withstanding the bulk of the German Condor Legion much longer."

"And I take it that it's the Germans that these friends of yours are interested in having me report on?"

"Yes, you could say that."

Allen had a sudden vision—a wedge of German bombers flying in the sun. He had seen them on a newsreel, hundreds of them, and one, even if grudgingly, had to admire their strength.

"Well, I'll do the best I can," Allen said suddenly.

"Oh I'm sure you'll do fine," Greyson smiled. "But there is one thing. I'd like it cleared with your dad first. Don't want to be

129

accused of breaking the family apart, do I?"

"Oh, you don't have to worry about dad. He knows I'm all grown up now."

They laughed again. But as Allen was leaving, the door half-opened and the snow falling softly behind him, Greyson started to talk about John once more. "Your father has a fine mind, Allen. One of the finest I've ever known. He senses things most of us are never aware of. However, much as I love him, I have to admit that he never was a striver. Do you know what I mean by that, Allen?"

"Yes, sir, I think I do."

"I'm sure you do, because you are definitely a striver, Allen. There's no doubt about that."

Years later, after all the agents had been sold down the river, after friends had been betrayed and promises broken, they would still call Allen Dancer a striver.

The night that Allen told his parents that he was leaving for Spain the house filled up with stoney silence. First, mother wept. Then she flung a book and it caromed off the wall. When she had stormed off with her nightgown trailing behind, there was still dad.

"Did Greyson Dow put you up to this?"

Allen shook his head. "It was my idea."

They were both looking at the disjointed skirting board where mother's book had cracked the plaster. The book itself looked dead. The spine was broken, and a page had torn off. The lamplight was sallow.

Dad shut his eyes and sighed. "I hope you're not doing this to please me, Allen. I'd hate to think that I was your inspiration to go down this path."

That was pretty presumptuous, Allen thought.

"I only hope you know what you're getting into," John added suddenly.

It was starting to get maudlin, so Allen snapped back, "Did you know what you were getting into when *you* went?"

130

"No, I suppose I didn't."

"And if you had known would it have made any difference?"

Then came a typical John Dancer confession: "I spent twenty years regretting something that happened in Russia," he said. "I'd hate for the same thing to happen to you."

"It won't," Allen said. He could have carved it out with a knife. He was that sure of himself. . . .

Allen spent six days training in a house that was not unlike that house in Oxford where his father had trained two decades before. There was also a rambling wooded garden in the back. It was filled with larkspur and ragwood, and the trees were white or the color of skin. Urns stood on the porch, and inside there were imposing rooms cluttered with dark furniture.

Instruction was informal. Mostly Greyson and Allen spent the hours chatting. There was a trick to getting information, Greyson said. The trick was ingratiating yourself with the enemy. The best spies were always glad to be of use. Sometimes you even played the slightly stupid fool. You did whatever it took to get what you wanted. Allen, as things turned out, was a natural.

Only on the last day were the actual objectives of Allen's mission discussed. The discussion was held in the garden where the moss on the stone path was so thick they might have been walking on flesh.

"What we want," Greyson said, "is a reliable assessment of German military capability. Naturally we don't expect miracles, but we think that if you keep your eyes open you should be able to help us."

The garden was darkening. They were treading over rotting custard apples. One or two squelched under their feet. "I've fixed it with your uncle," Dow continued. "You'll be going in as a correspondent from his magazine. Same as your father did."

"Yes, same as my father." It rang with a heavy irony.

"The important thing to remember is to make as many close contacts as you can. I have a feeling about the Germans. I have

131

a feeling that before too long we will need to know a great deal about them."

"Yes, I've had the same feeling," Allen said softly.

"It will really be a question of circulating on a social basis. I expect you'll be attending cocktail parties, and if you're lucky they'll ask you to breakfast the next morning."

If I'm lucky, Allen thought, they'll ask me to bed.

They came to the darkest end of the garden. Here the ferns were massive, strung with dew and spiderwebs. "There's one more thing," Greyson was saying. "I tell this to all the boys. Don't get caught. It wouldn't do for the Germans to suspect that we're probing them. It wouldn't do at all. So whatever happens, don't get caught."

"Oh I won't." Allen grinned, because in these early days he had still believed that he could outsmart the whole world. In the archives there remains something of a carefree, jaunty tone to these early days of Allen Dancer. There were wonderful vignettes of a sly, clever Allen bluffing his way across the Spanish plains. One story had him spiking drinks with sleeping pills. Another had him forging love letters. The truth was somewhat less than all this.

Allen sailed for Spain in the winter of 1937. He landed in Le Havre, then rode east along the Rhône until he reached the border. Snow fell the night he crossed the Pyrenees. He heard it hissing through the pines. It was deep and powdery, not bound to the earth at all.

Two days were wasted in Figueras waiting for the bus. He found lodging in the fortress above the town. The walls of his cell were seven feet thick, and the stone was very cold. All through the streets walked young men who had come to fight the Fascists. He bought them drinks, cigarettes.

From Figueras he rode into the western provinces. He was heading for the fascist citadel of Salamanca, but once he reached the Jarama hills he lost all control. Two nights into the countryside the bus was flagged down by Republican soldiers. Allen had

been dozing, and he woke to see the swinging lanterns and blackened figures through the dirty rear window.

The soldiers were ragged boys from the International Brigade.
There were Finns, Cubans and a few Americans. One boy was
badly wounded in the groin. He kept screaming, "Who's there?
Who's there?" The rest were silent, clutching their Remingtons
and Austrian Steyrs, but their helmets were French. Allen also
kept his mouth shut. He did not have anything to say.

It was dark when they reached the camp, and a warped, red
moon hung low above the plain. The dawn brought no warmth.
There was only an hour when the white mist rose off the frozen
ground, the tents and huts looking ghostly, the men with their
glowing cigarettes like phantoms.

Allen spent the morning in a sheepcote of thatch and fieldstone.
There was coffee, oranges and dry bread. He shared this hovel
with a lanky boy from California who he thought might have been
suffering from shell shock. He just sat there on his bunk, jabbing
a knife into the dirt.

"Been here long?" Allen asked.

The boy shrugged. "Long enough." He resumed stabbing his
knife in the clay.

"I only pulled in last night. I was on that bus that they commandeered to bring in more troops. Fellows must have been tired of
walking so I ended up taking a detour. But I guess that's war, isn't
it?"

"Yeah, that's war."

Between the stone doorposts lay a desolate view of sagging tents
and mudspattered trucks. Now and then the muffled thump of
rebel mortars came rolling in. Allen saw lines of limping soldiers
in long overcoats. He watched them tramp along the pitted road
and dip behind the ridge. Finally he said, "Can you tell me who's
in charge here?"

The boy did not respond for a long time. When he looked up,
his eyes were badly bloodshot. "What did you say?"

133

"I asked who's in charge here?"

"Kline."

"Kline?"

"Yeah, Robert Kline."

"What is he, the captain or something?"

"Yeah, he's the captain."

"Well, do you know where I might find this captain?"

The boy's eyelids fell. "Listen, will you please stop talking to me? I don't want to talk to you anymore."

Allen spent an hour slinking between rows of jerry-rigged tents before he found the captain's command post. It was a crude, planked shack with a scrap metal roof. An oil lamp hung from the rafters. The desk was a slab of wood nailed to an ammunition crate.

He leaned into the door and grinned. Inside were two men. One was squatting in the corner. The other was bent over the crate. "Captain Kline?" Allen asked, and grinned even wider.

"I'm Kline," said the man from behind the crate. He was thin and very young. He had wavy, reddish hair and large eyes.

Allen stepped forward with his hand extended. "Hi. I'm Al Dancer. I came in with that bus you people commandeered last night."

"We're sorry for the inconvenience," said Kline, although it was clear that he did not care.

"No inconvenience." Allen smiled. "What's a few hours anyway? This is war, right? Just so long as you can get me on my way."

"I'm sorry."

"Does that mean you won't let me leave, captain?"

"You can leave, but you'll probably be shot when you hit the rebel lines."

"I see. Well, I guess that pretty well cuts it, doesn't it? Any objection if I hang around here. I'm a correspondent, and I—"

134

"You can stay as long as you like, Mr. Dancer."

"Al. Call me Al. And thank you, captain. I'll try to stay out of the way."

Allen spent the afternoon nosing around the camp, not that there was much to see. Here in the wasted hills of the winter front Spain was merely a road with muddy tire tracks, ripped canvas and sullen men. At night the sky turned cobalt and was filled with too many stars to seem real. Dancer wandered out along the rutted path when the stench got too bad in his hut.

He saw Kline when he reached the ridge. The man was outlined against the black humps of the distant hills. He was cloaked in a woolen greatcoat, smoking a crooked cigar.

"Hi. Remember me?" Allen grinned.

They were standing side by side, facing the mountains. There was no sound at all.

"You're Dancer," Kline said.

"Yeah, I'm Al Dancer, the one who's here by accident."

"Yeah. There's been an accident."

"Or maybe it's not an accident." Allen laughed. "You know? Maybe it's fate." He had no idea why he said that.

"Could be," Kline said. "There's lots of things I'll never understand."

"Is that why you're here? To learn something? I know that's why I came. I came here to find something out."

"What?"

"Well, I don't know yet. But when I find it, I'll know." He was still grinning.

"How old are you, Dancer?"

"Me? I'm eighteen."

"How old do you think I am?"

"I don't know. You don't look too old."

"I'm twenty. I'm twenty, and that's all the difference there is between you and me, just two years. I've been here seven months, but the only real difference between you and me is just two years.

135

So stop trying to impress me. Stop trying to kiss my ass. I don't know any more than you do."

Later that night the boy from California screamed in his sleep and it shook Allen badly. He lay with his eyes open waiting for another scream. Finally he got up the courage to ask if the boy was all right.

"Fuck off," the boy told him.

"Look, I'm only trying to help—"

"Fuck *off.*"

Then the rain came crashing down, sending rivers of mud sliding into the camp. When the skies cleared German bombers came out of the sun. In the first strike Allen saw the boy from California take a piece of shrapnel in the stomach; it looked like red wine thrown from a bucket. Afterward everyone was walking around as if they were still in shock.

The rest of the journey was no less unreal. Allen rode with an ambulance crew through miles of blackened olive trees. All along the pocked trail were the rotting carcasses of horses. Entire divisions seemed to be functioning in a bad dream state. Ugly clouds kept boiling on the horizon.

He spent the last night before Salamanca in a white village, high on the plain. The town was half-deserted although faces kept leering at him from the doorways of sandstone hovels. In the late afternoon he walked into the central square. The light was so fierce that he had to squint, and clouds of dust were blowing through the streets. He was a solitary figure looking for someone to speak to in the empty square. His trousers were flapping in the wind.

Still, all that remained of these lost days in the Jarama Hills was the wry sketch that Allen later wrote himself, transcriptions that eventually found their way into the archives so that even the historians believed that Al Dancer spent two memorable nights with the flower of his generation, drinking local wine, toasting freedom and the future. Ernest Hemingway was there, and a morose Jew named Robert Kline . . .

136

Salamanca was arid. In the afternoons long shadows fell across the open land. Allen lived in a pink stucco hotel with black iron grills on the windows. Mornings he would coil his arms through the iron lace and watch the lizards on the blue tiles. The distant hills were tawny, although at times they looked red. Allen usually rose late in the mornings and spent an hour sipping coffee on the balcony under the flat, white sky. At eleven he went to the airy first floor gallery of the university for a press briefing. These briefings were usually conducted by Pablo Merry del Val, who loved to charm the foreign press but never told the truth.

Some journalists resented the lies, but Allen did not care. He filed what they gave him, and so his stories were filled with images of young generals on chestnut horses and banners in the wind. Still, a letter later written to Greyson Dow described the execution of nine Republican loyalist collaborators. The prisoners were taken to the backroads of town and then drowned in a tub of water. Allen indicated he had been upset, for a while.

Every day Allen spent several hours drinking and chatting with other journalists. When there was rain or cold winds from the north he would meet his friends in bars. In warm weather there were the open cafes that ringed the plaza. The city turned silvery in the early evenings. There were moments of happiness, but never well-being.

In time Allen began to circulate. He ate very good dinners at the Grand Hotel; roast suckling pig and sun-cured ham. It was also during these first days, Allen claimed, that he met Kim Philby, who eventually rose to the top of the British Secret Intelligence Service but all along had been a Soviet spy. Stories varied as to how close Dancer and Philby became. Certainly they lunched together, often in the company of Philby's mistress, Bunny Doble. Some forty years later when Philby was finally exposed as a traitor, Allen would hint that he had never been fooled. This was not true.

Allen's first score with the Germans was a young officer named

Kurt Lehr. They met one evening at the Grand Hotel and then went strolling out into the streets. Lehr was an elegant, fair-haired boy who had been a Hitler Youth and was now attached to the local intelligence unit. He did not smoke and drank nothing stronger than beer. He had perfect teeth.

The night Lehr and Dancer went for their walk, warm winds were blowing in from the surrounding hills. The moon, full and the color of red earth, cast blue shadows on the bricks and made the rose sandstone look unnatural.

At first they discussed only simple things. Allen said that the squid in Barcelona was very good, Lehr preferred cuttlefish. Next they talked of Germany. Lehr had been born in Schmelz on the banks of the old timber harbor. His father had owned a lumber mill, and they had lived in a breezy house with polished floors, gabled windows and a black slate roof. Matted reeds grew along the riverbank, and as a boy Lehr used to sail toy boats with long bamboo poles to guide them. Finally, after struggling through the Depression, Kurt's father had a stroke and his mother had to sell their house to a merchant from Hamburg. A Jew.

"It was always the Jews," Lehr said. "My father fought as hard as he could, but in the end there were just too many of them."

"Oh, come on now, Kurt, you don't really believe all that, do you?"

Allen was using his most reasonable tone.

"Perhaps I exaggerate somewhat. Still, there is a good deal of truth to this Jewish business. Look at the middlemen. Most of them are Jews, raising prices to suit themselves without any regard for the average fellow."

"Well, that may be, but it seems to me that you people are using the Jews as a scapegoat for complex problems." Allen smiled.

"Yes, perhaps this is true. Many of the more simple-minded laborers do need simple solutions to their problems. But also there is much truth in this Jewish business. I think they have done much

138

damage to German . . . uh, culture. Yes they have done much damage to German culture."

"Oh, Kurt. You Germans and your Jewish mania. You're like children afraid of the dark."

"Oh, no, it's you Americans who are the children. You don't recognize the danger when you see it. You don't want to believe how bad these Jews can be." His mackerel eyes were wide and sincere.

Finally they were like two gangling schoolboys, walking arm in arm, and when they finally sank to the curb the moon was throbbing at them, having now turned to bright ochre.

"Listen to me," Lehr said, "you really must come back to Berlin with me. We Germans are building a great new civilization and I wish you to see it." . . .

Over the years historians have returned to the archives again and again in an attempt to fathom the real depth of the Dancer relationship with the Nazis. There were those who believed that Allen went overboard in cultivating friendships with men like Kurt Lehr, those who could not accept that he was playing the role and nothing more. They proposed that as a young man he had genuinely flirted with fascism. Allen's defenders pointed out that regardless of his personal feelings he got the job done. This would always be Allen Dancer's defense . . .

Allen saw Kurt Lehr all through that dry summer of 1937. They often shared pitchers of beer in the early evening, and once they even shared a girl, one of the local whores, a washed-out child with smallpox cracks in her face. She took them to a squalid room above a bar and let them press her head between their legs. Allen stayed drunk through the entire unpleasant hour.

On more refined nights there were dinner parties at the German mission. Allen nodded and smiled while older men lectured him on the role of the German in the world as they knew it. There were

139

even Wagner nights in the plaza when all rose to sing the *Horst Wessel Song;* Allen loved those visions of the swaying women in tallow candlelight.

After Kurt Lehr had fixed it with the press officers, Allen was allowed to make weekly excursions to the front. Mostly he saw only long views of bursting shells as the German Heinkels, supporting the rebel Franco forces, bombed the barren hillsides. But then came the autumn, bad weather and three grim days at Teruel when Allen lay seven hours in the trenches below the burnt-out city. All around were the churned hills and wounded. Sunlight sparkled on the snow. Then the Heinkels came and the Russian quarter-to-one guns opened fire. Allen clenched his teeth so hard his jaws ached. Later he discovered that he had bitten through his helmet strap.

Kim Philby was nearly killed that day, and Allen saw waves of infantry cut down by machine gun fire. Afterward he walked in the violet light among the blank faces. A hush had fallen over the wasteland.

Allen left Spain not long after the battle of Teruel. He left as he had come, back across the plains and over the Pyrenees. Much of the way he shared a train compartment with a young nun who had stepped on a mine in Guadalajara. The explosion had torn off her left foot and her lower lip. It was terrible to watch her eat. She also kept talking about the Pentecost, and said that neither courage nor fear would save them. In her case, of course, she was right.

All through the landscape of flat salt marsh and open plain Allen wrote postcards and jotted down notes that years later would be collected in the archives and whose edge of sardonic humor would help shape the Al Dancer legend—it was eventually said that after he had charmed fascist Spain to her knees he set out for Berlin with hardly more than his wit, his trunk full of Brooks Brothers suits, and a letter of recommendation from a Nazi named Kurt Lehr.

140

Berlin was cold, and you felt it in your bones. On his first night in the city Allen saw frost in the girders of railroad bridges, in the iron balconies, in the grills and tramlines. In a garden below his hotel window the branches were black and frozen, and where the streets ended lay fields of snow and ice. (Allen would return to Berlin many times as the years went by. Something drew him back, and he would always recall this city as he saw it now: like a steel etching, a little smudged from an unsteady press. A city divided between austerity and perversion.)

The Lehr introduction eventually took him into the highest ranks of society. He even attended a luncheon in honor of Josef Goebbels. It was held in a rounded dining-room with a great vaulted ceiling. Beyond the enormous windows lay a long view of the boulevard. It was a bluish afternoon. Goebbels gave a speech and talked about his childhood. He made some joke about how his mother had wanted him to become a priest. Everyone, of course, laughed.

During the last week of Allen's stay in Berlin Kurt Lehr returned from Spain. He wired from a border village, and Allen met him at the station. He was standing in a crowd behind the turnstile when Lehr stepped onto the platform. The boy was deeply tanned and his cap was rakishly down over one eye. When they saw each other Lehr grinned and shouted, "Jew lover!" They embraced in the curling steam, but it was a man's embrace . . . they sort of clapped each other on the back. (*I moved from deception to deeper deception,* Allen later wrote. He did not define his terms.)

That night Allen followed Lehr up a flight of concrete steps into a modern flat of new apartment blocks. Each room was a cube with tiny squares of glass for windows and a cramped view of more concrete slabs; there was a portrait of Adolf Hitler and a crucifix above the door. The furniture was clean and tubular; the room had a naked, antiseptic look.

Lehr took a bottle of vodka and two glasses from a steel cupboard, laid them on the table and the men sat across from one another. Allen was gazing out the window to the flat-gray court and the parallel telephone wires that seemed to bend together in the distance.

"You see what a treaty can bring," Lehr said, and tapped his glass referring, of course, to the Hitler-Stalin non-aggression pact that would buy Hitler the time he needed to divert his war machine elsewhere.

"I thought you never touched the hard stuff."

Lehr shrugged. "Yesterday I heard that they pulled another body out of the Landwehr canal. It was the body of a fellow I once knew. A schoolmate. It was the Jews that killed him. These days it's not so bad, but there are still a few Jew knife killers left in the city. They live in old factories and come out at night to kill randomly. Once they caught one and when they asked him why he did it he told them that he couldn't control himself. Well, tonight I can't control myself either," and he tapped the bottle of vodka.

"You seem depressed,"

"*Ach,* I'm just tired. Long train rides make me tired."

"Yes, you look tired, Kurt."

"And maybe my nerves are bad too."

Lehr began to undo the top buttons of his tunic. Outside the wind was humming through the telephone wires. Shadows and stillness were adding up to some vague misery.

Suddenly Lehr ran his hands over his eyes. "I don't quite feel myself tonight."

"Are you sick?"

"No, but I feel strange. Yes, strange."

"Would you like me to leave?"

"No, stay with me. There's something I want to tell you, Allen. Something about the way I feel tonight. About feeling strange."

"What is it?"

Lehr's eyes were especially glassy.

142

"It's this . . . just this." Lehr's hand was like a crab, edging across the table.

Allen had to clench his teeth to keep from shivering the instant that their fingers slid together.

"It can't be bad," Lehr blurted out. "It *can't* . . ."

Their crab hands were coupling together. Allen's spine felt like a steel bar. His joints had locked. He could not move.

And then Lehr's entire body was like a crab. His pincer arms had locked around Allen's waist. Allen was like the fish. Allen could only think of how years before an old crab in a mossy pond had gripped the end of a stick he had held.

After it was done—yes, as they said, Al Dancer got the job done —the two of them wandered down the Steinplatz. The chestnut trees along the canal were bare. Reflections of their branches were wavering in the water. The two boys slumped down on the library steps. It was a relief to touch cold granite.

Lehr sighed, "I don't know what to say, Allen. How to explain. . . ."

"Don't talk about it," Allen told him sharply.

"But I couldn't control myself, didn't I try to tell you that?"

"Don't *talk* about it."

The city looked abandoned. There was a vision of the chilled, empty boulevard. Rows of streetlamps, doric columns and the Romanesque facades looked crystal clear.

Suddenly Lehr said, "There's going to be a war. I'm sure of it."

"I already know that."

"But we could be enemies."

"So what?"

"Well, perhaps we should—?"

"We should what?"

"Well, talk about it."

"What for?"

"Well, we could help one another?"

"If there's a war, Kurt, you can be sure I'll look you up."

143

In Allen's last impression of Berlin he was running in the deserted streets while Lehr was calling after him. Lehr was framed against the massive, stone columns, his legs apart, the rising sun behind him forming a halo around his body. He looked like the figure on a Nazi propaganda poster—prettified, unreal, terrifying. . . .

Two days later Allen sailed for America. He had difficulty sleeping so he often walked the decks at night. The North Atlantic passed in shades of blue and gray. Sometimes he heard seabirds mewing in the stillness of swells. There were many bad moments when he heard Kurt Lehr's voice inside his head. He often thought that he should have killed him.

Three months after Allen returned, his father also sailed in from abroad—from Russia it seemed. Allen was among the waiting crowds at the dock. Later they had a drink in a sawdust bar that overlooked New York harbor. Neither felt comfortable. Allen just kept staring down at the slow drifting barges.

Yet before an hour had passed he came to sense that something important had also happened to his father. Whether it was a good experience or a bad one, Allen could not tell. He had never been able to understand Dad.

Historians have always had difficulty sorting out the year and seven-odd months that followed Allen's return from Berlin. Some have been content to say that the boy merely finished his education and left it at that. Others, however, believed that Allen never really disengaged himself from the secret world, and even during these last college days he was still jockeying for position.

Although Allen continued to spend holidays at home, home was not the same. Small things had changed. Mother had developed a wasting cough. Allen heard her wheezing in the night. In certain rooms the wainscot was pulling away from the plaster. A windowpane in the scullery had been cracked and never replaced. A hinge on the kitchen door was loose. Whenever it swung open

144

or closed it sounded like a human being sighing.

Often Allen and his father took long walks together. They liked to trudge past the old church and out into the grassy fields. It was now 1939, and Hitler had entered Prague. John believed that England would be at war within the year. Allen agreed with him. He said it would probably come in the fall. Otherwise they never talked about anything consequential.

Next came Easter, and Allen met with Greyson Dow in Washington. They lunched at the Swann Club on a morning after a night of killing frost. Petals withered and broke off at the touch. All the ponds were frozen over. It was late afternoon, and the dining room was deserted. Through the large bay windows lay a garden filled with frozen puddles. (Greyson's diary contained only the most cryptic notes of his conversation with Allen, and so historians have never really known how close Allen had been to throwing in his lot with the Germans, not so much because he believed in them, but because he wanted to be on the winning side.)

He told Dow, "Do you know that Hitler has already decided how many pounds are going to equal a deutschmark? He's also got a man all picked out to be the English *Gauleiter*. They say he can take London in forty days, and I tend to believe it."

"Sounds like you've been listening to Joe Kennedy."

"Well, what's wrong with Joe?"

"He's an ass, stay away from him."

"But why?"

"Because he's going to be out on his ear. I hear he told the Germans they should change their line on the Jews, not stop the persecution mind you, just tone it down for a little while. Bad public relations, he said. Told them that public relations were very important. Roosevelt is just giving him enough rope to hang himself. So stay away from Joe Kennedy."

"Okay, but if Kennedy's out, then who's in? I mean, who's in that I should speak to?"

145

"This isn't a popularity contest, Allen. You're going to have to make a firm commitment."

"Yes, sir. I realize that."

"So I don't want to hear any more talk about German military strength. Those bastards are going to lose this war. I don't know how, but they're going to lose it."

"Yes, sir."

"And if you want to get anywhere in life you'd better start believing that."

"Yes, sir, but whom do I speak to?"

Then Dow lowered his voice, and took a deep breath. "Do you know who William Donovan is?"

"Donovan? The war hero?"

"Yes."

"Well, I've heard of him, but I don't really—"

"Find out about him. If you're any good at all you may end up working for him."

"Working for Donovan?"

"That's right. Bill will be heading Roosevelt's team."

"Team? What team?"

"You'll see. And while you're looking up Donovan, you might also ask about a man named William Stephenson. He's Canadian, but has been living in London for the past few years. He's something of an expert on radio links. The underground variety."

"And he's working for Roosevelt too?"

"No. He works for Churchill."

"Churchill? My God! You're not saying that there's going to be an alliance between Downing Street and the White House?"

"There already is, Allen. There already is."

"But how? What's the form of it?"

"Loose at the moment, but it should get stronger as time goes on. Stephenson will probably open an office in New York. There will be a coordinated exchange of information."

146

"I feel like a fool," Allen said. "How could I have missed the signs like that?"

Greyson answered Allen's question in the garden. They stood on the packed snow among the skeletal rose bushes. The sun was flaring on the ice and the lane filled with shadows. "I like you, Allen. I always have, but I'm beginning to see that you're something of an opportunist—no, don't interrupt me. This coming war will be terrible beyond belief. It will be fought to the last full measure, and no one is going to put up with your flippancy. So either you throw yourself into it wholeheartedly or get out of the way. This is no place for flimflam men."

(Years later, however, after Allen had surpassed them all it would appear that Greyson had been wrong. It would appear that the secret world was exactly the place for flimflam men like Allen Dancer.)

On the evening that the war began Allen walked the college grounds under cloudy skies. The night air was muggy, filled with moths. Later he would write that he had had a vision among the shadowy elms, that he had seen his entire destiny laid out before him. Actually he saw nothing that night, and his destiny was what he could get. Hindsight tended to seduce him—as it had so many others—into illusions of predestined significance. Still, by 1940 he had done very well for himself. He had reached the edge of Bill Donovan's fledgling intelligence organization, and the doors were open to him. The group still had no name, nor any formal jurisdiction, but at least the course was set, and Allen was lunching with all the right people. Denmark fell in April, then Norway. In May the Germans took Belgium, Holland and Luxemburg. (Allen got very drunk the night that Paris fell.)

For the first weeks of the war Allen lived in a kind of limbo. He had returned to his father's house, and every morning they took coffee on the terrace. The newspapers were full of war. There

147

were photographs of the German Panzer columns against cratered landscapes. Allen would read the articles aloud while his father nodded into space. It was late spring. On the day they began to bomb London, John did not come down to breakfast. Allen later found him knee-deep in the grass behind their house. He was just standing there with his hands hanging down. He said that they were living in an age which was moving progressively backward. It might have been considered a neat turn of phrase, but John Dancer was deadly serious. Allen made no comment.

By the closing months of 1940 Allen's story once again became lost within the greater drama. Here and there were references to young Dancer, but his role was largely overshadowed in the records by such figures as Stephenson, Donovan, Lyle Severson and the others of the old guard. It was during this summer that the British Security Coordination Offices were established in Rockefeller Plaza, and Stephenson began to work closely with American intelligence offices and press for American material aid.

By autumn it was a paper war for Allen. He had a tiny office in Rockefeller Plaza, and he spent his days sorting radio intercepts from the Caribbean sphere. It was boring work, but at least he was in the heart of a genuine intelligence effort, and now and then he saw important figures—Stephenson was there, so was Bill Donovan, and it was about this time that he met Lyle Severson.

In the evenings Allen sometimes had a drink with Lyle. They usually talked about John, who was also involved in the game, but no one quite knew how. It was said that he had something going with the Russians, not that Allen especially cared. It would be a long time before he crossed his father's path again.

And so the days truly just crept by. Allen had a recurring dream about a network of pneumatic tubes which fired bits of paper throughout the Plaza. He kept seeing himself speeding through the intestinal maze of pipes. His favorite bar was a place on Fifty-second Street, whose perpetual gloom and empty tables appealed to him. A sign on the wall read: *Those to whom evil is done, do evil in return.*

Allen was in Bermuda the day they bombed Pearl Harbor. He was there to help coordinate the interception of postal and telegraph traffic between Europe and the Western hemisphere. He arrived on a Thursday and spent two long days working with radio operators in the basement of the Princess Hotel. Saturday night all got drunk in the Gazebo Bar, and in the morning Allen wandered out to the beach.

He was a little shattered from too much rum. His gums ached. He could not quite focus his eyes. The eastern sky was pink. A line of sawtooth palms was set against the sky. When they told Allen that the Japanese had attacked he was conscious of *how* he was supposed to respond. It was important how one responded. People always remembered how you acted in a crisis, and they judged you accordingly.

Two weeks after Pearl Harbor, Allen petitioned for an English posting. England was the place to be, he had been told. England was where one could make a name. The petition ran four neatly typed pages. It was filled with words like duty and responsibility. In the end it was approved, but someone, probably a junior placement officer, scrawled this gibe at the bottom of the last page: *Who's this guy trying to kid?*

Allen left for England in the spring. The night he landed London was bombed. Up top against the sky figures in slickers spayed water into the fire until the canvas hoses ran flat. Afterward only the flare lamps illuminated the charred, wet wreckage. Allen lived through the raid in a sooty brick basement. He passed out Lucky Strikes until the pack was empty. "More where these came from." He kept laughing, but he was scared to death.

He left London the following morning and rode north through

green rolling hills past half-timbered cottages and grazing sheep. Training and operational facilities were in a grimy brick sprawl of a house which lay far into the Midlands. They called it the Flemming Estate, and it lay in a dingle surrounded by trees and open meadows.

Head of the Flemming unit was a walrus-faced Scot named Captain Jack Hawkins. Allen had tea with him on the first afternoon, and then they strolled around the grounds. Within the estate lay wobbly divans, dirty rugs, a minstral gallery, and mullioned windows. There were also many women.

Allen's office lay down one of the windowless warrens. Thumbtacks were in short supply so he had to paste up maps with chewing gum. He shared a servant's cottage with a boy from Manchester named Donnelly, but Donnelly had a girl and was rarely there so in the mornings Allen drank his tea alone, and wished he had real coffee. The kitchen table was fake Queen Anne with a weak leg. You had to keep kicking it into place. But Allen loved to watch the day break over the hills. London was forty miles away, and stray bombs rattled the walls a little. One night the plaster fell, and the gas jets flared to blue-green.

Flemming was filled with half-mad youth, children who had been raised on war and had difficulty remembering what it was like to have no war. The war was like their mother. The pervasive mood was cynicism laced with despair. They all spoke of living only for the moment. They made jokes about death. Most were superstitious. Many looked older than they actually were. Allen felt a little out of place.

Not long after Allen had arrived he bought Donnelly's vintage Jaguar. It was shiny red, and every Sunday morning Allen drove it into the countryside. He dreamed of meeting some girl and imagined her hiking up her skirt as she climbed in. He even started packing a blanket in the trunk, but all he ever saw were sheep.

Sometimes he drank in the scullery with the others. There was a case of prewar gin, and plenty of beer. Occasionally girls from

150

the coding room dropped by, and finally one of them even plopped down next to Allen.

"Got any gum, chum?"

He thought she was serious, and began to pat his pockets. "No, sorry, but I've got a Jaguar." It was his best line.

"Oh, so you're the chap that bought Steve's car. Does it run?" She was short and blond with a button nose, and she spoke with a London accent. Allen had seen her before through the rain-streaked glass of his cottage when she had paused under a yew tree to smooth her stockings.

This brick cavern was lit with candles and an oil lamp. The furniture was castaway: a burlap sofa with a rickety arm, a few sagging chairs, a table made of packing crates. The girl was kicking off her shoes, tugging at a thread on her heavy wool lapel. Allen could not keep his eyes off the nape of her neck. He also liked the way her hair tumbled down in easy curls.

"Oh, by the way," she said, "my name is Julia Mock."

"Mock, that's an unusual name. What's it from?"

"I don't know." She was trying to bite off the thread. "Mock turtle soup I guess. Dad was Welsh. He worked for the railroads."

Through the gloom and smoke came the thump of darts. They were popping open beer bottles on the edges of the furniture.

"You'll have to take me for a spin in that lovely Jag of yours," she was saying, but absently . . . she might have just been asking for the time.

"Oh, I'd love to. Whenever you want."

She gave him a quick smile. "How about now?"

"Now?" He couldn't believe it, after all this time of aching for a girl.

"Unless you think it's too late."

"Oh, well, I'm a big boy now, aren't I?"

"We'll see."

They followed a bridge of trees along a winding road until they reached the furthest crags. All the way Allen had been easing in and out of the gears as smoothly as he could. Her face against the breath-fogged windscreen was just another dimness, like the distant hills and passing heather.

He parked on a windswept rise. Below lay the fog like the face of a gray sea. They spoke softly. She talked about the blitz. She said she used to watch the searchlights sweep the sky and briefly light the quivering skins of barrage balloons. At one point he tried to say something profound, to pass along some sympathy for all the suffering. But she only laughed and said that it was pretty clear that he had never been through it himself.

The days grew warm, the trees were full of leaves and their branches spread across the gravel paths. Nights were usually still except for the distant rumble of passing planes or motor transports. Sometimes there were afternoons of lovely rain, and then the air smelled like a wet dog.

Allen found himself thinking more and more of Julia. He often lingered on the leafy walks, hoping to meet her, and when she did come they would stroll together. Once she even slipped her arm through his. It made his heart race. When they parted he watched her as far as he could until the path bent under the laurel and under a garden shed. He kept trying to hang on to the image of her. She had been bouncing along the gravel. There was just the merest glimpse of her nonregulation black slip beneath her murky wool skirt.

Allen soon came to realize that Julia was older than he. Not actually older, but *older*. The war did it, made the girls tough and wry. Wisecracks passed for sympathy. But if they were hard, they were also very real.

Three Sundays after they had met, Allen asked Julia to a picnic with him in the forest. She accepted without a moment's hesitation. He asked her as she was passing him on the path. She was straddling her bicycle, resting on the handlebars. Her sleeves were rolled above her elbows. Her skirt was tucked up a bit above her stockings. She flipped her head to the side and said, "Sure, I'll bring the chicken, you bring the vino."

They found a meadow filled with wildflowers, the sunlight was slanting through the trees. Bees were darting above the grass. Julia had prepared sandwiches spread with canned meat, mayonnaise and cucumbers. Allen had the Burgundy and his drab green army blanket. By the afternoon the breeze was rustling through the leaves above them. They were both slouched against an oak. Allen's hands were locked between his knees, the roots of the oak gouging into his spine. He wanted to put his arm around her shoulders but he was afraid. Finally he said, "Julia, there's something I want to tell you."

"No, I don't think you should."

"But you don't know what it is."

"Yes, I do. You're going to say that you like me. Well, I like you too, Allen. Only . . . I guess you'd have to say that there's someone else right now."

"Oh." He felt his chest tighten.

"It's not that I've meant to lead you on. It's just that . . . well, I thought it wouldn't hurt. You know, we would be friends. I've always had chaps for friends. Not lovers, just friends. But then I've had lovers too."

"Who is he?"

"Oh just some chap. He's a Yank like you."

"Do I know him? I mean is he stationed at Flemming?"

"Yes, but . . . well he's over the hill just now."

For an instant Allen did not understand. Then he realized what she had meant. "Is it France?" he asked.

"Who knows? They tell me he's supposed to be home by Christmas. I guess I'll get him a pipe."

"What's he like?"

"Oh, I don't know." She was wedging back her cuticles. "I guess he's sort of strange."

"How do you mean?"

153

She puffed a blond strand of hair away. "An idealist gone cynic. He used to say that he hated war, but he loved me so much he could kill for me. Maybe he takes the war a little too personally . . . but then, he's Jewish."

A phrase he had heard in Berlin suddenly flashed through his mind. *It must be genetic.*

All he said, however, was, "Do you love him?"

"God, I don't know. I suppose I love him, but I'm not sure I could actually marry him. He's not safe, like you're safe. Robert's more of the lone wolf. Fantastic, but a little scary."

"Robert?" Allen said, disbelieving. "Is that his name?"

"Yes," she said. "His name is Robert Kline."

Allen saw himself on that muddy Jarama hill again. Julia's lover was, incredibly—inevitably?—the brooding phantom with a crooked cigar. He did not know what to say. . . .

In time Allen became her confidant. They often talked until quite late at night. He found that she could be a distracted girl, never bothering to tidy up, always begging puffs on stale Woodbines. Her cottage was a mess. Panties and silk stockings lay where she had flung them. There was an old doll that glared from the mantelpiece, a few rusty seashells, a cracked bowl filled with nylon repair kits. She even scrounged ashtrays for cigarette butts.

In spite of all this Allen grew to love her. He loved the way she bumbled through her cottage or tramped down sodden lanes in her yellow Wellington rain boots. He never told her how he felt. He was afraid that he might frighten her away. Instead he only revealed himself with small acts . . . he brought her daisies, pinched from the captain's garden; he sometimes even brought her chocolate; but mostly he just listened to her while she talked about her troubles and her dreams. It was only bad when she talked about Kline. Kline was an axe that cut the bond between them. Allen kept seeing the damn image of the man, out there on the rainy hills of Spain. . . .

Soon England's sky was also stormy. The wind blew, rain fell

154

and the leaves were pounded into the gravel paths. Allen spent his days monitoring partisan radio networks. The lines ran north-east from Prague to Warsaw, then up to Stockholm and out across the sea. It was during this stage of his career that Allen formed his distrust of underground radio links.

The transmitters were bulky, heavy things. They looked like typewriters. Agents were given sets of crystals in a velvet pouch. Each crystal vibrated at a different frequency, but even when the crystals were changed every ninety seconds, the Germans still kept fixing on transmissions. For a while the Gestapo was pulling in a man a week. Once they got the section leader they could roll up the entire network.

So Allen came to only trust the courier lines. He liked telephone patter, written codes and commercial broadcasts. Once he even used cathedral bells along the Danish coast. The secret message lay in the interval of chimes.

The worst nights were spent in the receiving shacks. Drinking tea, chain smoking, while he waited for some tiny fluttering of life from a ruined network. They always seemed to signal just before dawn, and so hope came in like a garbled message from the moon.

But all in all Allen came to be very fond of this life. He loved the visions he had of his networks, the concept of those little, ragged people strung out across Europe. In time he became good at what he did, very good. He had, what was called, the proper touch. He knew when to gently prod and when to blow them out of the water. He was precise and impersonal. He understood that the entire game was ultimately reducible to mathematics. There were the odds of survival and the numerical value of success. Even the death toll was calculated in terms of percentages. All together these numbers formed something like an elaborate fugue. The melody ran between the counterpoints, and that was what under-mined the Germans. (Years later they would say that Allen had a dazzling war, but in truth he was only plugging into equations. The agents were abstractions to him. Not that he did not care

155

when he lost one, but the pain of failure and genuine remorse for a human life were different things. Allen was a deskman who could keep his objectivity. He did not fall to pieces whenever they hung an eighteen-year-old girl from a meat hook.)

Through that summer and into the early fall Allen's existence achieved a certain balance. There were the hours spent in his tiny basement cell with his maps pasted to the rough bricks and the naked light bulb strung from the ceiling. Then there were those moments with Julia. They met for drinks whenever they could, took long drives into the country. Allen liked to think that nothing would ever change.

The archives would place Robert Kline back at Flemming in October, yet no substantial link had ever been drawn between him and Allen Dancer at this time. It was noted that they knew each other, but the significance of Kline's return was never recorded. In fact there was only one brief mention of Kline in Allen's file. Apparently the two men were both cited for violating the rule about drinking in the receiving shed. They had been caught sharing a beer, and so it was always assumed that they had been friends. Nothing could have been further from the truth.

They first came together the night of Kline's return. It was Halloween, and Allen had stopped by Julia's cottage with a bag of marzipan. She was smiling when she answered the door. She took his hand and bent to kiss him on the cheek, but he was looking past her to where Kline sat on the lily-patterned sofa. The lamplight cut his face into hard lines. He looked about the same as he had looked that night in Spain.

The first moment was awkward. Kline was like stone. He spoke in a flat, low voice.

"It's been a long time."

"Oh, well, it certainly has." Allen laughed. "When was that? Uh, thirty-eight right? Definitely a coincidence, wouldn't you say?"

156

Julia opened another bottle of champagne at midnight. Then she and Allen were forcing laughter in their jokes, while Kline just kept glaring out from the cone of yellow light. Apparently he had had a bad time of it in France.

They became a threesome at Julia's insistence. Twice the first week she cooked dinner for them. A friend in the coding room had a line on stray chickens, and there were potatoes in the patch out back. There were many stiff moments when only the clattering silverware broke the silence, but generally Allen kept the conversation rolling. He was good at that.

One Sunday Julia got them all to pile into Allen's Jaguar and they went speeding down lanes covered with red leaves. More leaves sailed up from their slipstream. They picnicked in a meadow that lay in a circle of laurels. When the wine bottles were empty and the drumsticks had been tossed away Julia wandered off to wash the glasses in a brook.

Then Kline and Dancer were truly alone.

"She's a lovely girl," Allen began. It seemed like a safe thing to say.

"Yes," Kline answered.

"Not many like her around, are there?"

"No, not many."

They were squatting side by side on the blanket. Julia was a small figure weaving through the meadow ahead. The straw hamper was swinging at her side. The day was an odd break from darkening autumn. It was windless and hot.

"She talked a lot about you," Allen finally said.

"She talked about you too."

"Nothing bad I hope."

"No, she likes you. She wants me to like you too."

"But you don't like me, do you?"

Kline shrugged. "We met under difficult circumstances the first time. If I recall, you came on the third day of the counterattack. They had been cutting us down for nothing."

157

"I understand. Spain was tough on all of us."

Kline shrugged again. "Even so, I was unfair to you."

"You had a lot on your mind that day."

"Just the same, I'm sorry."

"Forget it. Friends?"

"Yes of course."

Kline clamped his hand into Dancer's. They were both smiling at one another.

"But there's one thing I'd like to ask you," Kline said.

"Yes, what's that?"

Kline's smile faded. "Why are you still trying to con me?" . . .

Allen did not see Julia much after that. Now there was only the war, and he threw himself into it as never before. He spent whole nights bent over maps, squinting into the weak light until the lines began to blur. His operating theater had changed. By these last weeks before Christmas he was helping to synchronize Yugoslavian resistance strikes with the broader Allied effort. His main agent was a gangster turned killer who led a pack of knife-men in the Black Mountains. They were men who had lost their homes and families. It was said of them that even if their legs were cut off they would still keep crawling forward until they dragged you down.

As for Julia, Allen sometimes saw her walking slowly down the Flemming paths, but Kline was nearly always with her and so Allen never approached her. There were moments when he missed her very badly, and one morning in particular he could barely keep from breaking down. He had been up for twenty-seven hours, plotting courier routes through the Ibar Valley of Serbia to the iron gates of the Danube. At dawn he looked out his office window and saw that the whole land was glazed with dew. A moment passed, and then he saw Julia standing on the rise of the frosted lawn. She was wearing a purple raincoat and her yellow Wellingtons. Otherwise the colors were gray and green-gray.

Later that morning Allen walked slowly through the mist,

158

kicked open the door of his cottage and fell onto his lumpy cot. He was half asleep, balled up under the wool and linen. For an hour he just lay with his eyes shut. Times like these he felt like a nasty, sweaty little boy, and outsmarting people was the best thing in the world. Finally he even began to chew his knuckles as the plan started to unfold . . . the whole question of ethics was reduced to a maxim: *Kline would do the same to you if things were reversed.*

The groundwork of his plan took two days. Then he went to see the captain. Hawkins was in his office in the central Flemming tower. Worms had tunneled through the paneling, and the wallpaper was rippling with mildew. Allen found the man bent over the electric fire. He was always complaining about the cold.

"I have a proposition," Allen began. He started to pick at the moulding. Below lay strands of fog in the black branches.

"Proposition or complaint, that's all anyone ever gives me," grumbled Hawkins.

The old Scot was wearing his natty cardigan. It was buttoned to the top. On the wall were charcoal drawings of Inverness. They were crude and too dark.

"Oh but I think you'll like this one. It solves a niggling problem."

"I'm listening. You have my undivided attention." The gas jets were hissing and sputtering behind them.

"It involves linking up all the networks with a single unvarying code."

"Unvarying, Allen? Nothing is unvarying. Look at the bloody weather. It's always changing for the worse."

"Oh well, of course you'll have your system of letter drops in case of forced transmission. But the trick is to keep it simple. I see one man bringing in the code, and the networks passing it along through cutouts. Given a week or so you could have an entire country neatly tied together."

159

"Too dangerous, Allen. They could roll up the whole damn show."

"Ah, but that's where you're wrong, sir. The networks don't need to be linked with personal contact. All they'll need is a frequency and call schedule. Say you want to set up a simultaneous strike over two or three sections. All you need to do is have the section leaders send out the word. Targets can be coded however you like."

Hawkins was staring at the pallid light through the oval window. Finally he said, "You're not thinking that this could be set up in the Balkans, are you?"

"No, I was thinking we might try it out in France."

"Yes, that would be the logical place, wouldn't it?"

"They're the tightest group we have."

"Not your area, though, is it?"

"No, it's not my area. It belongs to another man."

"Yes . . . Robert Kline."

And Allen echoed, "Robert Kline."

"All right, Dancer, tell you what I'll do. I'll put it up the lines and see if anyone cheers. If they go for it, I'll make sure you get a mention in the minutes. Brain behind the scenes, if you know what I mean."

"Oh, that really isn't necessary. In fact I'd rather you kept me out of it. Don't want them to think I've been messing with another fellow's pot."

"Suit yourself, but I'll keep you informed just the same."

"Yes. That would be nice. Thank you, sir."

Throughout this exchange Allen had been looking down at the burgundy rug. One brownish patch looked like Robert's face. The cigarette burns were his eyes.

Later, as the dusk mingled with the fog, the entire Flemming landscape became muted with the tones of full winter. Allen sat on the mossy steps of the garden shed until he saw Julia and Kline drifting by. They were framed beneath the trestle of boughs. In the

160

past whenever Allen had seen them strolling together he had experienced jealousy mixed with a deep sadness. Now, he felt nothing. He could have wrapped the last two days into a neat package and labeled it: *the things one does for love.* . . .

On Christmas Eve they wedged candles between the bricks of the scullery walls, and after a couple of beers, Allen kept seeing that light in long, fuzzy needles. Finally he was sick on the frosted lawn. By midnight Flemming was still and dark. Allen slipped on the flagstones, ripping skin from both palms. Then he nearly fell again when his shins banged into the box that had been propped against his cottage door. It was a carton of Lucky Strikes, and the card read: *Best wishes from Robert and Julia.*

For a long time he remained sitting on the bricks in a pool of moonlight. He caught whiffs of something rotting in his kitchen, and he had to keep on swallowing away the taste of bile.

There was only the merest hint in the records that Allen had anything to do with Kline's run into France. His name was mentioned several times in the early planning stages of the mission, and he was known to have later worked with radio specialists in formulating the call signals that Kline was to have passed on to his networks. The fundamental decisions, though, were beyond his authority. At best it could be said that Allen had merely dropped the seed into fertile ground. The bush that eventually sprang up was the work of others. . . .

Kline left for France about two weeks into the new year. He was flown over in a light plane that had been painted jet-black. It was a perfect night for a drop. There was a moon, but clouds cut the light. He was left in an open field a few miles from the train tracks which ran to Le Havre. The pilot who took him over was a boy from Canada. (His drop notes later became part of the record.)

In all Kline made four transmissions from France, two from the provinces and two from Paris. Things seemed to be going well. He reported meeting with section leaders and instructing them how

161

to use the new communications system and by the second week it was generally believed that Kline had succeeded in tying together the entire so-called Whistler Network. Then came the blackout.

Flemming radio operators spent three weeks in the receiving shed trying to contact Kline and waiting for his transmissions. There were rumors, snatches of arrest reports from the Parisian underground, but nothing could be substantiated. Finally an intercepted Gestapo cable told all that anyone needed to know. Kline had indeed been arrested, and was either undergoing interrogation or already dead. The latter if he were fortunate.

In the morning they sent a boy over from the operations unit to tell Allen. It was early, but Allen had not been sleeping much since the blackout, so when the boy came Allen was already up and sitting by the window. He saw the boy treading through the powdery snowdrifts that had fallen the night before. When the boy explained that Kline had been lost, all Allen Dancer said was, "Yes. I see. Thank you." Then he continued to sit and watch the light turn gold and finally gray, all the while telling himself that nothing like this was supposed to have happened.

Telling Julia was the hardest part. Allen found her in the canteen, sitting alone at one of the long tables with an untouched cup of tea. She may have sensed that something bad had happened because she did not speak when he approached.

He said only, "Will you take a walk with me?"

They went out among the trees and mounds of clean snow. Allen wore his tweed coat with the collar turned up around his ears. He was squinting at the glare. Julia wore her old purple slicker, but there was a new tear at the sleeve and her eyes were red at the edges.

Finally Allen stopped, turned and faced her. "It's about Robert. I'm afraid we've lost him."

For a long time she did not move. She was as stiff as any of the

162

twisted branches. There was a windless cold, nothing moved in the forest.

"Look, it doesn't mean that we can't get him back," he added suddenly. "It's happened before. The Paris group might be able to spring him. Or maybe he could make it out on his own . . . he's a very capable guy . . ."

Julia only shook her head. She had begun to cry now, although she was still unmoving, staring down into the snow. After a little while she said, "You really don't think he has a chance, do you?"

"No." He owed her that much honesty. "When they pick you up they usually take you to the Avenue Foch cells. The first rounds are pretty light, but after that comes the chambers at the Place des Etats-Unis. That's where they usually get you, or else they send you to one of the camps. I'm sorry, but I thought it would be somehow better if you heard it from me."

In the instant of silence she sank to the snow and began to scream. It was the same word over and over: *No.*

In the weeks that followed Allen saw her regularly. They were back to meeting after hours. Sometimes they would drink beer in the scullery, or else hot chocolate in the canteen. They also had this favorite spot, high up on the Flemming tower among the copse of radio aerials. They liked the northern view of the patchy forest and frozen ponds.

In time something between them started to change. They began to touch each other. She often pressed her body against his. Then came that evening on the steps of her cottage. It was midnight and the moon on the snow flung blue shadows across the grounds. Allen mumbled some sort of halting good-by, then bent to kiss her on the lips. When he had done it, he told her that he was sorry.

"It's all right, Allen. Really it is."

"But—"

"No, it's all *right,* Allen. Everything is going to be all right." Then she linked her arms around his neck, and just before they

163

kissed again he told her what seemed his darkest secret. "I'm afraid, Julia. I'm just goddamned afraid. Can you beat that?"

It won the day.

They continued to see one another, and at some point they became lovers . . . just fell into it. Sometimes he was her little boy, and his smoother, more formidable self collapsed all to hell. Then he could not help melting into her breasts. Once, after two of his agents were hung in Belgrade, he almost broke down and cried in her arms. It was no act. The entire day he had been playing the sober desk officer. Then they told him that he had lost two more, and he only nodded. But later that night Julia gathered him up in her arms, and he nearly wept.

At other times she was the child, going on about some girl in the coding room and a Spitfire pilot. He loved to watch her talk. Her hands moved like birds. Her eyes were flecked with copper. They often stuck candles on the dresser, and in the late hours Allen had to rub his eyes to get rid of the blur. Later he would realize that these were the happiest days of his life, although he could never tell that to anyone, because this was also the time that the secret world was suffering its worst casualties and one was certainly not supposed to feel happy. Only his son Jessie, some thirty years later, would actually admit that he loved war above everything else. John to Allen to Jessie . . . a natural progression. Evolution of the species.

There was a false spring that year. One morning the Flemming grounds were blanched with transitory blossoms, and for a week the weather remained warm. Then came a night of cold wind and winter returned. It was about this time that the last word of Robert Kline also came in from abroad.

Allen was in the briefing room, a long, raftered hall that lay in the east wing of the Flemming estate. There were dormer windows and benches that made the room look a little like a chapel. Hawkins was there, and two men from Churchill's office. The maps on the table were kept from rolling up by teacups and ashtrays.

As the meeting was adjourning, the men walking out the door, Hawkins caught Allen by the arm and pulled him aside.

"I'm afraid we've heard about Kline."

"When?"

"Last night. It came in from one of the Polish lines, and it looks pretty final. The Poles say he was finished at one of the camps."

"How reliable?"

"I'd say about eighty percent."

Further down the hall there were odors of wet blankets, and stale tobacco. A boy was mopping the floor. He seemed to be in a trance.

"We're going to call him missing for the moment," Hawkins went on. "I don't like to write them off unless there's absolute proof."

"Yes, sure . . ."

Before they parted Hawkins told him, "I'm truly sorry. I know how you must feel, Kline being a friend and all. However, one shouldn't lose all hope. There's always a chance."

As Allen walked out into the cool morning the word chance kept revolving inside of him. He waited until the evening to tell Julia as he stood in the half-light of the cottage doorway. She faced him from a dozen feet away. Her back was to the old stone hearth, his was against the battered oak door.

"We've just heard, and I'm afraid it's definite. No chance."

Afterward he had the oddest taste in his mouth. It was as if his tongue was coated with zinc. *No chance* that he could get rid of that taste in his mouth. . . .

They did not speak of Robert Kline again, or at least not if they could avoid it. There were his uniforms in the closet and his silver hairbrush in the bathroom. Whenever Allen hung up his coat he saw those uniforms. They were sort of scary. (And thirty years later Jessie would say that objects had no consciousness but they somehow acted on you.) Then one day the uniforms were gone.

165

Allen came to the cottage in the afternoon and there was only a gap in the closet. The brush was gone too. Julia said nothing.

Now all that was left of Kline was a ghost that sometimes made Julia's eyes glassy and her voice sound far away. Eventually they began to talk about marriage. Allen was the one who kept bringing it up, although whenever he mentioned it he became clumsy and shy. Sometimes his voice even cracked. Essentially, he promised her the world.

In time he must have gotten to her, because one night on the crag above the valley she agreed to marry. A southern wind was blowing through the open heath, and it took three matches to light her cigarette. Her hair was swept back. She was blinking into the gusts of wind just like a little girl.

Allen stood beside her, speaking to her profile. He kept swallowing and stuttering, and finally he broke down completely. "Ah, Julia, don't you see, you're the only one I can trust."

It was the last time he would ever really beg for anything.

Before they descended again through the tufted grass she said, "All right, Allen. I'll marry you."

They kissed, and it would have been a perfect moment, except that there was a distinct trace of reservation in her eyes. . . .

They were married in a country church, an old stone church with a crumbling nave, dry rot and woodworm. Wildflowers grew between the gravestones. The vicar had a glass eye. When they all stood to hear the vows read there was an odd, transient beauty— a little wind was rustling under the door, suspended dust was in the shafts of light.

Odd. Transient. Very appropriate for Allen Dancer and his life.

CHAPTER FIVE

SEVEN DAYS had passed since Allen Dancer had returned to Langley in the wake of the Yeats crisis. This was the time when each of the principal figures became committed to their respective roles, and there was no turning back.

It was also during this time that the second interrogation of Dusty Yeats began. Every night Allen questioned the prisoner, while Tony Nugent recorded what was said. Although these sessions were closed, it would later come out that Allen had conducted a rather sloppy interrogation. More than once he let his emotions get the better of him, and so failed to pursue important questions. One night he broke Dusty's finger, and on another night he put out a cigarette in the boy's groin.

167

Through all this Yeats was injected with drugs which Langley psychiatrists said had finally brought him under control. The irony was that because Allen believed these doctors he never did uncover the truth regarding the twenty-six missing pages of the Magic product list. It seemed that the doctors had told Allen that it was impossible that the boy could still be lying about the list's whereabouts, and so Allen accepted that the pages had been lost in the forest. It was only much later that Allen would look back and recall how, after the question of the pages had been passed over, Yeats had been smiling. He had quite clearly been smiling. He had been smiling like a tortured man might smile when, really, the executioner had gone too far.

It was also during this period that Humphrey Knolls made his first substantial breakthrough in his own investigation of the Dancers. It began with a photograph, an eight-by-ten glossy that everyone else had forgotten about. The photograph was part of a Bangkok station security check that had once been run on Jessie. Someone in that station had seen him talking with a strange man, not once but several times. An officer was alerted and a routine investigation was made, including the photograph which had been taken from a distance at night with an infrared flash. Nothing came of that security probe, Jessie was cleared and no follow-up was ever made. The material was merely sent back to Langley and placed in the Bangkok station file. There was not even a cross-reference to Jessie.

Still, two facts intrigued Knolls. The first was that the dates that Jessie met with the strange man corresponded with the beginning of everything . . . four months before Yeats sought admission into Langley, Jessie had been talking with that man; secondly, the man was later identified as a former Langley operative. No one knew his name, only that he was somehow connected with the secret world.

When Humphrey first found the photograph he hardly knew what to think. It was as shadowy and disturbing as any vision he

168

had ever had of Jessie. The boy and the man were two grainy figures on a stretch of desolate land between a Bangkok swamp and coarse sea grass. There was a long pipe above the water and the grass, and coils of barbed wire. Slanting spears of black steel were fixed against the sky. It looked like an abandoned place.

Jessie's back was to the camera. One saw only his lean outline. He was wearing a short leather jacket and jeans. He looked like a young punk. The man he was speaking to had been fully captured by the camera. He was clearly an old man, tall and thin. His face was cut with deep lines, but he had soft features, thin lips and high cheekbones. He was dressed in a long shabby greatcoat. From the angle of the shot it almost looked like he was standing in the swamp. So Humphrey called him the swamp man.

On the first day that Knolls had found the photograph he just laid it on his desk, and by the afternoon it was covered with other papers, coffee cups, candy wrappers, the overflow from the trash bin. Then by degrees the swamp man began to take a more prominent place in the story. First Knolls correlated the date that the photograph was taken with the record of Jessie's Bangkok movements. And yes, things had changed after the night that Jessie met with his swamp man. They were small things, variations in his working schedule, a trip abroad, travel into the countryside. It was also about this time that, according to Yeats, Jessie started talking a lot about Source Magic and occasionally about Sara Moore.

It was a growing fixation for Knolls. He hardly understood or even remembered how it all began. Simply there came a point when all his thoughts seemed centered around this swamp man. He could sit for hours in his room and stare at the photograph. He kept on telling himself that it was important, that it meant something. Finally when he could no longer stand the mystery, Humphrey made his first, truly risky move of the search. He stole a security pass from Severson's office, forged the signature and used it to pull twelve live files from the master operations safe.

It took an afternoon, and there were moments when he was so

frightened he thought he would die. There were hundreds of photographs of Langley operatives to look through. Yet when it was over, he had found the identity of his swamp man, and established one of the most important links of the entire story. This was the link between Jessie Dancer and Robert Kline.

Of all those who eventually found a place in the Dancer story, there was no one who baffled the researchers more than Robert Kline. Records picked up his thread four months after his escape from the German concentration camp. No one was ever quite sure how he had escaped. The notes of his debriefing were later transcribed for the archives, but they told nothing. Apparently Kline had little to say. He had a way of not responding to questions. He would just sit there. Silence did not embarrass him. . . .

The day Kline returned to Flemming there were warm winds blowing from the south. He had driven up from London, and the back of his uniform was black from sweat. When the jeep rolled into the courtyard Hawkins was waiting on the steps. The first thing he noticed was that Kline had taped a knife to his forearm.

"Would you care for some lemonade?" Hawkins asked.

"Thank you," Kline replied, but his voice was dead.

They stood before the tall windows in Hawkins's office. The room was fixed in a framework of afternoon light. Below were the tossing, green trees.

"We never thought that we'd see you again," Hawkins went on. "But then I suppose they all say that, don't they? I mean about coming back."

"Yes. They all say that."

"It's a pity that Allen and Julia aren't here. Or perhaps it's not a pity. That is, I'm not sure how you feel about it."

"Feel about what?"

"About their marriage. You were told about it, weren't you?"

"Yeah, they told me."

"And you feel all right about it? I mean no hard feelings? Anything like that?"

170

"Why should I care?"

"Well, as I understood it, you and Julia were, uh, rather close to one another. Then Allen . . . so naturally I assumed that you might possibly have felt a little bitter . . ."

Kline smiled, but it held no warmth. "Bitter? I'm not bitter about anything, Jack. I'm just anxious to get started."

Hawkins nodded nervously. "Yes. London told me about what you'll be doing, and I must say you have extraordinary guts."

"Oh, I don't know. What's it take to tag a few Germans? They go down like anyone else."

There was something terrible about the way Kline said it. Like the human stuff had been leeched out of him.

Officially Kline was listed in the records of the period as a Concentrated Terror operative. They called his sort the ruffians. At times they worked alone, at other times they worked with local resistance teams. They were trained at infighting and long-range killing. The risks were high, and after three runs you were considered an old man. Robert Kline became the best of them all.

He trained in the highlands of Scotland, a desolate place; the skies were always melancholy. Sometimes he would wander out across the moors. This was open land, and like the landscape of a dream it seemed to have supernatural possibilities.

He never came to know the people he trained with. Everyone was given a different name. Kline was Mr. Sly—the only American. The others were mostly foreign—Poles, Belgians, Frenchmen, Swedes. The camp commander told them that they were elite, the most direct punch of the Allied effort. Privately he believed that they were men who had just been pushed too far and now had come to make a stand. He admired them for it, but he was also a little afraid of them.

Kline's first run was in Poland. The target was the regional Death's Head commander, and former head of the Treblinka camp. His name was Bruno Steiner, and his assassination had been authorized on psychological grounds. Steiner was well-hated by

171

the Poles, and it was decided that his murder would give hope to the resistance. When Kline was first briefed about the job, they told him that this one was right up his alley—probably a reference to Kline's religion, because Steiner had killed hundreds of Jews.

Kline went in as an engineer from Munich, bound for one of the eastern factories. Local resistance was supposed to have furnished him with a car, but all they had was a motorbike. At first Kline was angry. He thought the bike would draw too much attention. In the end, though, he came to love that machine . . . streaming over the hinterland of flat treeless plain, he felt near-demonic, indestructible. He passed through many villages, each empty of life, and quieter than the open road because they gave a moment's shelter from the echo of the wind. At night there were few lights, only small specks on the horizon. He rode by compass, because there were no signs left standing.

The first night he slept in a grove of pines near the shore of a lake. At dawn the wind came sounding through the reeds, and the flapping wings of birds reverberated off the water. The lake was still and glassy, and Kline too felt still . . . he had the feeling that his entire life had been leading up to what he was about to do.

He could hardly wait.

The second night he slept with a girl. It just happened. He had come to a town and an old inn with weathered siding and rotting plaster walls. There was no hot water and the cold ran thin. His room was bare except for a stained basin, a desk, chair and a narrow bed. There was no carpet, just floorboards.

He was stretched out, smoking, staring at the water marks on the ceiling when the girl knocked at his door. She was a thin, doe-eyed girl with long, dark hair. Her German was bad. She had probably picked it up from passing soldiers. She said that her room was next to Kline's, and they began to talk. She could not have been older than sixteen, but she was already a little crazy.

Eventually they found themselves in her room, spread out on

the bed. There was a picture of a horse she had pasted on the wall, she'd torn it out of a magazine. Otherwise the room was as bare as Kline's.

She had a bottle of vodka, rank stuff. A soldier from Potsdam had given it to her. He had also given her some money, but that was all gone now.

"I guess you think the Germans aren't so bad."

The girl shrugged. "He only gave me that stuff because he felt bad. First he raped me, then he gave me money and this."

She listlessly tapped the bottle of vodka with her finger.

"Well, if I raped you I wouldn't have anything to give you afterwards."

"Maybe you won't have to rape me. Maybe I like you."

The drink made her sulky. Her lips looked bee-stung and moist. She had a kittenish way about her that was bizarre under the circumstances. It all added up to a contradiction between youth and what the war had done to it.

For close to an hour they just lay together . . . she had undone the buttons of his shirt and her fingers were playing on his chest. Finally she stretched, yawned and said, "I don't care about anything. I'm the easygoing sort." She kicked off her shoes and pulled the cotton dress over her head. She had small breasts, Kline could see her ribs.

"You don't have to do this," he told her.

"But I want to," she said, and sort of threw herself into his arms.

When he did not respond she took his thumb and rubbed it against her nipple.

"I'm cold . . . so cold . . . please . . ."

So he gathered her up, a long-legged girl, trusting. She pressed her lean thighs into his and ran her hands over his shoulders. There was a chilled, full moon through the window, and the room was washed in light the color of bone. She locked her arms around

173

him and would not let go. Once she moaned softly, then he saw that she was crying. When he kissed her nipples gently, her eyes rolled back. . . .

Later she would still not let him go. She had curled into the crook of his arm, her hair spread out on the pillow. Her lips were close to his ear. She whispered, "You're not a German."

He laughed a little. "What makes you think that?"

"You don't do it like the Germans. The Germans aren't good."

"Then if I'm not a German, what am I?"

She turned over on her back. She had taken his hand and was examining it. Then she started chewing on the end of his finger. Finally she said, "I don't know. Maybe you're a spy."

It made him smile. "I'm not a spy. I'm a killer. I have a knife in that rucksack. Two cutting edges. It's sharp as a razor."

She was grinning now and her eyes were the brightest they had been since he'd met her.

"Who are you going to kill?" she asked, looking more like a child than ever.

"Everybody," Kline said, and then he kissed her lightly, barely touching his lips to hers.

"Yes"—she giggled—"kill everybody, and keep on doing it until there's no one left but you and me. Then we can make a whole new race of people."

"I promise," Kline smiled, and kissed her again. . . .

Kline reached Cracow on the evening of the seventh day. He did not enter the city. He stayed in the woods and prowled the open fields for potatoes. Finally an old woman gave him shelter, some watery soup of leeks and turnips. There were also slabs of coarse dark bread.

The target was an ancient castle on a mountain above the city. Kline spent hours squatting in the cold field, gazing across three miles of brown earth at the high castle walls. Once Kline imagined that he had turned into a bat, and he saw himself skimming over

174

the grass, then flying through a turret window and down the corridor until he found Bruno Steiner.

He chose a windy night to make the kill. He left at dusk. First there was the long walk across the fields, then the climb up the mountain road. When a truck passed he rolled into the underbrush to avoid the headlights. He felt as sure of himself as that bat in his fantasy. There were guards at the gates, but he passed them easily by climbing a tree and slipping over the wall. Then he was moving through the compound and up the stone steps. He went in through a window and paused in the shadow of a ledge. In Scotland there had been a wooden model of this castle and he had studied it for hours. The feeling he had had while planning the kill was the same he had now. He was not afraid, just intensely interested.

He finally came to Steiner's bedroom. The man lay sleeping in the gloom. There were smells of hair oil and lotion. There was also the smell of leather. Underwear, a pair of boots and other shapeless objects lay about the room. A riding crop was propped against the skirting board. Kline waited until his eyes became fully accustomed to the darkness, then he crept to the bed. In the final seconds a kind of automatic pilot took over. Kline's wrist seemed to move of its own accord, drawing the knife, slipping the pillow over the face. As for Kline, it seemed as if his knife could cut through anything, every rotten memory of every minute since this war had begun. It made him grateful. . . .

There came a point when it seemed to Kline that he may have taken a step too far, crossed the line that most men call humanity, and now he was sick. Things were strange. People popped out and spoke, but it was difficult to understand them. He was always hungry, but he could not eat, always tired but he could not sleep. He felt as though he were impersonating himself.

They sent him to North Africa to kill a vacationing Gestapo interrogator. He arrived in the early morning and moving down

175

the esplanade the sea was an iridescent blue while the green of palm leaves textured a cloudless sky. The cliffs were white.

He spent the day sipping mineral water underneath a cabana. Sailboats were tacking into the sun, gulls were wheeling above, children cut up dead fish on the sand. He decided he would wait here until sunset. When the light turned purple he tramped back along the esplanade. Onshore winds were stirring the palms.

Night. He was climbing the hillside, slithering over garden walls, moving through bamboo groves, skirting goldfish ponds. Locks gave way at his touch. Windows rose soundlessly. It was part of his power now. He felt as if he could do anything, stepping from bed to bed, first the pillow, then the knife. . . .

So it went, from city to city. In Paris he killed seventeen, and they called him a psychopath and were not sure that he had anything to do with the war anymore. He might have just begun pulling them down randomly. It had happened before.

To himself he would say, Oh, I'm just a victim of a freak talent. After a good kill his nerves unbuckled. He would tread back up to his room or into a cafe or a train or a taxi. He would watch passing streetlamps, rainslick streets or night crowds and the blinking neons. It did not matter where he was; after a well-managed kill a kind of peace seemed to pass through him.

Still, it began to show. He could not quite keep it under control, and so people began to notice. They began to talk, to avoid his eyes, to watch him from a distance. It was as if they were witnessing an accident. They wanted to look, but at the same time they did not want to see.

In Antwerp he mutilated a body, he couldn't help it, the knife just kept working away, it wasn't his fault. . . . In Limburg he gutted a dog. The target had been a flabby *Haupsturmführer,* and Kline cut him down in the woods while he was out walking his Dalmatian. Afterward the dog had to go too. Kline was not sure why, it just had to. Then outside of Budapest and near Warsaw . . . same story as the ones before . . . the knife just took over. What

176

with the captured Gestapo reports and the newspapers, Kline's controllers had a fairly clear picture of what they were dealing with. They decided that Robert Kline needed a rest.

They sent him to Clovelly to sit on the beach. It was the end of the season and the town was deserted. He stayed in an old windswept hotel that the sun and wind had bleached white. In the afternoons he prowled the blown strand and returned with his trouser cuffs filed with sand. On the whole it was bad. The days were somber, the sea lay in shades of gray under gray clouds, low fog perpetually ringed the horizon. If they wanted to give him a rest, why didn't they send him to Hamburg?

Down the strand from his weathered hotel was an old fisherman's pub, oars on the walls and nets strung from the ceiling. It was always dark here, and a few old seamen were usually slouched at the tables. They would hang their slickers on pegs by the door.

Kline drank here nearly every afternoon. He would line up beers, and then lay his head in his arms. No one ever spoke to him. They may have been slightly afraid of him, as people are afraid of those who have been badly deformed. But one day, as he was slumped at the table, someone did speak to him. First he heard a soft voice whisper his name. Then the chair across from him scraped back.

He was groggy and at first all he saw was a halo of blond hair. Then he shivered a little, and even smiled. Because he was looking into Julia's eyes, and he could not quite believe it. He might have been emerging from a coma.

"How are you, Robert?" She was wearing a tan raincoat and a blue sweater. Her hands were trembling.

"How am I? What are you doing here? Of all the stinking places—"

"I had to see you. I kept asking, and finally I made them tell me."

"Come to haunt me, huh? You're a damn ghost. Why don't you go home?"

She began to cry. "Robert, I didn't know. They all told me you were dead and Allen was there and he kept on seeing me . . . it just happened."

"Sure, it's just one of those things."

Outside along the beach the fog was shifting. Gulls called but could not be seen. The surf was lapping on the sand. They were walking side by side, her hands inside her raincoat pockets, he holding her shoes. They walked with their heads down. The long silences were filled with the sound of the ocean and the birds.

"You've changed," she said. "You look different."

"Of course I look different."

"They told me about the camp. I'm sorry—"

"Is that what you came to say? I don't need it."

"That's not why I came. I don't know why I came."

Kline frowned. "How's Allen?"

"He's fine, he thinks I'm visiting dad."

"Oh, well, if you came to renew old times, forget it. I never cheat on pals." He didn't smile. "Besides they ruined me, know what I mean? For starters they stick these little glass rods up you, and then they break them. With women they use these little light bulbs. It cramps your style."

She started crying again. "Please, Robert, please don't."

He laid his arm around her shoulder, and they both sagged down to their knees in the cold sand. There was the circling beam of a lighthouse on the rocks across the bay.

"I'll take you back," he finally said, almost gently.

"No, I want to stay with you, I have to explain—"

"You don't have to explain."

"But I do . . . God, you don't know how it's been . . . wondering what happened to you, how you were getting on . . . what you thought about me. And after I heard you were here . . ."

Her ear was pressed against his chest, as though she wanted to hear his heart beat.

178

"It's going to be okay," he murmured, "everything's going to be okay."

"But you don't *understand?* I love you. I've always loved you and I don't love Allen like I love you, I never did. I love you so much it hurts, I swear to God it hurts me. Isn't that a laugh? Can you beat it?"

He kissed her and they got up, then started treading through the sand, crossing an open, windy beach.

In Kline's room the window was raised, and the white curtains were slowly billowing in and out. He unbuckled her raincoat and kissed her again. She was pliant, a little dazed. But when she was naked she glued herself to him. They lay unmoving for a long time. . . .

She stayed with him for three days, and then left. He did not see her to the station. They said good-by on the beach. It was another foggy afternoon. Flocks of gulls stood watching them. She brushed her lips over his and told him that she loved him. He had a notion to say something about Allen, instead he only smiled and said, "We'll get together again. It may not be for a while, but one day . . ."

So the bond was made, and Kline would recall this moment for the rest of his life. He would always remember how her hair had been blowing in her eyes. She was crying.

This was a moment no one believed could ever have taken place. No wonder they never fully understood . . .

Two months after Dusty Yeats had been captured, Humphrey Knolls found a photograph of Robert Kline and Jessie Dancer. They were fixed against a patch of desolate swamp on the outskirts of Bangkok. Dusty Yeats was still undergoing interrogation, and Allen Dancer was still staying in his father's house. No one knew where Jessie was, but it seemed to Knolls that his story was becoming clearer.

CHAPTER SIX

LATER THEY would say that after Humphrey Knolls had entered the name of Robert Kline into his notes the story became so complex for him that he had lost his ability to grasp it fully. They would say that his search then became haphazard, and that he had not been able to disentangle the various threads.

None of this was true.

In fact Knolls knew very well that the three days he had spent looking into the early life of Robert Kline had really been nothing more than an interlude in the larger story of Allen Dancer and Source Magic. Yes, he told himself, one day soon you will have to return to Kline, but essentially it was still Allen's story.

By now Knolls had seen Allen several times. He had seen him

walking through the corridors at Langley, joking with his junior staff in the cafeteria. Allen always ate peaches and cottage cheese and used his fork with deliberation.

Yet one day, not long after Knolls had returned to the Dancer files, he caught the image of another Allen. It was the late afternoon, and Knolls had wandered out across the lawn and into the first line of trees. All things seemed magnified and distinct: the pine needles, the rocks, the green ferns. But clearest of all was the outline of Allen standing on the grassy rise. Humphrey saw him from a distance and stopped. The man was alone.

There was nothing so equivocal in the records as this brooding Allen. In the records there was only a clever, dashing Allen, a young man who's smile never wore out. There were notes in Allen's own sweeping hand that described how he made bold cuts to the enemy's throat. He had the wildest schemes. One involved infecting Hitler's staff with venereal disease. Another had something to do with yellow fever. His program outlines always contained a joke or two. It was 1944 and Allen was having a terrific war.

Records had Allen and Julia living in a boathouse on the shores of Lake Geneva. It was an old timbered house with hardwood floors and blue shuttered Dutch windows. Faces of gnomes had been carved into the wainscot. The curtains were tied back with silk sashes. Rushes grew in the courtyard, and the garden was enclosed by a high hawthorn hedge.

In the evenings Allen and Julia sometimes strolled down to the harbor, where they liked to sit among the gently rocking boats and listen to the sounds of the straining ropes. Allen learned to sail here, and there remains a snapshot of a jaunty, grinning Allen in his captain's cap.

There were many parties, embassy affairs mostly and Allen attended them all. They were his mainstay, his operating theater, because it was within the small talk that he began to cultivate

181

friends among those of the Third Reich who believed that Hitler had to go.

It was a controversial affair that Allen was involved in. Here was an Allied representative openly meeting with Nazis and suggesting that if Hitler were ousted and the war ended, Germany would be permitted an honorable peace. Those opposing Allen's plan called it a kind of treason, but Allen maintained that he was a realist. The war, he would argue, was neither black nor white. It was gray, and there was nothing absolute once you stripped away the propaganda and the emotions. Allen, it was said, treated the Germans as if they were his clients.

Many of the records of this period were preserved by Greyson Dow, who had been acting as Allen's senior. This was to be Dow's last case, and some believed it was what killed him. They said it broke his heart. In truth, however, he had been ill for a long time and when he met Allen by the lake there was already death in his eyes . . .

Greyson Dow and Allen met in the morning about two months after Allen had first come to Geneva. It was a cold morning and Dow was exhausted from an all night flight in from London. He had taken a taxi to Allen's home, and then the two men wandered down to the lake. He wore an old overcoat, clutching it about his throat. His eyes were bloodshot, his voice was dreary when he spoke.

"I saw your father."

"Yes? How is dad?"

"He's well, he sends his best."

"I must write him, it's been too long."

"Yes, that would be nice, I'm sure he'd love to hear from you." From far across the water came a tolling bell. The fog was moving closer. Suddenly the older man said, "Listen to me, Allen. Your father asked me what you were doing here. I didn't tell him, and I don't think you should either. He hates the Nazis, and I don't think he approves of this business."

182

Allen was silent for a moment, then said, "And I suppose you don't approve of this business either, do you?"

Dow shrugged. "The other day I read a memo. Never mind where it came from. It pointed out that International Telephone and Telegraph owns two Focke-Wulf plants. So while ITT bombers are raiding our ships, ITT direction-finders are aiming our guns to shoot those bombers out of the sky. Now yesterday I heard you were dining with the I.G. Farben people. I understand they make the gas for the camps. So no, Allen, I do not approve."

Allen's cheek was lumped into a frown and he was nodding. Finally he said, "I didn't make the game, Greyson. I just play it."

"Yes, Allen. You do play the game."

"Look, what I'm doing here is going to save a lot of lives. Do you have any idea what the Germans are going to throw at us if we have to push across the Rhine? Or can't you bear to look at those figures either?"

"Allen,"—Greyson sighed—"please don't give me the logic of it all. I don't want to hear the logic anymore."

"It's not a question of logic. It's a question of *lives.* And whether you like it or not, Greyson, lives are important."

The old man shook his head. "What's important, Allen, is something called human dignity."

It's age, Allen thought . . . he's just past it . . .

They continued walking until they came to a green bench, where they sat down and continued starting out across the lake. A fog horn was sounding intermittently, mingling with the sound of the tolling bell.

"I've only got an hour," Greyson said abruptly. "I think you'd better just get on with your report."

Allen nodded. "All right. I'm supposed to tell you that these people I've been meeting with want some kind of commitment from Washington and London. They want it in writing. They see themselves as internationalists, and they expect to be treated as such if they play ball with us."

"Internationalists, eh? That's the best one I've heard yet."

"Look, Greyson, I'm telling you they're ready to move. All they want is a commitment."

"Yes, a commitment. Well, you tell them that there will be no commitment. Roosevelt won't go for it, and neither will Churchill. There's also the Russians to deal with, and the Russians don't want to talk peace with any internationalists from Berlin."

"All right, then, there's another way to go. Do you want to hear it?"

Greyson nodded, but said nothing.

"It involves a contact I have. It's someone I met in Spain. He's also in the game. Name is Kurt Lehr."

"I remember," Dow said softly.

"Yes, well, it seems that Lehr is looking for an escape hatch."

"I hate this," Dow whispered. "I don't know how you can deal with it."

Allen ignored him. "I think this Lehr can be useful in getting me to the top. Not just internationalists. Now I'm asking if I can pursue."

Greyson dropped his head. He was staring at his hands. "Frankly, Allen, I don't care what you do. You can climb right to the top of the whole damn dung heap if you like. Just don't ever tell them that I helped you get there."

Allen thought the old man was confusing the issue, thinking that he was talking about getting to the top of the hierarchy of the secret world.

Allen was right—except the old man did not believe he was at all confused.

Greyson Dow died in the fall. He went quietly, in his old bentwood rocker by the window that overlooked the river. He was alone, and the body was not discovered for several days. His papers were collected by some men that the President sent, and

184

in his safe they found his diary, which told about all those early years with the Dancers.

John Dancer attended the funeral, as did others from the secret world, yet the only mention of Dow's involvement was a brief mention in his eulogy that said he had been a patriot. Among the records of the incident was a short letter written by Allen and addressed to Dow's sister. Allen had sent the letter in care of the office where he knew it would be routinely opened and read. He wanted it that way. It was a simple note of condolence and it talked about how close he and Dow had been. It said that Dow had always been his second father, and that Allen would always remember him as such.

With Dow's death it seemed that there was no immediate oversight to Allen's activities, and he began to work unchecked. Three weeks after the funeral he made his first reach into the Abwehr and to Kurt Lehr. There were six more weeks of move and countermove. Allen held a dozen covert meetings with a go-between from the German Embassy. Finally a rendezvous was set for the forest outside of Basel.

Lehr had driven south through the Black Forest and crossed the border at dawn. Allen spent that same night in a white timber room not far from the Wettstein bridge. The maid woke him with coffee and two buttered rolls; all while Lehr sat shivering deep in the forest.

Allen proceeded to a clearing surrounded by pines and oaks, the earth was matted with leaves. Allen climbed the rise and then descended into the grotto. When he entered the circle of trees, Lehr stepped out from behind a mossy oak. There was a chill in the air, and the overhead branches made shadows below. Lehr was wearing gray trousers, baggy and wrinkled. His shirt was stained with perspiration. He had an old trench coat slung over his arm, and his skin looked pasty. It seemed he might have been made of wax.

All he said was, "Hello, Allen." Then he smirked.

185

"Been a long time, Kurt."

"Yes, five years, and you look better than ever. Is that what victory does, make the men handsome and the women beautiful?"

They sat on a fallen log. Lehr had lit a cigarette. He was unshaven, and the white of his eyes was full of red veins. His fingers were stained with nicotine. "I don't even remember what it's like to feel victorious. Isn't it funny how quickly one forgets. It feels like we've been losing for a thousand years."

"It doesn't have to go on, Kurt. Certain arrangements could be made."

"Oh, yes, I've heard about those arrangements of yours."

"A little courage is all it would take."

"A little courage? Then why did you ask for me, Allen? Don't you know that I'm a coward? We're all cowards back in Germany. The brave ones have been killed off. Now there are only cowards and crazy men."

"You don't change history by talking like that."

"Oh, *save* it, Allen. Spare me from it. I'm not trying to change history. I came here to save my own neck. What did you think— I wanted to make love to you again?"

"Shut up, Lehr. Just shut your damn mouth."

"*Ach,* who cares, Allen. We were young then and full of it. The world was beautiful, and we were two bucks"—Allen winced— "listen to me, Allen, I didn't really come here to bait you. I came to make a deal. It's better than this assassination business, much better—"

"You're a damn pig, Lehr, you always have been."

"But a smart pig, Allen, one who understands how the table will be set when the war is over. Now how shall I put it, Allen? Shall I say that I can help you? No. Let me paint a more complete picture. Let me say that when this is over I will have a key for you. It will be the key that you most need. Lo and behold, I will have a key to understanding the Russians!"

"The Russians are our allies," Allen said blandly.

186

"Ah, but for how long? Remember they were briefly ours as well."

"What the hell are you talking about?"

"The future. Our future. They tell you that the Russians are your friends, Allen? Surely you don't believe that. Surely you're too smart to believe it. The Russians are not your friends, the *Germans* are. It's economics, Allen. Everything is economics. Who do you think started this war? Hitler? Of course not. It was started by the bankers, and why do you think they did that? They did it as a prelude to a greater struggle. It's the struggle between the capitalists and the communists. It's God's struggle, for Christ sake," and he started laughing near-hysterically.

When he was quiet again, Allen spoke in that same flat voice. "All right, what is it? What have you got?"

"Papers."

"What kind of papers?"

"Oh, just some papers that the Gestapo entrusted to me to move for them. You see, these papers are very sensitive and it wouldn't do for them to fall into the wrong hands. But I don't think that your hands, Allen, are necessarily the wrong hands. In fact, I've always liked your hands—"

"Get to the point, damn it."

"Ah, the point. The *point* is, Allen, that I've stolen some of our files, and let me simply say that they represent the most detailed and conscientious sort of German work. They were compiled over the years by the very best Gestapo minds. Think of them as an encyclopedia of secret Russian affairs."

"Military?"

"And political. Oh, these papers have everything, Allen. Germans are so meticulous, I think we're the most meticulous people on earth. In fact we're so meticulous, I can't understand how we got to the point of losing the war." He giggled again. "Must have been the Jews, they must have stabbed us in the back again. Isn't that just like them?"

187

"Where are they?"

"I told you, I hid them."

"Where?"

"Ah, first you have to pay the price. Can't have a peek unless you pay the price."

"Well, what's the price?"

"*Ach,* they come so *cheap.* So cheap that you will laugh. You see, Allen, all you have to do to get these files is save one beautiful and charming Nazi boy—me. I'm the price, Allen. Keep me out of the internment camps when the war is over."

"You're right," Allen said. "They—and you—come cheap."

At the end of the war, Allen's stories became particularly tangled among the stories about the secret world. His weekly reports spoke of some vague eleventh-hour negotiations with the last of the fifth-column Nazis, but these reports were not totally believed. More probably, some felt, Allen was once again jockeying for position.

But they were also empty days, days when he got up in the morning and had really nothing to do. He often found himself staring out across the lake, watching the undulating mist. He could stand for hours, fixed at the window in his pajamas. When Julia awoke they usually had something to eat on the terrace if it was not too cold. Their conversations were halting and banal. It had been a long time since either had said anything meaningful to the other.

He did not know how to reach her anymore. She used to talk about having children, but that seemed over. Once he asked her the banality of all banalities—was she happy? They were sitting on the terrace. She was reclining in a rattan chair, wearing plain clothing, gray slacks and a blouse. It was a cloudy morning. Above the lake gray fingers of clouds were rising and falling like a hand that was opening and closing.

He said, "We never talk anymore."

188

She wasn't listening and he had to repeat it.

Then she said, "I know."

"It's been months."

"Has it?"

"It's been as long as I can remember."

"I'm sorry." Except there was no feeling in her voice.

"Has something happened? Is it something I've done?"

"No, Allen. It's nothing you've done."

"Then what is it? Don't you like this place?"

"I don't know. I suppose it's all right."

"You don't seem very happy."

She shrugged, finally said, "I suppose there's something I should tell you."

He felt what was coming like a steel band tightening across his chest.

"It's about when I went to see dad. I also saw someone else. In fact I slept with someone."

"Who?" It seemed as if the word was echoing back from the lake. "Who?"

"Robert Kline."

All he could do was nod. He was slumped over in the chair, his wrists were hanging over the rattan arms. He saw the glassy lake and the human shapes in the clouds. Well, he thought, it was inevitable.

That night Allen walked the strand. He had a few drinks in a hotel bar. The air was heavy and calm. He longed for rain, or wind, or thunder. *Anything* for a change. When he returned he found Julia sitting at the dining table. Her head was in her arms. A slow song was playing on the phonograph. She did not stir when he stepped in. There was just that spinning record playing: *If it wasn't for bad luck, I wouldn't have no luck at all.*

Allen leaned against the doorjamb and stood watching her for a long time. He had always liked the way her hair fell to her

189

shoulders, and now a rectangle of moonlight through the oval window made it look very blond.

Finally he said, "I'll be going away for a while. As soon as the war's over I'll be leaving. I think they're sending me to Berlin."

The phonograph was still playing, the singer's voice still crackling through the speaker. Julia raised her head. Her eyes were red . . . she must have been crying for hours, he thought.

But all she told him now was, "Don't hurt people anymore, Allen. You've got to stop hurting people."

Allen wrote seven petitions from the shores of Lake Geneva, and these too became part of the archives. Each letter was a carefully worded proposal that he be permitted to conduct an appraisal of the captured German intelligence organs. In essence what he asked for was a free hand to interview the Abwehr officers who were being held in Allied prison camps. There was never any mention of Kurt Lehr.

Allen got the job, though there were better qualified men available, and the military already had an existing apparatus for intelligence evaluation. There were, however, few other secret world operatives who wanted to spend the postwar days in a ruined Germany. . . .

Allen reached the Rhine sixty days after the war's end. Already the vines were starting to grow over the dragon's teeth—fallen Stukas, burned-out tanks. . . . On the flight across the Alps he was told that he would soon see something unbelievable—an entire nation laid to waste. But once inside the occupied zone, Allen had the strangest feeling that he had seen it all before. It was like reentering a dream.

He reached Berlin on a windy night and got a room in an old hotel on the edge of the Tiergarten that was now used as the foreign correspondents' villa. No one paid him much attention. There were only a few British journalists living here, and they were drunk all the time. Most of the windowpanes had been shattered and boarded up. It was early spring and the floorboards were scattered with fern seeds.

The first night he could not sleep. He lay in bed for a long time and heard rats scuffling in the walls. Finally he wandered into the dawn. Down the street lay a burned-out Tiger tank. Its paint was scorched, treads mangled and blasted off the drive sprocket. Beyond the tank were mounds of twisted iron and granite slabs. Old people in black were flitting among the debris, hiding in shops that had been looted months ago. Through the window frame of a tenement there was a girl, smiling and beckoning. Then she slipped her sweater down past her shoulder.

Eventually they gave him a jeep so that he could travel from camp to camp in search of Nazi intelligence officers. In between the camps he passed through cities where all the straight lines had turned to jagged rubble. Entire towns were roofless, and ruined factories lay on the horizon. There were stretches when all the sound was gone, as if it had been sucked into the craters.

Allen's status was vague. His papers should have given him the right to roam at will, but sentries kept smirking at his little cardboard pass and the Russians wouldn't let him into their zone at all. Allen had been out of uniform since the OSS had been dissolved, and his trench coat did not count for much. People were rude, or indifferent.

Work did not go well. The prisoners were either defiant or reticent; mostly they did not know anything. There was no sign of Kurt Lehr, and Allen worried that he was dead.

It seemed that the longer he stayed in this city the easier it all was to believe in. One night in a roofless section of the city he picked up a girl. It happened by accident. He had not been looking for one, he had just been wandering through the ruins. Here people lived in tarpaper houses. There was a rumor of typhoid, even the Black Death. He found the girl begging in the doorway of a burned-out dress shop.

She was blond and very young, not more than fourteen years

191

old. She wore a simple frock, gray now, but it must have been white once. The lace had been torn off, but she still knotted the waist with a purple ribbon.

She asked him if he had any chocolate. When he said that he hadn't, she started cursing him.

"You're a creep. You're a fucker creep."

"Where did you learn to talk like that?"

"Where do you think, fucker?"

All around lay splintered wood, slivers of glass, rat droppings, maybe even the bones of a cat.

"I'll tell you what I'll do. You have dinner with me, and afterwards I'll get you that chocolate. How about it? Want some real chow?"

"What do I have to do for it?"

"Nothing, except maybe tell me your name."

"It's Candy."

"No, your real name."

"After we eat."

He took her by the hand, and they moved through the shell-pocked warrens, past heat-fused grills and heaps of powdered brick. He took her to a nightclub, the only place around. Scrap wood benches served as tables. Blue tinsel streamers hung above the bar. There was a welcome sign for Yanks, but only Germans ate here.

By candlelight he saw that she was even younger than she had looked at first, with a perfect child's face and freckles.

"Thirteen," she told him.

"And the English?"

"Father taught me, because the cards told him that you were going to win the war and he wanted to be ready."

"Cards?"

"You know, the Gypsy cards." She pantomimed laying down the Tarot.

They ate blood sausage and pumpernickel. Prostitutes were

192

lingering in the back of the room. Allen ordered another beer. The waitress had dark, deep circles under her eyes, but the child's eyes were clever and bright. He also noted the way she kept wetting her lips.

"Where do you live?" he asked.

"Oh, lots of places." She was sawing away at her sausage. "I could live with you, if you want."

"What about your father?"

"Bombed."

"Mother?"

"All bombed. I was in school at the time."

"I'm sorry."

She shrugged. "Well? Do you want me to?"

"Want you to what?"

"To live with you?"

"I don't even know your name. You promised that when you ate—"

"Lise."

"Why, that's a pretty name. You should be proud of that name."

"Look, do you want me to or not?"

"God, you're just a kid."

"So what? I'll let you spank me."

Outside there were more ash images, camouflage nets burned into the concrete. All the doors had been blown off. The stucco was riddled with shrapnel. Allen and the child were walking slowly past puddles of black water.

"Now you have to tell me," the girl said. "I either go with you now, or I go my own way."

Ahead was a small park, but the foliage of the trees and hedges had been vaporized by incendiaries. Now there were only charred sticks.

"I'll do anything you want," the girl was saying. "You can be nice. You can spank me, anything you want . . ."

193

Allen just kept staring at the withered trees. Then he said, "All right, but just for tonight."

All through the streets he did not touch her, but when they climbed the stairs to his room he let her go ahead so that he could look at her legs. Once inside his room she began inspecting the walls and the furniture. She even fingered his cufflinks on the dresser. There were water stains on the ceiling, cigarette burns on the carpet.

Allen sat with his legs apart. There was a bottle of whiskey at his feet, a glass in his hand. No sounds came from the rooms below. It was nearing midnight.

The girl had washed and brushed her hair. She was stepping towards him, framed by the boarded-up window.

"Don't feel guilty," she told him. "If it hadn't been you, it would have been someone else."

The girl stayed with him for three weeks. He did not really understand her at all. At times she was just a little girl who desperately needed to be loved. At other times it seemed she would slit a throat for a chocolate bar. Once he gave her a wad of bills and she came back with an old moleskin coat, miles too big. He did not dare ask what she had done with the rest of the money.

In the end he was saved by a telegram from the Frankfurt intelligence unit. The message was cryptic. Someone was merely asking for him in Oberursel, but he had no doubt it was Kurt Lehr. After he read the telegram he shredded it and walked on through the shabby villa hallway. The Englishmen were drinking in the kitchen. When he entered his room he found the child curled up on the sofa, wrapped in the moleskin coat. As he crossed the room to kiss her, the floorboards moaned and she woke. There was fear in her eyes for an instant.

"Looks like it's over," he said.

She understood immediately. She must have been through it all before.

194

"I'll give you some money, and maybe when I get back . . ."

"Don't make promises," she said.

She had drawn her legs up to her chest, exposing her slim thighs. Her fingers were laced around her knees. No matter how old she sometimes sounded her hands always told him she was just a child.

Finally she said, "When do I have to go?"

"Oh, Lise, don't put it like that. It's not that I want you to go. It's just that—"

"When?"

"Tomorrow I suppose. Is that all right?"

She nodded, and there was no trace of emotion in her face.

"But look," he said cheerfully. "I'll take you out for a real fancy dinner tonight, how's that?"

"Sure, but if you want to touch me afterwards, you'll have to pay extra."

That night he could not help groping for her under the sheets. She tried to push him away, but she did not have the strength. He had never had any trouble before. Then he turned her belly down and yanked her panties off, but when he had her arms pinned and his mouth on her's, something happened that had never happened before. Not this way, in any case . . . Guilt started washing all over him, as if an artery had suddenly popped in his head, and he couldn't help saying, "What the hell am I *doing?*"

In the end he wrapped her tightly in the blankets, and cradled her all through the night. In the morning she left him with her first honest kiss, while he gave her all the money he could find.

Allen left for Oberursel at noon. He drove the backstreets to avoid the convoys. The mud across the cobblestones was so thick that it reflected the sky. On the outskirts of Berlin there were ruins that no one had bothered to clear. Birds flew in and out of broken windows. There were whole stretches of charred dirt covered with

195

fused glass and metal shavings. But beyond the city there was the scent of pines in full blown summer.

He reached the camp in the early evening. There were white-topped guard towers, barracks, coils of barbed wire; all against a rose-colored sky. A stone wall looked so brittle he thought he could kick it down, but inside the prison the bare bulbs turned everything solid again. There were nearly fifty yards of concrete tunnel. He met a sergeant who asked if he wanted a sandwich.

"I got salami. I got canned meat. How about it?"

"Uh, no thanks. Just the prisoner, if you please."

"Suit yourself."

A generator was humming somewhere. The tailgate of a big truck dropped. When they reached the cell block, the sergeant started fumbling with his keys.

"They used to keep the Jews in here," he said.

"Sure," Allen muttered. "The Jews."

Then the cell door opened. Allen stepped inside and there was Lehr, shirtless, stretched out on a straw pallet, a wad of dirty blankets wrapped around his feet.

"Ah"—Lehr grinned—"I see my knight in shining armor."

"How are you?" Lehr looked more like a fish than ever, a whitefish that had been tossed on the deck.

"When can I get out of here?"

"They're fixing the papers now."

"And I want a bath, and I want some clothes."

Lehr's eyes were puffed up. There was a bucket in the corner, a roll of coarse toilet paper on the floor. A little light fell through the bars in parallel lines.

"We'll spend the night in Frankfurt," Allen said. "Then I'll want the files."

"What files, I don't have any files."

Allen said nothing. He had not moved since he had entered the cell. His hands were in his pockets. All day he had been smelling traces of Lise's perfume.

196

"Okay"—Lehr smiled—"no more jokes for you. Do you have a rugged vehicle?"

"A jeep."

"Good, because we'll have to go deep into the forest, and high into the mountains."

"Don't fuck with me."

"Allen, what do you take me for? I had to hide everything."

"Where?"

"Bavaria."

"Where exactly?"

Lehr grinned again like that rat that he resembled. "You know the walls of these cells have ears, Allen."

Allen and Lehr took a southern route along the Alpine road through Munich and into Wolfratshausen. Then somewhere in the forest they stopped and tramped three miles off the road. It was early afternoon when they started digging, and it was growing dark when they finished. The files had been packed into three large trunks, lined with waxed canvas to protect the papers.

By midsummer Allen had been given a large estate on the outskirts of Berlin. It was an old stone house with a large garden. Iron bars were fitted to the windows, and there were double locks on the doors. Nine weeks were spent translating and decoding. Allen served as project leader, and his staff was German. They worked long hours, and Allen would say later that he had been driven by an overwhelming sense that something vital lay within those files. Yet this was not the whole truth, because Allen had never really had a mind for silent work and left it mainly up to Lehr.

It was autumn when Lehr first began to grasp the meaning that lay within those files. By now he looked like a ghost. Entire days had passed when he had not left the basement where the files were kept. He slept in a corner, on a filthy cot by an old water heater.

He shaved erratically in a rusty basin. He ate whatever was brought to him and never complained.

On the afternoon that Lehr had made his breakthrough with the files, he called Allen and the two wandered out into the estate's gardens. The air was chilled with the first hint of winter. Far across the city came the sounds of heavy construction. Berlin was being rebuilt.

They walked slowly along the dirt path until they reached an ornamental fountain, now dry and caked with sulfur. Lehr sat down on the fountain's rim. "If I died right now you would never know what is contained within those documents. Did you ever consider that, Allen?"

Allen didn't answer, waited.

There were odors of woodsmoke and decay. Above the garden walls and tangled vines was the top of a pulverized tower.

"I feel faint," Lehr was saying softly. "I believe I'm destroying my health for you."

"Let's hope it's not for nothing."

Lehr suddenly smiled again. "Oh it's not for nothing, Allen. You've definitely got your money's worth."

"All right, what is it?"

"Please, Allen, I can't just tell you like that. You must understand the full sequence here. You must understand the background. These files of mine are not merely a collection of documents. They are a story, a complex story with many levels of meaning."

"I could send you back to that camp in a minute—"

"Oh, Allen, when will you learn to love me?"

Allen turned his back on Lehr to look out over the tops of the vines to the burnt roofs of the neighboring houses and the tangle of drooping telephone wires.

Suddenly Lehr said, "Does the term self-serving mean anything to you?"

"What?"

198

"Self-serving, Allen. What does it mean in terms of an intelligence operation? How would you define it?"

"I don't know what you're getting at."

"Self-serving, Allen. It means that the overall objectives of an operation are only to serve the individual, not the nation."

"What are you talking about?"

"I'm talking about the files, Allen. I'm talking about how they show the existence of a self-serving relationship between someone inside the Kremlin and someone in Washington."

Allen sat down on the fountain's rim next to Lehr. He had taken a cigarette from his coat pocket but did not offer one to Lehr. The hollow sound of clanging metal was ringing in from far across the city.

"You'd better start from the beginning."

"Yes, the beginning." Lehr smiled. "Okay. According to the files three years ago the Gestapo caught a Soviet spy. It took them three days to break him. They used water to do it. The interrogation report runs about two hundred pages, but there is a short report that runs only about twenty pages. Consequently no one bothers to read the long report, which was a great mistake because in that long report the Russian talks about a certain arrangement between a Soviet intelligence officer and an American intelligence officer. It is an unauthorized, secret arrangement. They call it The Room, and it's dirty. It's very dirty."

"What do you mean?"

"Oh, it happens occasionally. One giving to the other. The Russian helps the American, the American helps the Russian. They both look very good and proper, while those around them look very bad."

"How would it work?"

"It could work many different ways, but essentially they trade material to one another. The Russian gives the American a speech of Stalin's in exchange for one of Truman's, or what have you. The point is that they trade. They give and take between them."

199

"Are you sure about all this?"

"Yes."

"So what do we do?"

"That's up to you, Allen. However, if I were in your position I would keep it to myself for the time being."

"What do you mean?"

"Well, let's say that you write it all up and turn it in to your superiors. Where would that leave you? They would give you a pat on the back and that would be the end of it. But let's say we were to track these people down ourselves. Then we could blackmail them into working for us. Do you see what I'm saying? We could turn this operation into our own tool."

"You're out of your mind—"

"But, Allen, you're the one who wanted a line into Moscow. Well, now I've got you one."

"I don't play that way, I'm not like you. I've got certain . . . principles."

"Of *course* you do, Allen. You're a real man of principle."

Allen looked away, then said, "All right, but we play it my way. Is that totally understood? You don't make a move without checking with me first."

"Of course, Allen, not a move." And he raised his arm in a Nazi salute.

A new phase began. Allen dismissed everyone, so it was finally just he and Lehr. The basement was vast, but the furthest reaches were dark. Only the actual work space was lit by a bare bulb and gooseneck lamp. Junk had been pushed into the corners—old chairs, trunks of clothing, scrap timber, brass and sofas—all infested with termites. There was no ventilation, and the dust never settled, just hung there in the spray of light.

There were despairing nights, nights when the files seemed to lead them nowhere. Then the depression became acute, and Allen would sit and stare at nothing for minutes on end. In the worst hours he talked about Julia, told Lehr that he missed her terribly. The German did not hear him.

The final stretch lasted two days and two nights. More files were brought in, not German ones but Washington estimates of Soviet probes into Berlin. Most of the material was dated, but this did not matter. Lehr was only interested in seeing how much the Americans officially knew. By now he was drawing links from small notations, watching for what had been missed.

Finally he found it. It was shortly after dawn, and Allen had been half-asleep. One arm lay across his face to block out the light. He had been seeing images of rattlesnakes.

Lehr said only, "I've got it. Allen? Here it is."

Allen rolled over. "What?"

"Come here."

"No . . . just tell me."

"It's in the dates, Allen. They're starting to add up."

"I don't know what the hell you're talking about."

"Time, Allen. Time is continuous. There's no end to it."

"No end to what?"

"To the link. Our fellow in Washington and our fellow in Moscow. They're still trading material back and forth. Look here. I have the sequence. It's all right here. It's in the gap between the inflow and the outflow."

Finally they went out in the streets. It was dawn, and they walked past ruins now hung with scaffolding. Women were digging trenches. Black water pipes were stacked along the curbs. From beyond the piles of rubble came the diminishing cadence of a work detail.

"Things move from east to west," Lehr said. "I think they move by hand, pieces of paper, little packages. Each one is carried by a man or a woman, just anyone in this sea of people. Maybe that woman over there, maybe that man, maybe someone you see on a train."

Down the street two boys were prowling through piles of gar-

201

bage that lined the pulverized curb. Beyond lay jagged ruins and patches of bare earth.

"What did you say it was called?" Allen asked.

"The Room," said Lehr. "They call it The Room."

"And you think we can trace it from here?"

"Yes. It can be traced from here."

"But what if I wanted to work from Washington. Couldn't we intercept it in Washington?"

"What's wrong, Allen? Don't you like Berlin?"

Allen frowned but kept on talking. "We know there's a man in Washington. Why not try and tag it there?"

"Because people will see what you're doing, and they'll start asking questions. You can't hide in Washington. You can only hide in Berlin."

"All right, but how long will it take?"

"I don't know. What's it matter?"

"The more time it takes, the greater the risk. I can't keep stringing them along forever."

"Why not? You think Washington is smart? They don't know anything. Every week I'll give you something to send them. It'll keep them happy."

"But how long?"

"I don't know. Maybe six months."

"Six months?"

"Well, what did you think? These things take time."

Berlin remained disjointed that winter. When the rubble had been cleared there were vast, empty spaces left, entire streets where the buildings had been leveled and there was nothing to stop the wind. In many quarters there were only minimal signs of life: notices stuck to the wall, advertising shelter, old clothes, lost people. No one knew where all the paper had come from, but the spidery notes were blown all over the city.

By now Allen's operation had been integrated into the Central

Intelligence Group, but it meant nothing. His reports were passed along until they were filed and forgotten. His seniors kept changing, and most of the time Allen did not know what was happening back in Washington. But then Washington did not know what was happening with Allen in Berlin. None of his reports ever mentioned anything about a secret link between an American intelligence officer and a Russian one.

In the early winter Allen and Lehr left the basement of their operations house and moved out into the field. On the first morning of their hunt they met in a small cafe near the Tiergarten. It had been their first meeting in over seventeen days. Allen had just returned from England and two weeks with Julia. She was living with her father now. The marriage was in limbo.

When Allen entered the cafe he found Lehr lounging at a laminated table on the glassed-in terrace. The German wore a faintly iridescent suit, blue suede shoes and a burgundy tie. Allen told him that he looked like a pimp, and Lehr laughed. The recently rebuilt cafe was painted in bright colors. Students chatted at the tables.

Through the glass lay a view of the construction sights. Steel girders rose out of mud flats. Cement blocks and iron rods lined the half-paved streets. There were fiberboard shops and groves of blackened trees.

"As soon as it gets cold, you watch and see them cut down those trees for firewood," said Lehr. He was smiling.

"You really love your people, don't you?"

"Naturally. I've always been a patriot. How's your wife?"

A plump blond girl brought them plates of greasy ham and powdered eggs. The coffee was sour and there was no sugar. From the tangle of surrounding German voices came a broken English phrase . . . *I'm so tired I couldn't clap my hands at a rat.*

Lehr ate delicately, slicing off small bites of ham, chewing them slowly. Finally he said, "I've done a little work while you were away. I believe I know where to begin now."

203

"I told you not to go charging around on your own."

"Yes, of course, Allen, but tomorrow night we meet a friend of mine. His name is Otto Krugger. You'll like him. He's a fine citizen. Old Waffen SS. Used to eat Russian children for breakfast. Your people would take to him—"

"You're a creep, Lehr, you know that? You're a real creep."

"Ah, but, Allen, this Otto Krugger used to work for The Room. He was one of the couriers. Now haven't I been a good boy?"

Allen Dancer did not reply.

Otto Krugger was built like a wrestler—squat, with a low forehead and dark pinpoint eyes. He lived in one of the roofless apartment blocks. When Allen and Lehr entered the cement shell they found Krugger bent over a fire. The carcass of a dog was turning on a spit. Krugger seemed embarrassed.

Lehr nodded at Allen, then said to Krugger, "This is the man I told you about, Otto. I want you to tell him what you told me."

Krugger scowled at the burned carcass, then said, "They call it *ein Zimmer.* The House."

"No, it's Room in English. The Room."

"Okay. It's called The Room, and it's a network. Very secret. Not too many know about it. Very dangerous to get too close."

"Where does it run, Otto?"

"From east to west, and west to east. Sometimes through Switzerland, sometimes through Turkey."

"And Berlin?" Lehr said softly.

"Yes, Berlin too."

"And what's the product, Otto?"

"Product?"

"You know. What do they send through the network, The Room?"

"Lots of things. Military, political. Lots of things."

"And when did it start?"

Krugger shook his head. "No one knows. It's just been going

204

a long time. Maybe before the war. Things move from east to west and then back the other way."

"Tell me about the other way." Allen said.

"Yes, sometimes they bring it out of Moscow, and sometimes they bring it out of America. Always it goes through The Room. The Room is special. The Russians have many networks that spy on the Americans, and the Americans have many networks that spy on the Russians. But The Room is special. The Room is the only network that spies on both."

"A trade-off," Lehr said.

"Yes, a trade-off. Both sides give to each other. The Russians think they win. The Americans think they win, but both really lose. Everyone loses, everyone except the masters of The Room."

"And who are they?" Allen said.

Krugger dropped his eyes. His head was set at a strange angle . . . he might have been facing a gale. "I don't know," he said. "No one knows."

Now all three men were watching the fire. The carcass had begun to sag on the spit. One flank was charred, the other still raw.

"What's he scared of?" Allen said suddenly to Lehr.

"What do you think?"

Krugger was still motionless. His elbows were pressed against his ribs. He was clutching his coat. Finally he said, "I'm not scared, I'm just cold."

"He means," Lehr said, "that he can't get back inside the network. They won't trust him anymore."

"But will he show us the door?"

Lehr smiled. "Look at it this way, Allen . . . we come knocking at The Room, they'll know someone talked and they could easily run it down to Otto. And Otto's a big boy. He could take a long time to die, if you see what I mean?" He looked at the dog on the spit.

"What if we get him out of here? We'll give him some money and a passport."

Lehr shook his head. "He doesn't trust you, Allen. Do you, Otto?"

Throughout this exchange Krugger had remained lumpy and wooden. Now his eyes were very dark. He was staring at the fire. "I'm cold," he said, "I'm very cold."

"Of course you are," Lehr told him. "I know how it gets, but will you give it a try, Otto? Will you try and get back inside The Room?"

"Tell him we'll make it worth his while financially—"

"Shut up, Allen. How about it, Otto? Will you make a play for The Room? Just one little play?"

Krugger finally nodded and said that he would, but he looked very frightened, and sad.

When Lehr and Allen left, Krugger did not stir. Down the corridor there were no sounds but their footsteps echoing through the honeycomb of deserted rooms.

The Room soon became an obsession for Allen. By midwinter he could not even speak the name without envisioning some vast interlocking network. He kept imagining a thousand people, clerks, prostitutes, bellboys, postmen—all linked together by The Room.

But deeper in the center, closer to the truth, there was Lehr. Weeks would pass when Allen hardly saw him. Then he would suddenly appear. Sometimes he looked ragged, strung out on coffee, cigarettes and maybe even Methedrine. At other times he was as sleek as any Berlin pretty boy grown rich off the black market. He never told Allen what he was doing, and if Allen asked him he would sidestep the questions. Finally he telephoned one afternoon and said that they were ready to move.

Allen again met him in the Tiergarten. By now the charred patches were green. Beech trees had been replanted, and the paths were clean again. The two men walked between the new shoots of flowers until they came to a patch of unrestored ground. Here there were clumps of dead brush, broken glass and rusting tin, and the skull of a horse.

Lehr had torn off a flower's head and was stripping the petals one by one. "I think tonight is the night," he said.

"What do you mean?"

"I mean that tonight we get our first glimpse of what's in The Room. Otto fixed it. He's back with them. He started yesterday. He picked up a briefcase from Dresden. Tonight he leaves it in a shop a few miles from here. We will have about twenty minutes to photograph its contents."

There was the heavy throb of a turbine from far across the city.

Allen was silent for a moment, then said, "Why the hell didn't we trace the line from Dresden?"

"Because Dresden is a dangerous city, and Otto didn't feel like risking his life for you. Do you blame him?"

"So now we're taking all the risks, is that it?"

Lehr shrugged. "Are you scared, Allen?"

Later there were drifts of rain moving through the city, and darker clouds churning in from the east. Allen spent the remainder of the day with Lehr. He did not want to be alone. That night they walked down the Bismarck-Strasse, Lehr gnawing on a roll and a dry sausage. The streets were half-deserted. Only a few desperate loiterers were out in defiance of curfew . . . girls cadging pfennigs, and for a mark they would take you behind a wall. The cobblestones were slick with drizzle.

They reached the Jacobistrasse and an old slum that had survived the street-fighting. Lehr walked so quickly that Allen could scarcely keep up. They passed beneath an archway and into a hollow courtyard. Each wall had faint traces of painted letters: *Erster-Hof, Zweiter-Hof, Dritter-Hof.* Lehr read them by matchlight, then grinned and crouched down to the gutter.

An hour passed. It was bone cold. Then came footsteps clapping on the stairs. Shadows moved among the masonry and the burning tip of a cigarette swept back and forth.

"He's done it," Lehr whispered. "Otto." Then he rose and yanked Allen's sleeve. They moved up a flight of stairs and along the balcony. Every window they passed was black, but all had human smells coming from them. The iron railing had fallen away. Chunks of plaster were missing from the walls. Lehr, stopping at the last door, pressed his ear against the wood, then pushed. The hinges strained on the rotting jamb.

Inside, straw was scattered on the brick floor. Moonlight fell through the rafters where the roof had been torn away. A table, a chair, and the fainter outline of the thin briefcase wavered in the blackness.

"Who lives here?" Allen whispered.

"No one."

Lehr groped forward, then kneeled and began fumbling with the briefcase lock. The latch clicked, and he bent closer.

Now the darkness seemed to be solidifying. Allen saw only jerky motions, Lehr's fingers digging through wads of shredded paper. Scraps of paper were fluttering out of the briefcase.

"We'd better get out of here," Lehr said.

Allen touched the shreds of torn newsprint. The briefcase had been packed with them.

"Get out now," Lehr whispered. *"Now."*

It was a blind sprint back along the alley, down the steps. Allen kept trying to grab hold of Lehr's coat and once he skidded into a patch of grease and ripped his trousers. He kept on running.

Finally they stopped, panting, beneath a mildewed arch.

"What happened?"

"Blown." Lehr told him the obvious. "We were blown."

"How? Otto?"

"I don't know."

"Maybe it wasn't meant for us." Allen's knees were starting to hurt badly. He was ready to slump to the gutter. "Maybe it was just a dry run for Otto."

208

"No"—Lehr sighed—"we've been blown. They know who we are."

"So it is Otto?"

"No. Otto wouldn't do this to us."

"Well, who the hell else could have done it?"

"Don't ever assume anything, Allen. Don't ever."

Down along the alley candlelight glowed from under doorways and board-shuttered windows. They tramped slowly now. Wind was blowing, rippling through pools of rainwater.

Lehr was speaking, but he might have been in a trance . . . "Tonight a briefcase passed along The Room, it should have been filled with documents . . . Russian war game reports, that's what it should have been filled with . . . instead we find only newspapers . . . so what can we surmise, Allen? What? What can we think . . . ?"

"My knee's a bloody mess," Allen said. "I think it's going to need stitches. That's what I think."

The narrow streets were winding and descending. They were moving through swirling drizzle. No sounds came from the tenements now.

Past an abandoned factory Allen said, "I suppose I don't have to tell you that it's over."

"Of course, you hurt your knee, so now it's over."

"I mean it. You had your chance. We played it your way. You messed up, and now it's over. I want a primary brief to send back to Washington. I'll want it in two days, and make damn sure it's documented."

"They won't believe you, Allen. They have no vision."

"What the hell do you know?"

Lehr smiled. "I've known them all, Allen. Known them all. They sit behind their desks and read reports. The world to them is just a little map on the wall with those little colored pins stuck in it. And that's all you are to them, Allen. You're just a little colored pin in the dot which marks Berlin."

"Shut up."

"And one day someone shoots you, and then they pull out your pin and drop it in a box. And that's the end of Al Dancer. So I come to you and give you a chance to have your own map and your own little pins. That's exactly what I've done for you, Allen. The Room is power. You take over The Room, and they'll never be able to say that you're just a pin. That's what power is, Allen. It's running both sides of the game. It's giving here, and taking there. It's playing both sides from the middle. And what do you do?"

"I said shut up."

On an empty corner the wind had died. There was only the silent drizzle, and low fog drifting through the broad, deserted street.

"Good-by Allen," said Lehr softly.

Then he turned and Allen saw him floating away. Hard angles of walls looked like clay in the mist. Lehr was framed against a row of blasted columns.

Allen was fixed on the corner. One hand was curling around a blacked-out lamp post. Lehr was moving slowly down the center of the shattered street. Then Allen heard the engine, and the squealing tires. It was a big car, and Allen thought vaguely about the new Buicks. The headlights threw long spears that diffracted in the drizzle, and Lehr was a perfect silhouette in the yellow. He tried to spin away, but the car picked him up and tossed him higher than the shaved columns. The car was already gone when he fell to the pavement.

Allen ran to Lehr and knelt down next to him. They were both wheezing.

"Don't talk," Allen kept saying, "don't try to talk."

Lehr's lips kept opening and closing. Blood was coming out of his mouth. "I've got to tell you . . . come closer . . ."

Somehow their hands had clasped together.

210

"Listen, Allen, listen to me, I lied to you . . . east end, the east end of The Room . . ."

"What? What, Kurt?" The name he hadn't used since Hitler died. "Kurt?"

"I know who's at the east end, I know, the east end of The Room . . . Listen, Allen, it's so big you'd never have guessed . . ."

"All right, Kurt."

"Then *say* it."

"Say what?"

"The name of the man at the east end. It's Servana. It's Valentin Servana."

So Allen said it too. "Valentin Servana." . . .

Kurt Lehr fell into a coma and lived for three days more. Allen must have spent thirty hours at the hospital, although he hardly knew what he was doing. He just sat by the bed and watched Lehr's face, listened to him breathe. On the last night he thought he saw Lehr's eyelids flutter and his fingers reach for something just past the sheets. Allen called out his name but Lehr died anyway, the internal bleeding too massive for the doctors to stop. . . .

Allen arranged the burial himself, and nobody attended. It was a pretty shabby funeral, but Allen did not know what else to do. The parson was senile. He thought that Lehr had been Allen's brother.

Afterward Allen caught a military air transport west. Below there was a greening countryside, and time-softened outlines of earthworks and villages that had been abandoned during the war. Julia met him at the bus. She wore an old flannel coat and those familiar yellow Wellingtons. She must have sensed that something bad had happened. Before their greetings had always been formal, strained. This time she accepted him into her arms.

They had supper with Julia's father. The old man had never really liked Allen, and the years had made it worse. Tonight he

211

looked like a white monkey. He kept mumbling into his food, rattling his teacup. He asked Allen why he was fraternizing with the Germans.

Later Allen and Julia walked along the beach. There was no light except the glowing sea and a rift in the clouds where some stars shone. A few curlews shrieked from the seaweed washed up on the crumbling walls.

"I won't be staying here long," Allen told her.

"You never do."

"But it's nearly over. Really it is."

"You've said that before."

"But this time I mean it. I can't tell you the details. You've just got to trust me."

"Why do you do it, Allen?"

"It's important, you know that."

"No, I don't know it. I don't know that it's important at all. In fact sometimes I think it's silly. You make it all up. You actually make it up. Communism. Capitalism. You people, both sides, make it up because you can't live without it . . . it gives you a purpose. You can pretend you're still important. It's stupid, I think . . ."

Beyond the breakers lay black rocks. A clump of seaweed looked like a body that had come in with the tide.

They walked in silence for a while. Then Allen said, "A friend of mine was killed last week. They ran him down with a car."

He had been waiting days to say it. He had even rehearsed the line.

She said only, "Does that happen often?"

"Often enough."

"Well, that makes it all the more stupid."

"But what if it had been me that they killed? How would you feel?"

"Lord, Allen, don't be maudlin. How the hell do you think I'd feel?"

212

Further down the strand lay sandy hillocks of tufted grass. The tide was turning in bars of moonlight.

Suddenly she said, "That friend of yours, who was he?"

"A German boy. A good fellow. You would have liked him."

"Why did they kill him?"

"What difference does it make?"

"I want to know, that's all. Why did he have to die?"

"Because he knew too much. It's always for the same reason."

She bit her lip. "Well, I think that's stupid, a stupid waste." She was gazing out across the sea to the black rocks.

Later that night he told her that he was about to do something that would change everything. He said that he would be gone a few months, but when he returned their lives would be set. She asked him again and again to tell her what it was he was about to do. Finally he said that he was going to hunt down two men, two men that were making a shambles of the secret world he cared about. Mocking it, betraying everyone.

After he said this she moved to the window. Down the hall her father was sleeping. She drew aside the curtains to see the ocean once more. Then she told him to grow up and stop acting like a cowboy.

Years later Allen Dancer would look back and say that this was the end of his beginning. He returned to Berlin, arrived on a night of blown rain. His breath was white on the air. Already there were some new brick monoliths. Everytime he saw this city he would return to find that it had changed.

He was alone now in his rickety house. There were only the guards from the Central Zone Command, two kids from Texas who spoke only to each other. They probably hated CIG duty, couldn't understand why they had to watch a bunch of old papers. Once a week an officer from the section intelligence board dropped by—a dry, cold man. He and Allen usually walked in the garden out of fear of microphones. There were no formal debriefings.

Allen would just ramble on about whatever came to his mind. The officer probably knew much of what was said was a lie but he did not care. He was just putting in time.

Allen spent many hours in the files, though he was never as deft with them as Lehr had been. Still, he was able to follow the signs. At the end of a month he was ready to pick up where Lehr had left off.

There was fog lingering against the stucco walls. Light from the new street lamps caught the raindrops on grimy windows. Allen met Otto Krugger down by the river, and for the first time in his career he carried a gun. It was a Walther PPK. They were the fashion, everyone in the trade carried them.

Krugger was waiting by the river wall. He wore the same drab coat. A dirty muffler was knotted at his throat. A knit cap was pulled down over his ears. His thick features were chapped and red. He looked more beaten than ever.

"I thought maybe you wanted to shoot me," Krugger said. "Because maybe you blame me for Kurt getting killed—"

"No, Otto, I don't blame you—"

"Because I didn't do it. Kurt was my friend, okay? I wouldn't do anything like that. That's all I got now is friends. Nothing else. I just got friends."

"What about me?" Allen forced a smile. "You want to be my friend?"

Krugger dropped his bullet head. "I don't know what you mean."

"I'm offering you a job, Otto. I want you to run interference for me."

"What do you mean?"

"To drive for me, to shoot for me. I need someone like you, someone with a little stick."

"My arm's not too good anymore. You know, I hurt my arm."

"I think you'll be all right. How about it? We pick up where

214

Kurt left off. There'll be some travel, some good money. I'll get you some new clothes."

Krugger turned and laid his hands on the wall. Below him oozed the slow water. The oil slicks reflected the light. There were no sounds but the lapping water.

Krugger was still staring down at it when he asked, "Where did you bury Kurt, Mr. Dancer?"

"In that little place near the Spandauer Damm. He's on the rise as you enter. I didn't know if he had a family. There was a notice, but no one came."

"I didn't see any notice," Krugger said. "No one told me."

"I'm sorry, Otto. I didn't think of it at the time."

Behind them lay a brick labyrinth of ruined shops. Barbed wire had been coiled into doorways to keep out street gangs. All Berlin still smelled of ash, sour cabbage and disinfectant. Money had no relationship to what it could buy.

"So how about it?" Allen prodded. "You want the job?"

Krugger did not look at him as he said, "They know who I am now. I can't get back inside the network, The Room."

Allen nodded. "We'll be playing it from the outside, so you won't have to get back in."

"And I don't know much. I only had one contact and I only saw him twice. The last time, he gave me that stuff. Then Kurt got killed."

"You were set up," Allen said softly. "We were all set up. Kurt just happened to have taken the fall, but it could have happened to any one of us. But now it's over and I'm just saying we should get on with it. How about it?"

Krugger shrugged. "What the hell, huh? What the hell?"

"Does that mean yes, Otto?"

"Yes. I'll shoot for you. I'll drive for you, you just tell me what to do. What the hell."

215

And then Krugger smiled, a lumpy smile, the smile of a man in search of a friend, in need of a master.

Now Allen's life became a single journey. All movement pointed to one end, but there was no single path. From Lehr's files and notes he made a list of people. Most were long shots, men on the fringe of Soviet networks, black market operators, washed-out Abwehr officers. They were scattered all over. . . .

Allen and Krugger drove into the Russian zone as far as Leipzig in an old Mercedes. Then the engine block cracked, and they took a train across the Baltic plain through marshland and brown villages. Krugger rarely spoke.

Some nights they spent on the road in open fields of high grass. There were also wooded stretches, and the fog lingered in the hollows. There were lost, unmilked cows crying along the highway.

With a north wind they came to a slow-withering city. There were hardly any children or young men left. The sign above the city gate, in burned bulbs and empty sockets, read *Zwölfkinder*. The sun caught long streaks of rust.

They found a room in a run-down hotel. The girl behind the desk was drunk. She made a fuss over their identity papers. There was only one bed and the mattress smelled of lice killer. Wind sounded through doorless corridors and voices came mingling from the other side of the walls.

In the morning they found a cellar cafe, drank coffee and ate black bread, then walked to the village square, where they were to meet a man. He was waiting for them under a sheet metal awning. He was thin and freckled, and when he stepped out into the sunlight all he said was, "Are you the one?"

Allen nodded. As always Krugger stood behind him and to his side. "Kurt Lehr sent me," Allen said.

"Kurt Lehr is dead. Don't stuff me with lies. You write me seven days ago and say you'll be here in three days. Every morning

216

I wait for you, so don't lie to me."

"I'm sorry, Dorum"

"And my name isn't Dorum. You got that wrong too. It's just Fritz. Okay? Fritz."

They began walking, Krugger following behind, and moved out of the sun and into the darker, cobbled streets.

Fritz coughed, then said, "So you're looking for The Room, huh?"

"Yes, we're looking for The Room."

"But you come to me and you don't even know me. You get my name off some old list, and you want to ask me about The Room. I think you're crazy. Your friend is stupid and you're crazy. Kurt would have never done anything like this."

"Kurt's dead," Allen intoned.

"Naturally Kurt's dead, but you're crazy. I don't know what's worse."

Fritz wore an old sailor's coat, but he did not look like he had ever been to sea He was pale and had thin, razor lips. Some of his blond hair fell in thin strands over his forehead.

"How many have you seen before me?" he asked suddenly.

"What's it matter?" Allen said.

"I want to see how crazy you are, and how safe I am. Every time you mention The Room to someone you take a chance. Did you know that?"

"I've seen about four," Allen said. "I've been all over Germany."

"And no one talks, right? So what makes you think I'll talk?"

Allen squinted. "It's like this, Fritz. It's stick and carrot. You know that expression? There's American dollars if you help, and nothing if you don't. But if you turn on me, Otto here will kill you."

Fritz smiled. "You got my name off the records, but the records are out of date. I don't have any connection with the organization anymore. Sure, I used to carry a little product, but that was during

217

the war. Now the whole world is crazy. You fit right in."

They had reached a courtyard ringed with tenements. Overhead were fraying wires. A dog slept in a doorway. There were no other signs of life.

They sat down on the edge of a dry well, now planked over to keep the children from falling in.

"Some of it I know," Allen said. "Some I don't. There's a hundred dollars for every piece of information that you give me."

"You're going to get us killed," Fritz said. "You're touching open wounds."

"There are two men," Allen persisted, "one is American, the other Russian. They used to meet somewhere. You were their travel agent. You used to arrange the meetings for them. Everything had to be covered, because these weren't small people. They were big people. So how about it, Fritz?"

The German breathed slowly. "I only worked the Russian end," he said. "I didn't know much—"

"But you knew where they met, didn't you?"

"Okay. You might want to leave Europe. It's too cold this time of year. You might want to go to a warmer climate. I understand that Turkey is very nice this time of year."

"Where in Turkey?"

"On the Russian boarder. There's a little town called Dogubayazit."

"Dogubayazit." Allen said the name silently. He was no longer watching Fritz. He was watching the patch of dusty cobbles, the shadows and the starving dog. "And now for a hundred more, Fritz. How often did they meet?"

"It varied. No more than a few times a year."

"Make it three hundred, Fritz. What made them meet? What was the signal?"

"There was a code."

"For a crash meeting?"

"Yes, crash meeting code."

218

"What was it?"

"Postcard with a photograph of a forest."

"Which forest?"

"Doesn't matter."

"And that's all?"

"No. You had to write something."

"What did you have to write?"

"I can't."

"Yes you can, Fritz. For another five hundred, Fritz. What were the words?"

The German had bent over. His arms were locked around his stomach as if he were sick. Finally he got out, "Enchanted. You write the words Enchanted Forest on the back of a postcard and you send it to someone in The Room."

"In English?" Allen asked softly. "Can you write it in English?"

"Didn't matter."

"So it's just the words Enchanted Forest, and then you send it to The Room?"

"Yes, The Room."

"And then how long until they came to Dogubayazit?"

"Two weeks."

"And will it still work? The postcard? What if someone sent it today? Would they still come to Dogubayazit?"

"I don't know."

When Allen and Krugger left the man he was still hunched over on the edge of the stone well. He had not touched the money that lay beside him. He sat with his toes turned in and his head down.

Somewhere along the road Allen did buy that postcard in a roadside shop. It was one in a stack of dozens. They were all prewar stock, photographs of the German Alps, and one special one of evergreens stretching for what must have been thousands of miles.

The shop was a little timbered hut on the outskirts of a lake

219

resort. It was a cold day. The shop's owner was an old woman in a black coat with a scarf around her head. Allen had the impression that she had not sold a postcard in a long, long time. While Krugger stood outside in the snow to watch the road, Allen paid her for the card. There was nothing else significant. This was just one more step to the end.

By now The Room was like a phantom railroad. He hardly knew where to send his postcard. Finally after weeks of charting routes in a small hotel outside of Dresden, he mailed the card to Prague.

During these days he often saw himself as living in another dimension. He was frightened nearly all the time. There were footsteps on the floorboards at night. The city was filled with Russian soldiers. He worked at a desk by the window. Below ran a pebbled lane and then a grassy hill with a few stunted trees. Beyond the rise lay the skyline of the fire-bombed city.

Krugger was always quiet. In the mornings he walked through to the city and out along the sandstone hills. He always brought back something to eat; smoked fish, a bit of cheese. While Allen worked, Krugger liked to lie on the bed and leaf through magazines. For a time he was also reading fairy tales from a child's collection that he had found in the market. One story told about an enchanted forest. Krugger thought that was ironic, and so Allen had to listen while the story was read aloud.

Finally came the last afternoon when Allen mailed the card. He and Krugger had trudged for miles so that the postmark could not be easily traced back to their hotel. At one point Krugger had wanted to hold the card. It might have been a religious object.

Afterward, back along the cliffs above the water, he told Allen that they should celebrate. Allen was tired. His ankles hurt. The whole world seemed blue-gray. "Why do you want to celebrate?"

"Because we're going to catch them now, aren't we?"

"I don't know."

An hour ago he had dropped the postcard in the mail. Now he

felt as if he might as well have thrown it in the river for all the good it would do.

"Yes. We will catch them." Krugger grinned. "I feel in my heart that we are going to catch them. I feel it."

"I hope you're right, by God, I do . . ."

"Of course I'm right. You'll see, Allen. They'll come. I would bet on it. I would bet you."

Turkey became the strangest end of it all. Even years later Allen would never be able to fit what he remembered of Turkey into a track of normal experience. Turkey would remain a suspended memory.

Through much of the journey he was ill from bad water in Istanbul. Then followed two days in Ankara at the villa of some character from the secret police. The man must have thought that Allen had influence in the Department because he could not do enough for him. Finally came the plains, flat, open land. Villages were only white specks along the horizon. Krugger had managed to buy a Land Rover. It had been left over from the war, but the Turks had rebuilt the engine. Allen slept most of the way, his head on his arm, leaning against the dashboard. Nights were cold, and the farmers were suspicious. A line of poplars in the distance seemed to take hours to draw closer.

Sometimes the only lights were lanterns fixed to the axles of passing carts. Once they hit a dog, and Krugger had to finish it off by clubbing it to death with the tire iron. The mountains were jagged and black, but the higher crags were filled with snow. There was no traveling in hard rain.

By the time they reached Dogubayazit the meager tread of their truck tires had been worn almost to the cord. Twilight was falling and the muddy track that ran between rows of brick shacks was black. The huts were thatched with grass, sagging on poles.

As they approached the village, figures shuffled out of the hovels and stood in the center of the road. Women in dark shawls, men

221

in quilted vests. The wind was sounding through the grass roofs.

An old man greeted Allen first. He wore a striped sweater and baggy, cotton trousers and acted as if he had been expecting them. He shook Allen's hand and led him into the largest shack. Cushions lay on the embroidered rugs, but the walls were smoked mud. Lanterns hung from the crossbeams. Red coals glowed in an iron pot. The old man had a weathered face, and said his name was Shall. Then they all sank to the cushions, and women brought tall glasses of mint tea.

"I am looking for two men," Allen said. "One is American. The other is Russian."

"Sure, you want the captains," the Turk replied. He spoke a ragged English.

"The captains," Allen echoed. His heart was beating very rapidly. He glanced at Krugger, but the German was stoney. He was watching the old man's hands, and the faces of the others that peered through the doorway.

"I call them the captains"—the Turk smiled—"they call me Shall. We are great friends."

"How long since you've seen them?"

The Turk began to chew on his knuckles. "Maybe a year, maybe more."

"How do they come?"

"From there." The Turk pointed out the door. "From the landing field."

"There's a landing field?"

"The American built it. So he can land his plane. He always comes with his pilot, but sometimes the Russian comes in a truck like your truck."

"And how do you know when they are coming?"

"They just come."

"What do they look like?"

"Like you, except that the American is older and the Russian has straw-colored hair."

222

"I think they may come again soon," Allen said slowly. "We would like to wait for them."

"Usually the captains pay us," the Turk smiled.

"We will pay you too."

The Turk began to rub his palm against his whiskers, smiled again and said, "Your friend looks very strong. Is he an American too?"

"No, he's German."

The Turk stared into Krugger's eyes. A German. Well, at least he was better than a German.

Allen waited three days. He and Krugger were given a mud hut of their own. A girl brought them bread in the mornings. There was lamb at midday and plenty of tea. It was cold, and Allen bought a pair of heavy socks. There was always the sound of chickens in the pen and goat bells from far across the rocks.

Each afternoon Allen would wander out to the rocks above the airstrip. He liked to sit up there and listen to the wind. Sometimes he lost hope. Other times he was very sure of himself.

On the day that the plane finally came he was thinking of nothing at all, trying to dull his anxieties. It was a silver Piper Cub, and it made a wide circle over the village. Allen was several hundred yards away from the landing strip. There was a long view over the rocks and open land.

Villagers tumbled out to meet the plane. Allen saw them as tiny silhouettes against the falling sun. His coat was flapping around his knees. When he saw the two figures emerge from the plane, he took out his automatic, instructing himself to remember which was safety-off and which safety-on.

Sunlight was glinting off the fuselage, and one of the men who had stepped out of the plane had started moving closer. He was climbing the apron of rocks, and Allen thought: he knows I'm waiting for him. He cocked the gun . . .

Years before Allen had stood at the edge of a field near a

country house where he and his parents used to spend their summers. Then too a figure had drawn closer from about three hundred yards away. At first Allen had thought that the man had been a neighbor, one of the farmers from across the valley. Then he had recognized that floating walk. It had been dad all along. Allen had just stood there watching for a long time. Then his father had called, and Allen had broken into a run. He had never forgotten how his father had smelled, and the feel of his bones.

And now it was the same. John Dancer stepped onto the rocky summit and stretched out his arms. He called Allen's name, but this time Allen did not run to him. He just stood there, shaking his head.

John Dancer sat down beside his son on a flattened volcanic slab. The summit lay in the path of the wind, and the wind was sounding through the crags. Allen's arms were pressing against his ribs. He was looking out across the landscape. In the distance the villagers were solarized in the dying light.

Minutes passed. Neither spoke. John wanted to put his hand on Allen's shoulder, but for some reason he could not do it.

Finally he said, "For a long time I've been wondering how I was going to explain when I had no other choice."

"So you've known all along? All along you knew it was me?"

"Yes."

"And you killed Kurt Lehr?"

"Not me, Allen. I didn't kill him. Someone else—"

"Who?"

Violet light was spreading over the horizon. Allen started to shiver. There was smoke curling from the village huts.

"Why is it called The Room, dad? I've never understood why . . ." He felt a little dazed.

"It's just a name, Allen. It doesn't mean anything—"

"And why didn't you tell me before? You could have told me—"

"I worried that you wouldn't understand. I worried very much about that."

Allen shivered violently.

"Maybe we should walk back to the village," his father said quietly.

"No. I want to stay here."

Far below someone had stepped out from a wall of white stones, the only figure on the muddy track.

"Is that your man down there?" John asked.

"Yes. That's Otto, but he's all right. He won't come up here. I told him not to."

"But what about afterwards?"

"No, it's okay. Otto's okay. He's not like Lehr was. Lehr wanted to move in and take over the whole operation—"

"And what did you want, Allen?"

Allen shook his head. "I don't know."

Another moment of silence then Allen stiffened, turned to his father and his voice rose. "But you've been passing them the real stuff. You're each other's moles! *You've been selling your own people down the river.*"

The words came back to them in a faint reverberation.

"They're not my people," John Dancer said softly. "That's the whole point."

That night John and Allen stayed together in one of the furthest homes from the village square. The mud walls turned faintly amber, from the light of the oil lamps. By midnight there were no human sounds, only the sounds of chickens, goats coughing and shutters banging in the wind.

It was not a question of forgiveness, John had said. He did what he had believed was right. Allen half-heard other phrases like that while he sat on the cushions. One side of his face was hot from the fire, the other was cold.

John told his story twice. First he went right to the matter, then

225

he told it circuitously. Deeper motives were the theme the second time. He said that if one were to take any route, one would still end up at the same place. He had the most difficulty talking about the woman. "Your mother doesn't know," he said. "How could she? How could I have ever explained?"

"What was her name?" Allen asked.

"Anna. Anna Servana."

"And why did she call him Valentin? Does that stand for something? Does it mean something?"

"No. It's just a name."

And then John talked about the Moscow station, how he and the boy had sat on the bench. Russian crowds were lifeless. Everyone kept their eyes fixed to their feet. Love of a country was just one kind of love, he said.

"But you must have realized what it meant?" Allen asked tonelessly. "All those people who've been hurt. The betrayal."

"We depend on each other," said John. "Val and I have come to depend on each other."

"So you pass things to him, and he passes things to you."

"Yes. But I had to do it, Allen . . . I hope you can see that, come to understand it . . ."

"You think it makes for a balance? Things are equal in the end? Is that it?"

"Perhaps . . . but that's not the point Valentin is my son. He's my other son. That's the point—"

"But you look good too, don't you? You look very good, dad . . . self-serving, that's what Lehr called it. He said it was self-serving—"

"That's *not* the point. The point is only that I needed to achieve a certain status to preserve the arrangement. I had to earn respect and trust in order to get access to the material that Val needed. Because it's hard to survive in Moscow. Val has to keep producing in order to survive. If he isn't valuable to them, they'll destroy him—"

226

"So you kept him safe by selling your own people down the river—"

"We never really hurt anyone. Plans maybe, operations, but we never *hurt* anyone—"

"What about Lehr?"

"The Room killed Lehr. There's an internal safety mechanism. He stepped on the catch and it sprang back on him. The Room works independently, in that respect."

In the first light the landscape looked unreal, as unreal as the story he had just heard. His legs were cramped. The cold from the mud bricks had seeped into his muscles. The western sky was amber, distant rocks looked molten.

Just before Allen fell asleep he asked, "But if you knew that I would be waiting for you, if you knew that it was a trap, why did you come anyway?"

"Because I didn't want to keep hiding from you any longer," his father said. "I thought it was time to bring you in." . . .

Valentin arrived that afternoon. Allen saw him first from a long way off. His truck was winding down the hillside. Once again the wind was tearing through the scrub. Allen sat in the hut, sipping mint tea. There was a strong draft under the door. He was calm, he told himself, he even heard his wristwatch tick.

Finally he got up and hobbled to the window again. Several hundred feet up the track John Dancer and his other son were walking. Black clouds were churning overhead. Valentin wore a belted woolen overcoat and leather boots. He had a lean body and blond hair. He and John were moving slowly down the road, John seeming to be speaking softly while Valentin nodded now and again. Watching from the window, even Allen had to admit that they looked like father and son.

That afternoon the entire sky turned black and rain fell in thick sheets. When it cleared, Allen and Valentin walked out among the rocks. Valentin was taller than Allen, and his eyes were lighter. He had a half-shy way of speaking . . . he might have still been

227

a young boy, but there were deep lines around his mouth.

When they reached the summit of rocks he said, "I heard about you. John has talked about you."

"Yes, John," Allen replied, because he could hardly call his father anything else now.

"Were you surprised? To learn that you had a brother?"

"Half-brother," Allen said.

"Yes half-brother. But were you surprised?"

"Yes, I suppose I was surprised."

Valentin stepped higher on the rocks. "Do you know what a pressure valve is?" he called back.

"What?"

"I said do you know what a pressure valve is? On old steam engines there were pressure valves. When the pressure became too great a little steam would be released so that the engine would not explode. I think perhaps John and I have served that function on several occasions."

Now Valentin was framed against huge boils of receding clouds, racing across the sky while the wind was spreading ripples over the sheets of muddy water below.

"This struggle between my country and your country," Valentin continued. "It's madness. You know that, don't you, Allen? There's no point to it. Each side sees only what it wants to see. They don't see the greater view. That's why I no longer feel guilty for what I'm doing. I see both sides. John also sees both sides. So we're like the parents of two fighting children. John and I. We are like the parents. Or do I sound pompous? I don't mean to."

Finally they were standing side by side. The wind was making their coats billow out.

"Does it mean anything to you, Allen? That we're brothers?"

"I suppose so."

"Because it means something to me. In a few days I'll be back in Moscow, and I'll remember you."

Allen said, "I've been thinking . . . The Room isn't really safe anymore. It should be changed . . ."

"It's worked for a long time."

"You were lucky, you were just lucky."

"So what do you want to do?"

What did he want to do? He was, almost without considering it, going along with what he'd been momentarily, at least, shocked by a little while ago. Well, he was a member of this family, wasn't he? If it made sense for his father and half-brother . . . He shrugged, buried doubt . . . What did he want to do? He would be creative, add a dimension . . . "Bring it out in the open."

"I don't understand," Valentin said.

"Look at it this way. You go back to your people, and you tell them that you've recruited another big man in Washington, but there's a problem . . . it's that he's got to make his office believe that you're really *his* agent. Do you see what I'm getting at? Your people think you've got a man, and this man told his people that he's got you."

"And you're that man, Allen?"

"Yes, but it's played out exactly the opposite at my end. On my end you become my agent who has told your people that I'm working for you."

"It is a mirror," Valentin said softly. "It is just like a mirror."

"It will justify the meetings, justify passing the product. After all, each of us will need to keep our agents supplied, won't we?"

Valentin nodded. It was a way to maintain what he believed in. "Yes, and perhaps we should call it that . . . The Mirror? Do you like that name, Allen?"

"No, I've already thought of a name. It's a name that no one will ever forget. Once they've heard it, they'll never forget it."

He paused to build a little tension, then said, "Magic. We will call it Source Magic, and I promise you that no one will ever forget."

The Langley archives contained nothing of what occurred in

229

Dogubayazit. Only one small reference in John's log even mentioned the journey abroad. Nor did Allen ever write about Turkey. His record went no further than Eastern Europe. Still, one clue, one ripple in the vast glassy pond remained . . . it was a photograph, and for years it hung in John's office. Then Allen had it for a while. Now it sat on the mantelpiece along with the other family portraits—Jessie's among them.

It was an old, brown, grainy picture in a simple wooden frame. One had to look closely to differentiate the human forms from the rock forms, the mountains from the clouds. But there against a ragged landscape three figures stood on a rocky crag. Dark shadows cut their faces, but it was clear that the central figure had his arms around the other two. It could have been a photograph of any three men in any stretch of wasteland. No one ever seemed to take much notice of it.

PART 3

CHAPTER
SEVEN

SOURCE MAGIC was born in that winter of 1948, although in the beginning it was not referred to as Magic. It was called merely Al Dancer's Eastern Link, and all through the summer it produced a series of remarkable submissions. The first was a seventy page transcription of a Moscow Center brief to satellite Apparat heads. Next came an eyes-only interdepartmental memo discussing tensions within Comecon. Allen gave no real explanation as to how he had obtained the material. He remained evasive, and a touch smug, some thought.

Eventually the secrecy proved too much for the powers in Washington. There was no end of infighting, no end of jealousy. The military, in particular, began pushing for an investigation, claiming that proper evaluation of the product could not be made

233

without an attributable source. So it appeared that Allen had been actually forced into a position in which he had no alternative but to reveal his source. In fact Allen had not been pushed into anything. He had been in control all along, and the eventual unveiling of Magic was a brilliant piece of showmanship.

No one ever conducted a thorough study of Source Magic's birth, nor ever reviewed its birth in relationship to the larger Dancer story. So the notes that Humphrey Knolls compiled eventually became regarded as the family's most complete chronology.

By the third week of research, Knolls's notes had taken the form of a time-track . . . dates were penciled in the margins and beside each date were notations of important events: Allen's trip to Spain and Germany, John's Russian affair. Some of the notations Humphrey filled in from memory, some he had estimated, and some he had stolen from sealed files throughout the Langley archive system. The notes were on yellow foolscap, over fifty pages in all. Humphrey would read them on the floor of his apartment. He always kept a burning candle and a tin of lighter fluid handy in case the door burst open.

In the end, when these notes became part of the larger record, chroniclers at first found them a little baffling. They were filled with odd cryptograms, lines crisscrossed in and out of one another. In places the handwriting was almost illegible. This much, however, was immediately clear to those who read them. On about the fourth week of his search, Humphrey Knolls had found a common thrust among everyone involved. His chronology had reached the year of 1948. Allen Dancer was becoming an untouchable force in the secret world; John stood silently behind him, and between the two of them Source Magic had begun. But also within Humphrey's record there was a deeper, hidden force, and it was moving rapidly toward the birth of Jessie.

1948 was a settling year, a time for laying down the foundations of Source Magic. Allen and Servana met twice during the months of February and March. Both meetings were held on the outskirts of Zurich, where Allen had purchased a four-bedroom safe-house. The house was christened Sorcerer . . . it came to Allen one night while riding on a train. Magic . . . Source Magic . . . Sorcerer . . . He liked it.

The house was an old brick estate. The upper rooms were dark and narrow, the plaster yellowed. Dryrot had loosened the floorboards. The scullery smelled of stale food. The bannister was pulling from the staircase, which was also somber and twisting.

The house was surrounded by a wild garden filled with vines and waves of ivy. Beyond the garden was a grove of birch trees, and beyond the trees lay a narrow highway that ran twenty miles into the city.

Ostensibly the house was owned by Otto Krugger. His signature was on the deed, his name on the brass plate at the entrance of the garden. In truth, he was only an employee of the Magic organization. He would live in this house, take care of the grounds, and most importantly aid Allen Dancer. A ladder, set against the garden wall as if someone had been repairing the masonry, was the sign that all was clear; no ladder meant the opposite. Krugger was also taught to work the tape recorders, to set the alarms, and during meetings he kept watch from an upstairs room that gave him a view of the highway for miles in all directions.

Allen came to Sorcerer a day early for his first meeting with Servana. He told Krugger that he had come early in order to check the signals and test the alarms. Actually he had come early so that he would have one free evening to explore, to prowl the rooms, open drawers, cupboards. He wanted time to get to know this house, and so convince himself that it was really *his*. He wanted Servana to feel like the visitor, not himself.

It was cold and clear the morning that Servana arrived. There was snow on the distant mountains and frost on the black ground. Allen was watching from an upstairs window when Servana's taxi rounded the hill for the last six-mile stretch to the garden gates.

They met in the dining room, a long high-ceilinged room with a window overlooking the frozen garden. Allen sat at one end of the oak table, Valentin at the other. On the wall hung a still-life of a butcher's block heaped with vegetables, a wine bottle and a freshly killed hare.

Valentin wore a coarse, ill-fitting suit, but even in these clothes there was a trace of elegance about him. It was in his eyes, his soft-spoken manners, the way he gestured. It made Allen feel uncomfortable.

"How was the flight?" Allen began.

"Very nice, thank you."

"No problem crossing over?"

"No, none at all."

"Would you care for breakfast? I can have Otto do you some eggs."

"No thank you. I ate on the plane."

Which was a shame, because, as Allen had learned years ago, it was always an advantage negotiating with someone while they were eating. You could stare at them and make them feel self-conscious. Providing, of course, that they didn't do the same to you . . .

Later, without any real thought, the two men found themselves wandering through the vast, gloomy house, peering into rooms, trying out the furniture, examining the paintings in the drawing room. Valentin seemed particularly entranced by a moody landscape of Lake Lugano.

"I don't think that one is worth much," Allen said.

"Perhaps, but I think it's interesting just the same. See there. See how he does the light on the water. That's like Russian light."

Allen shrugged and sat down in a dusty wing chair, began toying with the tassels on a lampshade. "Listen," he said suddenly. "I want to talk to you about Italy."

"Italy?"

"Yes. I want you to know where Washington stands on Italy."

236

"But I know already where they stand, Allen. They're going to try and fix the election. Is that the phrase? Fix the election?"

"I need this one, Val. I don't want to lose the Italians."

"I did not realize that it was your operation, Allen."

"It's not, but you know what I mean. It wouldn't look good if the Communists win that election. It wouldn't look good for anyone."

"It might look good for me." Valentin smiled.

"I'm serious, Val. You've got to help me on this one."

"Very well, Allen. What would you like?"

"Washington has ten million to back the Christian Democrats. It's in a so-called stabilization fund. The game plan calls for the money to be laundered through individual bank accounts and into the hands of key people. What I want you to do is to fix it so that Moscow thinks there's at least thirty million, and that the money didn't come out of Washington. I want them to think it came from the Vatican. Can you do that?"

"So, Allen, you think you can discourage Moscow with thirty million dollars and the Vatican?"

"Don't you?"

"I'm not sure how they will react, but if this is what you want—"

"It's what I want, Val."

Servana had moved from the painting to a Dutch chest with peeling marquetry. Beside the chest was a couch with sunken springs. He sat down in the couch, but then got up again and walked to the leaded window.

Allen was watching him intently. "And there's something else, Val. It's about what we discussed the other day."

"The bomb," Servana said.

"Yes."

"What about it?"

"Well, it's a pretty tall order. I've been thinking, and it looks like it's going to be a tall order."

"They will all seem like tall orders, Allen."

"This is different."

Servana shrugged. "Let me tell you something, Allen. By the end of the next year the Soviet Union will test her first atomic bomb. This is fact. Regardless of what you do or do not do we will still be testing next year. However, it would help my standing—and so our arrangement—just now if I could give them something tangible. Yes, it is merely a gesture, because we do not need anything from you, although I doubt your people will be able to accept that. But it would increase my position, which is important to both of us, if I could deliver something—"

"Like what?"

"Perhaps a sketch of your detonation system."

"Good God! You've got a dozen agents on the board. Can't they get you that?"

"Well, Allen, they're not actually my agents."

"It's not going to be easy, not for me. That kind of stuff doesn't cross my lines."

"I think perhaps that if you try you will find that it is not too difficult."

"All right, but I'll need at least eight weeks, and even then it's not a promise."

"Eight weeks will be acceptable."

"And when it's over, I'll need someone."

"Someone?"

"You know what I mean. Look, after you people set off a bomb there's going to be some real frustration around Washington. They're going to talk about Communist conspiracies, spies . . . I mean there's going to be some real heat. So when it starts, I want someone I can give them. Someone they'll believe in."

"Oh yes, I see. You want a scapegoat."

"Call it what you want, but give me someone, Val. Give me someone big. Like those two leftist Jewish intellectuals, for example. They'll look like idealists to their friends and probably be pleased to take it on themselves. They're martyrs at heart, though

238

I doubt they'll get more than a stiff prison sentence. After all, they're parents and one of them is a woman . . ."

"The Rosenbergs?"

"Yes." . . .

Valentin left that evening. Allen saw him as far as the garden gates, where there was a view through the frosted trees of the black highway, and from which the red lights of the taxi Allen had called only an hour ago were visible.

They had gone a dozen feet in silence before Servana said, "I wonder, Allen. I wonder if you find what we're doing distasteful."

"Why do you say that?"

"Oh, I don't know. It's just that I sometimes find it so. And then there's Father. I know that he does not always enjoy this. In fact he once told me that a man would have to be made of stone not to feel some guilt some of the time. So I ask you, Allen, does it ever bother you?"

"I'll get used to it."

"No. I don't think you will, Allen. I don't think that one ever gets entirely used to it. Whatever the rationalization."

Three days after the meeting Allen left for London. He arrived in a cold spell, the entire city was numb with it, not to mention what the war had done. He spent the morning drinking beer in a pub near the station. When he felt drunk enough he rented a red Jaguar, and drove southwest to see Julia.

Julia still lived in her father's seaside cottage. Allen hardly spoke at all. He brought the old man a pipe and an Irish shawl for Julia. In the mornings the old man took him fishing down by the breakwater. Allen got to bait the hooks, then would sit on the rocks shivering while the curlews screamed all around.

As always Allen slept down the hall from his wife. That was how her father wanted it. Then late one night she heard him moving down the stairs. Some time later she found him sitting at the kitchen table, staring at an empty plate as if it were an object of some importance. He wore an old flannel robe, worn through at the elbows. There was beach tar on his feet. He had sliced his finger cutting cheese. When Julia entered the room he smiled and said, "Hello."

Two days later she decided that she would return to America with him. He seemed so mournful.

Spring was unfolding when they reached Washington. The days were crisp and clear. America was the greatest nation on earth, and this was her capital. On the first Sunday after their arrival Allen took Julia to see the Lincoln Memorial, the White House and Arlington National Cemetery. They walked along the cool green lawns between ranks of gravestones until they came to the Tomb of the Unknown Soldier. Julia wore a belted mackintosh and a long yellow scarf and stood there silently while Allen explained the significance of the burning flame and the marble arch. Later they fought because she would not make love to him.

They lived in a small brownstone not far from Foggy Bottom, which was the headquarters of the new Central Intelligence Agency. Their bedroom window looked out onto a tangle of vines and ivy covered bricks. There was a damp smell of leaves in the hallway, and on windy nights the branches of an oak scraped against the shingles. There were evenings with men from the office, and weekends with old John. Julia had begun to study painting.

Julia had no friends, none at all. She did not like the wives of the men in Foggy Bottom, and they did not like her. There was a cloistered, academic feel to those early days of the CIA, and Julia did not fit in. Allen had started smoking a pipe. His library was filled with books, and Oriental rugs had been laid on the floor. He wore tweed suits and ivy league trousers with blazers and some of his jackets had leather patches on the elbows. Two evenings a week he spent at his club, and he made much about corresponding with friends who lived abroad. He was obviously enjoying life.

But Julia did not write letters to anyone except her father. Nor did she use the telephone. She could not remember the names of streets, and she always forgot to carry money. Sometimes Allen would return home at night and find her sitting in the darkness listening to old records.

Julia never asked what Allen did. Not that there was much that he was permitted to tell her, but she never asked anyway. She knew only that something called Magic had blossomed and now everyone respected Al or envied him. But it did not seem to matter to her one way or another. She did not like the Central Intelligence Agency. She did not like the entire secret world and the people within it. She particularly did not like the people.

Some days she would just wander through the neighborhood. Fall was her favorite season . . . she liked to stroll among the swirling leaves, she liked to stand at the edge of playgrounds and watch the children through the black iron fences. She marked the passing months with odd events . . . there was the day that Allen broke her father's crystal vase, the one he had given them for their wedding; there was the day that a man from Allen's office killed himself; and then there was the day that old John took her hand and said that he also knew what it was like to feel out of time and out of place.

It had been a warm day. She and Allen had spent the night in John's house. She got up early and wandered out into the garden, wearing a white pleated skirt. When she came to the stone bench she sat down. An empty bucket lay rusting in the grass. The sun was still low in the sky, and the light fell through an apple tree. She had been sitting only a few minutes when John stepped out from behind the hedgerows. He smiled and sat down beside her.

"I have a friend who spends every weekend in his garden," he said. "His name is Lyle, and every weekend he's in his garden planting, pruning, digging up the weeds. He says my garden is a disgrace."

"Oh I don't know." Julia smiled. "I sort of like it like this."

Clumps of his weeds were glinting in the light. John was looking at a particularly shabby bush. He had never bothered to learn the names of his plants, they just grew. Then he said, "Allen used to play here when he was a boy. I built him a tree house over there.

241

He used to sit up there and spy on people."

"Too bad it isn't that easy now," she said softly. "Imagine all the spies up in tree houses. I'd send Allen off to work with a sack lunch."

John's voice dropped. "You don't like what Allen does, do you?"

"No, not very much."

"What would you rather have him do?"

"I don't know. Something straightforward . . . a carpenter maybe."

The sun started breaking through the higher branches. Now whole new patches of the garden were glowing, cobwebs were glinting . . . "Tell me," she said suddenly, "is Allen good at what he does?"

"Yes, of course."

"No, I mean is he very good? Better than nearly all of them?"

"Well I'm not the one—"

"Please tell me."

"All right, yes, Allen is very good."

Later that day Julia stood on the porch and watched Allen swing golf clubs in the grass. Clumps of turf sailed high into the air. Finally he threw down the club and swore. And then she thought she understood. After all these years she finally understood. The players in the secret world were dangerous not so much for what they could do to themselves, but for what they could do to others . . .

Months passed. By now Julia had done a whole series of playgrounds in muted tones; she liked to let the watercolors run together. Every week there were dinner parties, and always the talk was political. The most popular stance was a sort of tempered liberalism, with no question getting a simple answer. Julia rarely listened to what was said. For some time now she had been having a recurring dream . . . She kept seeing herself asleep in her bed-

242

room, it was late afternoon and the walls were milky white. Suddenly the whole room shook and warm air gushed in. Through the billowing curtains, far along the horizon, she saw a rising mushroom cloud. She had that same dream twice a week . . .

The first snow fell two weeks before Christmas. Julia rose late. Allen had left hours ago, and so there was only the sound of the snow brushing on the windows. The city streets were filled with slush. Carollers drifted out of department stores. Julia bought Allen a cashmere sweater for his ivy league image, then moved on down the boulevard past Salvation Army bands, past plastic holly wreaths stuck to the lamp posts. She was just moving in a crowd of other shoppers, mostly women like herself, when a hand fell gently on her shoulder.

It was Robert Kline, and he was looking directly into her eyes.

"It's me," he said.

"Yes. How are you?"

Neither of them smiled. It might have been taking place in a dream.

"I'm fine. I saw you but I wasn't sure it was you. Do you . . .? Can we talk some place?"

"Yes, of course."

They looked around while the crowd flowed past them. Finally they located a coffee shop and drifted to a table in the rear. Fairy lights were blinking on the walls, the radio was playing "Silent Night."

"I saw you once before," Kline said. "You were riding in a taxi. I never thought I'd see you again, but now you're here—"

"Yes, I'm here."

"How have you been?"

"I've been all right. How about yourself?"

"Fine. I've been fine. And Allen?"

"Never been better. And what have you been doing?"

He shrugged. "Traveling mostly."

"Business?"

"Sort of."

"And what brings you to Washington?"

But Kline shook his head and turned away. He looked as furious as he ever had in the war.

"What the hell are we doing, Julia? What?"

"I don't know what you mean?"

"Yes, you do."

She nodded, shut her eyes and when she opened them again they were filled with tears.

"Let's get out of here," he said softly.

"Where?"

"Some place . . . I want to go some place where I can lie down beside you. I want to do that . . ."

They drifted through the crowds again. Darkness was falling, Christmas lights were glittering everywhere. The trance was so complete that they hardly had to speak to one another. She just followed him up to his room, and then actually lay down beside him.

Kline lived in a small, cheaply furnished apartment near the university. There were chairs covered with burlap and a couch with distorted cushions. Students lived in the neighborhood and the faint strains of jazz were always drifting up from the coffee shops. It was the kind of shabby place that people took for granted.

Kline had rooms like this throughout western Europe. They were his safe-houses, and he had been living in them since the war. Officially he was known as a transient operative. He worked between the seams of Lyle Severson's network, and some of the Hungarian routes. No one was sure who had admitted him to the CIA. He had just been absorbed naturally, because he had been around at the right time and they all knew him. He was not what they called a career man. He lived on the fringes, and they paid him six hundred dollars a month though there were bonuses for the nasty jobs.

On the first afternoon with Julia he hardly talked about himself.

244

He told her that he was still working in the trade, but not much more. He said that he did it because it was the only thing he knew. On the second day he explained that he manipulated people, and he met them on street corners and in train stations. Some needed money, some needed protection and some needed a sense of belonging. Kline explained that he was mostly a candyman for a dozen frightened men and women who spied for the United States.

Beyond all this Kline had little else to say. There was his work and little more. He went from place to place, day to day. Paris, London, Berlin: every city seemed the same. He had no women to speak of, but there were always a few girls along the way. Through it all, Julia realized that he was calmer than he had been five years ago. When she told him this he shrugged and said he supposed he was.

On the second day she came to him in the late morning. She found him washing dishes in an old pair of jeans and a cheap drip-dry shirt. His sleeves were rolled up above his elbows. When he answered the door his hands were still damp. They stared at one another for a moment, then she broke down and fell into his arms.

They lay side by side. His mattress was narrow and lumpy. There were water stains on the ceiling and the nightstand was marked with cigarette burns. There was also the dripping tap ringing on the dirty dishes that her arrival had kept him from washing.

For a long time they did not speak. Then Julia took a long breath and said, "We're crazy. You know that, don't you?"

Kline shrugged, said nothing.

"What can this possibly lead to? We don't have any future, so why do we go on?"

"Why did you go back to Allen? Why didn't you wait for me?"

"I don't know. Why do people screw up their lives?"

Outside the light was blue. Cold shadows were filling the room. The soft riff of a saxophone was drifting in from the cafe below. Finally she ran her finger along his lips and said, "I don't know why I'm with Allen. Sometimes I think I just made a mistake. Other times I think he tricked me."

"What would he do if he found us together?"

"I don't know. Maybe nothing, or maybe years from now he'd kill us. I don't mean literally. I mean in worse ways. Allen doesn't look dangerous, but he is."

"No he's not. He's not what you call dangerous. He arranges things to happen to people. He's a manipulator."

They had both grown very still. The dripping water and the distant saxophone were the only sounds in the room. Suddenly Kline said, "What if I told you that Allen was a traitor?"

"What do you mean?"

"I mean literally a traitor. I mean that he's been telling secrets to the other side, important secrets."

"There are no important secrets. It's a game. He just plays it like a stupid game—"

"Everyone thinks that he's got himself the Kremlin's favorite son, but in fact it's just a deal he worked out. He and that Russian, they exchange things so they both look good."

At some point she had started crying. She was still lying on her side, her cheek resting on her arm, her tears were soaking through the sheets.

"I don't care," she said. "It doesn't make any difference what Allen does. Don't you *see* that? It's all a big joke . . . communism, capitalism—they're just words some people have invented to keep us all fighting each other. And the joke is that the men who invented them have forgotten they invented them. They believe it too . . ."

Another minute passed, the dripping water on the coffee cups. Finally she said, "He'll beat you if you try to fight him, Robert. He's got all the power now, and if you try to fight him he'll kill you. He'll kill us both." . . .

They hardly spoke about Allen again. They hardly spoke at all. She would meet him in the late mornings because she could not

246

stay away. Sometimes they would just stand side by side in his dirty little room, stand and look out the window to watch the falling snow and the traffic on Thirty-seventh Street. The underlying feeling of these moments together was that time was running out. They could only eat when they were famished, only sleep when exhausted. Once he made a joke that cut them both to the bone . . . something about playing chess in an empty room while waiting around to be murdered.

Occasionally they took a chance and met outside, sometimes in the park, sometimes in a museum. In public, Kline was always different. He was wary, kept watching the faces of people around him. The whole world might have been against him, and worse, it seemed as if he welcomed the fight, as if he wanted to go down fighting. Once while he was sleeping she stretched and her fingers touched something that was hard and cold. She pulled the mattress back a little and found that he had a snub-nosed revolver taped to the headboard. They never talked about the future.

They never spoke to one another on the telephone. Kline did not trust telephones. Once they had agreed to meet at the Lincoln Memorial . . . It was a cold day, and Julia arrived in the early afternoon. A few tourists came and went and then she was alone. She waited more than two hours but he never came. The next day he told her that something had come up but he had not been able to call her and cancel their meeting. This was how it was, living so close to the edge.

Once, just before falling asleep, she had a kind of vision in which Robert had killed Allen. She imagined Robert and herself staring at the body. The force of the bullet had thrown it against the wall. In the vision she was numb and silent, while Robert was simply matter-of-fact. He said that no matter how far and how fast they ran, sooner or later they would be caught. The next morning she woke up with these words circling in her mind: *sooner or later.*

Their last day was the day before Christmas. They met in some dark Greek restaurant whose sooty windows looked out onto a

247

row of tenements with blackened fire escapes. Earlier they had walked through the tatters of Christmas streamers. The city was adrift with lights, purple and red. At some point on the rain-slick streets Kline had said that he would be leaving in the morning, that Christmas was a good day to travel. Every station was empty.

Now she told him, "I'd like to know where you're going."

"Why?"

"So I can think of you as being in a certain place, a room in some city. Otherwise it will be just as if you've vanished."

Kline glanced at other tables. There were girls laughing in the corner, and a boy with sunglasses. The air looked faintly yellow. Oil was hissing in the corner.

"I'm going east," Kline finally said. "I'm going to the other side of Berlin."

"How long will you be gone?"

"I don't know, maybe a week or two."

"And afterwards?"

"Don't talk about afterwards. Things just happen and you try to make the best of them."

"I don't understand what you're saying?"

"Yes, you do."

She dropped her eyes. The silverware was blurring through her tears. "It's Allen, isn't it?" she said. "You're going out there so you can get him, so you can prove he's been cheating."

He bit his lip and nodded. On the counter sat a plastic Santa Claus. A red bulb was glowing in its belly. Kline was watching it when he began to speak. "Have you ever heard," he said, "of the theory that everyone has two people in their life who are inextricably linked to them? Two people we can never avoid. One we love, the other we hate. And we can never escape either one of them. We're like comets. The orbit may take us a million miles away, but it always brings us around on a collision course with the same two people. That's what's happening now. You, me, Allen—one day we're going to collide."

248

Outside the air was moist. Evening was falling and the mist was mingling with the drizzle. Robert and Julia lingered in the yellow pool of a street lamp. For a while she just clung to him, then she let her arms slip free from his shoulder. Ahead lay an empty street shining with rainwater and the blinking traffic lights. The last words she heard him say were, "No matter what happens, I want you to remember that Allen Dancer isn't your husband. I am."

Robert Kline had been gone ten days when Julia woke up in the morning feeling faint and nauseous. She went into the bathroom to be sick, and hanging onto the towel rack, staring at her own reflection in the toilet bowl, she knew . . . there was going to be a child. She remained kneeling for a long time, feeling the smooth chrome of the faucet, listening to the dripping tap. When the nausea passed she moved out into the kitchen. Allen was there, banging around with the pots and pans. He can't hurt me anymore, she told herself. There was going to be Robert's baby. Robert *is* my husband.

She waited two weeks to tell Allen about the baby. It happened over breakfast on a Sunday when through the windows she could see the breeze flattening the trees, spinning leaves down the avenue. He spilled his coffee when she mentioned Kline's name, then sat for several seconds and did not speak.

The coffee had begun to drip on the floor now. A few drops had splattered across the linoleum. He said, "I've known all along . . . not about the baby, of course, but about you and Kline. I've known that for some time."

"I see, you spied on us?"

"Not really, but every time I called you were gone. Then I found out that Kline was in town, and well . . ."

"You're a real spy, Allen. No question. You're also a bastard."

He had turned to the window. Julia had chosen the curtains, yellow poplin with a pattern of daisies.

"What do you want to do about it?" she asked.

249

He was shredding the paper napkin in his lap. "Nothing."

"What do you mean?"

"I mean nothing. You're going to have a baby, and I think that's wonderful. I hope it's a boy."

"It's not your baby, Allen."

"How do you know that?" He smiled. "There was last week, and the week before. Maybe you shut your eyes, pretending that I was Robert, but that doesn't make it his baby."

"I said it's *not* yours—"

"But you can't be sure, can you, Julia? You might never be sure."

"God, I hate you."

"You'll get over it."

"No I won't. And I'm leaving you, I'm going to live with Robert."

Allen looked directly into her eyes. "You're not going to live with Robert, now now, not ever. Because Robert isn't coming back."

"What are you talking about?"

"He went over to the other side, didn't he? Well, they caught him four days ago."

"I don't believe you."

He shrugged. "Well, it's true. He was picked up by the East German police. It's probably going to make all the papers. Apparently they're going to stage a show trial."

"You're lying."

"No, Julia, I'm not lying. And you should also know that this time there's no chance of getting him back. He had no business being there, and that means he doesn't warrant the effort as far as the Agency is concerned. So you might as well get used to the idea all over again. Kline is gone. Forget him."

It was odd how the furniture seemed to be growing larger as she looked through the kitchen door . . . the sofa, a potted rubber plant, all of it seemed to be expanding.

Then she heard him speaking from what might have been light-

250

years away . . . "For whatever it's worth, I'm sorry."

"Oh my God, you're *sorry? You're* sorry?" Then her head fell to the side and a voice that was not quite hers began to scream. "You *did* it, you made it happen to him. I know damn well you did. You made it so they would catch him . . ."

As he climbed the stairs he heard her still screaming after him. The words were gone now, but she was still sobbing furiously. He wanted to press his hands to his ears, but if nothing else, Allen Dancer had learned to be a self-controlled man.

The child was born in the fall. Julia had left Allen some time before, so the child was born in her father's house along the English coast. It was an easy birth, with very little pain. They all said that the boy looked like his mother, not a bit like Allen. She named him Jessie for no reason in particular. She had just always liked that name.

In the months that passed, Allen came to see her several times. They would often walk out along the seawall, just as they used to do years ago. After a while he even began to talk about Kline. He told her that there was some hope that he would be exchanged for a Soviet spy. He told her that he was personally trying to arrange it. And he finally managed to convince her that he had had nothing to do with Kline's arrest and was doing his best to get him back. It was a lie, but she finally came to believe him. She badly needed to, even though they were divorced that winter.

The young child Jessie's nursery lay in a loft beneath the peak of the cottage roof. Through the window swelled the sea, and Allen used to tell the boy that the black rocks beyond the breakers were actually the humps of whales. He also used to sit up there and watch the sleeping child. He liked to leave the night-light on so he could study Jessie's face.

His son's face. He repeated that lie to himself, hoping, as with his other lies, that he could make it the truth.

251

CHAPTER EIGHT

THE TRIAL of Robert Kline lasted seven weeks. It was held in a large hall that had been built by the Nazis, partially destroyed in the war and then rebuilt. A red star made of plywood hung from the ceiling by three loops of wire. The prosecuting attorney was a thin young man named Oskar Luft. Over the weeks he wove a brilliant case against Kline, all with soft-spoken sincerity. Even Kline was impressed.

The proceedings were well covered by East German radio and newspapers. Kline sat at a long, unpolished table, wearing a gray prison uniform. His hair had been cropped short. He seemed to be listening intently to Luft, or else lost in thought. He was given fifteen years.

252

In the beginning he was imprisoned in an old monastery that lay somewhere to the east of Berlin, surrounded by miles of dark forest and rolling hills. The walls of the monastery were blackened granite and the roofs were slate. There were also prefabricated quarters for the guards, and the entire compound was surrounded by coils of barbed wire.

The cell was a windowless cement room, five by six feet. There was a tiny straw mattress and a little round stool welded to the stone floor. A fifteen-watt bulb encased in the ceiling and protected by a wire cage burned all the time so there was really no day and no night. When undergoing interrogation prisoners were kept in cells fitted with twenty-five-watt bulbs. The brighter the light, presumably the more disorienting.

The door was made of thick steel, and there was a panel so that plates of food could be slid inside. There was also a peephole so that the prisoners could be observed. On good days, when he felt strong, Kline would lie down and imagine in great detail how, with a length of stiff wire, he could spear the eye of someone who was observing him. They would probably kill him for it, but at least he would have a few seconds to celebrate with his six inches of bloody wire.

Every tenth day the prisoners were given a warm shower. It was all Kline had to live for. There were also exercise periods, but these were erratic. Sometimes they walked him in the courtyard, other times he only had the length of the corridor between the cells. Then again, days would pass when he was not let out at all. For a while Kline tried to keep up his strength by doing simple exercises in his cell, but as the months passed he more or less lost interest.

In addition to the regular routine there were small incidents of cruelty. Once they tried to feed him rat's meat. Once he was beaten. He could not understand the reason for these incidents. They had already tortured him in an effort to find out what he knew, but of course torture did not work. Kline was accustomed

253

to pain, so they finally gave up. But then why these incidents of cruelty? Then he stopped thinking about the reasons why any of it happened.

From the start Kline had marked the passing time with faint lines scratched on the wall of his cell. Because there was no day or night when the window was shut, he used meals as his standard. Whenever he was fed he made one small scratch on the wall. He was pretty sure that he was fed twice a day. After about six months had passed, a guard noticed these lines that had been scratched into the wall and Kline was taken out in the hall and beaten. When he was pushed back into the cell he found that the lines had been obliterated. That was the worst day of his life, and he actually broke down and cried.

With time taken away, he felt there was no hope. He would sit and count the inches off, up one wall, then across the other. He had never been very good with numbers, but when he reached the millions, strange things began to happen. Sometimes the cell would become filled with silvery light, and once he had the oddest feeling that he was hovering high above the prison. He was staring at the wall, but in his mind he saw the trees, some very distinct. And once he even saw Julia sleeping in her bedroom. In his mind he saw her very clearly. Then it was over, and he was back to the wall, counting inches.

He happened to be counting on the day the guards opened his cell and told him to follow them. They led him down the long vaulted corridor, then down a winding flight of stone steps. There were smells of coffee and a generator was throbbing somewhere. He passed guards and a woman smoking a cigarette. Finally he was led into a circular office where, behind the desk, sat Oskar Luft.

The room was stark. There was an old wooden desk, two chairs and an aluminum tea cart. There was also a row of small windows, but the shades were drawn.

Luft motioned to the straight-backed wooden chair, and Kline

254

sat. The walk had made him dizzy and he felt that he had to hold onto his chair to keep from flying away.

"Would you like some tea?" Luft asked.

Kline could not help grinning. He felt like a mad animal.

"Milk and sugar?"

"Thank you."

They both drank in silence for a moment, while Kline shut his eyes.

Oskar Luft was a small, intense man. He had dark hair and a long face. He wore steel-rimmed glasses and dressed in baggy suits. During the trial he had been strangely polite to Kline although he had asked for the maximum sentence short of death.

When the two men finished their tea, Luft drew back the window shades to reveal a wide view of the countryside, and Kline could not stop himself from rising from his chair and walking to the glass.

"You have no idea," he muttered.

"I'm sorry," Luft said, "I wanted to come earlier but things got in the way."

"Yes," Kline said, "things are always getting in the way."

Below grass lay in silver spears of light. There were distant rocks with yellow lichen and a passing truck on the road below the hills.

Finally Luft said, "Would you like to take a walk in the forest?"

"Huh?"

"I said would you like to take a walk out there? I mean *out* there, out beyond the walls."

"What the hell are you talking about?"

"I'll take you for a walk into those woods. Right now you can be walking in those woods if you only agree to help me."

"Probably full of mosquitos," Kline mumbled.

"I'm sorry?"

"The woods. I said they're probably full of mosquitos."

And, incredibly . . . to Kline, at least . . . they both laughed.

255

They sat on a fallen log. Kline had picked up a pinecone and was holding it very tightly. From here they could not see the prison, surrounded as they were by a twisted grove of hawthorns. There was also a stream and reeds growing by the water's edge.

"You're Jewish, aren't you?" Luft said.

Kline nodded. "So what?"

"During the trial I was always bothered by the fact that you're a Jew. My father would have been very upset if he knew that I had prosecuted a fellow Jew."

"You were just following orders." Kline said it with a straight face.

Luft sighed. "You don't know the half of it. I was actually saving you. Everything I did was calculated to save you."

"Well you surely did one hell of a job."

"Listen to me, I know you must hate me. You have every right to, but just listen to me now. During your interrogation you said that you came over to prove a point. You said it was an important point. You said that there was a traitor in your camp, and that you wanted to expose him. Do you remember all that?"

Kline scowled. "What I remember is that you were standing in the background while they turned the voltage on. That's what I remember, Luft. And now I should kill you."

"I think you'll feel differently when you hear me out—"

"Great, so make me feel different. Go ahead."

"We had to put you through the trial and the interrogation so that Moscow would have no reason to intercede. You see, they did not want a trial here, but once we started it they could not stop it. It would have looked bad. So we had to do it all, because otherwise Moscow would have killed you. Yes, they would have killed you. They wanted you quietly dead."

"Quietly dead." Kline said it back. It was what, for all practical purposes, he'd been.

"Moscow was afraid of you," Luft went on. "Someone there was afraid of what you knew."

256

"Yes? So what did I know?"

"You knew something very important about two men. One of them is in Washington, and the other is in Moscow. Do you know what I'm talking about, Robert?"

But Kline did not answer. He was squeezing the pinecone in his hands, watching it crumble away. Finally he said, "What the hell are you doing?"

"I'm confiding in you, Robert. I'm telling you that we've also had a rather bad failure rate over the last few years, and one can't help speculating. Moscow is doing very well, but some of the satellites. . . . Well, you know how it is, don't you? Last year two of our agents were caught in Paris. The year before there was a boy shot in London. What else can I say?"

"You can start by telling me what you want."

Luft smiled. It was the first time that Kline had really noticed his smile, and it reminded him of the smile of a little boy. Luft's whole face lit up, and there was even something rather kind in his eyes. But what he said was, "I want you to help me trap Allen Dancer and whomever he's trading with in Moscow."

They had begun to walk. Here the forest was the dampest. Green bulbs grew in the black soil. Kline was prodding a silver slug with a stick.

"What put you on to Allen Dancer?" Kline said at last.

"I will tell you . . . three years ago I had an agent in Berlin. We'll call her Olga. She was an attractive girl, and after some months in the field she managed to become the mistress of an American general. He was a NATO advisor, not too big a fish, but at least the yield was as regular as clockwork. You know the situation. The general was one of those who could keep a secret only between his ten best friends. Then one day Olga comes to me and she reports that her general has become involved with an American transport operation. The operation involved sending some radio equipment over the border. Well, I think to myself that this is very good news. I need only to have a team follow this shipment of

257

radio equipment and it will lead me right to the door of some agent. A week goes by. I send in my report, and I begin to ready my team. It all looks very good to me. Except that what finally comes down from the top is that I mustn't interfere with this American transportation of radio equipment. Well, I tell myself, okay, I've played these kinds of games before. Obviously the people at the top have their own reasons for keeping me out. Except that there is one thing which bothers me. You see, the man who is in charge of this radio business is none other than Allen Dancer."

"So you knew him, right?"

"Not personally, of course, but I knew about him. He had been stinging my people for years. One here, another there. I'd lost at least four good men to Dancer, and now that I had the chance to get even with him—well, you can understand, can't you?"

"There are lots of reasons why Moscow might want you to keep your hands off something like that."

"Oh, sure, I thought about all that. I looked very hard at all those other reasons, but they did not quite fit. No, Robert, the only reason why Moscow would order me not to track that shipment of radio equipment was because he's really their man."

"No, they don't own Allen Dancer. It's a trade-off. I may not be able to prove it, but I'm sure of it. There's Allen Dancer, and there's someone else."

They had come to a circle of mossy trees where green light fell through the branches, and for a moment it was as if Kline had forgotten where he was. He was motionless, gazing at the smooth trunks of the birches. Then he said in a distant voice, "You're State Security under Willy Zaisser, aren't you?"

Luft smiled. "Very far under. I'm a Jew. You know how it is."

"Do you have any friends in high places? People who will back us up?"

"A few, I suppose, but—"

"But essentially you're an outlaw, is that right?"

258

"Well, yes."

"Then we haven't got a chance."

"But things are changing, Moscow is trying to become less visible. They want our German Democratic Republic to stand . . . on her own feet. Is that the term? Stand on the feet? Yes, and it all means that Moscow won't always be watching like they used to. It means that we will have the latitude we need to conduct our investigation. So what do you say, Robert? Is it a deal?"

"Tell me about the trial. Tell me what happened behind the scenes?"

Luft shrugged. "Well, as I said, Moscow Center wanted you from the start, but they made no overt demands. You know how it is. They hint about this and they hint about that, but they are careful not to demand. After all, legally you were our prisoner, and as I said encroachment is a big issue. Satellite is a dirty word. You know how it is."

"Did they send a man down to see me?"

"Mikhail Brezin from the First Division. He's an old hand but he's weak on diplomacy. He didn't know what to do when I told him that you were mine. Finally he went home."

"What about when they learned you were going after a front page story with the trial and then just prison. Who screamed the loudest?"

"Bruno Pontecorvo. He's also First Division, but he's not our man. I know Bruno, and he's not the type who would sit down with someone like Allen Dancer. He loves the party, and he's stupid. Besides he's lost too many people over the years. He's the one who lost the Caligari apparat in Boston. You remember Caligari. The newspapers called it a major victory for the FBI. Well, I know the FBI, Robert, and they could never have rolled up Caligari unless someone tipped them off. So I have this theory . . . I believe that Allen Dancer was given Caligari and then passed it along to Hoover. I've seen the pattern over and over again. I've seen it dozens of times."

259

"And who is it over here, Luft? Come on, you must have some idea. First Division Moscow Center, and who's been looking like the champion?"

Luft shook his head. "I will tell you something. What I cannot seem to understand is how Dancer worked it out. I've been through it a thousand times, and I simply can't understand how he first made contact with Source Magic. You see the problem, don't you? A trade-off of the sort that we are discussing entails a tremendous amount of trust on the part of both sides. They would have to have had a long relationship before they could have begun. This is not something that one arranges at a party. Trade-offs are very dangerous. It's too easy to betray the other fellow. So I ask you, Robert . . . how in the world did Allen Dancer do it? How did he establish the relationship?"

"He didn't." Kline smiled. "Allen Dancer couldn't buy himself a bloody Arab, much less work a deal with a Moscow Center section head. So you've got to stop thinking in terms of Allen Dancer, because he didn't start Source Magic. His father did— John Dancer."

"How do you know that?"

"I don't for sure, but I remember that in the war old John was considered *the* Russian man. He's been over there twice, that's common knowledge, and he gets on well with them. So it seems very likely to me that he could be the one."

"And this John? He's like his son?"

"No. There's no one like Allen."

They entered a clearing filled with ferns. The trees around them had grown thicker and darker, and the ground was spongy, smelling of rot.

"So will you do it?" Luft asked softly.

"Do what?"

"Help me break Source Magic. Together we can do it. I'm sure we can."

Kline thought for a moment. "Will you get me out of the monastery?"

260

"Of course, but you must promise that you will not try and cross the border."

"Promise?"

"Yes. Give me your word of honor."

Kline laughed. "You really think you can trust me?"

"Why not? We're both Jews aren't we?"

It was the spring of 1950 when Robert Kline was released from prison into the custody of Oskar Luft. It was a secret move. Kline was taken to Luft's apartment, which lay on the outskirts of East Berlin. It was one of the postwar buildings, concrete and drab. A window looked out to a courtyard that was crisscrossed with telephone wires. In the dusky hours Kline and Luft would sit by that window and drink bitter coffee while outside the wind blew over the city, tossing bits of paper around the empty streets. Old people collected bottles and sold them illegally. This was a city of naked light bulbs and rainy streets. There were long blocks of prefabricated apartment buildings. There were odors of gas leaks and boiled vegetables. In the summer garbage rotted quickly. In the winter your breath was white on the air.

Kline slept on a camp bed next to the stove. Luft slept in the adjoining room. They got up early each morning, drank coffee and ate dark bread. Then came a long walk through cold, treeless streets. Everyone was always moving. No one was lingering. The light was always steely gray.

Luft worked in the Ministry building down on the *Unter den Linden,* a grim place with narrow passageways and concrete steps. The entrance was through an iron gate, then along a dingy brick corridor and up two flights of winding stairs. There one pressed a bell and waited for the sentry. Lunch came on an aluminum plate, food from one pot. There was an electric fire in Luft's office, but it never seemed to work.

The others in the Ministry were suspicious and sullen. Everyone seemed afraid of everyone else. The women all wore coarse wool skirts and layers of sweaters. The men dressed like Luft, in ill-cut suits. Luft and Kline spent much of their time in the basement, where the central files were stored. It was like a dank library, except that the shelves were fitted with metal screens.

From the start Luft made it clear to Kline that what they were about to do would be dangerous. He said that it would not look good if they were caught investigating Moscow's most secret operation. So every step they took was masked, every hour otherwise accounted for. The others who worked in the Ministry knew only that Kline had been a prisoner of the State but now was working for them. He was supposedly helping with NATO penetration. Yes, they were pleased to have him on their side, but custom had it that after an agent turned once he could never be trusted again. So most believed that Kline was a coward who had agreed to work in exchange for his life. Had he been a brave man, they said, he would have remained loyal to the West. This was what they felt about Kline at first, but as the months passed and they began to know him better it seemed that everyone finally at least came to respect him. They said he was unstable and had a hair-trigger temper, but he would be a good man in a fight.

In the beginning Luft and Kline kept mostly to the files. Luft would wheel them into Kline on a trolly. Some papers went back to before the war. There were field reports from early German Communists to the Comintern. Apparently the Soviet apparat had placed an agent in the Reichstag, but he was later shot in Saxony. During the war years the central figure was the Ministry head, Wilhelm Zaisser, who recruited German prisoners and fed them back to the Nazis. Links were maintained with courier service and shortwave radio. Luft had been one of Zaisser's agents, and what the files did not contain he knew firsthand.

After the war came Vladimir Seminov, an envoy from the Politburo with a direct line to the Kremlin. Seminov ran the denazification programs, organized trade unions and ran thirteen networks into the West. He paid his agents fifteen dollars a month and lost them at an alarming rate. A few defected, more resigned and

262

others were blown by what Seminov believed was betrayal in the highest echelon of the Soviet machinery. Then Seminov himself vanished, some said murdered by one of his own men over a woman, while others said he was murdered by a Swedish killer in a joint operation with the British. There was, however, a third possibility, one that took Kline three months to establish. Yet in the end he was left with a memo written by a district officer from Leipzig who believed that Seminov had in fact been killed by a West German assassin named Otto Krugger, a man who worked exclusively for Allen Dancer.

In time Luft and Kline became entirely absorbed in their search. At the end of seven months they had constructed a timetable of events and flowcharts that showed the possible lines from Moscow Center to Allen Dancer. But beyond these pages of notes, all handwritten, coded and stored beneath the floorboards in Luft's apartment, there was nothing tangible. To believe, Luft would say, is different from knowing, and proof is different still. These three conditions often looked alike but in fact were very different.

Sometimes after a day at the Ministry the two men would walk out into the evening together. It was on such an evening that Kline, in frustration, said that they could make things simpler if they just killed Allen Dancer.

"I'd do it," he said. "I'd do it in a minute. In fact I'd like to do it. I'd like it very much."

There were gray shapes of children playing down by the foggy canals. Trucks stood along the embankment. Russian soldiers were milling around the bridge. Far away rose pillars of factory smoke, and there was the sound of trains rolling in.

"It would be an easy operation," Kline went on. "You spring me to the West and I can get Allen in . . . oh, maybe sixty days."

"Then what? You come back. You stay? You wouldn't be safe on either side."

"I wouldn't care, right now it would be enough just to do it."

Luft was leaning on the iron fence above the canal. There were bottles, papers and green scum drifting below. Berlin, at least this part, did not seem a very proud city; people threw trash everywhere.

"You know," Luft said, "I don't believe I've ever met anyone quite like you, Robert. A man who does not seem to have any goals."

Kline smiled. "I used to, but I found that the closer I came to achieving them the further I slipped away."

"All right, then, I'll make you a deal . . . you stay with me for another year, and if at that time we still haven't found Dancer's man in the Kremlin and definite proof that a trade-off is occurring, then I'll take you over the border and let you take care of him. Does that seem fair to you?"

"Another year, huh?"

"Yes, just one more year."

By the winter of 1952 they had entered a new phase of the search. At Kline's urging, Luft dispatched agents to gather data from the field. Some traveled to Paris, some to New York and even to London. Others went east. Each was given only specific targets, and none was told the complete story. Even so Luft did not like bringing others into the search. No one, he said, could be trusted. Still, what came back from abroad eventually led Kline to a point where he could make his first reliable estimate about where the eastern end of Source Magic lay.

Kline's estimate began the only place it could begin: with an actual sample of Magic product. The product was delivered in the late afternoon. Luft picked it up from an agent along the Karl Marx Allee. Kline kept watch from beneath the city gates. There was ice in the gutter and the bluish gloom of winter made distant figures appear ghostly.

When they returned to their room and opened the thick envelope they found thirty-three handwritten pages. The pages were the minutes of a Kremlin meeting in which several Center Division heads had discussed the penetration of the Westinghouse electronics plant in Philadelphia.

It was nearly daybreak when they went to bed. Luft's eyes were raw. Sleepless nights were very hard on him. Outside the window there was frost forming on the telephone lines. Both men had wandered to the window, were standing side by side. And then came a gesture that was also representative of these days . . . Luft put his hand on Kline's shoulder.

"Goodnight," he said.

And Kline smiled. "Goodnight, Oskar."

Their voices were very tight. It was a unique experience for both of them.

Kline worked another seven weeks on his estimate. At the Ministry, hunched at the desk between the steel cages, he made only obscure notes, faint cryptograms that appeared to be extensions of his NATO work. But when he returned home each evening he transcribed these notes to a yellow pad of paper. Sometimes he sat on Luft's old sofa, a piece of junk with a missing cushion. Other times he worked by the window, and in contemplative moments he liked to watch the foot traffic treading down icy streets . . . people looked as if they were sleepwalking.

The basic premise of the estimate was that the minutes of a Kremlin meeting could only have come from one of the eight Division leaders of the State Security Committee. Given these eight, Kline was able to eliminate another five by checking their success rates. From the remaining three he narrowed it down to the most likely one.

Now he and Luft took to the streets again. It was a soft night, full of heavy mist and the rumble of convoys. Years ago this neighborhood had been alive with whores and entertainers, now it might have been an abandoned movie set. Weeds had grown up among the ruins of war.

For the first three-quarters of a mile Kline spoke only about

265

how he had come to arrive at his estimate. Then they reached a section of small factories with roofs of rusted sheeting. Kline stopped at the edge of a muddy street, his hands jammed in the pockets of his raincoat. "Tell me what you know about Valentin Servana," he said.

Luft whistled softly. "So now we've reached the . . . major leagues? Is that the expression? Okay. Valentin Servana. I met him once, in . . . oh, about 1947. I was part of the Presidium sent to Moscow for the All State Security talks. Servana lectured on the first and last day. I can't recall what he said, but I remember that he was a very personable fellow. He had a soft voice, and he's very handsome. They say that he never loses his temper."

"Background?"

"I believe his mother was an actress, and his father died in the early days of the Revolution. Incidentally, he uses his mother's name. Father's name was Diderot, but since the twenties he's been calling himself Servana. No one knows why. While he was still a boy he became Jan Brezin's secretary, and remained with the army for many years. Then in 1945 he was transferred to the First Division. Now he heads Section Three, which is the American sphere. They say he's a steady producer, but not brilliant, and for this reason it's difficult for me to see him as our man."

"But there's another way to see it," said Kline. "Let's say that brilliance is a liability. Other boys get jealous if you're too good. They begin to wait for you to take a fall. It might be better to play it modestly. A steady producer with no ups and downs. Just keep it coming in. You see what I'm getting at, don't you?"

"But Allen Dancer is flamboyant."

"Yes, but I think that Servana is probably a good deal smarter than Dancer."

They passed an army garrison that the local police had taken over. An ammunition dump was grown over with birch and willow. There were cobblestones here, some still blackened from the war raids.

266

"I'm through with the old files," Kline was saying. "From here on out we need to see the current status of Source Magic. I want to know the distribution routes. How is the product handled? Who does the primary work? What's the layout of the Enchanted Forest?"

"Why don't I just bring you Harry Truman, Robert? It might be easier."

"I never said it would be easy, Oskar."

"You never said it would be impossible either."

"Just start with Allen. Put a man on him. Let's see if we can't get some idea how he spends his time. And his money."

"What about Valentin?"

"I don't know. How closely can you watch the head of Section Three?"

"It depends on several factors, but I'm sure I can at least pick up a little gossip."

"All right then, concentrate on Dancer. He spends a good part of the year in Switzerland, you might want to look into that."

They took a few more steps, then Kline stopped suddenly. "There's one more thing," he said. "I'd like you to do me a favor."

"What's that, Robert?"

"There's a woman. Dancer's wife actually. Her Christian name is Julia. If it's possible I'd like a profile on her. Do you think you could manage that?"

"You say it's a favor, Robert?"

"She doesn't know anything. I just want to find out about her."

"But why Allen Dancer's wife, Robert? Isn't there something more I should know?"

Kline only shook his head.

And so in his own way Robert Kline returned to the essential story, to Julia, and of course to Jessie. Luft received word of them on the first day in spring, a day when Berlin was at last swept clean by the westerlies. Earlier he had met with a stringer just in from

267

London. He had met the man down along the railroad yards, then in the early afternoon he and Kline drove out along the Autobahn until they came to a patch of open land. Luft parked his battered Volkswagen at the rise of a grassy knoll. A radar installation stood above the distant pines and further still lay a stone wall.

There were seven pages relating to the woman and the child; Luft's agent had inserted them in the lining of an attaché case. Neither man spoke while Kline cut the pages free with a penknife.

Kline hardly breathed after he read the pages. He merely continued to stare out at the blown landscape. After a few moments he said, "I'd like to know when the child was born."

"The child?"

"Yes. There's a child, a son, and I'd like to know when he was born."

"I don't see—?"

"Please, Oskar."

Luft could not recall when Robert Kline had ever used that word. . . .

In all Kline received five reports relating to Julia and the child. They were like his long-range telescope: There were details about her daily life, and mention of the money that Allen sent her each month. Apparently he made erratic visits, always brought gifts but never spent the night. Finally there was even a photograph, slightly blurred and taken from a long way away. It showed Julia and the child crossing a street in Nightsbridge. She wore a belted mackintosh, Jessie was in her arms. The camera had captured her full in the face. She seemed serious, well caught up in the routine of life.

The photograph had essentially been a gift to Robert from Oskar, who by this time knew how his friend felt about the woman. It was one evening while they were having dinner together, and Luft said he had a present for Kline. Then he handed him the photograph. Kline did not know what to say. It was a quiet, good moment between the two.

268

Sometimes, when he was alone, Kline would prop that photograph in the windowsill, or lie down with it and put it on his knees. He liked to look at the faces long enough to get their images fixed in his mind so that whenever he shut his eyes he could still see them clearly. He also liked to study Jessie's face.

And more than once he told Oskar that when Allen and Source Magic had been run to the ground he would return to Julia. He used those words: *run to the ground.* In this way Luft came to know Kline as no one had ever known him before, and after a while some secret part of their beings seemed to merge. They even began to think alike.

What would eventually be seen as the end of the first stage began with a request from a watcher of Luft's who claimed that he had uncovered a vital key to the workings of Source Magic.

Two days after receiving this message Kline left for Zurich. He traveled under diplomatic cover as far as the Rhine, then burned his passport and crossed the border as an industrialist from Frankfurt. In Zurich he made contact with his watcher, and together they spent four days following a beefy, middle-aged man in a woolen overcoat and homburg.

Luft never knew exactly what went wrong, how he was blown. But on the fifth day his watcher was murdered along the Alpen Quai. Luft found his body bent over the steering wheel of a Volkswagen. It took two more days for Luft to find a safe route out of the city. He was frightened every moment.

Kline was waiting for him at the train station. When they saw each other they pretended that they did not know one another until they were sure that neither had been followed. Then they went walking together through the train yards. Steam was rising from behind the waiting rooms. They walked to the end of the track, where junked locomotives lay rusting.

Luft said, "This may be the last time we will be able to walk like this."

"That bad?" Kline's voice showed no emotion.

"I imagine that right now the wolves are heading this way, and Servana is leading the pack."

"How does it happen over here? Do you disappear, or will there be a trial?"

"Oh, there will be a trial. Trials are always the favorite route. They tend to wrap it all up with bows and ribbons. They end the talk for good."

"It's too bad, we were close—"

"Yes. We were close. Did you know that I very nearly found it in Zurich? Dancer has a safe-house there. It's called the Sorcerer House, run by that fellow Otto Krugger."

"Well, maybe there's still time, Oskar. We could use a couple of your Poles. They're pretty tough. Send them out and have them burn Krugger. I mean, we can't just lie down and get kicked, can we?"

They had crossed the yard and stood at the edge of flat open land. A mile of track ran through a marsh. A waiting train sent puffs of white steam into the darkening sky.

Luft had begun to shiver. "Did you know that they used to load the Jews from here?" he said. "This very station had trains that took the Jews east. Whole trains full of them and bound for the camps."

"Well, they didn't get us, did they?" Or had they? Finally? Then it was the Nazis. Now it was anybody, even your own . . .

Another space of silence, filled only by the hissing steam and their feet on the gravel. Then Kline was speaking again, his voice rising. "So what can they really pin on us? We made some investigations. We ran a little surveillance job on one of Allen's people. We took a peek at some Center files. I mean Servana can't hang us for that, can he?"

"Yes, he can," Luft said, and there was an unhappy smile on his face.

"Well, Jesus, Oskar, I thought you had friends in high places."

The same unhappy smile. "I told you, Robert. I'm a Jew, and nothing has really changed."

"So that's it? We just sit here and wait for them to pick us up?"

"I don't know what else we can do—"

"Well, we can at least run, can't we?"

"Where to? The borders are closed."

"Then we can hide."

"Where, and for how long?"

"Well, then what the hell? At least they can't say we didn't try."

They were arrested two days later, taken from their apartment just as dawn was breaking. The eastern sky was washed with violet light, and the buildings and telephone poles stood against its black silhouette. The streets were littered with political leaflets, some from the East, some from the West.

In the ensuing tribunal Kline and Luft based their defense on the Ministry offensive failure rate, and the intersection of Magic product with Section Three of the State Security Moscow. Those thirty handwritten pages of the Center meeting became a key document as well as Kline's estimate of the Seminov scandal. But in the end the prosecution's case was damning. They were charged and found guilty of instigating an unauthorized investigation of the Section Three operational routes with the intent of betraying those routes to a foreign power. The sentence was far more severe than what had been expected. They were given twenty years, and the difference between Oskar Luft and Robert Kline was that Luft was astonished at what was happening to them, while Kline shut his eyes to conjure one clear image of Julia and her son—his son? —Jessie.

The prison lay on a marsh to the east . . . Kline was never sure exactly where. From the window of his cell he had one long view of brown land to the horizon. Sometimes he would see horsemen off in the distance. It would take them more than an hour to move out of sight.

In winter it was cold, and the land became a sea of mist. They had him working in the engineroom, which was considered to be

271

a good job because it was warm. After a while he came to love the greased drive shafts and heavy wheels. He also liked the steady throb of the generator, liked to lie back and listen to the rhythm of the pistons.

In all it seemed to Kline that time was passing in stages. First there were the early days when he just learned to make the best of it. Once he had to cut down a bully who kept trying to steal his cigarettes. Then there was his apprenticeship in the engine-room, where his teacher was an old Hungarian who had been inside since the war. Over the years Kline and this old man became good friends. They would talk while the generators hummed in the background. Finally, though, the old man died, his heart gave out and they buried him outside the prison walls. Kline was given a day to, as the warden put it, "reflect on his grief." It seemed that the warden had a sentimental streak.

The final stages of Kline's life in the prison came toward the end of his sentence. It was 1978. He was old himself by now, and the guards did not bother him much. They knew he did not have the strength to make it past the marsh even if he were able to get through the gates. So Kline more or less came and went as he liked. Most saw him as a quirky, leaky-eyed harmless old man. He used to wink at the younger ones and tell them, "Don't lose hope. Destiny waits." Or some such. It kept up his image.

Which in a way was true, because in the final stage of Robert's life the wheel came around again. It began when a prison near Dresden was closed and its inmates were sent to other prisons throughout the country. Kline was in his cell when the first trucks rumbled in. He heard them in the courtyard and raised himself to the window in order to see what the commotion was. And there among the ranks of new arrivals stood a bent, white-haired Oskar Luft.

When Oskar saw Kline, he broke into a limping run. The two men fell together and embraced. Others stood around and watched, but no one snickered or laughed. They all knew how it was with old friends. What else was there?

272

Later that afternoon the two men wandered into the lot behind the engineroom. The sky was gray and fading. Mud was frozen here, and brittle weeds grew among discarded tool cribs, galvanized vats, coils of barbed wire. In the distance lay forty feet of earthwork, covered with willows.

They had been sitting for more than an hour, perched on two barrels. A guard had passed, but he only nodded. No one cared about these two old people alone in the afternoon.

"Do you still think about it?" Luft asked after a long silence.

"Think about what?" said Kline.

"Why, Magic, of course. Dancer, Servana . . . don't you still think about them?"

"Sure, I still think about them."

"What do you think? Do you think about getting out and starting again?"

"Sometimes."

"Well, I never used to think about it much. Oh, in the beginning perhaps, but after a while I sort of stopped caring. Then something happened. It was just a few weeks ago. Something really quite unusual happened. It was when they were moving us. First in the trucks, then in the trains. Finally we all had to spend a night in a kind of marshalling shed near Holunderthal. Well, I can tell you that it was cold, Robert. Everyone was stamping around trying to keep warm. The guards were trying to keep the boys from the girls. Then the fuse went, and we had to light candles. Well, I remember thinking, 'This is it for you, Oskar. You'll never make it through this night. They're going to find you stiff as a board in the morning.' So I just sat down against the wall of the shed and started to say my prayers."

Kline smiled. "You can't petition the Lord with prayer, Oskar. Haven't they taught you that by now?"

"Yes, go ahead and make jokes, Robert, but I'm about to tell you something extraordinary. There I was, sitting and shivering, and beside me was this little girl. Crying."

"What do you mean little girl?"

273

"I mean a little girl. Oh, not a real child. She must have been about . . . oh, perhaps twenty. And pretty. She was beautiful. Blond hair, blue eyes. So I say, 'What's the matter?' or something like that. She says, 'I'm cold.' So then I say, 'I've got a nice, warm blanket here, I'll let you come on in with me.' Well, naturally she's suspicious, but then it is awfully cold, and so finally the two of us are as close as a fish in the can."

"Must have been a strain on your heart." Kline even laughed.

"No, listen, Robert. We were together, this girl and I, and after a time we began to talk. I tell her a little about myself, she tells me a little about herself. She says that she's English, and her father was a colonel or something. Well, pretty soon I get her whole story . . . Her name is Sara Moore. Her mother used to work with codes. Sara entered the service when she was eighteen and went right into the file room at Whitehall. That would be the Circus, Robert. Do you follow? This girl is working for the British Secret Service, and she has a view of everything. Then one day she begins to notice that there are certain odd little things happening. Papers are missing, and they wind up in the wrong places. So she begins to investigate, and what do you think she finds? She finds everything that's missing crosses the American lines. In other words she finds that it's an American who's leaking secrets. Do you see what I'm saying now, Robert?"

"Magic," Kline intoned. "She'd run right into Magic."

"That's right. She worked on tracking down those leaks for months. Then one day she hears about a security officer in Moscow Center who's willing to tell her about a certain relationship between Allen Dancer and Valentin Servana. Well, she's not field-trained, but she decides that she just can't pass up this chance. So the next thing she knows she's on a plane to Berlin to meet this man. He's supposed to have been the section adjunct, but it might have been a trap, because Sara is only in the city for a few hours when they pick her up."

"But she knew something, is that it?"

"Oh, not really. She had plenty of theories about how Dancer

274

and Servana worked the trades, but she didn't really know that much. In fact, I'd say she knew a whole lot less than we do. So, no, it's not *what* she knew that's important. It's *who* she knew."

"Allen Dancer? She knew Allen Dancer?"

"No, Robert, it wasn't Allen that she knew. It was the boy, Jessie. She knew Jessie Dancer. They lived together as lovers for more than a year, and what do you think she told me? She told me that Jessie doesn't like his father."

There was a pause now. Both men were watching the girders fading in the twilight. A warped moon was above the marsh.

Finally Kline said, "We're going to have to talk with this girl. You know that, don't you, Oskar?"

"It's going to be difficult. She's on the other side of the compound in the women's section."

"Well, I don't care what it takes. We've got to talk to her. We'll fix it with the guards. We'll do anything, just so long as I can see her."

When they got up to make their way across the yard, through the weeds and into their quarters, Robert Kline was no longer shuffling. He was walking like a man half his age.

The intersection of Robert Kline's life with Sara Moore's was perhaps the single most important event in the whole Dancer story. It took weeks and several hundred cigarettes in bribes for Kline to arrange a meeting with the girl. Finally, though, came a morning in an allotment shed on the far northern edge of the prison grounds.

The shed was a small wood frame hut filled with rakes, shovels, a garden hose and bags of fertilizer. Kline reached the shed just as the cold sun was rising over the marsh. He wore his woolen coat, but he was still shivering. Finally he saw two figures approaching, black outlines against the red sun. The guard was a big man, and the girl looked particularly frail beside him.

Kline was standing in parallel bars of light and shadow when the girl was pushed into the shed. He said nothing at first, and she

275

only gazed blankly around, as if she were in shock. Her eyes were sleepy, large and blue-green. Her features were small and sprayed with freckles. Her hair was blond, almost white, and she had a thin boyish figure. She wore a drab, prison dress and clutched an old blanket around her shoulders.

Kline looked through the slats to see the guard standing thirty feet away, smoking and gazing out to the marsh. The girl was watching him as a frightened rabbit might watch a predator. She was looking at him from the corner of her eyes.

Kline smiled and said, "Hello, I'm a friend of a friend. He's an old man. You met him a few weeks ago. Do you remember?"

At first she did not seem to understand him, and only said, "You're American, aren't you?"

"Yes, but that's beside the point. What's important is my friend and the things you told him. Do you remember?"

She nodded. "Oskar . . . his name was Oskar."

"That's right, and do you remember what you talked about with him?"

She had a small mouth, and very thin lips. She was shaking now.

"Listen to me, Sara. I'm a friend, this isn't an interrogation. This isn't a trick . . . this is real and I'm trying to help—"

"But I don't know what you want . . ."

He nodded "My name is Robert Kline, and I don't believe in Magic either."

Now they were both fixed, perfectly still in the bars of light. Even the dust was suspended. The girl's eyes were filling with tears.

Finally Kline said, "Now will you tell me, Sara? Will you tell me what you told Oskar?"

She closed her eyes and nodded. Tears were streaming down her cheeks. Then she managed to say the name. One word, and it was barely above a whisper. Jessie.

"Yes, Jessie," Kline echoed softly. "Will you tell me about Jessie?"

276

She spoke haltingly and very quietly . . . "We met at a party. He was working in the embassy. I had just started to . . . you know, Source Magic . . ."

"Yes, Magic."

"So when I heard that he was working in London I arranged to meet him."

"Then it wasn't a chance meeting?"

"No, not chance."

"You met him because you thought he might know something about Magic."

"Yes. I thought he might be able to tell me. I had to know—"

"And did he help you?"

"He didn't know anything. He didn't want to know anything. He didn't want anything to do with his father."

"Did he tell you why?"

"He said that he didn't like his father. He said he even thought he hated him . . ."

"Yes, but why? Why, Sara? Why did he think he hated his father?"

The tears came again, and she shook her head. And before he could press her further the guard was coming for her.

In the next few months Kline met the girl several times. He would wait for her in the shed which overlooked the marsh, or else they met in an abandoned laundry room. Either place it was always the same. They would stand together talking softly while the guard smoked another cigarette. It was in this way that Kline formed his first impressions of the apparently remarkable Jessie Dancer.

When they first met, Sara said, Jessie had just come back from Vietnam, and the war was still very much inside him. In the embassy they had him filing bits of paper. He never had a kind word to say to anyone. Enemies were what he preferred.

"We fought at first," she said. "He knew I was only trying to use him. He knew it from the start, and he became very angry. I thought he was going to hit me. He's like that . . . when he gets angry he's different."

"But you did become friends eventually, didn't you?"

"Yes, eventually."

"Close friends?"

"Yes," and it made her start to cry again.

Kline waited a moment before he spoke again. The fog was swirling far off in the distance, fog that the sun would soon burn away.

"Jessie didn't have any other friends," she said. "Just me."

"And what about Magic? Did he finally help you?"

"No. He didn't want me to do it. He just wanted me to leave it alone."

"But you couldn't, could you?"

She shook her head. "I never told him. We never talked about it. It was just something I did."

Before she left she told him that Jessie did not know she was here. He probably didn't even think she was still alive . . . he would have come for her if he had known. He wouldn't have let her stay here, she was sure of it. And then she began to cry again. She had cried a little every day, but this time Kline could not help reaching for her. So when the guard finally rapped against the side of the shed, Kline was holding her in his arms.

The last time Kline saw the girl was a month before his release. They met in the half-light of the deserted laundry room. Through the grimy windows he could see steel girders strung with barbed wire outlined against an evening sky.

The girl had a thin cut above her forehead and a bruise on her cheek. When she saw Kline she hesitated, then called his name and ran into his arms. He held her while she wept. Later she told him that the women in her cell had stripped her, tied her down to a bunk, and then beat and raped her.

But in this deserted room, among old water troughs, splintered

278

benches and pressing irons, a kind of healing took place for both of them.

"They're going to let me out pretty soon," he told her. "I won't forget you, *that's* a promise. One way or another I'll get you out of here."

She pressed his hand to her lips. "What are you going to do?"

"I don't know."

Suddenly she broke away from him. She was standing straight, and in her own way she looked quite fierce. When she spoke again her voice was hard and cold.

She said, "Find Jessie. Do it. Find him and tell him that I'm here. *Please . . .*"

Kline and Luft were released from prison on a spring day. They were just two old men being driven back to Leipzig in a truck. The driver had a transistor radio wedged between the dashboard and the windshield, playing *It's been a long, long, long time.* You can say that again, Kline thought.

In the late afternoon they found themselves on a dirt road that ran between wavering meadows of purple flowers. They were walking into a steady wind, their caps pushed down over their ears, their coats flowing behind. They might have been two lost, quirky fools heading for a city they had never seen before. The whole landscape was like a running watercolor, the wind seeming to smear the trees and flowers together. When they began to pant they sat down under an oak and shared a chocolate bar. Kline started pulling off flowers. He was idly shredding them and dropping the petals on the ground.

"You shouldn't be doing that," Luft said. "The groundskeeper might see, we might get into trouble."

"To hell with trouble," Kline said, and a handful of petals came raining down on both of them.

Luft shook his head. "Imagine the two of us trying to tie up a bundle of snakes. And at our age?"

"Well, we've got to try, Oskar. It's all we've got."

279

"What do you want to do, Robert?"

Kline paused and glanced around the meadows, then said softly, "I want to get a product list, a Magic product list."

"You mean a list of the material that Dancer has been receiving from Servana? You mean an actual list?"

"I do."

"But you'd have to steal that out of Langley—"

"I know."

"You're crazy, Robert—"

"No, listen to me, Oskar. Why did we fail the first time? We failed because we couldn't get proof, isn't that right? Well, if we had an actual list of the material that Servana has passed, then we could get them both. All we would have to do is to trade that list with Moscow for a similar list of the material that Dancer passed to Servana. Do you see that, Oskar? Langley thinks that Dancer is passing Servana chicken feed. Moscow thinks that Servana is passing Dancer the same. In fact they're both passing each other gold, but the only way to make Moscow and Langley realize what really goes on between them is to show them each what the other side has been taking in."

"You're still crazy, Robert, and even if we could get such a list, how would it help Sara?"

"Once we have the Magic list, we don't necessarily have to make an exchange with Moscow. All we have to do is to let Dancer and Servana know we have it. Then they'll get her out for us. I can assure you of that. They'll move mountains for us once they know we have the list."

"They could kill us, it's dangerous."

"Of course it's dangerous, but at least they'll give us Sara. They'll do it to buy time for themselves, if nothing else."

"Time to figure out a way to kill us."

Kline shrugged. "We're old men, Oskar. What have we got to lose?"

"But why Langley? Why not first try and get one of Servana's

280

product lists, then threaten to trade it with Langley for one of Dancer's? We can get her out that way too. It would work just as well, and the east is home now, for you too. Surely it would be easier to operate in the east—"

"Yes, it might be easier for *us* to operate in the east, but we're not actually going to be operational in this one, Oskar. Someone else is."

"What are you talking about? We don't have anyone—"

"We will."

"Who?"

"Jessie Dancer."

"You mean Allen Dancer's boy? You want to recruit Allen Dancer's own son for this?"

"Yes, and I'm going to see him about it."

"But you don't know anything about him, Robert. You don't even know where he is."

"I'll find him."

"And then what?"

"I'll talk to him."

"But you don't even know him. He might laugh at you. You're an old man, after all."

"Well, at least I can try," and then Kline began to grin like the wolf that he sometimes resembled. "Besides, Oskar, I have a good feeling whenever I think about Jessie. A very warm, good feeling . . ."

Not long after their release, Oskar Luft died. He and Kline were known to have been living in Zurich, a clear indication that their hunt had never ended. For a while they shared a flat in a working class section, and later there was a cottage in the country. They liked to take the crosstown bus all the way to the botanical gardens and walk along the paths between the roses. It was here that Luft died. In the weeks before he had suffered from cramps and begun to lose feeling in his limbs, but when he died it was an oddly simple

281

gesture. The two friends had been staring at a hundred stalks of perfect roses. Then Luft was just toppling over, reaching out for Kline, and finally collapsing in his arms.

Not long after Luft had been buried, Kline left for Bangkok. It had taken him nine weeks to locate Jessie, discovering his whereabouts by tracing the passport through an old contact of Luft's. Then he simply left. Once in Bangkok he became an insubstantial figure on the edge of marshes, strolling through the twilight along the brown river. He bought a jade beetle for no reason at all. The nights were muggy and warm. He went from place to place, searching for Jessie. Finally they met in a small cafe along the waterfront.

Purple light fell from paper lanterns. A moth, trapped in one, kept beating its wings against the rice-paper skin.

"What do you want, old man?" Jessie had a way of speaking through his teeth, as if he were perpetually enraged.

"I knew your mother," Kline said.

"So what?"

"And I've seen Sara Moore."

Dancer yanked the old man out into the night so that they could speak without being overheard.

On the next night they met on a marsh near a crumbling sewer plant. Jessie had just come back from the jungle, where he had cut his ear stalking through the elephant grass. His hands still smelled of cordite, and his pockets were filled with hollow-point bullets. When Kline entered the marsh, Jessie was waiting for him by a large steel pipe. A warm wind rippled through the bamboo.

All Jessie said was, "I've decided to help you."

Kline allowed himself a smile, and shut his eyes for a moment. As if giving thanks.

PART 4

CHAPTER NINE

A FEW days after the encounter on the marsh, Jessie Dancer spoke seriously with Dusty Yeats about infiltrating the Magic apparatus. From his own account as extracted by Humphrey Knolls, Yeats had been receptive to the idea from the start. The objective of the infiltration had clearly been to obtain material which could later be used to secure the release of Sara Moore.

Jessie remained in Bangkok only a few days after Yeats had arrived in Langley. Then he traveled across Asia and into Switzerland. There he stayed in Kline's cottage, which lay along the lake outside of Zurich. In the afternoons the lake flowed into violets and darker tones. It was a shockingly tranquil place to be after a war.

285

Kline's cottage lay in a dingle off a narrow, shady lane. The rooms were filled with simple country furniture. There was a black stove and a butcher block in the kitchen. The floors were red brick, worn smooth over the years and covered with coarse rugs. You could hang your coat on a door peg, and in the corner was an old wing-chair. There were discolored washbasins and porcelain bowls. Roots had cracked the chimney stones. The windows looked out into green tunnels of foliage. The first thing Jessie asked Kline when he saw the cottage was, "Hey, are there any snakes around here?" It was meant to be a joke, but Kline had never fought a war in a jungle so, at first, he did not understand.

In the mornings Jessie would frequently stroll out into the forest and line up empty beer bottles. He had a long-barreled semiautomatic Beretta that he had picked up en route to Switzerland. The weapon had been modified to accommodate lighter loads . . . the spring in the blow-back mechanism was loosened, and the barrel was grooved for a silencer. It was a killer's weapon, and most days Jessie spent hours among shadowy trees, squeezing off shots.

While Jessie was away Kline usually worked on the files. It was an academic effort. There were really no secrets left, and he worked mainly because he had always worked. He was like any of the old historians; entirely consumed in the intricacy of the past. He hunted for the sake of hunting. After so many years it was part of him.

Much of his research seemed to have led him to the Bay of Pigs fiasco. For years Kline had believed that Source Magic had played at least a role—maybe a decisive role—in the operation, but he had never taken the time to study it. Now for some reason he felt compelled to understand.

He had begun with the day of the invasion. April 17, 1961, when the fourteen hundred Cuban exiles landed at the southern inlet. The day before the B-26s had struck the Camp Libertad airfield outside of Havana. It had gone badly from the start. Ten planes were downed and ten pilots killed. The following morning the

286

landing began, and the misery compounded. Soon after hitting the beach the heavy mortar and artillery opened up, and the exiles were decimated. Cuban aircraft, which were supposed to have been destroyed by the initial bombing raid, caught the brigades in the open. Finally Castro unleashed his heavy Stalin tanks, and the day was finished.

Who was to blame for the Bay of Pigs? There were those, Cubans mainly, who said that the operation would have succeeded had only President Kennedy authorized an eleventh-hour support team. Then there were the strategists who said that the operation had been doomed from the start. They said the Cubans had been poorly trained, Castro's retaliatory force underestimated, and the bombing strikes badly coordinated. Yet in the mind of Robert Kline, the Bay of Pigs had always stood juxtaposed against Source Magic.

Logic, experience and hunch played their roles. Besides, there were moments when it seemed to Kline that he had an almost eerie insight into events . . . and then the past ceased to be a broad perspective and became a string of crystalline visions, and it was as if he saw events through tiny fragments of glass. Which was the way it was for him with Source Magic and the Bay of Pigs. He saw the story in his mind . . . The initial talks in Guatamala city, where the CIA station chief met with a wealthy coffee grower and arranged for the secret training camp, then the arrival of the five groups of Cuban exiles who'd been organized into a revolutionary front, and finally Allen Dancer and Servana.

Kline guessed that they'd met in Switzerland about, say, seven weeks before the invasion. He could visualize them speaking on the balcony of a rented villa, Allen wearing a gray suit, his tie undone . . . Valentin listening with his head down and to the side. Allen had probably only been able to give Servana the barest bones of the invasion plans, probably hadn't known the exact dates or the size of the exile army. Maybe all Allen had known for sure was that the CIA had furnished the ten bombers, but given the way

287

things eventually fell, that had been enough. Servana's contacts had only to alert Castro about approximations, and they could take it from there through their contacts. It was a pretty rinkydink operation all on its own . . . hardly needing to be compromised from outside. A perfect setup for Magic . . .

One night, several days after he had begun to research the connection between Magic and the Bay of Pigs, Kline made the mistake of mentioning it to Jessie. The boy was particularly morose that evening. He was sitting at an awkward angle in the rocking chair, his shadow moving back and forth on the wall. When Kline told him his theory the boy only sneered. A cigarette was glowing between his fingers.

"You think I'm wasting my time, don't you?"

Jessie shook his head. "No, I don't think you're wasting time."

"But you don't believe it's possible, do you?"

"Anything's possible."

"But not likely. Isn't that what you're thinking?"

"I'm thinking that there's a difference between what's real outside and what's real in here." Then he tapped his finger to his skull. "In here."

Kline tried to tell the boy how it was actually to have seen the vision of the two men talking on the balcony of a rented villa. But Jessie did not listen, and Kline realized then that only old men understood how strange things can happen after one has spent a very long time immersed totally in a single subject. Obsession?

More often, however, their evenings together were passed in silence. Kline prepared simple meals, usually just potatoes and vegetables from a haphazard garden he had planted without really thinking about it, then he and Jessie would drink an inexpensive table wine and subside into their respective worlds.

It was a strange relationship.

But there was one night, several weeks after Jessie had come to stay here, when Kline could not resist pulling out a few of his old jazz records and putting them on the phonograph. Then instead

288

of silence the room became filled with the rich tone of a clarinet while a dreamy, whiskey voice sang: *I've got no chance of loving you—no chance at all . . .*

"Do you hear that song?" Kline asked him. "Your mother used to love that song."

"Is that right?" said Jessie listlessly. He had been staring at an empty wine bottle for an hour, and he had the strongest urge to shatter it.

"She mostly liked the sad ones," Kline went on. "She used to listen to them with the lights turned off. We used to listen to them together that way . . . a long time before you were born."

As if Jessie cared at all what had happened before he was born. Including his mother and Kline . . . But Kline kept on talking, first about himself, then Allen, then Julia.

Later, after going upstairs to Oskar Luft's old room, Jessie found himself trying to remember a few specifics about his own life. It was very still now, and cold for the first time in the year. Outside the window blackberry bushes were glittering. There was even frost on the windowpanes. Before he knew it he was printing big letters in the frosted glass: SAR—then he rubbed them out. . . .

Not long after Jessie's birth his mother's father had died and she and the child had moved to London, where they lived in a working-class flat. In the early evenings Jessie used to lie in bed and hear the rough kids playing ball in the courtyard. Eventually he would become the roughest of them all. There was a photograph taken: Jessie and his mother on the steps of their flat. She was smiling, but one could still see faint traces of the pain around her mouth. Jessie's eyes were wistful, distant. He looked about a thousand years old.

What Jessie remembered best was that his mother was always afraid. She was afraid of the streets, crowds and Sunday afternoons. What she liked were small, warm rooms filled with yellow lamplight and a slow clarinet playing on the gramophone. She

289

used to tell Jessie that he was her little man and that they must be a team against the world. But no matter how hard he tried, he was just too small to stop her from being afraid.

When it came time for him to attend school, Allen sent him to a place called Mitgangs. "You must get a proper start on life," Allen had told him, but what one got at Mitgangs was hardly that. There were sessions when the older boys beat the younger ones. They would tie you to a water pipe and flog you with wet towels. Once they held Jessie down and put a snake on his face. Worst of all, though, was knowing that he had only been put in Mitgangs so that Allen could have mother all to himself.

Finally there was that night when a boy named Crabbe tried to pull down his trousers in order to whip him with a belt. Something boiled up in Jessie so quickly that even he did not know what it was. All he saw were Crabbe's lips sort of curled above his teeth. And then the whole world was a bursting ripe tomato with the sound of bone on bone. Afterward, when they all stood around in shock because Crabbe was bleeding so badly, Jessie felt like he was floating in a placid, dreamy calm. He'd cut his knuckles on Crabbe's teeth, and the blood tasted like a pencil, only saltier.

After that life became a nightmare that only his pride could get him through. He had no friends . . . the other boys were afraid of him or else paid him no notice. On Sundays he was given peaches and cream and then herded into the chapel, where they lectured about God. But Jessie already knew all about God. God played dirty tricks . . .

In retrospect memories from these years tended to be all clotted together. He remembered the sound of slamming doors, and how his mother used to fight with Allen. Late at night he would hear the tangle of their voices. Allen's was always so damned smooth and reasonable . . .

But most of all he remembered one summer evening with his mother. He was lying on her bed, idly toying with the contents of her jewelry box. It was filled with junk mostly, although there

290

were silver thimbles, strings of yellow pearls and a tiny jade horse that was what he liked best. There was also a gold locket, and when you unclipped it there was the photograph of the man with the strangest eyes in the world.

"Mum?"

"What is it, Jessie?"

"Who's this?"

Mother was at her writing desk. All evening she had been sorting bits of paper, while Jessie had been dangling his feet, squinting at the face inside the locket.

"That's just an old friend," she finally told him.

"Yes, but what's his name?"

She thought for a moment, as if she could not remember, or else was afraid to tell him?

"It's no one you know, dear."

"Yes, but what's his name."

Then she sighed. "His name is Robert. Robert Kline."

Later she started to cry, for no reason at all that he could understand.

Through these years his mother still painted, and her paintings became more and more real, although they also became sadder ... landscapes always gray, streets always dark and empty. Finally she did a portrait of him, only he didn't think that it looked like him. It looked like a boy who had grown up to look like the portrait she had done of Robert Kline. . . .

Jessie was thirteen when his mother was killed. The headmaster pulled him out of class to break the news, then took him for a stroll down a leafy path until they came to the chapel. In the end the headmaster left him alone in the chapel so that he might receive some sign from God. Well, there was a sign, all right. His whole body seemed taken over by rage. He was struck by rage, as he might have been struck by lightning.

Later he found out that his mother had been attacked by a gang of boys for the change in her purse, and had died from a knife wound in her spine. Allen Dancer did not attend the funeral because he was supposedly involved in vital government business. But seven weeks later he flew into England and took Jessie on holiday to the north of Scotland. They spent a fortnight together in a small cottage near Innerleithen. Jessie spent most of the time tramping through the gorse. The light was gray-blue in the afternoons and the streams were filled with toads. Allen was always trying to be a pal, but he just couldn't do anything right.

Throughout the next years Jessie recalled that he saw Allen nearly every holiday. Their relationship was reserved, but polite. Often they went to Switzerland and France. There were also a few summers spent at his grandfather John's house. The old man always did his best to please Jessie, and there had been moments when Jessie sort of felt he and his grandfather understood each other, had at least more in common than he and his father.

One incident stood out above the rest. It occurred of an evening when he and Allen were on holiday at Lake Lugano. He had been out all morning wandering along the waterfront. When he returned Allen was waiting for him in the doorway of their hotel. The gold locket was dangling from his fingers. It was unlatched so that Jessie could see the photograph of his mother's friend.

"Where did you get this?"

"It was mum's, and you had no right taking it—"

"No *right?*"

And Jessie felt the stinging slap across his face, after which Allen stormed out of the room. A moment later Jessie watched from the window as Allen stood at the lake's edge and threw the locket far out into the water. It was a bad throw. No grace or rhythm to it. . . .

At seventeen Jessie lived in a small shabby flat in London's Little Venice. Women came and went. Everyone was smoking hashish and sleeping with everyone else. The Beatles played at Albert Hall, and a lot of people believed that things were actually getting better. Jessie thought he knew better.

292

You woke up in the morning, got stoned and went out looking for a girl. More often than not you would end up in a dirty tenement with a mattress on the floor and a dozen others nodding off on grass. The Rolling Stones were playing on the radio, singing, *I want to see the sun torn out of the sky. I want to see the whole world painted black.* . . .

At eighteen Jessie started working at the American Embassy in London. Allen got him the job, and they put him to work addressing envelopes and typing correspondence. Allen had told him that it was important to make himself well-liked, but Jessie did not care whether people liked him or not. Eventually he started sleeping with a girl named Mary Pram who worked in the Embassy's confidential section. It was Jessie's first real brush with the secret world.

Later she told him that she had only been sleeping with him because he was Al Dancer's son, and she thought it might somehow help her career. When she confessed all this she cried, but Jessie mostly thought it was funny. As though he was an open sesame to Allen . . .

Jessie could not remember exactly why he decided to go to Vietnam. There just came a point when it seemed to him that Vietnam would be the only place in the world that was real. In a war, he figured, things would get reduced to simplest terms. Dumb people would get killed quick, while the long-time survivors would be better and very wise. Beyond all that, Allen had been pressuring him to go for quite a while. He said that service on the edge of a combat zone would look very good on his record. Except Jessie did not want to be on the edge of the combat zone. He wanted to be right in the middle of it.

Jessie spent his first three months in Saigon. He lived in a room off the Lam Son Square and hung around the milk bars in Broddards and La Pagode. In the late afternoons the city became desolate and the long boulevards held nothing but refuse: wind-blown paper, neat piles of human excrement, firecracker casings

293

from the Lunar New Year. The trees along the main streets looked as if they had been scorched. After curfew the emptiness was total. There were only the police patrols and a few children running newspaper kites into the swamp wind.

It soon became clear to Jessie that Saigon was a city that was corrupt to its roots. Most white men hated to even step into the streets . . . the locals took odds on their lives. There were five known Vietcong sapper battalions in the Saigon-Cholon area, and every night someone got killed. But Jessie never worried about getting killed in Saigon. It was a city that seemed to accept him into its fold. Within only three weeks he had the moves down.

In Saigon they had him working in liaison with Army Intelligence and the Drug Enforcement Administration. His job involved helping stop the heroin flow from the Meo tribes in Laos to the Corsican Mafia in Hong Kong. Not long into the game Jessie decided that many of the agents from the Drug Enforcement Administration were as corrupt as the Mafia dealers, and so after three months he set up two Americans who had gone dirty. He waited until they tried to sell him nine kilos of number four, then he shot them, and threw their bodies into the river. After that, he left Saigon and moved out into the delta to fight the war for real.

Next came the life that he might have been waiting his whole life to lead. Things happened at night in the jungle that in the morning he could not quite believe had happened. He often felt as if his pupils enlarged until the entire whites of his eyes were wide, like some animal's. When that happened, even on moonless nights the jungle appeared crystalline, as if seen through an infra-red scope. The nights were best, perfect.

When Jessie arrived at the delta station there were three other men there. Then one afternoon a sniper shot two, and then there was only Dusty Yeats. Yeats had been a Green Beret Bushmaster who, after three tours, had been told that he was too unstable for regular duty. He was deeply superstitious and addicted to amphetamines. The first night that he and Jessie went into the forest they caught the tail end of a Vietcong patrol in a crossfire. It was a clean kill among the moss-bound trees. After they returned to the station, a silent understanding, a bond was built between them.

Often the jungle represented an entirely separate reality. In the afternoon there were blue-green shafts of light, mingling with the purple fuchsias, spider webs and translucent fronds. Further out lay the mango groves, which had been laid with Claymores and German razor wire. Deformed banyan trees grew along the estuary. Jessie and Yeats used to pass through these trees in the early evening, then move out into the damp, warm stillness of the jungle floor. It was not a war they were afraid of, and they fought it with total concentration.

There was no sense of finality to the end of the war. Merely there came a day when it was over. Yeats had long ago decided that he would return to California to live with his sister, while Jessie had no plans at all. He had been offered a position in Langley, but he did not want it. By now he had come to believe that the world was pretty much divided between people who were neutral, and people who were evil. Those in Langley, he told Yeats, were the latter, and if he lived among them he would not be able to control himself. He was afraid there would be an incident.

Jessie spent his last weeks of duty back in Saigon. By now the war was clearly lost, not that Jessie much cared. He had always known that Vietnam could never be conquered, only destroyed. He spent his days doing nothing. He lived on brown rice, vegetables and vitamins. The city was filled with gutted buildings, puddles, wet newspapers and broken glass. It was during this time that he began to sense that there was something special about him. Not good, but special. He could not look at objects impassively. A lamp, a chair, a table, a bottle . . . there was always something about their presence that annoyed him, as if they kept trying to encroach on *his* presence. Also, people were always avoiding his eyes, and little things made him furious. He told Dusty—and believed it—that all one had in the end was dignity, self-respect

295

maybe, and that it was better to kill than let someone take that away from you. On the flight back he found himself sitting next to a lawyer from the Internal Revenue Service. The man started telling Jessie how it was important to believe in what one did for a living. He, for example, fully believed in law enforcement and the importance of taxation. Jessie kept trying to think of something he could say that would answer the man. Nothing, short of murder, came to mind. . . .

Finally he returned to London, if only because London was an easy choice. His position at the Embassy was still available, and they had even kept his flat for him. Also, London was neutral and passive. He did not believe it was a city that would fight back.

So he fell into the regular ranks of society, and killed each day like normal people killed time. He woke every morning in his contemporary flat, then wandered into the kitchen and waited for the kettle to boil. There was a view through a sooty window of a gray backcourt; zinc garbage cans, laundry lines, telephone wires. He spread two slices of bread with canned meat and mayonnaise, pressed them together with lettuce and stuffed it into a paper bag with a thermos of orange juice. Later he would eat his lunch alone in the park. He dressed in modest clothing and then moved out into the streets to catch the bus. The next six hours were spent mechanically sorting through embassy correspondence. He rarely spoke to anyone and never did more than what was expected of him. At the end of the day he would file back into the streets and return to his flat, where he would eat a frozen dinner and stare out into the bluish London air.

It was a bearable existence. There were no undue pressures placed on him, no unusual demands. His only real concern was that one day someone would try to take advantage of him, try and humiliate him, try and rob him of what little self-respect he had. Then there would be an . . . accident in the streets, and everyone would be terribly shocked.

There were people who felt sorry for Jessie. They saw him as

296

a sad, lonely, oddly simple young man. Women in particular were taken by him . . . after all, he was blond, quiet and seemingly polite. Jessie, though, avoided conversation, because whenever he spoke to people he felt as if some kind of machine were speaking for him. He never knew what he would say, and his voice always sounded disembodied to him. It was particularly bad whenever he spoke with someone in a position of power. Government officials, bankers, doctors, lawyers: these people who could step on others out of indifference or arrogance, and Jessie was continuously afraid that one of them would try to step on him. Then he would have no choice but to pull them down. So the war was not over . . . you just had to be a little more careful how you fought it.

Jessie's supervisor at the embassy was a frightened little man named Cork. Cork was always trying to help Jessie, probably because the boy terrified him. Jessie had only been working three months when Cork called him into his office. Cork's office was paneled with fake rosewood. There were two leather chairs for visitors and Cork's own massive swivel behind his desk. In the corner was a trolley laid with cups, saucers and a coffee pot on a hot plate. Cork had been born in Boston, but after years of service in London he spoke like an Englishman.

"Won't you sit down?" he said when Jessie entered. There followed an awkward exchange of amenities, and Jessie began to sweat.

"Tell me," Cork finally said, "how are you getting on here?"

"Fine, thank you."

"No personal problems? Nothing bothering you?"

"No. Everything's fine."

"I see. How about the work? You don't find it too dull, I hope."

"It's fine."

On the mahogany surface lay an ebony letter opener, a leather cup filled with pens and pencils, neat stacks of paper in silver mesh baskets, a cigarette lighter, a marble ashtray, and another marble slab that held a gold fountain pen. Jessie kept glancing from object to object as if they were about to explode.

297

Cork was saying, "I don't usually make a point of prying into the personal lives of staff, Jessie. However, in your case I've decided to make an exception . . . well, quite frankly I'm a little concerned about you—"

"Something wrong with my work?"

"Oh, no, it's nothing like that. It's just that . . . well, you seem to keep to yourself an awful lot . . . never join in with the others. You missed the picnic last month . . . I can't help wondering if there isn't something troubling you."

"No, nothing's troubling me."

Except that every object on the desk had begun to smirk at him.

"Yes, all right, but I do wish you'd make more of an effort to meet the others. They're a good bunch, really. I know they'd be only too happy if you opened up a bit."

At that moment Jessie had a quick vision of himself opening up in a mango grove with the selector switch of his M-16 on full automatic—

"Look, this isn't meant to be a lecture, Jessie. It's only that I'd like to see you join *in* more. For example, there's a party Friday night. Our British cousins put a little affair together for us every year. The whole staff is invited, and I'd be very grateful if you came."

"Thank you, I'll try to make it."

"I wish you would. I'll leave an invitation in your box."

It got very bad before the conversation ended. Cork kept going on about how pleased he was to have had this chat, while Jessie kept staring at the objects on the desk. *Okay, he wanted to say at them, you made your point. . . .*

The party was held in a large reception hall. There was a long buffet table covered with white linen, crystal and silver. Uniformed servants circulated among the guests with champagne and hors d'oeuvres. The men were dressed in black tie, the women in expensive gowns. They congregated in circles, and Jessie stood at the

298

edge of the largest circle and pretended that he was one of them.

He might have stood like that all evening, smiling when jokes were told, moving on to other circles when his presence became noticed, except he sensed a girl was watching him.

She stood surrounded by young, confident men, but her gaze kept falling past them and settling on Jessie. He supposed she was very pretty, with blond, almost platinum hair and large blue-green eyes. She had small features and freckles, which made her look like a child. There was also an odd, sleepy look in her eyes, as if she had just woken up.

He had no intention of speaking to her, none at all. He was sure he would never have been able to carry it off. But later, while filling his plate with food he would not eat, he heard her speaking behind him.

"Hello. You're new around here, aren't you?"

He turned. "Yeah. I'm new."

"Do you work at the Embassy?"

She was definitely on the make, but he wasn't sure why.

"Yes."

"How do you like it?"

"It's fine."

"Were you transferred from somewhere?"

"No, not exactly."

"So what were you doing before?"

"Before?"

"I mean before you were working here?"

He took a moment to think, because suddenly he had lost all track of where he was. It happened a lot. Then he saw an image of the jungle and said, "Vietnam. Vietnam, I was there."

As always the word cast a kind of spell. It was a bad word, and the girl dropped her eyes. She looked as if she was concentrating very hard.

Finally she said, "I didn't realize."

"Yes. I was there." He still was, for that matter.

299

"Well, I imagine it must have been a rather difficult experience."

"Difficult?"

She tried to smile. "I mean with the war and all."

So he smiled back. "Oh it wasn't difficult. Not at all. Just the opposite."

She left him standing beneath a chandelier that was flaring with spikes of light. He supposed this was what they called having an adjustment problem. . . .

Jessie rarely thought about women during these days. He figured it had something to do with the war, the thought of making love seemed, somehow, wrong to him. He wasn't sure why. It just seemed that way. But later that night when he had returned to his flat, he found himself thinking about the girl. He kept seeing her eyes, hearing her voice. He might have gone on brooding about her all night, but then the doorbell was ringing and she was standing in the porchlight.

"May I come in?"

He shrugged and turned his back on her. She followed him in, and sat on the edge of the sofa. She was wearing a black raincoat, and black was his favorite color. He was facing the window.

"I've come to apologize," she said.

"What for?"

"Well, I was rude to you, wasn't I?"

"I don't know."

"Yes. I left you standing there."

"So what?"

"So I'm sorry."

He turned and faced her. "Look, what the hell do you want from me? You come 'round here playing cat and mouse. Well, I didn't ask for this, and I guarantee you I don't need it. So what *is* it?"

300

She lowered her head and took a deep breath. "You're Allen Dancer's son, aren't you?"

All he said was, "fuck," but it came out very softly.

"I heard you were here, in fact I asked about you."

"Who sent you, the London Station? Circus? Is that it? You're one of the London girl guides? Well, let me tell you something, you'd better stay away from Al Dancer. He eats little spies like you for breakfast."

"But you don't even know what I want—"

"Yes, I do."

She had risen from the sofa and walked to his side. Now they were both looking out across the empty street to where the lamplight fell on the puddles.

"You don't like your father, do you?"

"Whatever gave you that idea?"

"It's obvious. Besides, you wouldn't be working in the Embassy if you were close to him—you'd be working with him."

"Well, you're wrong . . . everyone likes him, he's a hero—"

"Is he? And I'm not talking about everyone . . . I'm talking about you."

"What is this? You want to recruit me? Is that it? This is London's move to muscle in on Mag—? Well, you tell your people to screw off."

"It's not like that," she said calmly. "I came here on my own, and my name is Sara Moore."

"Is that right?"

"Yes"

"No boyfriends in the street?"

"I told you, I came alone."

"In that case I think you'd better leave right now. I'm not a very stable person, and if I were in your position I'd leave, just leave."

She wasn't afraid, not at all, and just before she left she told him that he was nuts and that she never wanted to see him again.

Later, though, long after midnight, it occurred to them both that they had fought as if they had been old lovers. The thought came to them near-simultaneously. Jessie was again at the window, watching the fruit trucks pass. Sara was lying in her bed, staring at the ceiling. And yet suddenly both were thinking this same thought, even though they were miles away from each other. . . .

So when she came again he was not surprised. It was as if a secret understanding had unfolded itself in them both. It was a clear day in the park. Jessie had come there to eat his lunch as he always did. His bench was at the end of a shady path that ran between high hedgerows. He had just begun to tear open the paper sack when she emerged from behind the foliage and sat down beside him.

"Hello." Her voice was gentle, without the artifice of the first time.

"Hi."

"How have you been?"

"Okay. Yourself?"

She shrugged. "I've been thinking about you."

"Yeah. Well, I guess I've been thinking about you too."

Their eyes met, they smiled, and several moments passed before either felt there was anything more to say.

In the end she shared his sandwich, and then they went walking past the hollyhocks and beeches through a maze of sculptured hedgerows. Finally the passing clouds turned the light to oyster tones, and they were standing beneath damp oaks.

He said, "I've got to get back to work. I'm already late."

"Me too." She smiled.

"But I'd like to see you again, if that's all right."

"Yes. I'd like to see you too, Jessie."

"Maybe tomorrow then? At the same place?"

"Yes. Tomorrow."

Then very softly, very lightly, she kissed him on the lips.

When he returned to the Embassy he found that three hours of

302

his life had passed, and he had not even realized it. Three hours: it had been years since time had passed without each separate minute ticking away in his head.

Every afternoon now, Jessie and Sara met in the park. Soon she started bringing lunch, and once she even brought a hamper from Fortnum's. They often strolled along the Serpentine. Sara liked to pelt the ducks with bread crumbs. They would sink down together in the grass while the wind tumbled through the trees and spread ripples over the water. Once they sat so long together that before either had realized it, the day was over.

Evenings they often had dinner together. Sara knew all sorts of places where the food was good but not expensive. They never talked about anything that mattered. The relationship was still in its fragile stage. Each night they kissed and said good-by, and afterward Sara would lie in her bed and worry that she would lose him.

Finally she decided that she would make love to him. It felt odd to have to make a conscious decision rather than just letting it happen naturally, but Jessie, she had to come to realize, was an odd person. He could be so hard one moment and soft the next. She planned the evening out to the last detail. They had a candlelight dinner, then went strolling through Hyde Park. Finally she said that she wanted to go home, so he found a cab and rode with her to the doorstep. As always there was an awkward moment under the porchlight, but this time she did not let him run away from her. She looked into his eyes and bit her lower lip.

"I want you to come with me." She could scarcely get the words out.

"Do you mean upstairs?"

She had never seen him look so vulnerable.

"Yes. I want you to come upstairs."

He glanced over his shoulder, then said, "Listen, I've got to explain something . . . I mean it's sort of been a long time since—"

"Come on."

"But the cab's waiting."

"Jessie, forget about the cab."

They made love shyly, a little desperately. She was long-legged and cool, while he was still and warm. There was a candle on the nightstand, throwing gold light on the ceiling and walls. When her dress fell away and she bent down to kiss him, he felt the wings of a protective bird had engulfed him. . . .

Afterward, while they lay in the darkness together, he could not help thinking about Allen. Since his mother had died, Allen had gone through dozens of women. In Jessie's mind, he seemed to treat them like something he got out of a can.

One night Jessie, of his own accord, began to talk about his father. It was toward the end of their third week together. They had had a passable dinner in some basement restaurant and then started drifting through the streets. It was a dark night, and once more the rain left puddles on the cobblestones.

First he told her about the Allen he had known, how he had never been close to the man, how their time had been spent in polite conversation which had been meant to cover deeper feelings. Then he talked about the Allen that others knew, and finally he talked about Magic. He said that he did not really know very much about the organization. It was something that Allen had never trusted him with, but he was aware that there had been this Magic for as long as he could remember . . . it was an institution.

They reached a neighborhood of old houses, grimy and subdivided into tiny flats. There were smells of oil and spiced food. The road dipped and rose into the blackness. A solitary bell was ringing far away.

"Jessie?"

"What?"

"I want to ask you something, and I want you to answer me honestly."

304

This was one of his harder nights. All evening he had been watching objects from the corner of his eye.

"If you knew that your father was cheating, would you do anything to stop him?"

"It depends . . ."

"Depends on what?"

"Look, why do you care anyway? It's not your game, Sara. It's got nothing to do with you."

"Yes, it does. It has a lot to do with me. Listen . . . about two years ago I had a friend, a good friend. His name was Peter. We worked out of the same office. We saw each other quite a lot. In fact we even thought of getting married. I mean at least he . . . well it doesn't matter now. You see, seven months ago he shot himself. He had been handling very sensitive material. Soviet sector stuff. One day some of that material wound up in the Russian embassy. They said he did it, they said he did it for money. Only, there wasn't any money, and besides, I knew him. He wouldn't have done something like that. Still, they had a closed hearing. For his defense he made a list of everyone who had access to that material. Allen Dancer was number three on the list."

"It doesn't prove anything."

"Wait a minute, let me finish. At that time Allen was handling a lot of the routing between London and Washington. Apparently there was some deal he worked out with the Circus . . . I don't know the details, but I do know who the other people on the list were, and I know that the only one of them who could possibly have done it was Allen."

"But no one bought it, huh?"

"They're afraid of Allen Dancer. They're all afraid of him. Anyway, Peter didn't handle it very well. He was a sensitive person . . . I guess he couldn't take the strain. He killed himself before the trial even ended . . ."

They had wandered to a neighborhood of brick tenements, backlots filled with rotting mattresses, broken glass, wet paper.

305

There were only a sprinkling of lights. From somewhere behind them came the rattle of kids dragging empty gas cans over the cobbles.

"He's dead," Jessie said after a long silence. "I'm sorry, but there's no significance to it, he's just dead. So stay away from Magic."

"I can't, Jessie, I've got to stop it."

He turned to her. "Listen to me, Sara. You go after something like Magic and maybe you think you're just going to be chasing pieces of paper around. Well, it's not like that. You go after Magic and you got to be willing to take it all the way. You got to be willing to really stick it to them. Because that's the way they play. For keeps. Most people, they'll tell you that they're ready and willing to take something all the way. They'll tell you that they're really ready to mix it up if it comes to that. But they don't even know what it means. They don't even have a clue. I know, I can assure you of that, Sara. So don't ask me about Magic because I can't tell you what I'd do. Only, if it ever comes to that, it's going to be bad. It's going to be very bad and I wouldn't want you around to see it. Okay?"

This was the last time they ever spoke openly about Allen Dancer, Source Magic or anything related to the secret world. It was a Thursday, and rain was falling intermittently over London. For the rest of the evening Jessie was a little strange, almost a stranger again . . .

Eventually he came to depend on her as he had never depended on anyone before. He was not very good at dealing with the ordinary events of life: paying bills, shopping for food, cleaning, cooking. He was a little like a person from another planet, a planet that was almost, but not quite, like this one. He never memorized the names of streets around him. He often forgot to carry money. He tended to think in terms of absolutes. He saw importance in odd places.

306

In time he did become calmer, less insular. He began sleeping nights and eating regularly. He rarely lost control of himself. Only one incident stood out to remind Sara of how he used to be. It was late one evening in Chelsea. He and she had become lost in a maze of half-lit streets where the walls were covered with spray paint. Suddenly three Jamaicans stepped out of a doorway. One of them tried to grab Sara's purse, but Jessie moved with remarkable speed, sliding in close. He was precise and fluid. Two were hurt badly before Sara even realized what was happening.

She cried in the taxi on the way home. Jessie said nothing. It had begun to rain, and he merely stared out the window and watched the passing reflections of street lamps, the fog on the rooftops. Later that night Sara kept seeing the two men falling. Jessie had clearly broken their ribs, and she would not let him touch her for hours after. (Years later, while standing in that prison laundry room with Robert Kline, she remembered how it was with Jessie when he moved in close to people he hated.)

In the end Jessie gave up his flat and lived with Sara. She had a flat in Putney above the Thames, and every morning they took the district line from Putney Bridge Station. In the evenings there were barges drifting past the Tower Bridge, crowds tramping beneath their window in the violet light. Jessie would never forget one Sunday afternoon when he and Sara did nothing but talk, and listen to her stereo. She wore a white, flowing robe, and when she stood at the window he could see the faint outline of her body through the thin material. Mozart was playing in the background, and eventually it occurred to him that this was the best time of his whole life. Right now, it was the best time of his life. And then he became afraid, because he knew that nothing good ever lasted. This much, though, would always remain. He was learning early what John had learned late, and what Allen had never learned at all. . . .

The end, when it came, was as sudden as any that had come

307

before it. All Jessie knew was that Sara left on a Friday evening and said that she was only going to Paris on routine business and would be back the following Monday. In their months together she had never given him the slightest reason to believe that she was still chasing after Source Magic, and in the hours before leaving she had shown no signs of nervousness, no apprehension. Just sort of excited.

Their last moments together were relaxed and happy. He took her to the station. She wore a blue coat and a scarf around her neck. The wind had brought the color out in her cheeks and her eyes had never seemed brighter. His last image of her . . . she was standing on the ramp, waving a cheery good-by. (Later he would realize that she must have sincerely believed that she could actually beat them.)

It was Sunday morning when the man from the Special Branch called on Jessie. He was a lanky, crooked man with gray hair and a weathered face. He wore old tweeds and a battered hat. He said his name was Harry Holms, and he had a hesitant, blinking way about him.

There were river sounds: a clanging bell, the moan of a barge. Holms sat with his legs apart, his hat on his knee. While he spoke he stared at his hands. He said that Sara had not acted with the complete knowledge of her superiors, although several others from her department were involved. No one was quite sure who received word that an East German clerk had information to sell, but most believed that the offer had in fact been genuine. The operation only failed then because it had been poorly planned, and the security had been abominable.

"Details are still vague," Holms went on. "We're only just now putting together a complete picture of what happened. Seems that she crossed the border late afternoon Saturday. Contact was to have been made that evening, but they picked her up as she was stepping off a bus."

308

Jessie had gotten up from his chair and walked to the window. Although the day was clear, all color seemed to have drained away ... there were black barges and cranes, the skyline and river were gray.

"Why are you telling me all this?" he finally said.

"Well, I was given to understand that you were very close to her. So naturally—"

"No. I mean, why are you telling me the truth? You don't usually tell the truth to outsiders, do you?"

"Yes. Well that's the whole point, isn't it? I mean you're not really an outsider, are you, Mr. Dancer?"

"What's that supposed to mean?"

Holms got up and went to the window. Now they were both gazing out at the colorless city ... billowing factory smoke, and a row of birds on the telephone wire.

"Sara and I were also friends, Jessie. Rather close really, considering the age difference."

"She never mentioned you."

"No, I didn't think she would, but nonetheless the fact remains —Sara and I were friends. As a matter of fact I was largely responsible for bringing her into the service, and you know how those kinds of things are ..."

"No. How are they?"

"Well, let's just say that I've always taken a keen interest in her, and as a result she tended to confide in me."

"Why don't you just get to the point, Holms?"

"All right. I know: Officially Sara Moore went on a little shopping trip to East Berlin to buy some low grade stuff from an unhappy clerk, something to do with troop strength. She bungled the run and now they've got her. At any rate that's the official version, but it's not the truth, is it?"

"How should I know?"

"Because the truth is that she was trying to buy evidence that

309

would open up Source Magic, and Allen Dancer is your father."

Jessie nodded alightly. "She didn't tell me she was going," he said quietly. "I thought she'd given it up—"

"Well, she hadn't. It was supposed to have been a two-day job. In and out. I was to meet her at the station on Sunday."

A long silence, both men still gazing through the window at the passing barges.

Then Jessie said, "Okay. What do you want?"

"I want you to talk to your father. I know that you're not very close to him. Sara told me. But it might help if you spoke to him. Because, you see, Sara didn't bungle it. She was set up. Somehow they knew what she was trying to do, and they sucked her in with the story about the clerk. Then they picked her up. It was very neatly done."

"Where is he?"

"You can't mention my name, it's very important that I remain—"

"Where's my father?"

"Switzerland. Here's the address."

Jessie stayed staring out the window for a long time after Holms had left. Later he cooked himself a meal that he did not eat, and finally, very late, he fell asleep. He awoke in darkness, forgetting that she had ever left him . . . until he reached across the bed and remembered. It was the first time he had cried in many, many years. . . .

Now began the days of Jessie's decline. He lived moment to moment, in and out of time. He did not return to the Embassy. He did not even call in. He just stopped going. The worst part was opening closets and drawers and suddenly seeing objects that used to be hers. The dresses in the bedroom were especially upsetting . . . they always seemed to be waiting for him.

It was also during these days that Jessie made his first attempts to contact Allen Dancer. He left messages all over. Finally Allen phoned from Zurich. Their conversation was brief. Allen's voice

310

was very faint through the static. Jessie said only that it was important that they meet.

Allen arrived in London two days later. Jessie met him in the lobby of the Ritz, and Allen suggested that they have a drink. Jessie did not want one. He wanted to walk, anywhere, so they went out into the streets and the wavering mist. Streetlights were glowing as if seen through fogged glass. Allen was wearing a charcoal-gray suit, a woolen overcoat and soft leather brogues. Jessie wore a cheap cotton jacket and running shoes. The ends of his bluejeans were frayed, the cuffs of his shirt undone. He had not shaved.

"I know what this is about," Allen began. "I spoke with some people in the Special Branch and they told me about the young lady. Now I'd like to say I'm sorry for you—"

"I don't want your sympathy, I want your help."

"You must have liked her very much. This is the first time in years that I can recall you asking for help."

"Yeah, it's the first time in years."

"Have you known her long?"

"Long enough."

They were both staring at an empty street. Puddles of rainwater were reflected in red neon. Abruptly Allen said, "I've never liked London. I don't know how you can stand it."

"I get along."

"How? By sorting letters in the mail room? Why don't you come back to Langley with me? I'll get you a seat on the South American desk."

"I don't want a job, I want you to get Sara back."

"Yes. Sara Moore. You know what she was trying to do, don't you? They told me you had nothing to do with it, but still you knew about it, didn't you?"

"What does that have to do with anything?"

"A great deal. Here is my own son living with a woman in the British Intelligence Service, a woman who is effectively planning

311

to compromise my own unit. Just how do you think that looks?"

"We're talking about her *life*. What do I care how it looks?"

"It's jealousy, you know. The British have always been jealous of what I can produce. So what's their latest solution? They send some poor little girl out to buy some two-bit clerk who claims he can give them Magic on a platter. *Damn* them—"

"Listen to me," Jessie said, "I don't care about Magic, I just want her back. Do you understand what I'm saying? I'm down on my knees, I'm begging you. Help me get her back. Please." And that last word was as unnatural for him as it was to a man named Robert Kline . . .

Allen dropped his head and was gazing into his own image, rippling in a puddle at his feet.

"I'd like to help you," he said easily. "I realize that you and I have not been particularly close and I would like to take this opportunity to tell you that I do care about you, Jessie. However, there's nothing I can do. Do you follow me here? Absolutely nothing I can do. They gave her thirteen years, and there's just no chance. I'm sorry . . ."

Dawn found Jessie still tramping through the gray streets. Fog hung clotted among the tenements, mixing with chimney smoke. There were smells of coffee and wet fur. No city had ever looked this disfigured to him. Once he saw two amber headlights growing larger in the mist, and he had an urge to just fall under the tires. But in the end he couldn't do it. In the end he could only fall back on himself, and he very badly wanted to destroy something.

Jessie remained in London for six more weeks. He spent days in the waiting room of the Foreign Office, but no one would see him. There were days when he forgot to shave, and his shirts were always grubby. Eventually people got tired of telling him that Sara Moore was a lost cause, and then having to face him.

He had become an embarrassment.

Finally he became a kind of shambling figure, running out of

312

money. Shopkeepers knew him because he was always patting his pockets for change, and he could never remember the price of things. Once or twice, friends of Sara's came to call but he did not answer the door. Neighbors heard him pacing the floor at night, but they were too afraid to complain. He was always scowling when they passed him on the staircase.

He supposed that he had just lost hope. There was a last encounter with Holms. They met in the park after a night of rain. There was a clean stillness, and the sound of droplets falling from trees. Holms asked what Jessie planned to do with his life. Jessie said that he was not sure, but two days later he placed a long distance call to a freelance recruiter in Washington. The man remembered Jessie from Vietnam. There was a brief exchange of greetings, then Jessie asked if there was any action abroad. A week later he was in California talking to Dusty Yeats, and a week after that they were both in Thailand, organizing strike teams to hit the Vietnamese in Cambodia. It was about this time that Jessie remarked to Dusty that you could forget anything in a war, a statement later repeated to Humphrey Knolls during the first series of interrogations of Yeats.

It was an insular, professional war. Most of the Cambodians whom Jessie recruited had been trained by American advisors during the Vietnam years, and they deeply hated the Communists. Jessie and Yeats would meet them in the evenings about a mile from the border. Then they would all sit in the tall grass, smoking, chatting, taping clips together for faster reloading. The most popular weapon was the AK-70, although Jessie carried an M-16 and an M-79 grenade launcher, cut down and fitted with a special stock. He'd put a lot of work into it, and it became one of his few well-loved objects.

In time it seemed to Jessie that his life had become like a slow walk down a long, dark tunnel. He passed each day with the same calm intensity. He enjoyed watching his teams fan out through the marsh and vanish into the tree line. In the rainy season the valleys

313

became blanketed with thick, white fog. He supposed that if he stayed long enough he would eventually be killed, because those were the odds. But he did not really care if he died. This was his life. Without Sara.

The whole story might have ended even before it began if one evening, about a year after he had arrived in Thailand, Jessie hadn't walked into a shabby, waterfront bar and found Robert Kline waiting for him.

CHAPTER
TEN

OVER TWO months had passed since the capture of Dusty Yeats, and now came the events that eventually would be called "the final phase of the Dancer story." In all, this last phase would take up nineteen days.

It began with the return of Jessie Dancer from Switzerland, where he'd been with Robert Kline when Yeats had been captured. He stayed there throughout the interrogations because it had taken him so long to learn about the capture, thanks to the contact procedure that relied on a postcard system that could only be originated out of Zurich. So it was not until Yeats had failed to respond to three such postcards that Jessie began to suspect that something had gone wrong. Next he made a series of calls to

315

unsuspecting Langley employees, and finally he learned what had happened. This had been on a Thursday. The following Monday he caught a night flight out of Zurich, and the last nineteen days began. . . .

There was a storm on the night that Jessie returned, and there had been a storm when it all began. The storm began not long after dusk. First clouds mounted in the north. Then came the wind, and finally more rain.

In the early evening Allen and John nibbled cold cuts and sipped diluted whiskey under a lampshade that had once been pink but was now the color of dust. Then they moved to the library. John read some dog-eared brief on Soviet dissidents, sat there with his chin almost on his chest and occasionally mumbled. Once he asked, "Do you think that Jessie remembers his mother at all?"

It irritated Allen. "What's that got to do with anything?"

"Oh, it was just a thought."

"Well, of course he remembers her."

There had been many evenings like this during the previous two weeks. Long silences lay like fog, then John would suddenly speak. Afterward the silence would engulf them again. Allen had not been telling his father much. Dad was a little too slow, and with Jessie he tended to get sentimental. After John had gone to bed Allen went upstairs, looked into rooms that were shut for days at a time. The furniture looked cold. When the rain began to fall, the light and ghostly water made him feel uneasy. Finally he sat down on the window seat of his old room and began to leaf through the transcript of the Yeats interrogations. As the hours passed, the storm became a solid wall of wind and rain. Leaves were torn off. The whole house shook with thunder.

As for Humphrey Knolls, and how close he knew he was to a complete understanding, this has always been a mystery to Agency record keepers. In later testimony he would claim that he had known only fragments, and these fragments were lost among unanswerable questions. The record, though, hinted at a greater understanding. Within the last entries of his notes on the case two themes were most prevalent. First, Knolls had returned to the place he'd started from. His final notes were filled with references to Dusty Yeats. There were snatches of half-remembered phrases that Yeats had told him in the early days of questioning. There was even a crude, scribbled diagram of the compound with stick trees for the forest, and broad strokes for the open grassy land. His second theme was even more to the point of the overall story. Two crooked lines had been drawn on the bottom of the last page. The first was labeled Robert Kline, and the second, Jessie Dancer. Their point of intersection was labeled Bangkok. Beneath this sketch there were two thrusting arrows, as if to indicate motivation. One was labeled Julia Dancer, and the other was Sara Moore.

When the storm broke and the rain began to funnel down, Knolls also sat by the window. Finally he got up, shuffled to the kitchen and poured himself a glass of milk. But the milk was rancid so he drank water from the tap. Then he splashed more water on his face as if to clear himself for one last question.

(Later, after the record keepers had deciphered his notes, they too would ask this question: on the last night before it all opened up, had Knolls known enough to warn security that Jessie was about to return?)

Next there was Yeats, and for his story there is only the medical records. It was known that he had been given fairly large doses of sodium Amytal and LSD. Much of the time he was only semi-conscious. Thought was always slow, time even slower. Early on he had tried to slash his wrists with the shattered remains of a glass. Then he lapsed into passivity, and from passivity into pleading. He would reach for the hands of his interrogators whenever they approached his bed. He would reach to press his lips to their hands. A harsh word could make him cry for hours. They'd done a job on old Dusty, all right.

And finally there was Jessie. His plane was the last to land before the storm, and the wind had already begun flowing in from the north by the time he had reached the Virginia hills. He rented a Chevrolet, and began the final preparations. He used a forged security card to enter the main gates. The gate guards had not been alerted that he, or anyone else, might have been attempting an illegal entry, and so he was routinely let through. Then, wearing the white overalls of a hospital orderly, he passed through the foyer of the testing center. A hospital guard vaguely remembered seeing him walking briskly down the first corridor but did not consider the possibility that the young man was anything else than he seemed to be. So it stood; Jessie slipped through a slack security line, and the deception was over.

On duty the night, shortly before midnight, that Jessie entered the testing center was a prim young nurse named Ginger Land. She did not see him until he had grabbed her, clamped his hand over her mouth and ordered her to lead him upstairs to where Yeats was being held.

Once they reached Yeats' room Jessie bound and gagged her with torn-off strips of sheets. Yeats was in a drugged sleep, and it took Jessie some time to wake him. For several minutes Yeats did not seem to recognize Jessie. Then Yeats was calling out Jessie's name, bursting into tears. Jessie and Yeats were now moving out the door, and for an instant Jessie looked at Ginger Land full in the face. The light from the hallway was glinting in his eyes, and it seemed as if the pupils were growing larger until the whole white was gone.

The nurse was not discovered until the next morning. Then security was called in and not long after daybreak all the principals had assembled. John and Allen drove in. Lyle Severson had come. Humphrey Knolls was there, pacing the corridors, retracing the steps that Jessie had taken. There was coffee and donuts on a trolley, but nobody touched it except Knolls.

Discussion centered around two questions. The first was how Jessie had known where to find Yeats. Later this was solved when

318

they discovered that Yeats had inadvertently been listed on the duty roster as a patient in the Testing Center. All Jessie had done was telephone the central directory, ask for Yeats, and the computer automatically fed out his location.

The second question dealt with what measures should be taken to capture the fugitives. Normal procedure would have been to enlist the aid of local police, but Allen would not hear of this. He wanted the situation handled internally.

When the discussion ended and the two Dancers had left, Knolls and Severson walked out of the testing center and out across the Langley quadrangle. Here the walkways were littered with leaves and branches. Dark clouds were still heaving and rolling across the sky. The wind was damp and cold. Knolls wore a dirty blue parka and wrinkled trousers. Severson had on the same coat he had worn when it all began. The two men tramped slowly until they reached the middle of the square. Then Severson said, "I take it that you're not pleased with the way Allen is handling things."

"Why do you say that?"

"Oh come on, Humphrey. I saw the way you looked at him. You were scowling. You were definitely scowling."

Knolls shrugged. "All right, I'm not pleased."

"Is it because you don't think that Allen will find them?"

The wind was bending the grass, tossing leaves everywhere.

Suddenly Knolls was clutching Severson's sleeve. "Lyle, listen to me. I want you to put me back on the case. I want to have complete freedom to move. There's something very wrong here . . . I feel it. There's something wrong with the way Allen Dancer is handling this."

"What on earth are you talking about?"

"I'm talking about Magic. I'm trying to tell you that Allen Dancer will do anything—not to protect his son, but to protect Magic. And I mean anything . . ."

"Oh, for God sakes, Humphrey. The man is Jessie's father. One

319

doesn't go about shooting one's own son."

"Then why the closed hunt? Why is he only using his own people? I'll tell you why, because he wants people who are loyal to him and him alone. Look at Tony Nugent. The man is a six-cylinder hood. You don't send Nugent after someone you care about."

"Are you through, Humphrey?"

"Yes . . . no. There's something else you should realize. Jessie is no ordinary person. He's an extraordinary fighter, I mean that literally. Have you ever looked at his record? Well, it's sort of frightening. Very scary, in fact."

"So?"

"So I don't care who Allen sends after him, if Jessie gets cornered he's going to fight, and then I promise you it's going to get bloody. Then try and explain that one to the Director."

In the distance three gardeners were moving across the grass into the tree line, dark figures, stooped and walking slowly, one of them swinging a bucket.

Finally Lyle sighed. "All right, Humphrey. What do you want?"

"I want full authorization from you. I want two or three security people. Tough ones, and I want full access to the Magic files. I also want to put a bug on Allen Dancer's telephone."

For a moment Lyle was very still. Then he said, "Oh, dear God."

"If you don't want to give it to me in writing, then okay, but I want it verbally, and I want it now."

"If you get into trouble I won't bail you out. Is that understood?"

"Yes."

"And it's only for a ten-day period. Ten days."

"Make it twenty. It's going to be all over one way or another in the next twenty days."

Like Knolls's, Jessie's sense of an ending also came that morning. He had driven through the night while Yeats slept in the back seat. By dawn they had reached open country. Fog lay mounting in the gullies. When Yeats woke up he found that they were parked by the side of the road. His first clear image of the day was of Jessie sitting upright on the hood of the car. He staggered around to where Jessie sat, leaned up against the warm grill. "How long have I been out?"

"About seven hours," Jessie told him.

"Seven hours, huh? Then I definitely got no sense of time. You know what I mean, Jess? Whenever I think about something or say something it feels like it happened a long time ago. It's weird."

"You'll be okay."

"Yeah, but right now I'm not. They kept shooting me up with stuff, and now my sense of time is warped all to hell. Hey, I need a rest."

For a moment there was no sound at all, then just wind in the branches and a few birds sailing overhead. Jessie was watching a car on the road behind him, tracking it, watching the glinting reflection through the trees.

"Listen, Dusty, this is very important. Last night you talked about the product list. You said you got it, but you had to stuff it in a pipe. I've got to know about that."

"I was under pressure, Jess. You know how it gets. I figured maybe my chances weren't too good, so I dropped them. But I dropped them in a good place, man. I can tell you that. It was a classic."

"Do you think it's still there?"

"Yeah. I mean the first thing they asked about were the papers. They couldn't figure out why I wanted an old list, so they kept asking. But every night I'd just sit there on the cot and tell myself that the stuff was gone. I mean it was gone. Lost. Pretty soon I sort of got to believe it myself. I guess you could say that it was my coolest move."

321

"Do you remember where that pipe was?"

"Oh yeah, I remember. I might not be able to remember my own name, but I remember where I dropped the list."

The twenty-six pages that Yeats took from Central Reference listed thirteen documents which Magic had produced over an eighteen-month period. Each document was titled, numbered and briefly synopsized.

The list contained undeniable proof that Valentin Servana had been betraying Moscow Center; no question it would have willingly been accepted in trade by Center for a similar list of material that Allen Dancer had given to Servana. Jessie had known exactly what he had the moment he laid eyes on the pages.

That moment came on the morning of the second day. The night before Jessie and Yeats had returned to the tenement and vacant lot where the papers had originally been hidden. It had been a black night and very cold. The city streets had been deserted and littered with blown refuse. Jessie circled the block twice, saw no one, and minutes later he had the documents.

Then came another long drive through the night, and into the Virginia hills. Through it all, Yeats again slept fitfully. He kept complaining of headaches and marginal hallucinations. He said that it looked like there were rats scurrying out of the darkness, faces in the passing trees.

Morning came on a back road that ran through open pasture. It was here that Jessie felt the safest now, here among the hills and long highways. He spent an hour studying the documents while Yeats dozed in the back seat.

Then, just as the sun was rising, the two went walking through the grass.

"Did I do okay?" Yeats asked. "I mean is that what you wanted?"

"Yeah, you did fine."

"So you can use it, huh?"

"I can use it."

"And it's going to get the girl back, right?"

"Yes. It'll get her back."

"Do you think you can tell me how? I'd kind of like to know. I mean after all this time I'd kind of like to know what's going to happen."

They were both squinting into the distant hills where the light was falling on mountain tops. Jessie seemed to be watching something with great intensity. Finally he said, "Magic is operated on a give-and-take basis. Do you know what I mean by that? They exchange things. They give this, they take that. It's a scam. Nobody owns anybody. They both work for themselves and each other. The proof is in the lists. You hand that list into Center and you blow the Moscow end right then and there. You get one of Center lists and you cancel the other ticket. You cancel it right then and there."

Yeats was gazing into empty space. Finally he began to speak in a low, halting voice. He said that when this was all over he did not believe that he would want to go on working inside the secret world. Jessie said he understood.

There was a taut, bizarre quality to the next two days, and all the principals felt it. Allen and John Dancer spent a lot of time mooning around their house. They would pour themselves drinks and gaze out into the garden. John kept asking questions that Allen refused to answer. Allen was taking Valiums every afternoon.

For Knolls, too, the next two days were especially tense. He had the telephone and mail taps on the Dancer home, but nothing of consequence had been revealed. The initial excitement had worn off, and now he was locked into the grinding drudgery of spying. Whenever he saw Lyle, the old man avoided his eyes.

As for the search for Yeats and Jessie, all that had occurred was that Tony Nugent had spent two days contacting motels, hotels, car rental agencies and service stations along the highway leading out of Langley. He eventually found the girl who had rented Jessie his first car, but she had nothing to say other than the boy had cold eyes and had not looked like a very nice person.

Yeats and Jessie kept running. It was Jessie's belief that the airports would be watched, and so he had decided to put time and distance behind them before they would attempt to catch a plane to Switzerland. And so the two days were spent entirely on the road. They slept in the car, ate at truck stops and fruit stands. The land was unchanging, fixed in greens and browns, although mornings often glittered with frost.

Through it all Yeats kept complaining about the cold. He also complained about bad dreams and that he still had no sense of time. Seconds, he said, seemed too long, while whole hours would pass before he knew it. He became deeply concerned about small events. When Jessie's watch stopped, for example, he spent the entire day brooding about it. It was a self-winding watch, and he could not understand why it had stopped. He said that it was very bad, the very worst kind of omen. Jessie had started giving him large doses of vitamins, but they did not seem to help.

Finally they caught an afternoon flight to Mexico City from New York, and it was a rough flight. Jessie had chosen Mexico because it was an indirect route. He called it the soft route, but for Yeats it was pretty hard. He hated Mexico. He always had. He said that the Mexican police were among the worst in the world. He said that they were animals.

In Mexico they stayed in a pink stucco hotel with pink tiles in the courtyard. Room service brought them their meals, Jessie mainly ordering fruit. They did not leave their room. Yeats watched a bullfight on television for an hour, then Jessie made him turn it off because it was obviously making him upset.

The next morning they caught a flight to Switzerland. Again it was a rough flight, and the only thing that saved Yeats from complete panic was his belief that they could not possibly die in

324

an airline crash. He said that it just wasn't meant to be, not in his Karma, or some such.

For Jessie the flight was also bad. He had been thinking a great deal about Sara . . . once he shut his eyes and saw a distinct image of her silhouetted against the London skyline. He often found it hard to believe that he might actually see her again, but for a few minutes during the flight it had seemed very possible. Then he started imagining what she must have experienced in an East German prison camp. The thought made him clench his fist until the veins stood out all long his arm.

They spent the night in a hotel near the Zurich airport, the sort of place where one expected clean sheets and little else. The rug had been woven into geometric designs, there was a copy of one of Picasso's geometric women above the bed, and the wallpaper was also a pattern of rectangles. For a while Jessie just sat and ran his eyes from one hard angle to another. It was getting very bad, very bad . . .

They rented a car in the morning, and then began what Kline called the homecoming, the procedure the old man had worked out to ensure a safe return . . . First Jessie made a phone call to a cottage outside of Zurich that was about a mile down the road from Kline's. A woman answered, a not too bright little woman who always wore cardigans and bedroom slippers. Kline paid her a few francs a month to take his messages. She thought that he was an antique dealer.

Jessie made a second call to the woman thirty minutes after the first. This was the tag call, and the woman told him that seventeen Graham mantel clocks were arriving on the evening express. This was the clear sign.

The final approach began as the sun was passing the tops of the distant mountains. Jessie had driven to a narrow country lane that ran between green meadows. Great oaks grew on either side of the road—and the trunk of one had been recently slashed with a knife. The six-inch scar was the sign to proceed. Long morning shadows

325

were falling across the lane, and out of those shadows finally stepped Robert Kline.

He wore his old gray overcoat, his wrinkled flannels and his shabby brogues. He stood among the hanging branches and watched as Jessie approached. His hair was closely cropped and he looked thinner than ever. His cheeks were hollow, his eyes dark. He might have been some scrubby tree unable to control its limbs. . . .

The night that Kline and Jessie reunited was the night that they began to plan the final moves. They worked in Kline's study which had a view through the garden to the lake. The floor was strewn with stacks of documents and notes. The mood of this room may have been set by an old china lamp with a flowered shade that cast rings of yellow light on the ceiling and desk.

At the center of attention was the product list. When Kline had first seen the list he had picked it up and held it to the light, then he slumped down in his chair and read it again. Finally he just sat there and stared at the papers as if they represented something holy.

There was a faintly haunting quality to the night of planning. There were moments when Kline could not help but see himself as the young man that he once was. He worked on sheets of unlined foolscap, and in the end there were nine pages of these notes. They bore the stamp of a pragmatic, wartime operation. Each step was numbered and labeled.

Essentially there were two parts to Kline's operation. The first involved a package which would be sent to Allen Dancer. The package would contain a sample of the stolen product list and instructions telling him to take the next available flight to Germany, where Jessie would be waiting for him with the demands. He was to come alone and to talk to no one. If he violated any of these terms, the product list would be sent east and exchanged with Moscow Center for a list of material that he had passed to

Servana. Within the trade this was known as a burn, and the reason for that was obvious. Allen would be burned . . .

The site for the confrontation between Jessie and Allen was the German seacoast town of Lubeck, chosen for its long wooded stretch of East German border, a stretch that Sara Moore could easily be taken across.

The second step of the plan involved the exchange; the girl for the product list. As Kline saw it, Sara would be taken to the border where Jessie would meet her. Her crossing should be at dusk so that Jessie would have both the light and darkness to work with.

There would be a three-day lapse between the time that Allen heard the demands from Jessie and the actual crossing. During that period Kline envisioned that he, Yeats and Jessie would wait in a house not far from the border. The house, he said, had to be fairly secluded and rented in absolute secrecy. When Kline explained these details to Jessie, he only nodded, but it was clear to him that this was not the first time that Kline had done something like this.

Once the girl was safely in their hands, Kline said that Jessie would take her away and hide her. He and Yeats would also go underground for a while. It was further understood that Sara's release would not in itself be the end. The end would be the final destruction of Magic. Neither Kline nor Jessie ever spoke about how or when this would occur, but it was understood between them that when Allen freed the girl he was really only buying himself a little more time . . . .

It was eleven o'clock in the evening when Kline finished addressing the envelope that would be sent to Allen. Dusty was sleeping down the hall. Jessie lay on his back on the floor, smoking and sipping beer. There was a map of Europe on the wall that had long since rolled past the thumbtacks which threw shadows on the plaster.

Kline said that for the first time in his life he felt very close to success, and it scared him.

"I don't know why" he said. "I suppose I should feel elated. Instead I'm scared."

"It happens like that sometimes," Jessie mumbled. "It doesn't mean anything."

"But I keep thinking that Allen won't come."

"He'll come."

"And how will it be for you to talk to him? To stand there and tell him that you're going to blackmail him?"

"It'll be fine."

"You know that he may try and appeal to you on an emotional basis. He may try and reduce the situation, down to a lower level. He may tell you that he'll be only too happy to try and get Sara out. Do you see what I'm saying? He may try to appeal to you as a son."

"He may try to kill me too"—Jessie smiled—"one never knows."

Earlier, Kline had imagined how it would be for Allen when he first opened the envelope. He had imagined him very clearly in his bedroom, in a white cashmere sweater and charcoal-gray slacks. He might crumple the envelope until his knuckles turned white.

Now Kline saw that same image of Allen in his bedroom ... this time in even more detail: a fire burning in the tiled hearth, two silver-backed hairbrushes on the oak chest ... Then the image was gone, and he turned to Jessie again. "There's something I've always wanted to ask you," he said, and his voice sounded distant. "It's about your mother."

"What about her?"

"Well, I've been wondering. Did she ever mention my name to you?"

"I told you, she said that you were a friend."

"Yes, and she had the locket, the one that Allen threw into the lake."

"Yeah, there was the locket."

328

"But she never said anything else?"

"No."

"Nothing about you and me?"

Jessie sighed. "Look, what do you want me to say? You want me to say that you're my old man?" He surprised himself with the words . . . that he had actually said them finally, instead of just thinking them.

"Well, wouldn't it mean something to you, Jessie? Wouldn't it mean a little something?"

There was so much pain in Kline's eyes that Jessie could not help but let it out . . . "Yes . . . it would mean something to me . . ."

They left for Lubeck two days later: Jessie, Kline and Dusty Yeats. Once there it took Kline four more days to find a house where the last hours before the crossing would be spent. During the planning stage Kline had imagined renting a partially wooded country estate. He had to settle for a crumbling stone farmhouse.

The place was damp and filthy, and smelled of cats and wet wool. There were no carpets, only flagstones, and the wind blew under the door. A narrow staircase led to a bedroom where there was a bed, a dresser, a chair and a mirror. On the wall of the kitchen was a print of Lubeck Harbor, and on the mantel were seven china figurines. There were also three Prussian soldiers, three sailors and a tiny ballerina with only one arm. When Jessie first saw the ballerina he thought . . . that's for Sara. It was not the sort of thought he'd ever had before . . .

Around the farm lay fallow ground filled with grass and high weeds. There was a muddy cow path that led past a brick granary and rows of wooden cattle sheds. In the barn was an old pickup truck, although on the first day Jessie rented an Audi because he said that they might need a fast car.

The same day that they moved into the farmhouse Jessie mailed the envelope to Allen. In his own mind it was not a particularly significant step. It was just the first step . . . like grouping ammunition clips for faster reloading or adjusting an infrared scope. It was just something you did before a fight.

After the envelope was sent there seemed to be nothing to do but listen to the wind rattling through the shutters. The sky here was vast. Yeats, more than any of them, seemed disturbed by this country, telling Jessie that he felt as if this place was the end of the world.

On the day that Allen was due to arrive, Jessie drove to the crossing point to wait for him. It was late afternoon when Jessie walked out onto the hill to look across the Eastern border. From where he stood there was a clear view of the skeletal watchtowers, and he could hear the wind whistling through the strings of barbed wire, knocking together the dangling soup cans that had been hung to warn the guards. It was also cold, and he was about to return to the Audi when he saw Allen's car winding down the road in the distance. A silver Mercedes. Even now, Jessie thought. Even now he drives a car like that.

The car stopped before it left the main road, so Jessie assumed that Allen had seen him. He was looking down across a hundred yards of grass and fern. Next Jessie heard the muffled thump of the slamming door, and Allen was standing there, gazing directly up the hillside.

It took five minutes for Allen to climb the hill, during which time Jessie stood there very straight and still. He was chewing on the end of some grass. He was wearing his raincoat like a cloak over his shoulders, and there was a silver bangle around his left wrist.

"I told you to come alone," he said when Allen approached.

Allen shrugged. "I don't go anywhere without Nugent."

"You weren't supposed to bring anyone."

"Is that so? Well, let me tell you, I've taken enough from you. Just who do you think you are?"

There was no expression in Jessie's eyes. They were facing one

330

another across ten feet of grass, and they stood at the very top of the hill. All around was open land and the towers against the darkening sky.

"This is how it's going to be played," Jessie said. "You've got three days to contact Servana and have him bring the girl there." He pointed to the border, that lay below and behind him.

Allen also turned to see the border, then muttered something and shook his head.

"You'll have her here at four o'clock," Jessie went on. "That's four o'clock in the afternoon. How you get her here is your business, but Servana will have to fix it with the guards. That means that the towers will be clear. I don't want him just to keep them from shooting. I want the towers and the land around it completely cleared, but that shouldn't be too much of a problem for someone in his position—"

"What do you know about his position? What do you know about *anything?*"

"I'll be coming here at four to get her. I will not have the product list on me. Kline or maybe Yeats will have it, and unless they hear from me within thirty minutes past the hour, they'll contact Moscow Center. There will be an offer of our list for something that shows what you've been giving Servana. Do you have any questions?"

"I can't really believe you're doing this."

At least, Jessie thought, he didn't say 'my own son' . . . "You had better believe it, because it's really going to happen. It's going to happen just like I said."

"You're crazy, do you know that? You're crazy."

Jessie smiled, but it was a terrible smile that had long ago lost its direction. He might have been smiling at death.

He continued looking at Allen for a moment, then turned and started moving back down the hill. It was then that, out of character, Allen tried to hit him, stumbling forward and swinging blindly. Jessie hardly moved to avoid the blow, but when it was over Allen was on his knees, clutching at his stomach, and there was blood in his mouth.

Minutes after this first encounter, there below the hillside while Allen lay bent over the hood of the Mercedes, he said to Nugent, "Tell me what you would do. Right now, without thinking about it, just tell me what you would do."

"I'm not sure what you mean, sir."

"Yes you are, you know exactly what I mean."

Across the border the sun was dropping behind the pines, sharpening the coils of barbed wire. There was blood on the silver hood of the car.

"Well, sir," said Nugent, "I'd begin to play it like they want it. I'd call the East and get them to send that girl out. That's what I'd do first. Get that girl headed for the border, because then no matter what you've got yourself covered."

"And then?"

"Then I'd go to the Germans. They owe us a favor, and I'd collect."

"What kind of favor, Tony?"

"Well, sir, I think we can assume that these people—your son and the rest of them—are going to be operating in this area. So it's just a question of doing the legwork. See what I'm getting at, sir? Foreigners moving into this area, renting a room somewhere . . . there's bound to be a trail."

"And you say we use the Germans to find it?"

"Yes, sir, I do. I know some Germans here who are very good at this kind of thing. They're very clean people, if you know what I mean. Do a lot of work for the Special Branches, and they don't ask questions. They just do a good, clean job."

"We blow it, Tony, and they'll be down on us hard."

"Yes, sir, I realize that. I realize that we've got to tag them while they're still holding onto the paper, and by paper I mean what that Yeats character took from Central Ref."

"Timing, Tony. Your timing has got to be very, very good."

332

"Yes, sir, but the way I see it we really don't have a big margin of error. I mean we'll have started it rolling as far as the girl goes. She'll be coming just like they want it, and if at any point we run into a snag, then we can just deliver like they want. So like I said we're covered either way, and if these German boys score, then it's a pretty simple job from that point on."

Suddenly Allen's voice was hesitant. "What's a simple job?"

"Well, sir, I think that this is not going to be resolved until we, uh, completely deal with the problem—Kline, Yeats—"

"And Jessie?"

"Well, sir, that's a question that, uh, only you can really answer. I mean, I realize that this is a pretty difficult situation for you. However, I think that it's something that, uh, should be looked at now, because sooner or later . . ."

"Yes . . . well, sooner or later."

An extraordinary quiet seemed to have fallen from the sky. Every leaf, every blade of grass lay unmoving in the sunlight. Wild flowers in a distant meadow looked like the heads of strangled birds. Allen's hands were pressed against the hood of the car, and he was staring into the reflection.

"Sir?"

Allen sighed. "You know, Jessie might have been killed a hundred times in the last few years. First there was the war, then that Cambodian thing. It could have happened any number of times."

"Yes, sir, that's a very good point. And I imagine that he's going to continue to live that kind of high-risk, one might even say self-destructive existence. I mean, given the sort of person he is, I'd say that if it's not one thing it's going to be another. I mean, you've got that whole weird life-style. You've got your drugs and the rest of it. So I'd definitely say that if it's not one thing it's going to be another—"

"How would it happen? I want you to tell me how it would happen?" Allen did not quite identify the words as coming from him. Even he had trouble with that.

333

"Well, sir, as I said, we start by getting the girl moving—just in case. Then we get these people I know to start looking for the trail. If they find it, then they, uh, just move in and tag them. They do it right after, uh, Jessie moves out to pick up the girl. That way he isn't involved in anything this side of the border. I mean, he's going to be meeting the girl when she crosses, right? Well that puts him pretty close to the wire. And, well, lots of things *could* happen as far as the East Germans go."

"He wants the towers completely cleared, he won't move until he sees the towers cleared—"

"Well, we can have a couple of guys stationed on the hill above him."

"And if he doesn't cross the border?" The "he" was no longer Jessie . . . only an impersonal pronoun . . . an enemy problem.

"Well, as long as he's found on the East side, sir. I mean, it's only a few yards one way or another, isn't it?"

Allen had still not moved. His hands were still pressed to the hood of the car. He might have turned to wax.

"Sir? Sir, if I can just say one more thing here. I realize that you probably have some pretty strong personal feelings connected with this problem, but I just want to say that I sincerely believe that this is the only way to handle it. I mean this is really his game, and unless we, uh, stop it right here and now it's just going to continue until . . . well, until everything is gone. I mean, sir, we've just got to face it. Your son is actually endangering, well . . . everything."

"He's not my son, Tony."

"No, sir. He's not."

"You don't know what I'm talking about, do you?"

"I'm not sure, sir."

"No. You don't know what I'm talking about."

An odd wind was rising from the southwest when Jessie returned to the farmhouse, bringing with it smells of grass and

334

livestock. Yeats was waiting on the porch, and Kline was in the kitchen laying down strips of bacon. He had always said that in moments of stress it was important to eat. But no one felt hungry that night, and so they just drank cheap gin and nibbled at a few slices of cheese.

It took Jessie an hour to describe his meeting with Allen, not because he had much to say but because Kline kept asking detailed questions. He was particularly interested in how Allen had reacted. He said that he wished he had been there. He said that he would always regret not having seen Allen Dancer's face.

There was an unreality, a sense of timelessness to the next thirty hours. Yeats seemed particularly ill at ease. On the second evening he had wandered out across the fields, and when he returned he seemed shaken . . . he said that he had met two German farmers who had not looked like farmers. He described them as well-built men in blue nylon jackets. He said that they had been driving along the dirt road that skirted the edge of the farm. One spoke passable English. They had been driving a black Volkswagen van, and it was the van that bothered Yeats. He could not understand why farmers would drive a van.

Yeats told all this to Jessie while they were standing on the porch. It was twilight. There were long twilights in this part of the country, darkness seemed to gather at the top of the sky and then seep down slowly to the horizon. Jessie listened, now and then asking questions. Yeats said that one of the farmers had a harelip. Jessie thought about this, decided Dusty was still seeing things, or reading things into what he saw. Besides, it was too late to change things now. Not now, when they were so close. Sara . . .

The last day, and the night before, were like the dead time before a battle. Kline lay awake in his bed until very late, listening to squirrels or perhaps rats in the attic, which reminded him of prison. Before he fell asleep he had the strangest feeling that he was lying on the grassy hillside above the border, and looking down the barrel of his old rifle, the one he had used in the war.

335

First he saw the moon in his sights, and then some kind of bird. Before he fell asleep, though, he saw Allen. He shot, but missed . . .

Jessie got up early in the morning only to find that Yeats and Kline were already in the kitchen, Yeats still talking about the farmers he had met. There was coffee on the old stove, but it was sour. The sky was clear, white, and you could see your breath on the air.

During the last hours the three men stayed close to one another, spoke in short, broken sentences. Again they were not hungry, and again Kline cooked a meal anyway. It was still something to do. He made corned beef and threw in some eggs. Yeats said it was a bad sign that the yolks had broken.

There were two good-bys, one for Kline and one for Yeats. With Yeats, Jessie walked out into the back fields behind the cattle sheds. There was a broken fence in the distance and a garden that had been partially plowed but then left to the weeds. Yeats wore a blue windbreaker, Jessie his short, black leather jacket. They walked side by side until they reached the granary and a view of the open land.

"You got to go, don't you?" Yeats said.

"Yeah"—Jessie sighed—"I got to go."

"You nervous?"

"Sure."

"Me, too. I don't know why. This isn't any worse than hunting dinks, but I'm nervous as a cat. Last night I couldn't even sleep. It's the waiting I guess. You're going to be out there, and I'm going to be sitting here like a jerk, chewing on the furniture."

"It'll be over before you know it."

"Yeah, that's what they always say. They cut off your arm, and they tell you that it'll be over before you know it." Then he laughed. "This lady you're going to get, she better be nice. You know what I mean, Jess? She better be real nice."

It would have been a fitting ending right then and there. Both

336

were looking out across the blown land. Dead leaves were rattling around them. Yeats was still smiling. Jessie was about to turn back to the farmhouse when Yeats suddenly took hold of him by the sleeve. He looked terribly afraid.

"Jessie, I got to tell you, man. I got to tell you something."

"I'm listening."

"Well, it's just something. I don't know, it's just maybe something's wrong—"

"Nothing's wrong, Dusty. Everything is going to be all right."

"Yeah, but I got this feeling, Jess. I don't know how to explain it. I just got this sort of feeling. It's a *bad* feeling."

"It'll be all right," Jessie said quietly. "Everything is going to be fine."

But when they shook hands, and Yeats managed to get out a good luck, there were tears coming down his face. At first he was ashamed. "I don't know what's wrong with me, it must be that shit they gave me, I just can't control nothing . . . I must look like a fucking idiot."

"No, you look fine. You look just fine."

Then Yeats was grinning absurdly, mumbling, "Yeah. I'm fine, I'm looking real fine . . ." He did not walk back to the farmhouse with Jessie. He just stood there in the fields, feeling more alone than he'd ever felt in his whole life.

As with Yeats, Jessie's last words with Kline were subdued and resonant of fear. They stood by Jessie's rented Audi on a muddy patch of ground in front of the farmhouse. Jessie was leaning on the fender of the car. Kline was staring at the tires, his thoughts far away.

Finally he smiled weakly. "Wouldn't it be funny if it didn't start?"

"Well, there's always the truck in the barn."

"Oh, yes, I forgot about the truck. I guess you could pick her up in the truck if you had to."

337

Several seconds of complete silence, Kline watching the road and the far line of pines, Jessie looking in the other direction, to the farmhouse and cattle sheds.

Finally Kline said, "You won't go in too fast, will you? Take an hour to watch. There's no hurry."

"Yeah. I'll take some time to check it out first."

"Did you bring your pistol?"

"It's in the car."

"I know I always used to feel naked without one."

"A knife is quieter." It was an old joke, but neither laughed.

Again there was that last moment before Jessie got into the car when Kline could have said good luck and left the ending at that. But like Yeats he may have had a sudden vision of something.

"I want to tell you something," he said quickly. "It's about what happened between your mother and me. It's about . . . well, *I am* your father, Jessie. I'm sure of it now . . ."

Jessie looked into Kline's eyes. "Yes . . . well, there is a certain resemblance. I mean I can sort of see the resemblance," and they were both grinning at the absurdity of it. . . .

When Jessie finally drove off, Kline stood and watched until the Audi had left the muddy track and vanished behind the line of pines. Then he turned and walked back into the house. Yeats was sitting at the kitchen table. There was a bottle of gin in front of him, and a glass in his hand. This was the moment that Yeats had said he was always afraid of.

He and Kline just sat, not talking, both sipping the gin and occasionally slicing off pieces of cheese with a stainless steel knife. Kline, without really thinking about it, had picked up the product list and was idly fingering the pages. Then it just lay on the table between them, still in its folder, creased down the middle. One of the edges was even a bit torn.

Twenty minutes passed like this, and still neither man had spoken. Yeats had not even moved his hands. There was the wind

338

through the shutters, and further off the rumble of an engine.

"Jessie?" Yeats asked.

Kline shook his head. "How could it be so fast?"

"I'd better go take a look."

"Bring the gun."

"Where is it—?"

There was a sound of splintering wood and falling glass. Yeats was half out of his chair, had picked up the knife. There were two men in the doorway, both in blue nylon jackets. One had a harelip; they both had automatic rifles. The French make them, Yeats thought vaguely, he had seen them in the war. Then he thought how he had really known all along that this would happen, even before he had met these two men on the road. We should have waited it out in the city, he thought.

He was leaping forward, thinking he might cut just one of them with the blade, but then both rifles fired, and he was lifted into the air and tossed away. Through it all he was calling out Jessie's name, calling to him . . .

Kline too saw an image of Jessie as the rifles swept around, but then he was also falling back, and it was like staring into a light bulb when they hit him . . .

He felt nothing now, only the warmth spreading in his stomach while his limbs were cold. He lay still for a long time, heard the footsteps of the killers and their voices. They were German, and wasn't it just like Allen Dancer to hire a couple of Germans?

He heard them leaving now, the engine of their van fading into nothing. He coughed out Dusty's name, but the boy was clearly dead. You could see his eyes. And I should be dead too, Kline told himself. If they had really been any good at all I'd be dead too. In the old days he always checked the bodies if there was even the slightest doubt. Trust Allen to save a few dollars by hiring second-rate killers who forget to check the bodies.

From where Kline lay he could see across the flagstones through the door to a patch of floor where the light fell. By now he also saw the sequence that had led up to this. First Allen's men tracking them down here, then the teams, one for him and Yeats, another for Jessie.

Now instead of Jessie's face, there was Oskar's face, and Kline saw him as he was falling in the garden. You're an old man, Luft used to say. We're both old. But I have to try, Oskar. I have to try and warn him, don't I?

So Kline raised himself on an elbow and looked around him. Things seemed very solid. There was the table, and one of the chairs had fallen. Yeats lay in the corner, doubled over, but his head was back and his mouth was open. There was quite a lot of blood seeping from Kline's stomach, but he was breathing well enough. He supposed that he had only been shot once, and that the bullet had lodged in the tissue. When he finally managed to get up and stagger out into the sunlight the sky had never appeared so overwhelming.

There was so much blood by the time he reached the barn that he was afraid he would not make it. But then he had the barn door open and he was resting, hanging onto the side of the truck. What if there's no key, he thought suddenly. But there was a key, right there in the ignition.

The truck was an old faded blue Ford. There was chicken wire in the trailer and pieces of old lumber. Kline had never been lucky with machines. They were always falling apart on him, except the motorbike during the war. You could ride that motorbike to the moon.

The engine sputtered and stalled. He tried again, but it still wouldn't turn over. Please. Just give me this, he said, although he had no idea who would do the giving. But then the engine was roaring, shaking the cabin, rattling the timber in the trailer. He waited, counting. It was just like counting off the inches in that prison cell. He had never had a chance to tell Julia that he had actually seen her in a vision, sleeping in her room, all while he had been counting off the inches into the millions.

340

Now on the narrow road between the fields Kline saw every-thing running together . . . the landscape was like one of Julia's watercolors, the tones were muted and the sky and foliage seemed to be merging. He kept one hand on the wheel and pressed the other to his wound. Not that it stopped the blood.

Then he was thinking of Jessie, and saw him clearly in his mind. The boy was still sitting on the hillside above the border. He imagined how it would be pulling off the road, shouting out. It was a damn shame that the horn didn't work. He would have liked to have rolled in there with the horn blowing like hell.

In Spain there had been sirens on the German bombers. Allen had been terrified of them but to Kline they had merely been a dirty trick. It was a shame that Allen hadn't been killed in Spain, and then Kline wondered if things would have been different if he'd been more polite to Allen when they had stood together on that muddy hillside in the rain . . .

Now the road was starting to blur into green puddles. He passed a ruined church and vaguely thought that he had only a few more miles to go. He was very certain that he would make it. He was entranced at the wheel. The accelerator was pressed to the floor. The truck was jolting and rocking, but Kline did not mind . . . he was just trying to hold on to an image of Jessie.

Except in the end he could not hold onto Jessie. He could only see Julia. The steering wheel had turned to rubber, and he was sailing off the road, submerging into the green. As he died he kept pressing on the horn. He had forgotten that it did not work.

Just as Kline had seen him in his mind, there was Jessie waiting on the hill. It was nearly four o'clock, a few minutes before the hour. The light was fading and the sky was turning from blue to indigo. When the wind blew through the grass the fields looked like the sea. His mother, Julia, used to say that when the wind blew it meant that God was taking stock of the future. It was a nice thought . . .

341

Jessie had been waiting here for an hour. There had been no sound and no movement, except that once again the wind was whistling through the strings of barbed wire, knocking the dangling soup cans together. He was waiting now, just as he used to wait for combat. For a while he studied the landscape, noting how the hills fell away to the marsh, the pine groves opened onto bracken and the deeper hollows. He thought of nothing in particular, but beneath it all there was a sense of finality, the last twist of the matter.

It was night, and he was thinking that everything that had ever happened might only have been for this moment, all pointing to one end. He felt as cold and heavy as a stone man.

In the last minutes it seemed to Jessie that the world had become particularly fragile. Anything could happen, he thought. Anything could have happened to Sara. Wait without hope, John used to say. Nobody understood what he meant, but now Jessie believed he understood, waiting in the darkness. His ears were filled with the wind, and then, above the wind, he heard the drone of an approaching truck.

He strained to see through the shifting night, and there far across the border two headlights swept in a long arc over the landscape. It was a military truck, slowly skirting the saltpan. Jessie got to his knees. The truck had left the road and was swaying toward the border, rising and dipping in the grass. A mile closer and it stopped, although the idling engine still droned.

Jessie began to live out a dream he must have had a thousand times . . . Far below a girl stood silhouetted in the headlights of the truck. She was a small, thin figure in a greatcoat, treading toward the border. For a while he watched her, then he stood up and began to descend the hill.

He saw her clearly when he reached the open ground. She was less than two hundred yards away, black against the yellow headlights. He saw her hesitate, then raise her arm, and finally she was stumbling toward him.

342

At fifty yards he even heard her call his name, and then the whole world splintered. He felt the pain before he heard the shot ... like the whip of a steel rod beneath his ribs, and he was falling, rolling into the black vines. He could not quite believe it—too sudden. But three more shots rang out of the hills and cut the grass, while Sara was still calling from somewhere out there in the night. . . .

The surrounding hills had taken on a dream perspective. Time too was dreamy, and Jessie was acting out his worst dream moves. He lifted the flap of his jacket and shirt, dabbed at the blood. It wasn't so bad, he told himself, just a deep slice where the bullet passed. The blood was seeping down his thigh, but the pain was containable. With disciplined thought, he'd learned, nearly all pain could be controlled.

He waited several seconds, concentrating, then started crawling through the grass. There were odors of leaf mold and blood. Twenty feet more and he was up, heading for the wire. The ground gave away beneath him, and three more shots sounded, but he was already diving under the wire, kicking at the rotting staves.

Eventually he was zigzagging, half-bent, for a line of black trees on the horizon. The truck had pulled away, he could see the red taillights bobbing in the distance. For an awful moment he was afraid that Sara was in that truck, that they had taken her away again.

Then she was rising out of the grass, and with her hair floating behind she looked like a ghost that he had seen in a dream.

She was real enough, though, when they finally fell together.

It seemed that a long time had passed, that they had talked for hours and now there was nothing more to say. No need to say more. They lay in the bracken under the pines. The night sky was dark purple. Sara had torn out the lining of her old coat and folded the cloth into bandages. When she had knelt close to him to clean out the wound he had been able to see her face very clearly

343

... there were circles under her eyes and she was thinner than he remembered, but she was still Sara, and for that he was grateful.

When she finished cleaning the wound she put on the bandage and told him to hold it tightly in place. Their hands were covered with blood from his wound, and it was on the grass and her gray prison dress.

"I don't know how long you can go with that," she said, "I can't get the bleeding to stop."

"That's okay, it'll stop."

"But we need some tape and disinfectant—"

"We'll get some."

For a while they just sat there . . . Jessie slouched against the tree, she huddled in her coat.

Finally she asked, "Who are those people? Who shot you?"

"I guess they work for Allen."

"So it's come to that? Between you and Allen—it's come to *that?*"

"Yeah, I guess it has."

"And it's all because of me? All this is happening because of me?"

"It was supposed to be a burn, get him right where he lives."

"But they were shooting . . ."

"I know, I guess we must have screwed up."

"Can we get out?"

"I've got a car on the other side of these hills. We'll cross the wire and follow the tree line around."

"Then what?"

"I don't know, I guess we'll try and make it to the city."

"And Robert? Is he with you?"

"I don't think he is anymore. I think they got him. If they're up there now, I think it means they got him and Dusty."

"Dusty?"

"He was a friend of mine."

They fell into another silence. Sara was looking without seeing into the grass . . . it was a look that Jessie had seen in her eyes before.

Finally she said, "I always knew that you'd get me out. I used to lie awake at night and think about how it would be, and now it's happened." She looked up at him. "Well, it *has* . . ."

Before they got up they became very serious. Jessie had taken the Beretta from his shoulder holster, cocked it, flipped the safety on, and laid it on his lap. They walked west, following the line of pines. The pain under his ribs was spreading to the bone. It was cold, but he was glad about the wind . . . it would cover the sound of their footsteps.

By the time they reached the edge of the pines the pain had become acute. He knew that he had to control it, come to terms with it, but it kept cramping the muscle. Then, too, there was Sara; he also had to come to terms with her presence, because during the war there had been no women and right now he needed it to be exactly like the war.

When they came to the edge of the flatland, they knelt in the brush. Across the wire lay the hills from where they had shot him, but all he saw now were the outlines of pines and stunted oaks. The pain had risen to his shoulder, but pain was like pride—you could feed on it. Even when they had to crawl under the barbed wire, crossing back to the West, even then he was able to do that.

They rested in a hollow of vines and spider ferns. Jessie lay on his back, pressed his arm hard against the wound. By now his shirt was drenched with blood, but his mind was very steady.

After a few minutes Sara said, "That was the border, wasn't it? We just crossed the border into the West, didn't we?"

"Yeah, we crossed over."

She dropped her head in a silent laugh. "It doesn't feel like I thought it would."

Which made him smile, thinking: *She's just like me.*

345

The overtones of the dream returned . . . The hills were black humps against the sky. The wind, rushing in gusts through the pines, slashed the broader leaves together, clattered over the ridges. There had been nights like this along the Mak Mun trails in Cambodia, Jessie remembered, and he wished he had brought his old M-70. With the M-70 it had been like throwing lightning bolts. Once he had literally vaporized a truck.

By the time he reached the rise of the hill he felt himself growing weaker, which he supposed was due to the loss of blood. Still, he was sure he could go on for another hour, maybe even two. He told himself again to think of it like the war.

He saw Allen's hirelings the moment he reached the crest of the hill, saw them through a long tunnel of leaves and crossed shadows. They were waiting by his Audi, fifty yards below in a cluster of dark pines. One was slouched against the hood, the other was obscured in the darkness so that Jessie could only see the glowing tip of a cigarette.

For a long time he was motionless, silent. Sara knelt behind him, and he could hear her breathing. All right, he told himself. You're going to go and do it. He released the safety on the Beretta. Before he moved on down the hill he turned to look back over his shoulder, and it was as if he were looking at her for the first time. She moved her lips, but did not speak. She thought he had the oddest, almost wistful smile.

Then he was gone, slipping quietly through the ferns, gently picking aside the vines. He paused in a patch of strange purple flowers, then moved on in the next flurry of wind.

There was slatted moonlight where the hill fell away. Beyond two men waited in the trees. He had a good view of them now. They were bulky figures in nylon jackets. One of them had a hunting rifle propped against his hip.

Lying in the vines, he thought: this is what you do best. He eased the Beretta down and fired, man and gun merged in perfect union. . . .

346

When it was done he rose unsteadily and turned to face Sara, who was still kneeling on the crest of the hill. All she saw of him in the darkness was his thin, crooked figure. One arm was pressed to his side, the other was slack, the Beretta dangling from his fingers. He signaled her with a nod, and she began to climb down through the twisted brush. No need to talk. They understood each other perfectly.

The bodies lay in the bracken by the side of the highway. At first Sara saw them as only black, amorphous shapes, but when she came closer she turned her head away.

She got into the driver's seat, still without speaking. Jessie sat doubled over beside her. His clothing was covered with blood, and his face was very pale in the moonlight. It was almost as though they had played out these roles before, and now they were performing by rote.

She drove awkwardly at first, stalling and then lurching onto the highway, but as they gathered speed a sense of life, of relief passed over them both. Jessie lit a cigarette and let his head fall limply to the side. Sara breathed deeply and settled back behind the wheel. They passed a grove of shadowy oaks; dark, monotonous hills were on the horizon and frost hovered in long shrouds across the fields. On a rise above the hills they saw the lights of Lubeck in the distance. When Jessie risked shutting his eyes he felt as if he could sleep for a year.

Half a mile further on Sara laid her hand on his forehead. He hardly stirred, but her thought was that he had a fever. She also felt that the worst was over now, it was only about fifteen miles until the city—

And then she saw it, a blacked-out van moving off the gravel shoulder a thousand feet ahead.

"Oh my God, Jessie—"

The van had stopped broadside to block the highway, figures scattering in the headlights.

"Turn around," he told her quietly. "Go back the other way."

347

She braked hard into a wide screeching turn, skidding on the gravel, and then they were gathering speed again, heading back the way they had come through a long curve and the shadow of the hills—

A second van pulled out of the trees and stopped like the first across the highway.

She heard Jessie's voice, but it seemed to come from very far away. While the van was coming closer, growing larger in the headlights.

Time had slowed, and she thought she might as well keep going now. That's what Jessie would do. He'd just smash right into them and that would be the end of it. Except she couldn't do it, and in one disintegrating moment she swerved for the blackness and the trees.

As soon as they left the road the windshield filled with leaves and splintering branches, and they were plunging into the high swirling ferns, and finally they rolled into a wooded meadow, ghostly birches spreading out before them in the headlights.

They came to rest in deep brush. Behind them was the rattle of approaching vans, and someone was shouting. But all Sara really heard was Jessie's voice as he led her out of the car. . . .

It was black, the air was cold. Up a mossy slope grew the denser pines, and Jessie thought that if he could make it to those trees he ought to get at least one clean shot. But he was bleeding even worse than before. He also must have hit the dashboard when they left the road, and he knew he did not have the strength for the climb. So he took Sara by the hand, walked a few feet, and then sank down to the ferns. When she realized that he was not going any further she gave him a questioning look, but he shook his head as if to say, this is far enough.

Now there were only forest sounds . . . dripping water, crickets, wind. The night seemed thick around them, broken

348

only by moonlight on the leaves. They had both grown calm, nearly passive, and Jessie could not help thinking that it must have been like this for Dusty that night they chased him through the Langley forest . . .

He heard voices from the highway, footsteps through the brush. A spotlight swept across the foliage. Jessie cocked the Beretta and laid the barrel on his knee. He was sighting into the blackness. *You can come out now,* was his simple thought. *I'm ready.*

"Jessie?"

The leaves rustling. Footsteps, and he heard the voice again. "Jessie?"

"Who is it?"

"Jessie? Don't shoot." And a hesitant, squat man shuffled out of the shadows.

"My name is Humphrey Knolls," he said.

Jessie Dancer and Humphrey Knolls. They stood in the gloom under the trees. There were other figures in the background and footsteps on the sodden ground. A spotlight broke through the branches. Sara sat a few feet away on a gnarled stump, her hands wedged between her knees.

Knolls wore an old raincoat, torn at the cuff. His shoes were wet and covered with mud. For an awkward moment he just stood, feeling bewildered and a little afraid. Finally he said, "I work with Lyle Severson's office, I was the one who first talked with Dusty Yeats."

"I know who you are," Jessie said. "What I don't know is how you got here."

"We had a mail tap on your father's house. I saw what you sent him."

"Okay, so now you've got me. First it's Dusty, and now me."

"It's not like that, Jessie."

"Then how is it?"

Without answering Knolls reached out and gently touched Jes-

349

sie's sleeve. "You're bleeding," he said, "you've been shot."

"They got lucky." Jessie smirked.

"Was it Allen's people?"

"Maybe."

"Where are they now?"

"They're dead. I shot them."

"Did it happen at the farm?"

"What do you know about the farm?"

"We picked up Tony Nugent. He was on his way to Hamburg. I suppose—"

"What about the farm, Knolls?"

But Humphrey did not answer, just kept looking at Jessie's feet.

Jessie shook his head, breathed deeply. "They got them, didn't they? Dusty and Kline . . ."

"Yes."

"And Allen?"

"We don't know where he is. Nugent isn't talking, so at this point we just don't know."

The silence fell again, and they were three awkward people standing in a forest clearing. It might have been a painting.

"There's a first-aid kit in the van," Knolls said at last. "And we can arrange for a doctor in Lubeck."

"Oh? Well, that's all you're going to arrange, Mr. Knolls."

"I don't know what you mean, Jessie."

"I mean Sara and I are getting out of here in the morning."

"I know that."

"And if anyone tries to mess with us—"

"I told you, Jessie, it's not like that. We didn't come here for you. We came to . . . contain your father. We came for Allen. I want you to believe that . . ."

Jessie and Sara reached Lubeck within the hour, riding with Humphrey Knolls in the back of the van. Sara treated Jessie's wound with the first-aid kit while Jessie stared out at the passing landscape. Twice Knolls tried to start a conversation, but neither

Jessie nor Sara seemed to have anything to say. So in the end he also sat quietly, sometimes gazing out the window, sometimes stealing glances at Sara. He had not imagined that she would be so pretty, not after all that had happened.

They entered Lubeck through the side streets, across a deserted railroad yard, past factories and a schoolyard. There were smells of grease and fish. The city was like a ruin. It was a Thursday evening, but Jessie did not know exactly what time it was. His watch had stopped, which Dusty used to say was the very worst of omens.

The bodies of Robert Kline and Dusty Yeats were discovered the following morning, and Humphrey Knolls proceeded to write his report:

Allen Dancer had enlisted the support of the German secret service, and in a massive effort managed to discover the location of the Lubeck farmhouse. He then hired two professional assassins, Germans and unnamed. The killers spent about nine or ten hours watching the farmhouse, and when Jessie had left on the afternoon of the final day, they came down and killed both Kline and Yeats.

As for the girl, Sara Moore, there was only this to explain her presence. Tony Nugent, interrogated in Hamburg, admitted that the girl was to have been used as bait. Specifically, he said that she was to have been their edge against Jessie. He said that with someone like Jessie you needed an edge. He also professed to have a real admiration for Jessie, because of his record in Vietnam.

Sara would also have a story to tell, but it was a story too fragmented to be fully entered into the records. She would describe how she had been taken from an East German prison by two Russian State Security officers. They had treated her neither kindly nor roughly. The journey had been by car, and it had taken about fifteen hours. For a long time she had not known whether she had been traveling east or west, because the clouds had ob-

351

scured the sun. Also, there was this incident which occurred just as she was being led from the cell. There, down a long stone corridor, she had met a man. He had been walking in the opposite direction, and when he had seen her he had ordered the guards to stop. He had approached her slowly, and very gently taken her face in his hands. He was tall and thin, and had fair hair and soft eyes. Before he left her he told her in English that everything would be all right. Then he smiled. It was only much later that she found out that this had been Valentin Servana, and he was not at all what she would have expected.

And finally there was Humphrey's own story, which detailed how he had left by an afternoon flight from Langley and had arrived in Hamburg ill from too much coffee. He had never traveled well. In Hamburg the party requisitioned two consulate vans and drove at high speed to the border, where he set up the roadblock in an effort to intercept Allen Dancer or any of the other principals. It was a move he was later reprimanded for . . . the roadblock was said to have endangered government property and caused a potential hazard to innocent motorists. In Humphrey's mind, it was his finest hour.

Such, then, were the essential details that filled the first draft of Humphrey's report. Later that report would be revised and a new prologue would be added. There was, however, something which was never contained within any of the Knolls' reports, and this was a description of how it had been between Jessie Dancer and Sara Moore.

Knolls spent a lot of time wrestling with the problem, wondering what, if anything, could be said. It seemed that he best remembered them together in the morning after the border incident. They had spent the night in a Lubeck hotel, two doors down from Humphrey's room. White light was streaming through the mullioned windows, accenting the paint blisters on the brown woodwork. Across the sooty courtyard was a woman's profile framed in the muslin curtains. Knolls and Jessie talked for about an hour.

352

Then it was over, and they said good-by. It was all very matter-of-fact.

Yet, in Humphrey's mind, an image of the lovers remained, and even days later he found himself brooding on it. It was an image of them in that hotel room. There was Sara, sitting on the edge of the bed, combing out her hair by the window, Jessie watching her reflection in the mirror. Both of them were caught in the glow of morning light. Knolls was no expert on lovers, but somehow this picture seemed to him to be one in a million. One that few people before him had ever seen, let alone known.

EPILOGUE

IN CONCLUSION Knolls wrote: "We have reached the end. Everything of relevance has been passed to Lyle Severson, and so now you know as much as I have ever known. I cannot stress enough the importance of a historical approach. The early days are particularly vital, and please do not forget the women, as they seem to have been a catalyst for everything. You should further remember that this story must be seen as a whole, because the last generation was a consequence of the first."

This was written about three days after Knolls returned to Langley. It was a period of limbo. The final snows had melted, but the air was still chilled, the branches bare against the wintry light.

Then came a night of warm wind, and spring descended in the morning.

Knolls spent a lot of time sitting around his bedroom in an old matted robe that his mother had given him years before. He liked to stand at the window and watch the blossoms on the plane trees. He munched cold cereal and stared at the cornflakes box. One evening he went to the city and wandered among the crowds. When he returned he singed his eyelashes trying to relight the oven. He also kept having an urge to call Jessie Dancer.

The inquiry began the following week, and as Knolls had predicted, nothing of much significance was revealed. Allen spoke obliquely about the Magic retrieval systems, security measures and the general character of his Kremlin link. It was essentially what he had said at the unveiling of Magic some thirty years ago.

When asked about his relationship with Jessie he sadly shook his head and intimated that the boy was seriously disturbed. He also claimed that he had never meant him any harm, and had only been trying to take him back to Langley for treatment. It was at this point that the inquisitors, in the interest of good taste, dropped all discussion of Jessie.

All in all, then, the first days of the inquiry had a rather convivial air. Allen joked with inquisitors. They in turn joked with him. There were moments of lively banter, and also moments of hushed compassion for a man who had been disgraced by his son. Allen wore an exquisite Donegal tweed from Savile Row with a tight, budded yellow rose in his lapel.

This might have been the final scene: Allen leaning back in his chair, his mouth set in a lipless grin while his colleagues laughed appreciatively. As it happened, it was not the finale.

That came on the third day of the hearings, when Knolls placed a long-distance call to Jessie. No one was ever sure what was said, but the following day Jessie again returned to Langley. Knolls met him at the airport and saw him first from a distance. Jessie had always had a distinctive, almost feline walk. One hand was in his

355

pocket, the other poised at his waist. He wore a beige cotton suit, brown loafers and a drip-dry shirt with the collar undone. He was a Jessie that no one had ever seen before in Langley; a diffident, vaguely uncertain young man. . . .

It was eleven o'clock in the morning, and old John Dancer's garden lay in a green-gold haze. A breeze was stirring the scent of roses with the odor of decaying leaves. In the shade of the hedgerows a grove of speckled toadstools had shot up from the compost.

When Jessie arrived, John was sitting at a blue garden table with the remnants of his breakfast. It was cool under the hanging willows. Jessie and the old man spotted each other from a ways off as the boy moved down the flagstones, but they did not speak until Jessie was also sitting at the table.

"I thought maybe you'd be coming," John said. "I don't know why, I just had the feeling that you'd be coming. Premonition, I suppose."

"How are you?" Jessie said softly.

"Oh, I don't know. Knee gives me a little trouble, and they tell me the bladder's going some. Other than that I'm all right . . . How about yourself? I heard someone shot you."

"It was just a graze, it's pretty much healed now."

There seemed nothing else to say. John was sucking on his mustache ends, Jessie was toying with a coffee spoon.

"Did you come alone?" John said suddenly.

"No. I'm with Humphrey Knolls. He's waiting in the car."

"Of course, Humphrey Knolls. Funny little man . . . Your father hates him but I've always rather liked him . . ."

"Where is he?"

"Allen? At the hearing. Comes in late at night. Leaves first thing in the morning. I've been alone quite a bit lately. You won't be staying, will you?"

Jessie shook his head. "No. I think I'll only be here for the day."

"Yes. I didn't think you'd stay."

356

Another pause. The old man was looking past a blur of white hibiscus, past the bamboo reeds to a green reflecting pond. His goldfish had died years ago, and no one thought of restocking the pond . . . they said that John would never remember to feed them.

Jessie said, "I guess you know why I came."

John nodded, but did not look away from his garden.

"It's got to be done," Jessie continued. "It's gone too far."

"I know. Too far."

"And it's got to be done today. Now."

"Yes, today."

"I can have Knolls call so they'll be ready for us."

"It wouldn't be as dramatic though, would it? I mean as the two of us walking in unannounced. Imagine the two of us walking in like that. Lazarus back from the dead, that sort of thing . . ."

They walked back to the old house so that John could change his clothes. Dust was suspended in the sunlight falling through the shutters, a vase of wilted roses was on the mantel. It took what seemed a very long time to find John a clean shirt.

John's testimony lasted about seven hours, although Jessie spoke for part of that time. It began with all that had happened in 1917, and ended along the German border in Lubeck. Later each point of the narrative would be studied, annotated and compared with the records. It was a process that would last for weeks. But regardless of the care taken with detail, there was, as always, something missing from the records—the underlying feel of that afternoon, how it had been to hear old John speaking slowly, softly, staring at his hands on the table. And then too there was Jessie, answering questions in clipped, hard sentences, sometimes looking menacing, sometimes only bored. When he had left, some of those present would find that he was still a little unreal.

Ironically there was still one subject which neither Jessie nor John would discuss in any detail—the women. Not much was ever made of it, but the fact remains that Jessie refused to talk about

357

Sara, and John would not discuss Anna Servana. . . .

It was not until that evening that anyone saw Allen. During John's testimony he remained in the adjoining chambers with Tony Nugent and two men from Security. Food was brought in: coffee, sandwiches, salads in plastic bowls covered in cellophane. For the most part Allen did nothing more than stand at the window. There was a view through smoked glass of the lawns and the forest where it had all started, and Allen kept returning to the window. He would stand there, smoking, drinking mineral water, all while the white sky turned dark.

It was not until the hearing had adjourned that Allen and Jessie finally saw each other. Actually they met by chance as they were leaving the assembly complex. Allen, Nugent and the two security officers had left by a rear entrance and were moving along the walkway, skirting the lawn. Jessie, Knolls, Lyle Severson and John were descending the broad steps. When Allen and Jessie saw one another they stopped. It was dark with only the path lights and the intermittent glow of offices in the buildings around them. They were separated by the wide circle of lawn and the rising mist of the sprinklers. Each looked into the other's eyes, but it was difficult to tell whether either acknowledged anything. Or everything.

It was nearly nine in the evening when Jessie and John finally reached the old house. They had driven in silence, but when they arrived Jessie got out of the car to walk with John at least partway up the flagstones.

The air was warm, humid.

John said, "I didn't know about the girl. Allen never told me."

"No. I didn't think he did."

"And if I had known I would have done something."

"I know you would have."

"Because, believe it or not, I know how it can be—between two people, I mean."

358

"I know you do."

"And the others . . . Robert Kline, Dusty—I didn't really know about them either."

"Well, you do now."

"Yes. I do now."

Jessie started to speak again, but stopped. All he finally said was, "Look, I'll be seeing you, okay?"

"I hope so."

"Sure. I'll be seeing you."

They turned and started moving in opposite directions—John toward his phantom house, Jessie to his rented car. But after a few paces it was as if Jessie suddenly remembered something. He stopped, spun around and called out, "Hey! I really will be seeing you."

And even as his voice trailed off they still went on staring at one another, as though something quite remarkable had happened between them.

For all sorts of security reasons there were no formal charges brought against anyone, but of course the secret world was badly shaken.

Allen left Langley on a summer evening. He was driven to the airport by one of his staff, while others lined the road to wave him off. Later that fall he accepted a position with one of the major oil companies. Apparently they wanted him for their international relations department, because after all he was still considered a well-connected man.

About Valentin Servana, only this was really known for sure. Less than a year after the fall of the Dancers he retired to a villa along the Black Sea. Consequently it was assumed that the essential lie of Magic was never uncovered in Moscow. The Soviets probably believed only that Valentin's agent had been blown, which they probably thought was bound to happen, given the risks that Allen had been taking on their behalf.

359

Still, there was also talk that John and Valentin met one last time along the Turkish border and talked over the possibility of Valentin's defection to the West. In fact, this was true, but Valentin told John what his mother Anna had told him years before . . . that they had had their chance, and missed it.

John, of course, denied ever having seen his son again. He claimed that he had only gone abroad to see Jessie, and the stamps in his passport went no further east than England. But according to Lyle Severson, when John returned from that trip he had a photograph with him. It was a picture of an old woman standing on the banks of a river, and the landscape beyond was vast and flat to the horizon, and surely there was no place like that in England. . . .

Finally there was Humphrey Knolls. For a long time after the close of the Dancer case he continued to live in a kind of solitary limbo. He thought about Jessie a lot and once even tried to phone him, but the number had been disconnected. He later heard that Jessie was in London with Sara, although no one quite knew what else he was doing.

But regardless of what was said, for Knolls, at least, Jessie would always remain a little unreal, a little larger than life. He could simply not imagine Jessie falling into the orderly ranks of society. He could only imagine him perpetually stalking through cities, moving on the very edge of things. He knew without question that Jessie had come to hate deeply the secret world and everything that it stood for, but then the secret world did not much like Jessie either.

In the end they would portray Jessie as nothing much more than a particularly savage killer, which was what eventually led Knolls to realize that in the end this story of the Dancers did not belong to the historians at all.

They, for God's sake, had missed the whole point.